THE AGATHON

Book One

Colin Weldon

Copyright © 2016 Colin Weldon
All rights reserved.
ISBN 1519139683
ISBN-13: 9781519139689

For Lorena, for keeping the ship on course.

On August 15 1977 Jerry R. Ehman detected a signal while working on the SETI (Search for Extra Terrestrial Intelligence) project. The transmission was a strong narrowband radio signal coming from the constellation Sagittarius. It was determined to be of non-Terrestrial and non-solar origin. It lasted for seventy-two seconds.

1

September 3 2339 – Mars Colony 1
Gamma Event T Minus Forty-Seven Minutes

Carrie Barrington stood at the edge of the lake of black liquid and watched her mother die.

"John! I love you. Save Carrie." The black liquid covered her mother's reddened eyes, as she clawed at the soil trying to escape. She gave one final muffled scream before the violent scene calmed and she relinquished control to the inevitable. "Goodbye, Carrie," she whispered with her last breath.

Carrie opened her eyes and sat up in bed. She gripped her soaked t-shirt and held her hand against her chest. Her heart was beating so quickly that her breathing was laboured. Every night was the same dream but this one had been more intense. It seemed so real. The smell of burning in the room alerted her to look around to make sure nothing was on fire. She examined her sheets to find small burn holes scattered throughout them.

"Not again," she sighed. She looked at the palm of her hands and saw how red the tips of her fingers were. She closed her eyes and clenched them.

She sat up and stared out through her blurry eyes at the lights of the colony laid out across the red Martian soil. She looked at the clock that read nine p.m. She was late. Again. In the distance a burst of blue light rose from one of the Atmo processors. It cast a momentary blanket of blue and silver shimmer over the living pods and curved domes of the main habitat. She swung her legs out from under the sheets and placed them gently onto the ground. The hard cold surface of the metallic floor sent a shiver up her legs as the residual images of the night's memories lingered behind her eyes. Her voice echoed off the walls of her quarters, as she recited the mantra her mother had taught her as a child. The gentle hum of the life support duct overhead helped slow her speeding heart. She opened her eyes and stood up slowly from the bed. She made her way to the bathroom, removing her soaked shirt in the process, before stepping into the sonic shower. She placed her head against the wall and activated it.

The comm link chirped next to her. She paused the washing cycle and tapped the pad next to the mirror.

"This is Carrie," she said.

"Ms Barrington, the data relay from the Jycorp orbital began twenty minutes ago," a stern male voice said over the comm system.

"Sorry, Doctor Tyrell, I'm on my way. Five minutes."

"Hmm," he said gruffly as the comms clicked off. Carrie sighed and reactivated the shower. She looked at the palms of her hands again and turned them over. She thought that maybe the time had come to talk to Meridian about what had been happening to her. Before someone got hurt.

Main Observatory Mars Colony 1
Gama Event -T minus Thirty-Three Minutes

"Computer initialise array diagnostic phase two. Authorisation Doctor Tyrone Tyrell, alpha one seven three," Tyrell said into his console, as the main doors to the lab opened.

"Yes Doctor Tyrell," the computer's female voice said. He raised his head and watched Carrie Barrington enter. He sighed quietly to himself.

"What was it this time?" he said, looking back at the console. He felt her sigh as she moved across the lab to the viewing chamber.

"My apologies, Doctor Tyrell. It will not happen again," she said, tapping some commands into a console attached to a large transparent chamber that lay in the centre of the lab. "Imaging chamber is powering up," she said.

"Hmm," Tyrell grunted back, as he attended to his readings. "A good scientist is a punctual scientist, Ms Barrington," he said. "Your father assured me you would be reliable." He knew that arguing with John Barrington was futile and, in the end, he would have resented him for not taking his daughter on and that simply would not do. He kept his gaze fixed on the incoming data stream that was scrolling across the screen on his workstation. There was a moment of silence and when Tyrell raised his head he found Carrie standing next to his desk, looking intently at him. There was something in her striking blue eyes that unsettled him, but he made sure never to show it.

"Doctor Tyrell, I assure you it will not happen again. I have been having some difficulty sleeping lately, but Doctor Brubaker has given me some medication that is working a little too well. I will be seeing her later on tomorrow morning to discuss this. I apologise for my tardiness. Now would you like me to continue with my analysis or would you like to report me to my father who can have me reassigned?"

Tyrell cleared his throat.

"Please," he said, motioning to the imaging chamber. She nodded politely and walked calmly back to the chamber. He was surprised at her tone. She hadn't shown a hint of frustration with him in the six months that she had been his assistant. He would of course not be reporting her to her father.

"Any change in the signal data from the Monolith today?" Carrie asked, keeping her attention on her control panel.

"Same old, same old," Tyrell replied. He was not winning any popularity contests with the rest of the colonists and as such kept a noted distance from them and almost never attended social gatherings. A point the commander had raised on more than one occasion with him, but he had always found a way of deflecting the conversation with some new discovery on some other Earth-like world light years away. His distance had been respected by most and even Meridian had given up, after a few weeks of calling the lab with idle threats of dragging him to some silly event or other aimed at improving the social bonds of the colonists.

He loved this time of night usually, when the colony was quiet, and the power output levels were low. There were months where he would go undisturbed, observing and cataloguing the cosmos. He felt connected with it somehow. On the edge of understanding yet knowing nothing. The signal from the structure on the small moon orbiting above refused to give up its secrets. He loved working at night. It had the added benefit of limiting his interaction with the rest of the colonists. At sixty-one years of age, he had availed himself of Jycorp augmentation therapies, which had given him the appearance of a man in his late thirties. He wore a well-trimmed silver beard and was classically handsome with dark brown eyes.

The lights of the imaging chamber caught his attention and he glanced up at Carrie, who was now sitting in one of the elevated chairs in front of it.

"Let me guess," he said looking over at her. Carrie didn't look back.

"Just taking some rotational readings, Doctor. It won't take long," she said. Tyrell raised his eyebrows. The chamber went black as it activated and seconds later its centre burst to life, with flickers of bright lights that reflected off the walls of the lab. The transparent chamber filled with the three-dimensional image of a spiral galaxy. Its leading edges touched the inside walls of the enclosed space. Carrie tapped some commands into a hovering panel just above her head. The stars raced towards the walls of the viewing chamber, as if it were travelling through the galaxy itself. It passed through planets and gas clouds and asteroid belts in a matter of seconds, before coming to a stop. Earth filled the room. Represented in perfect holographic form. The blue planet rotated slowly in front of them. Tyrell hated it.

"I really do not know why you waste so much time on that silly little planet. You weren't even born there," he said. Carrie looked around at him.

"I just like the colour blue," she said, smiling. "Why have you such a dislike for it?" she asked. Tyrell did not know how to best answer her question. Was it Meretti? he thought to himself. Was it the fools at Berkley? He wanted to tell her that he thought the entire planet was a petri dish long past its sell by date, but decided to keep it to himself. Anyway he had the feeling she already knew the answer to his question.

Jycorp wanted "progressive thinkers" on the Phobos and colonial projects and so Tyrell had played along.

"There are over a million catalogued star systems, so far as we know, that have habitable worlds capable of supporting life. I just think our attention should be focused on the future of the human race, not its past, don't you?" he finally said.

"That's easy for you to say," Carrie replied, turning her head back to the image. "You've been there."

"You're not missing much, Ms Barrington. Believe me." There was a moment of silence as Tyrell turned his attention back to his readings.

"It looks so peaceful," Carrie said.

"Well it isn't," Tyrell said. "Don't be fooled, Carrie, much blood has been spilt on your little dream world. More than you can possibly imagine." Carrie didn't answer.

"By the way, I need you to run a containment diagnostic on the sample of The Black, when you're done there. Your father needs it by the morning." He knew that would bring her back to reality.

He knew that there was something different about this girl. The tragic loss of her mother to 'The Black' as it was now known, weighed heavy on all the inhabitants, but her father had been clear that she was to be given no special treatment. Tyrell had been a member of the scientific council that had begun its investigation into The Black following its gruesome discovery. Her aptitude for the sciences was off the scale, even by Tyrell's standards. She consumed information and regurgitated it with creativity and a level of understanding that was unheard of for someone so young.

Tyrell watched her, as she stared at the slowly rotating ball. Fascinated that someone could be so interested in something so completely unimpressive and even repugnant, yet here she was, eyes unmoving and with a wonder and stillness that secretly he found soothing. Tyrell made his way across the lab. It was one of the largest structures at Colonial 1 and he was very protective over it. At the centre of the room stood the enormous viewing chamber. Like an empty glass box, it stood as his gateway into the universe. Jerome Young himself had designed and commissioned the impressive piece of technology and had cut the ribbon when it had been first activated in a ceremony six years earlier. The backdrop had been the very same image that Carrie had been watching a moment earlier, as the packed lab had ooo'd and aah'd at its capabilities and astonishing image resolution.

Tyrell remembered Chase Meridian cheering, "I can see my house," to laughter and toasts.

He approached the young woman and stood by her side.

"Did you hear me?" he said. She jumped slightly.

"Sorry, Doctor, I didn't hear you come over. Yes, I heard you, I will run the diagnostic." Tyrell nodded.

Carrie's gaze returned to the image as she raised a hand and tapped several commands into the free-floating control panel. The image in the viewing chamber began to expand outwards, past the outer boundaries. Landmasses began to reveal intricate detail of the continent she was focusing on. Tyrell always found the accuracy of the motion to be unsettling, especially now following a particularly heavy meal. The holographic image showed floating cities and thousands of vast tubular formations that connected to each landmass.

"The planetary connection grid is spectacular to see at this height," Carrie said, as she paused the image and sat back. Across the viewing area was a sea of activity. Billions of humans travelling in glass pods like a luminescent bloodstream. Carrie smiled.

"At night the harmonic resonance of the charged particles inside the tubes makes each pod luminescent," she said.

"Yes, I am familiar with the phenomenon," said Tyrell. "I would have thought your focus would be on the prevailing Monolith signal. Why are you so fixated on a planet that is so backwards you refuse to look forward at the wondrous possibility of other sentience in the galaxy? Your father will not be happy about you spending this valuable time studying this planet. You know how important The Agathon project is to him, not to mention this colony." He paused and looked Carrie in eye.

"Doctor, why do you try and decode the signal?" she said, meeting his gaze.

"What do you mean?" he asked.

"What do you hope to learn from it? You have been analysing the alien transmission for most of your life, have you not?"

Tyrell crossed his arms. "I have," he replied.

"Why?" she said, looking at him with her almost glowing blue eyes. Tyrell had never seen anything like them and had concluded that they must have been a result of a chemical reaction with something in the Martian atmosphere, when she was born.

"Because whoever they are, they may know the answers to it all," he finally said.

"You mean your answers to it all," she said. He smiled.

"Perhaps." He kept his eyes on her.

"By the way, the computer logged you into the containment chamber yesterday morning for two hours?"

She looked up at him. "Yes, Doctor, I thought I would get a head start on that diagnostic. I remembered it was due shortly. I was just taking atmospheric readings," she said.

"I see," he replied, not believing a word of it. "Carrie, you are not supposed to enter that room without my authorisation. Another thing your father was quite clear about. And you need not lie to me, Carrie. I know very well why you went in there."

She lowered her head. "Yes, Doctor, I apologise. You are right. I went in to take some readings of The Black. I had a thought a few nights ago that it may react to barrionic particle saturation. I didn't want to wake you."

Tyrell sighed. All he needed was the commander's daughter to be killed in some insane experiment on his watch. That wouldn't do at all. And there was something different about this girl. Something that had intrigued him since she was a little girl. At colonial functions she had had a little party trick her father used to make her perform in front of other guests. She would be handed a pad and without any questions, draw perfect renderings of colonial family members back on Earth. All she did was look into the eyes of the person. It was a party trick that stopped after her mother's death. He had seen her exchange glances with her father on numerous occasions, as if they were speaking to each other. But only briefly. He was sure she was telepathic on some level. He had never asked directly. Science was observation. So he quietly observed.

"It could have killed you," he said quietly. She turned and looked at him with an unsettling gaze. She looked off into the distance.

"I have to know what it is," she said.

"We all have to know what it is, Carrie, but that knowledge will not do either of us any good if that thing liquefies you in the middle of my lab," he said, his voice raised.

"Can you imagine that conversation with your father?" She didn't answer. "I've entered a code word clearance, only on the containment lab. You are not permitted back in again without my explicit permission," he said, turning away from her and heading back to his main workstation. She turned back to the viewing chamber slowly.

"Yes, Doctor Tyrell, I understand," she said.

"Now, if you wouldn't mind, we don't have that much time this evening, so if you could reposition the orbital array towards Phobos. I would like to get a visual on the Monolith quickly, on its next orbit."

"Of course," Carrie said, tapping some commands into her control panel. The image of the Earth regressed in the viewing chamber, as Carrie pulled back from the blue planet. The stars zipped by as the Earth vanished from sight. Seconds later the image filled with the familiar red planet. An oddly shaped orbiting ball of rock began to appear from behind the Martian haze. As the imaging chamber crept closer, the surface of the orbiting moon became more detailed. A computer voice confirmed the target lock of Phobos. Miles of fluorescent pipes spidered across its surface, crisscrossing at large cubical structures, making it look like a pebble trapped in a glowing spider's web. Tyrell frowned. While his access to the Monolith structure and signal data had been unrestricted, he was never given permission for data from any other structures that Jycorp had attached to the base of it. Jycorp had been busy the last century, spending much of its resources on this mysterious little hunk of rock.

It was rumoured that over three quarters of Jycorp's research and development division were now stationed here, along with entrenched military bases and orbited by two space stations, Phobos One and the Jycorp orbital platform, which was restricted to military personnel only. Observing the Jycorp station was restricted by the viewing chamber at the behest of the supreme chancellor and CEO of Jycorp, Jerome Young. The image of the moon filled the viewing chamber. As it reached the surface, both observers looked on at the focus of Carrie's attention, which became the prominent feature in the chamber.

The two mile high, rectangular structure, stood ominously before them. Mirrored on all sides, it reflected the surrounding area and almost cloaked to the human eye, depending on what angle it was viewed from. One could be fooled as to its sheer mass, unless one was face to face on the surface. There it stood peacefully. A monument to an ancient civilisation. Surrounded by a hub of monitoring platforms and miles of duatronic cabling, which monitored every wavelength of energy emanating from the structure. Silently, it looked out into the universe and played its song over and over. Tyrell looked at the structure. More familiar with it than anything he knew. It had been his life's work on Earth. Every inch of its surface plagued his dreams. The Monolith signal had been steady over the last hundred years and the human race was no closer to understanding what it meant. Not as far as Tyrell was concerned. The algorithm relayed Terabits of information every second on a carrier wave so strong it had been theorised that the only way it could have been compressed was through subspace. Tyrell knew one thing. The origin.

"Image locked, Doctor Tyrell, relaying data now," said Carrie.

"Thank you, Carrie. Hold it there for now," he said. Tyrell linked his console with the relay on the orbiting moon and began downloading the daily updates on the signal. He sat back and watched it, as it streamed past his screen. Thousands of symbols flooded his console. He rubbed his eyes and yawned. His latest set of algorithms had revealed no pattern to the random stream of data. Again. He was beginning to grow weary of the chase. He raised his eyes and watched as Carrie looked on at that rectangular structure being represented in the viewing chamber. He watched her closely.

Carrie stared on at the black rectangular Monolith and moved the viewer in for a closer look at its flat polished surface. A familiar gentle hum began to resonate in her mind. The sound felt strangely organic and it always stopped when she repositioned the array away from the moon. She likened it to a cat purring and, when mentioning the sound to Tyrell a few weeks back, she'd realised that she was the only person able to hear it. She had opened her mind to the structure on many occasions but had learned nothing from doing so. It just hummed gently in her mind. She actually found it relaxing.

"Carrie, reposition the array to the Aristaeus system, will you? Let's say hello to our friends," said Tyrell from behind her.

"Yes, Doctor," she said, tapping in the commands for the target star system. Visiting the home world of the signal makers, or what was thought to be the home world of the signal makers, was a daily trip for Carrie.

"Quickly now, I would like to get a closer look at that large orbital we were locked into yesterday," said Tyrell. Carrie took a breath. His tone was grinding her more than usual this evening and she had begun to find it irritating. His proximity lately had begun to send shivers down her arms. His mind had always been difficult to read. His thoughts were highly organised and she could tell he made great efforts to conceal information from her. It was more than secrecy. He had disciplined his mind to focus in such a specific way when he was near her and she could feel the strain it had on his concentration. He was hiding something from her mind. And so they played their little game of hide and seek.

"Inputting target coordinates now," she said. The image pulled away from the surface of Phobos and past the red planet, before zipping through the stars. At six hundred light years away, the array was only able to show the system at a distance. After several minutes the viewing area slowed to a gentle halt, revealing a bright star.

"Aristaeus system locked," came the soothing, female computer voice.

"Lock in Aristaeus Three," Carrie said into her command panel. The viewing chamber flew past a small rocky planet and past another large gas giant, before settling on the target world. At this distance, Aristaeus III resembled Earth. It was a large blue oceanic world, with swirling cloud masses orbited by the two moons Hemera and Groma.

"Would you like to complete the gravity readings on Hemera, Doctor Tyrell?" she asked.

"Not today, Carrie, try and get us closer to object Delta," he said. She tapped in target vectors and moved the array.

"Scanning," she said.

"Object Delta cannot be located at this time," said the female voice.

"Dammit!" said Tyrell.

"It probably burned up in the atmosphere. It was in very close orbit," Carrie said.

"That doesn't explain why it had a stable orbit yesterday, Carrie," Tyrell retorted gruffly. Carrie bit her tongue. There was tension in the air.

"It couldn't have been a meteor," he said.

"Any impact on Hemera or Groma would have left residual debris and we would have seen any incoming projectile on the previous days' scans of the system." There was silence in the lab.

"Whatever it was, it's not there anymore," Carrie said passively. She could feel Tyrell approaching the viewing chamber and straightened her back. The tension between them began to increase when a low frequency alarm sounded, attracting Tyrell's attention. A female voice came over the comms.

"Signal frequency change in aspect. Doctor Tyrell, please come to Astrometrics." Tyrell stood beside Carrie and tapped the console on her chair.

"Tyrell here, I am on my way," he said, looking sharply at Carrie.

"Keep looking; it may have been flung out into the star system by an asteroid impact or something," he said, turning away from her.

"I may be a while, so if you still don't find anything in the next half hour complete those soil samples for Doctor Meridian and place them in the refrigeration unit. The last thing I need today is her breathing down my neck," he said.

"Yes, Doctor Tyrell," she said, feeling at ease as he made his way to the lab exit. Tyrell took an instrument out of one of the lockers behind the workstation and left. The hiss of the door column left the room deathly quiet. The only sounds were the quiet chirps from the instrument panel above Carrie's head. She was finally alone with the Universe at her fingertips. She tapped a few commands in the panel and redirected the array back towards Earth. She magnified the planet so that the equator filled the space in the viewing chamber and relaxed into her chair, watching it spin silently.

As the minutes drew past, she began to lose herself in Earth's abundance of life and light. She began to feel her eyes close as she followed the continents. As she began to drift off to sleep, the rhythm of unconsciousness was interrupted by what looked like a bright beam of light. Her eyes felt too heavy to look at it any further. It began to brighten. As her mind drifted off to sleep, her mother's voice began to echo in her mind.

Her eyes open as she feels her hand slip from the inside of a weathered cave wall, while she manoeuvres under a protruding rock face which lies directly ahead of her. The red soil is loose and, although untouched in millennia, it falls from underfoot with ease. She draws in a strong breath as she steadies herself and checks in with the team, who follow closely. She checks her suit for tears and does a visual on her oxygen levels. She catches a glimpse of her reflection in her arm display. She has long brown hair framing a soft and sallow complexion. She has an athletic physique and can feel the adrenalin flowing through her veins as she makes her way through the cave. Her husband is watching intently from miles away, while her daughter sleeps soundly under the watch of Doctor Chase Meridian.

"Easy, guys, it's loose underfoot here," she announces to her colleagues who follow closely behind. The cave is dark and she tells the team to activate their overhead lamps. Her two companions follow closely and light up their path with white light. One of them is a young cadet by the name of Charlie Weston. A rather serious twenty-seven-year-old who fills out his suit to bursting point. John had insisted on taking backup. Physical backup, should she run into trouble. While Charlie is pleasant company, he isn't much of a talker and usually wears a stern and serious expression on his face as he prepares himself for combat at a moment's notice. She had objected initially but finds him to be a comforting addition. Her other companion is a pretty Japanese mathematician by the name of Jin Li Chun. She has an intoxicating sense of humour and loves to cook little treats for her for their all night lab analysis sessions. As they continue their descent she begins to feel the ground beneath her soften.

"Romeo Two to Aquaria base," she says.

"Aquaria base here. Go ahead, Jennifer." Carrie hears her father's voice coming through the comms. She feels her mother's heart beat calmly at the sound of his voice.

"John, I'm taking Romeo team into the cavern now. There are high deposits of iron in the cave, so comms may be intermittent," she says.

"Aquaria base acknowledges. Proceed with caution, Doctor. Aquaria base out." Carrie's mind leaves her mother's and travels across the Martian desert. Through the blinding sand storm and towards the light of the colony. She sees her father standing at a curved window and enters his mind. Their thoughts begin to intertwine as a new set of emotions layer themselves onto her own. For a moment the floodgates of feelings overwhelm her, but it quickly dissipates and they become one. She feels her father's anxious heartbeat.

"Fucking planet," he whispers under his breath. He paces behind the monitoring station. "Weather report," he says to one of the men at a control console.

"That dust storm is right on top of them, Commander. I would have them stay put for at least twenty-four hours," he says.

"Perfect timing, Jennifer, as always," he mutters under his breath. He strokes his unshaven cheeks. Carrie feels her father's muscles tense. He a fit forty-year-old man. He feels tired and is in need of a night's sleep, but his mind is sharp.

"She'll be fine, John. Jen's a tough cookie. Tougher than you, I might add," comes a female voice from the corner of the room. He turns to see Doctor Chase Meridian staring at him. She smiles. He notices the little smiles on his crew and walks over to her.

"I would appreciate you keeping comments like that to yourself, Chase," he whispers. She puts her hands up in mock apology.

"Sorry, Commander, my bad, but that woman flew a very long way to an alien planet with you. Not to mention gave birth and recovered from nearly being blown up by some lunatic. So I think she can handle a little camping trip. She's in her element John, she needs this," she says. Carrie sees the look in Meridian's eyes and feels comforted by it. She has a spark in her eyes, has tightly cropped blonde hair and has youth still carved into her cheeks. She has an air of authority that her father deeply respects. He nods and turns back.

"Aquaria Base, this is Romeo One. We have entered the canyon. Readings indicated something a hundred meters north of our current position and seventeen meters down. We are proceeding." The commander's brow furrows.

"Aquaria base acknowledges. Watch yourself, you didn't bring your lucky dice." He looks over at Meridian who meets his gaze. There is a pause on the comms system, as the unusual familiar tone that the commander uses is understood.

"Aquaria base, that is a negative. Romeo One has it firmly in her atmo suit," she says. Meridian smiles.

"Aquaria base acknowledges," he says, smiling.

Carrie's mind shifts, leaving her father and floating across the red soil. It finds her mother's mind and merges with it. She feels her hands grasping at the cave wall as she makes her way inside it. At first, she thinks the soil is giving way before she looks down and starts to see the rocks have started to become smooth and uniform. She stops in her tracks and turns to the others.

"You see this, Jin?" she says

"Yes, Doctor, very strange. Seems to get flatter the further we go down. Some sort of erosion from a lake or freshwater source?" Jennifer shakes her head without answering and continues on.

"The passageway opens up in twenty-two meters," Jin chirps over comms. Their lights begin to disperse as they approach an opening slowly. The ground is dark. Black. They pause and take in their surroundings. Jennifer reaches over to the side of the cave wall and runs her fingers over the surface. It is smooth, like polished stone.

"Jin, are you getting any readings?" she asks.

"Mapping it now, Doctor. One moment," she replies, as she points a long cigar-shaped instrument around the inside of the cave and along its floor. Charlie holds firm, directing his lighting array onto the cave floor.

"Why is the ground black?" he asks. Jennifer looks on.

"I really don't know, Charlie, but it looks like some sort of ice formation," she says. Jin finishes up with her scans and looks bewildered at the results on her pad.

"My God, it's organic," she says in awe.

"What?" Jennifer says, as she makes her way over to confirm.

"The cave floor," Jin continues, "it's not ice. It's some sort of organic matter." Charlie bends down and reaches a hand out. The two scientists do not see him do it. His fingers slip into the ground easily.

"It's not solid, Doctor," he says, immersing his whole arm beneath the surface.

"Charlie, step back," Jennifer says. "We don't know what we're dealing with here."

Charlie looks at Jennifer.

"Sorry, Doc, wasn't thinking." He does not move. Jennifer steps closer to the young man.

"Charlie, I said step back," she repeats, annoyed that she has to tell him again.

"I am trying to, Doctor, but I appear to be stuck." Charlie starts to jerk his arm backward to no avail.

Then the screaming starts. His mouth opens and his eyes turn red. Jennifer realises there is something very wrong. She moves quickly towards him and tries to pull him out. She cannot. Carrie feels panic begin to well inside her mother's chest as her heartbeat begins to increase. Whatever has him has a firm grip and is pulling his arm in deeper. It looks like thick black liquid. He begins to flail widely, in agony, unable to speak. Jin grabs his other arm and jams her feet into the ground to get resistance. Charlie jerks forward and the momentum of the motion throws Jin straight into the black fluid. She gives a last shocked scream before disappearing from Jennifer's view under the surface. Charlie begins to sink.

"Jin!" Jennifer shouts, while trying to keep a firm grip on the manic security officer. He looks at her as blood begins to flow from his eyes. She tries one last time to hold on as he is pulled under the surface. She lets him go and steps back to the edge of the blackness. She is out of breath and tears of shock begin to stream down her face.

"Jin!" she screams into the darkness. No answer. She stands up slowly and keeps quiet, trying to listen for voices. Nothing. She turns to pick up the scanner and loses concentration for an instant. She loses her footing on a smooth rock and slips into the dark fluid.

"Fuck," she says. To her surprise, she is able to stand in it. Knee deep in what feels like warm mud. A tingling sensation begins to creep up her legs. Then the pain. It shoots through her legs like a high voltage shock. She cannot scream. The shock of it has knocked the air out of her lungs. Her feet go *numb. Her mouth is wide and eyes bulge. She begins to sink into the black fluid. Her legs go numb. As if they are no longer there. Carrie feels the pain. She feels her mother's panic. She feels her helplessness. Her thoughts begin to merge and blur. She can feel herself losing consciousness and grabs the comm panel on her arm. It activates. Now chest deep. No feeling in her torso. She has no muscles contraction in her lungs. She cannot breath. She finds the strength in one last breath and gives it to her husband who she desperately hopes can hear her.*

"John," she screams, her throat beginning to fill with blood. "I love you. Save Carrie!" As the black liquid covers her eyes and fills her lungs, she can only mouth the name of her daughter as the organism takes her.

What seemed like an eternity later, Carrie awoke screaming. Grasping at her chest. She looked into the viewing chamber. The Earth was gone. What looked like an asteroid field was now swirling through the chamber. Huge sections of rock and fire were floating past her slowly. She caught her breath and tried to clear the images from her recurring nightmare, as she righted herself in her seat. She closed her eyes and took in several deep breaths, before looking around at the empty lab. Tyrell was still out. She was alone.

"Computer, time," she asked, feeling groggy.

"Time is zero three zero ten," said the soft, female voice. She looked on at the asteroid field.

"Computer, realign array Earth," she said.

"Alignment currently locked to those coordinates," said the voice. Carrie looked at the rocks. She looked at the control panel above her and checked her readings. Twice. She felt confused. She tapped in the coordinates for Earth's moon. The image in the viewing chamber shifted out to show the moon. It was definitely Earth's moon.

"Aspect change to Earth, viewed from lunar surface," Carrie said. The viewing chamber obeyed and took Carrie to the white powdery surface of the Earth's moon. There, looking up from its surface, were masses of floating rock.

"Where is the Earth?" Carrie asked.

"Planetary body cannot be found. Gamma radiation detected," said the calm, female computer voice.

"What?" Carrie said. "What do you mean, it cannot be found?" she asked. "Gamma radiation?" She reached up and tapped some commands into the control panel.

"Computer, show me the last thirty minutes of recorded data," she said. The images in the viewing chamber froze and went black.

"Time index commencing at three seven," said the soft, female computer voice, not sharing a hint of the anxiety Carrie was now feeling. The imager came to life, showing the blue rotating Earth.

"Okay," said Carrie to herself. "There she is. Now what the hell happened?" She allowed the critical scientist voice to take over. "Has to be an array malfunction," she said. "Computer, when was Gamma radiation detected?"

The viewing chamber began to speed the image up, then it stopped. The Earth's rotation returned to its normal smooth self. Then a bright flash of light made Carrie place her hand over her eyes. After a few seconds she looked at the viewing chamber in time to see the Earth exploding from the inside out. Its atmosphere bleeding out into space as the detonation from its centre engulfed the entire globe in a hail of fire and light. It had happened so quickly. Chunks of rock floated outwards towards the edges of the viewing chamber. Carrie's mouth remained wide open. Her lips were dry.

"My God!" she said. "Doctor Tyrell!" she screamed at the empty lab. No answer. The debris field filled the viewing chamber. She leapt from the seat and ran towards the door of the main lab. It hissed open and there stood Doctor Tyrell. He looked down at her. His eyes were red and crazed. He looked at Carrie and then up at the viewing chamber.

"Gamma Explosion detected," repeated the female voice.

"Doctor!" she said, pointing to the viewing chamber.

"I know, Carrie," he said, placing a hand on her shoulder. "Remain calm," Tyrell said with a firm and almost surreal tone to his voice. "Come with me." He turned her back towards the diagnostic tables.

"Computer, pause viewer and discontinue alert," he said assertively. The alarm stopped and all went silent. He turned to Carrie. "Sit down, Carrie," he said gently. Carrie began to shake but obeyed him.

Tyrell turned and walked over to one of the diagnostic tables and started punching in commands. Carrie sensed something from him. It was faint, but the more she opened herself up to it the stronger it got. For a moment, she thought it was excitement. But she dismissed it as her imagination. His adrenalin was probably playing havoc with his emotional state. Something in Tyrell's eyes didn't sit right with her. She looked back at the now empty viewing chamber. The room was silent. Only the chirps of the computers filled the void. Tyrell sat down and looked over at Carrie.

"What just happened, Doctor Tyrell?" she asked. Tyrell looked at the empty viewing chamber.

"Too early to tell, but it looks like some sort of Gamma radiation. The entire planet has broken up." He paused. "Your father is on his way here now. In the meantime I am going to conduct some more observations to see if I can ascertain what we're dealing with." He turned back to his diagnostics display and began sifting through the data being transmitted by the array. Carrie closed her eyes and, for a moment, she thought she could hear the faint sound of screams.

Phobos Orbit
Gamma Event T minus seventeen minutes

Jerome Young stopped the manoeuvring jets on his harness and positioned himself just over the equator of the small moon. There, he hung weightless in emptiness and stared down at the surface of Phobos. His EVA had lasted longer than he had scheduled but it had been a particularly beautiful view of The Agathon dry dock and he wanted to watch the construction for a while. Besides, it was the first moment he had had to himself in over two weeks. The only sound was his own breath inside the faceplate of his helmet.

"Young to orbital," he said into his comms.

"Orbital here, go ahead, Mr. Young," came the swift response of a young, male voice.

"Patch up the signal to my comms, will you?" he said.

"Patching now, sir," the young voice said. The silence in his helmet was replaced by the steady rhythmic clicks and harmonies of the signal. He closed his eyes and listened. He allowed himself to drift in the emptiness, as the sound reverberated through his mind. Maybe this time he would crack it. After all, true inspiration came when one was totally isolated from distraction. His father had never cared for signals from other worlds. A ruthless and violent man, he had preached to Young that power was the only true constant in the Universe.

"One either has power or one is a slave. There is no in between." Young had listened and had learned to appreciate what his father had meant, but had always looked to the signal.

The signal. What good was power when the Universe continued to perplex the mind? Power without knowledge haunted him. When his father died the plans for the orbital platform on Phobos went ahead with the full resources of the company. Protected by Jycorp Military personnel and its pitfalls. It was hard for Young to find privacy anymore. Even out here, floating above the surface of Phobos, he had a tracking detail of three security personnel a half a kilometre away in case he got into difficulty. He loved the view from this angle of the Monolith. Almost perfectly perpendicular to the top surface of the mirrored structure. He had often viewed that section as the antennae cluster, even though no real evidence existed to support it. He had thought that if he stood directly on top of it, then the signal would flow though his body and give him the means to decipher it. He stretched his arms out and closed his eyes to listen. His comms chirped.

"Mr. Young, we have an incoming transmission from the chancellor," said a male voice. Young's heart quickened. The title of chancellor wasn't quite befitting the beauty of Sienna Clark, whom Young had appointed to the position less than a year earlier. As head of state to the planet, her elegance was matched only by her fierce intellect and legendary ruthlessness. Yet, her charm and humour was infectious. They had shared an evening of passion, unbeknownst to the world, after her inauguration dinner.

"Put it through up here, Lieutenant," he replied. The comms chirped again

"Jerome, this is the chancellor, I hope I am not interrupting you?" said an assertive, female voice. Young smiled in his breathing plate.

"Not at all. I'm actually looking at you right now." He flicked his eye up to Earth. "What can I do for you on this fine summer's day?" He redirected his manoeuvring jets and began his descent onto the surface of Phobos.

"Well, I normally wouldn't disturb you when you're out 'jogging', but our listening post on the surface of Mars relayed a signal change from the Monolith a few moments ago. I have contacted Doctor Tyrell and also advised our listening posts here on planet to advise. Have you had the same readings?" The surface of the moon grew closer as Young slowed his descent towards the Monolith. He hadn't heard anything from either orbital platforms, but that wasn't surprising, as he had left strict instructions not to be disturbed.

"I haven't checked in yet, Sienna, but I'll do so now. I'm on my way to the surface as we speak. I'll link up when I'm inside the main hangar bay in thirty minutes. Any idea what the change signifies?" His curiosity had made him lower his guard and his tone towards the chancellor had now become very familiar. She snapped him back to reality.

"Please do, Mr. Young. I will speak to you then." The penny dropped.

"Of course, Chancellor. Young out." His comm snapped closed and there was again silence.

A change in the frequency was something that had happened on only a handful of occasions. It usually signified a galactic event like a supernova or black hole that had interfered with the data stream. He watched the Monolith, as it grew closer. His escort followed his descent on the surface of the moon. It was a manoeuvre his detail had not been fond of. His atmo suit's thrusters were automatically programmed to bring him to the surface with relative ease, but there was always a little nervousness in case they failed.

He had programmed them to bring his descent perpendicular to the edge of the Monolith, so that he could almost touch it on the way down. Few humans were able to get this close. The bases and power cables that surrounded the perimeter glowed neon blue. The light from the main hangar deck was now tracking him. As the Monolith passed him by, he gazed at the unmarked surface. His reflection gazed back as it watched him fall towards the surface. For a moment, he thought it had smiled at him. He dismissed the illusion and continued downward towards the base of the structure. His jets fired and he came into a soft and controlled landing. He faced the Monolith and reached out the palm of his hand, touching its smooth surface. His mirrored hand met its reflection. His comm chirped.

"Mr. Young, main hangar is prepped for your arrival. I will see you inside," said a male voice, much older than his.

"Good to see you, Tosh, be two minutes. Young out." His only true companion out here, Doctor Daniel Tosh, was a physicist in his early seventies. In need of genome treatment and paralysed from birth due to a severed spinal column, Tosh had been a pioneer in both FTL drive technology and interstellar communication systems technology. With a dry wit and love of fine dining, he was often the honoured guest at Young's table. They would debate morality issues, democracy, and war, but above all else the alien life forms responsible for the signal and the Monolith.

Getting Tosh to Phobos had not been easy. He had failed all medical criteria and Young had to outfit the transport carrier with specialised medical equipment just for the trip. He needed him though. He had been instrumental in the analysis of 'The Black', which had proven lethal and elusive on the surface of Mars. He and Tyrell were alike, in that they both liked to work alone. He had always known that great minds always sought isolation. He made his way over the surface of the moon towards the large black structure to the north. He gave his jets a light tap, bringing his feet gently onto the surface of the moon. Behind him his security detail followed suit. As he approached the front of a large hangar, the main doors hissed open. He glanced back at his detail that was following close behind.

"Come on, fellas, last one in is a rotten egg."

The two Marines quickened their step, which was not easy in this low gravity. They entered the hangar door and waited while it sealed slowly behind them. Atmosphere filled the entrance and they removed their breathers. Young revealed a thick head of greying hair and manicured but stubbled face. The inner door opened, revealing an overweight man in a floating wheelchair. A gift from Young that enabled its user to traverse any terrain with ease. The man in the chair wore a white faded shirt with the sleeves rolled almost up to his shoulder. A pair of glasses hung from a slightly torn breast pocket. His features were soft and he had an air of quiet confidence. He was holding a metal tool in one of his hands.

"Hello, Tosh, how ye been?" asked Young with a light slap on his shoulder. Tosh gave him a warm smile.

"I was doing just fine until this damn rock of yours went berserk a half hour ago." They moved along a long white walled corridor, with many doors springing off to various labs. Tosh floated easily through the hall and kept pace with Young, who walked with purpose.

"What's been happening?" he asked.

"Well, three minutes ago the subspace frequency went dead. Like totally dead. Kaput, for the first time in a century. We thought it was a wormhole or some other phenomenon, so we did what any good scientists do. We waited. Sure enough, it came back, but with a power and frequency we have never seen before. The signal is changing from transmission frequency to an energy pulse." Young stopped in the hall and turned to Tosh.

"A what?" he said.

Tosh replied, "It's an energy pulse. And it seems to be emitting Gamma radiation." Young looked him in the eye and began walking quickly now.

"What is its focal point?" Young asked.

"It's directed at Earth's Pacific Ocean."

Young moved quickly now down the hallway towards his destination. They reached another corridor and stepped onto a small gangway, which led to a lift. Young motioned to his security detail to remain behind. They stepped onto the gangway and began to descend. After several minutes the platform came to a stop, revealing an enormous array of machinery scattered throughout a technological sprawl of sensor arrays and holographic interfaced computers. Technicians were scurrying about and the floor area was buzzing with activity. Nobody seemed to notice the new arrivals. Young and Tosh headed over to one of the computer stations. A female technician was sifting through endless amounts of algorithmic code, which was spinning past her display.

"What's the situation, Dana?" Tosh asked. The attractive girl turned her head and stood.

"Mr. Young, I'm sorry, I didn't see you there." Young held up his hand.

"Nice to see you, how are things with the signal?" They sat together at the desk and all looked at the code.

"It started about a half hour ago. The Monolith started resonating a photonic pulse, originating from the Aristaeus system. The pulse is being directed at a focal point in the Pacific Ocean. It seems to be causing some sort of quantum fusion effect within the Earth's core."

Young looked at the data. then glanced at Tosh.

"What do you make of it, Tosh?"

"Looks like an attack," Tosh replied.

Earth
Office of the Chancellor
New York City
Gamma event T minus nine minutes

Chancellor Sienna Clark's day had begun as it usually did. She rose at five a.m. and went for her customary five K run around Central Park. It was a cold morning in New York. She had programmed the Holo-display for a brisk morning with the dew still fresh on the grass. She missed being able to run in the real outdoors, but being Chancellor had precluded such luxuries. The facsimile was impressive with the sounds of the morning metropolis emulated in almost perfect detail, from the smell of the freshly baked bread at the patisserie on East 60th Street to the sounds of the Holo-boards as they displayed Jycorp advertisements. She was a fit woman at forty-eight, with a strong frame and angular complexion. At five foot eleven, her presence was felt in a room long before she ever opened her mouth. Her confident and assured stride commanded social occasions with ease. Running was the only time she had to really process her thoughts. Tyrell had told her to wait while he analysed the data from the signal change that morning, which gave her a window to hit the bricks. It wasn't to last as long as she had hoped, as a square viewer appeared overhead with her Chief of Staff, James Ryder, looking down at her. He never smiled and even though dressed impeccably he always looked like he hadn't slept in weeks.

"Chancellor, sorry for disturbing you, I have Doctor Tyrell on the line," he said, floating in mid-air.

"Put him through," the out of breath chancellor replied. The image flickered and Tyrell appeared overhead.

"Hello, Chancellor. Thank you for being so patient. I have been running diagnostics and liaising with Doctor Tosh. There is a definite shift in the polarity and nature of the signal. Mr. Young is currently on an EVA. There is no definitive data as to the cause of the shift as of yet, but we do know that it is emitting Gamma radiation and that it is being directed at the Pacific Ocean." She looked up at the doctor and tried to catch her breath.

"I will contact you when I have more."

"Thank you, Doctor Tyrell. Keep me appraised." The screen went blank. She turned and headed for the exit of the Holo-chamber. At one thousand meters tall the Jycorp headquarters was a formidable structure, modelled on the architecture of the Monolith with its mirrored surfaces reflecting the cityscape. The chancellor's office was located on the top floor suite, with an impressive glass surround offering breath-taking views of the cityscape. She had positioned her white glass desk beside the east-facing wall to watch the sunrises. The spectacular bursts of light as they sliced through the skyscrapers in the morning were breath-taking. It made her feel almost godlike, watching the humbling beauty of the world.

She arrived at her office after a quick phone call to Young, who was out taking the views of Phobos. She sat at her desk and asked an aide to prepare her a cup of Jamaican coffee. Black with one sugar. She was often amused at how far human civilisation had come on the back of beans. It was a wonder that nature had not incorporated caffeine into the human genome through some sort of Darwinian adaptation. She sat at her desk and started looking through the communiqués of the morning. Her chief of staff was always her first call in the morning and he usually joined her when she arrived at the office. She was early today so took advantage of the quiet moment she had to catch up on the latest developments. The signal shift would probably take up a significant amount of time today, so she quickly sifted through the council's manifest to see if there was anything she could bump until later in the day or tomorrow. She was scheduled to speak to Commander Barrington regarding The Agathon project later in the day. The FTL ship orbiting Mars was nearing its completion and was only twenty months away from its first test flight. A few minutes later, the door chimed. James Ryder entered and nodded to the chancellor a good morning.

"Quite the morning, eh, Jim?" she said with a grin.

"Yes, Chancellor," he said sombrely. "I don't like what I see on Phobos."

The chancellor smiled. "Jim, the damn thing has been on there for a hundred years. I think if it was a hostile move they would have done it by now, no? Let's just wait for Tosh to get to grips with it and take it from there." Ryder's usual furrowed brow and pit bull-like appearance told her otherwise.

"In the event of any hostile action, we need to consider the evacuation protocol. I suggest preparing a number of drills over the next twelve hours. As you know, your executive shuttle pod is manned twenty-four hours a day, but I would like to go over some scenarios with you so that we can cut our response times."

The chancellor's expression began to change to one of frustration. She hated this area of her position and she didn't like to be handled, but her regard for Ryder won out and she nodded her head in reluctance.

"Okay, Jim, but let me finish my coffee first, all right?" Ryder acknowledged and handed her a briefing labelled 'Agathon Project Code Black. Security Clearance Only'. The sun was streaming in through the window as one of the chancellor's assistants laid a tray of steaming coffee on the table.

"Would you mind dimming the windows, Laura?" she asked.

"Of course, Sienna," she replied. She caught Ryder's disapproving eye as she did. Her chief of staff was not fond of aides using her first name, but it had been something the chancellor had insisted on when she was sworn in.

"People are less likely to betray a friend," she had once told him. The windows darkened with a command from the aide.

"Is there anything else I can help you with, Chancellor?" said Laura.

Sienna shook her head and Laura turned quickly on her heels and made a discreet exit.

They read over the progress reports of The Agathon project and Ryder updated her on launch protocols and timeline reviews. When they were finished, they turned their attention back to the signal. The comms system chirped.

"Go ahead, Anna," the chancellor said

"I have Jerome Young on the line." The chancellor's back straightened.

"Mr. Young, what news?" she said with as much officialdom as she could muster.

"Chancellor I think you need to consider relocating to the Orbital platform." His voice was different. She could tell when a sentence with very little information was intended to communicate more, and his tone of voice was rock solid. She wanted more. Ryder shot a glance at the chancellor.

"Mr. Young, I have a schedule which precludes me from leaving Earth right now. Can you elaborate?" She thought she felt a small vibration in the floor. She dismissed it as Young answered.

"Tosh and I have come to the conclusion that whatever the signal is doing, it seems to be affecting the core of the planet at a subatomic or quantum level. Deliberate or not, the calculations are becoming somewhat alarming, so I think we need to get you and your staff off surface for the time being, while we continue to observe. I don't want to make this an order, Chancellor, but if needs be—"

The chancellor interrupted, "Jerome, you don't think that sends poor signals to the populus? The chancellor abandoning her people every time Jycorp snaps its fingers? I honestly believe we need to think carefully about this and wait for more data on what the changes in the signal mean, without creating an unnecessary planet-wide panic. You appointed me to this position to lead by example, did you not? And you assured me that Jycorp would not overrule me. This was your first step in giving power back to the people of this planet, Jerome." There was a moment's pause and then a clear response.

"Okay, Sienna. If it's okay with you, I would like to speak to James to go over evacuation protocols for a few minutes, in case things start to heat up. Please be available on comms at a moment's notice."

"Of course. Be my guest," she replied. Ryder picked up the portable earpiece and placed it in his ear. He was silent while Young spoke. He gave brief answers.

"Yes, sir. Of course, sir. I understand, Ryder out."

The chancellor frowned.

"That was quick."

"Yes, he was just confirming that protocol black is still ready to go at a moment's notice. He likes to cover all the bases."

"Of course," she replied. For the first time in their professional relationship, she knew that he had just lied to her. On the table, her coffee cup began to vibrate.

Young hung up the transmission and turned to Tosh. Tosh looked at him.

"She's a full head of steam, eh?" he said.

"That she is," he replied.

"You think Ryder got the message?"

"He got the message," Young replied.

"How long do we have?" Tosh turned to the display.

"The uplink from the Earth orbiter is beginning to show tectonic activity. I think we need to talk to Tyrell."

"Get him on the line," said Young. The comms chirped and Tyrell's face appeared.

"Dr Tyrell, I am afraid whatever is happening up here is not a friendly hello anymore. Do you concur?" said Young

"Mr. Young, I have been monitoring the changes in the signal and, from what I can gather, it is becoming evident that this is some sort of energy weapon being directed at Earth's core. We have no current defence against a Gamma radiation of this magnitude. Judging by the intensity of the pulse, I would say we are looking at an extinction level event." There was a silence.

"Jesus Christ, what can we do?" Young asked quietly, almost rhetorically.

Tyrell responded, "Save as many as you can and send them here. There isn't much time. I'm going to speak to Barrington now. If you will excuse me, I think we need to get moving... fast. Tyrell out." The transmission closed and Young and Tosh looked at the technicians who were now focused on them. Panic was starting to fill their eyes. A young Asian manning the communications station beside Tosh looked up.

"Sir, can't we just blow up the Monolith?" he asked.

Young put a hand on his shoulder. "The station doesn't have anything powerful enough to damage it. We tried every explosive and particle weapon we had five years ago, to try to get inside. Not a scratch."

"Get me Ryder on the comms. Secure the channel." Young placed an earpiece in his ear. After a few seconds he was connected.

"Ryder, this is Jerome Young. Olympus has fallen. This is not a drill. Acknowledge. Do it now." The comms clicked. He looked at Tosh.

"I want to speak to John Barrington now."

Main Observatory
– Astrometrics lab - T minus six minutes

"This is Tyrell," he said, raising his voice but not taking his eyes of the holo-comp display.

"Tyrell, it's Tosh here. You seeing what I'm seeing up here with the signal?" Tyrell was studying the data on his display carefully.

"Tyrell, you there?" Tosh said. An urgency in his voice piqued Tyrell's interest. Tosh was not one for displaying emotion easily. Tyrell looked on for a minute, to see what he was on about.

"One second, Doctor, I have not been observing it as of yet." There was no doubt there was an increase in the amount of data being transmitted, but there was something strange about the way the data was being organised. It had begun to pulse. The stream had never done that before, but there was something else. There was a definite energy signature now being emitted by the signal. Tyrell couldn't believe it.

"Tosh, I'm seeing an energy pulse embedded in the stream and it seems to be increasing. You concur?"

"Yep, that's what we're seeing up here. I don't like it Tyrell, our sensors are going berserk. It's highly focused and directed towards the Earth. If it keeps going it's going to cause destabilisation in the core. I've got Young coming in from an EVA now." Tyrell took a moment to take in what Tosh was saying. He needed time.

"Inform the chancellor immediately, Doctor. I will monitor and contact you in ten minutes."

"Okay, will do," Tosh replied and the comms clicked off. He stared at the stream for a moment and then tapped some commands into the clear panel on the desk

"What is the nature in the change of signal?" he said to the computer. A few moments later, a soft, female voice responded.

"Signal composition increase by 7000%. Composition now 42% Gamma 13% photonic with unknown elemental variants being observed."

Tyrell continued, "Speculate as to unknown elemental variations."

There was silence, then the voice responded. "Standard analysis of the variants is not possible under current analytical conditions." Tyrell looked at the data and tapped a few more commands into the panel.

"Begin a comparative analysis on the interaction with known particles and electromagnet field generation from a planetary body."

The computer acknowledged, "Beginning analysis. Please stand by."

Tyrell's heart rate began to increase as he did some computations on his own palm computer. "It couldn't be," he whispered to himself, as he looked at the numbers.

The female voice clicked in. "Particle analysis complete. Gamma ray synthesis is possible in a planetary core, given the infusion of known particles."

Tyrell's eyes widened. "Speculate as to probable outcome of Gamma ray interaction with core of planetary body."

The female voice responded coldly. "98% probability of annihilation of planetary body." Tyrell sat and watched the signal as it flowed like a river across the holo-comp display. He wasn't entirely sure why he felt so energised. Surely he should call Barrington. The end of the world was coming. Earth had been chosen. Its people could not respond to the signal and the creators had grown angry and frustrated with its ignorance. It was time. He had been chosen. To live. He had escaped. The universe knew that he needed to find the true nature of it all. And the meek shall inherit the Earth.

"And the meek will die," said Tyrell. He hadn't noticed the incoming transmission from Tosh. His eyes were still fixated on the signal. The comms continued to sound.

Tyrell finally answered, keeping his tone subdued. "Tosh? I'm seeing a Gamma burst being focused at the core. With that level of energy I think we're looking at a cataclysmic explosion."

Tosh replied, "Jesus fucking Christ, why would they blow the planet?"

"It seems they've run out of patience. I advise you to get who you can off the surface. There isn't much time. I need to call Barrington and advise him. I'll keep observing. Tyrell out."

Tosh was in the middle of replying when the comms went dead.

Office of Commander Barrington

Commander John Barrington stared at the two colonists sitting across his large oak desk. His mind had been wandering for the last several minutes and he was having difficulty focusing after his thirty-six hour survey of the orbiting Agathon dry dock.

"Commander. Do you hear me?" Doctor Chase Meridian asked.

"Hmm?" he said, realising that he hadn't.

"I said that we have now been waiting for three days for the transfer of the micron inhibitor and the good doctor here is refusing to give it back until he's finished with his silly little analysis of the microbial—"

"Now hang on just a second," interrupted a flustered young man sitting beside her. "You gave my department total discretionary use of the equipment for a period of three weeks, not two!" he said in a thick Scottish accent.

"Oh for God's sake," retorted Meridian. "Commander, Doctor Kyle McDonnell knows full well what my conditions were for relocating that machine, and the fact that we are sitting here..."

Barrington raised his hand. "Doctors, please..." he said, sighing. He leant on the table and placed his thumb and forefinger on the bridge of his nose.

"I am sorry, Commander, I realise you must be tired from the last few days. We can discuss this when you've had some rest," said Meridian. Barrington could hear the concern in her voice and looked up, giving her a smile.

"Kyle, you have until the end of the week, then transport the inhibitor to the biology lab. Will that be satisfactory to you both?" he said wearily. They both nodded and stood to leave.

"Doctor Meridian, a moment if you will," he said. She turned and nodded to McDonnell, who gave her a cheeky smile as he left. Barrington was in no doubt that there was something between those two, but had never confronted her about it. She sat and pulled her dark hair behind her ear. She was a plain woman in her early forties, with simple features and a well-kept physique. She was a disciplined and meticulous biologist with a dry wit.

"Drink?" he asked her, knowing the answer.

"Constantly," she replied with a smile.

"How is she doing?" she asked.

Barrington fixed her a neat whisky and handed her the large-bottomed glass. He sat in a long lounger chair next to the wall and stared out the window. "At this rate, we'll never get done. The damn hull plating is still absorbing way too much background radiation. It will just break apart the second we go into sub light. We have to find a way to make the polarising resin thicker or all this will be for nothing." He swirled his drink around his glass.

"That is nice," Meridian said. "But I was referring to your daughter." He looked over at her and smiled.

"Oh right," he said. "That's even worse."

"She still having nightmares?" she said. Barrington nodded. He looked out the window again.

"I wish Jennifer had let me take them both back to Earth. I never wanted to bring up a daughter on this hunk of rock. Let alone bring one up alone. I'm a military commander. What the hell do I know about raising a woman?" He took a thick gulp of his whisky and let it burn his throat, before he stood up to make himself another. Meridian laughed.

"What's so funny?" he said.

"It's the same as building a starship, John. Once piece at a time. I think you're doing okay," she said, dropping ranks. "Jennifer knew the risks of doing what she did and she wouldn't have married you if she didn't think you were up to the job. When was the last time you had a good night's sleep?" she said.

"Twenty one years?" he said, giving her a grin. He looked out at the networks of pods and connected walkways of Mars Colony 1. Off to the right he glanced at the main control centre of Aquaria Base. The thirty-storey pyramid structure was the focal point of the colony and shone a beacon of light into the night sky. A nice touch by the designers, keeping the inhabitants in touch with Earth.

"I miss her," he said suddenly. There was a moment of silence before Meridian stood and walked over beside him. She placed a hand on his shoulder.

"We all do," She said. "But you have something special in Carrie. We both know that. She is important, John. You have to turn to her now. You have to let Jen go." Barrington didn't answer. He had to restrain a sudden and unexpected flood of emotion that threatened to overcome him. It was probably tiredness.

"Any change in her telepathic abilities?" she asked. He shook his head.

"They are strong," he said. "She's hiding something from me. I thought it was just the usual secrets, but there is something else." Meridian nodded.

"You might have better luck than I," he said. She laughed.

"We may be close, John, but she still keeps me at arm's length. Give her time," she said. "She will have to say something eventually, John. There are already rumours."

"Not yet," he snapped back. "I will not have Carrie the subject of colony gossip. I have enough to worry about with Jycorp brass breathing down my neck every minute of the day, without having to deal with that."

Meridian took a breath and looked away to break the tension.

"Where are you on the latest batch of results on The Black?" he asked under his breath.

"Nowhere," she said, placing her empty glass on the table. "It is highly resistant to everything we throw at it." He nodded. "Get some rest. If you want I'll get Brubaker up here to give you a tranquilliser." She paused. "Or something better."

Barrington laughed. Brubaker's romantic interest in him was no secret between them. "Don't tempt me," he said. She nodded and turned for the door.

"Let's do dinner tomorrow. We can chat some more," she said. Barrington gave her a thankful nod and she headed out into the hallway. The holo-comp on his desk came to life with a light flurry of activity, indicating an incoming call. Without shifting his gaze he answered.

"Barrington here."

A young male voice answered, "Commander, it's David. I am passing by, can I have a word about The Agathon?" Barrington sighed, wondering if he would ever get any sleep this evening

"No problem, Lieutenant. Come on in," he said.

Lieutenant David Chavel stood at the entrance to the commander's office. The thirty-two-year-old pilot stepped in and gave a familiar salute to the commander, who reciprocated casually. They had spent so much time together over the last several months that protocol was starting to lapse. Barrington had reminded himself to keep an eye on that, but for the moment he couldn't have cared less. Jycorp had increased the materials shipments in recent months and new personnel were coming in almost weekly. Chavel had been a key player in handling the logistics of the build. Barrington was fond of the young man. He had an enigmatic personality and took initiative well.

Chavel had come to his attention a few years earlier, following an accident in which he had earned the Daedalus Medal of Honour for bravery in the course of action. He had been a pilot at the helm of a transport ship bound for the Jycorp mining operations facility on the moon when it had been struck by a micro meteor shower. With the temperature of the command module falling and oxygen depleted, he had managed to seal the crew and passengers into an aft compartment and pilot the stricken vessel safely into orbit around the moon. When the rescue team had finally reached them he had been clinically dead. Chavel took a seat opposite Barrington and placed a display pad on the desk.

"Drink?" Barrington asked politely.

"No, thank you, sir. If I have a drink now, God only knows where some of these engine parts will end up." Barrington smiled lightly.

He could tell the young officer had been up for well over twenty-four hours and was operating on pure adrenalin at this stage.

"So how's our baby doing?" asked Barrington. Chavel tapped some commands into the pad and with a smooth flicker of particles a three-dimensional image of a ship was born from the light. The two men looked on at the ship. A large disc-shaped object rotated slowly before them. Jycorp had completely redesigned their interstellar concept designs by removing all external fusion engines. The Alpha class vessels, which ferried supplies and personnel between planets, were extremely reliable and efficient but had been bulky in order to accommodate the drive sections of the ships. The Agathon had been built without the need for fusion drives, allowing its simplistic and streamlined design. The rim of the ship spun independently on its axis at varying speeds, creating an electromagnetic field. The FTL drive section was powered by a secondary spinning ring, encompassing the ship and was located perpendicular to the edge of the vessel. This ring was locked in place next to the rim of the fuselage while not in use. Windows and lights peppered the vessel, giving it a grand scale even while viewed at this size on Barrington's holo display. The ship was clearly unfinished, with at least a quarter of the aft exposed to the vacuum of space. Corridors and quarters were visible like an open dolls' house.

Barrington addressed the young lieutenant. "She's a work of art, David," he said.

"Yes, sir. She sure is. She needs a lick of paint, mind you, and we've got some issues with FTL ring deployment. The architecture of The Agathon was designed so that its symmetry facilitated the transition of the hull smoothly from normal space to faster than light speeds, with as little stress as possible to the outer hull.

"As you know, sir, the relatively large surface area of the ship was causing an odd mass variable during gravimetric simulations," Chavel said. Barrington nodded.

"The problem is the radial alignment of the FTL ring when it reaches full rotation," he continued. "It creates its own mass in the middle of the space time singularity, so we have to adjust the rotations per second by a millisecond or so to allow for the effect. Otherwise the stress on the hull might tear the ring clean off the ship."

Barrington sat back in his seat. "A millisecond, huh?" he said, smiling. Chavel looked back up from the image of the rotating ship and reciprocated.

"Yes, sir," he said.

"I think I can live with that, Lieutenant."

Chavel nodded. "I thought you would, sir. We can't get a full test done until we can lock up the hull on that aft section," he said, pointing to the unfinished part of the craft.

"Where are we at on that?" asked Barrington. Chavel blew a sigh out.

"Eighteen to twenty-four months at least, at this rate. We are getting heat from Jycorp on our latest personnel request. Seems there's politics in play on the flight crew allocation. Until we can get confirmation on the last batch, we're gonna be waiting on the remainder of the hull alloys." Barrington nodded and tapped a command into the display pad, and the ship sank back into digital oblivion. He sat back in his chair and addressed the young man.

"Been quite the year, hasn't it?"

He smiled. "Yes sir, it has."

"David, I realise you have been under tremendous stress and I want you to know that I am not in any way unsympathetic to the weight that has been thrust on your shoulders. I have been forced to improvise in order to build this little world of ours and also try and spearhead the greatest leap our civilisation has ever attempted. I am not sure I have ever thanked you properly for the sacrifices you have made, not only for me but for the colony." He paused and looked at the surprised expression on the young man's face

"I owe you a great debt, David. If Jennifer were here today she would agree with me. I just wanted to express that to you, as I thought it important."

"It's my honour, sir," he replied, shifting somewhat uncomfortably in his seat.

"I am concerned about my daughter, David." Chavel raised an eyebrow.

"How so? She seems to fit in very well, no?"

"You don't have daughters, do you, Lieutenant?" Barrington returned with a light smile.

Chavel reciprocated, "No, sir. How can I help?"

"She is becoming increasingly isolated. Much like her mother used to be. Forgive me for being so blunt, but how well do you know her?"

Chavel shifted in his seat. "Not well, sir. She seems to shy away from conversation. We've talked. She's bright and very capable. She seems guarded, but if she is having difficulty she seems to hide it well."

The commander contemplated the young man's words. "Thank you, Lieutenant. That will be all." Chavel stood and collected the pad off the desk

"Anything I can do, sir," he replied as he made his way to the door. It slid open with proximity and the young lieutenant made his way into the corridors. Barrington's thoughts wandered as he leaned back in his chair, once again turning to face the exterior view of the glowing colony. His eyes drifted towards the observatory, as the peace of the moment weighed heavily on his eyes. He began to drift into unconsciousness.

The smell of freshly cut grass on a summer's day fills his senses. It is Mars. But different. Alive with lush green landscape. He feels the soft ground beneath his feet and the sun's warm rays on his face. He looks up and sees his wife across the field in her colonial jumpsuit, back to him.

"Jennifer," he shouts.

The silence and bliss between the two of them is palpable, as they stare at each other across the open field. Scattered throughout the landscape are a

variety of forests and streams now teeming with life. Overhead the skies are alight with broken cloud formations, splitting the Martian sunlight into beams of striking colours. The sounds of life on this new Earth drown the senses. They are separated by a quiet flowing river, which flows effortlessly over the uneven ground. Light breezes play with her hair, as the warm glow of the distant sun warms their faces. It is a happy moment. He never moves towards her. As if they glance at each other across some impassable terrain. She mouths something to him. Every time the same. He can't quite make it out.

It looks like, "I love you." She repeats it in slow motion over and over, always smiling. He begins to hear the faintest sound of a woman's voice being carried on the wind. Jennifer's voice begins to echo in his ears. The words are not, "I love you."

She is softly saying, "I'm melting." It is the moment right before she begins to sink. A pool of black oil like fluid forms beneath her feet.

Barrington calls to her. "Run, Jennifer," he cries. She looks on calmly, still gently smiling as she slowly begins to submerge into the black. Barrington screams to her to get out. She pays no heed. Her smile remains as her torso and upper body begin to submerge. "Please, Jennifer! Don't go." She closes her eyes calmly and accepts the black fluid into her mouth. Still smiling.

Barrington howls, "No!"

He woke suddenly, looked around the room finding it empty and dark. As he wiped away a tear the holo-comp bleeped, indicating an incoming call.

"This is Barrington, go ahead."

The voice on the other end was shaky and frantic, "John, this is Tyrell. We have an emergency. I think you should come to the observatory immediately." Barrington's heart jumped.

"What's going on, Doctor, is Carrie all right?"

"Yes, John, she's fine, but there is something happening to the signal. Please come down here. I am declaring a colonial emergency."

2

Main Observatory
Gamma Event T plus ten minutes

John Barrington stared at the viewing chamber. The view had been taken out to encompass the debris field. He rested his hand on Carrie's shoulder. Tyrell was hunched over a console, punching in various commands. Watching the ever-expanding flotsam of rock as it floated serenely outwards into the black of space, held a strange meditative quality to it. The orbiting arrays, satellites and space stations had been obliterated in the blast. The shockwave had carved a chunk out of the orbiting moon and it was left alone without its owner like a wounded and abandoned pet. Carrie had not spoken since her father had arrived at the observatory. She seemed unable to take her gaze from the viewing chamber.

"I don't understand, Father, it was right there. I was watching it all night. It was so alive. Am I dreaming?" The commander lowered himself to meet her eye level and glanced back at the floating rock, still grasping at his own straws and in awe of the devastation.

"I don't know, Dice," he said, calling her by her childhood nickname. "Why don't you go back to the habitat ring and try to get some sleep. Doctor Tyrell and I have a lot of work to do before the rest of the colony wakes up and finds out what has happened."

Carrie was quick to respond, "I cannot, Father. I have to stay here with you. Please, I have to stay with you."

He turned his gaze back to the viewing chamber. "Okay, Dice. I could use your help anyway. I need to talk to Tyrell for a moment. Do me a favour and contact Lieutenant Chavel on comms. Tell him to come to the observatory immediately, for a briefing. Don't tell him what has happened here until we figure this thing out, okay? I also need you to get a hold of Doctors Meridian and McDonnell. Tell them all to get here quickly, but do it calmly, Dice."

Carrie's face blushed slightly at the mention of the lieutenant's name. Her father knew that response well, but he did not have time to get into it with her.

"Yes, Father." She paused. "I'll get on it." She stood from her perched observer chair, went to a nearby workstation and sat behind one of the computers. He watched her. *John, I love you, save Carrie.*

"John?" Tyrell's voice said from behind him. "We should really think about where we are at. Take stock of the next steps. There are decisions to be made."

The commander acknowledged the doctor with a small nod and made his way over to meet him at his workstation. He took a seat next to Tyrell, while keeping an ear tuned into his daughter's voice as she tried to reach the others. He addressed Tyrell in his soft monotone.

"Talk to me, Tyrone, what the hell happened here tonight? Why wasn't there any warning?" Tyrell closed his console down and addressed the commander directly.

"Commander, we were just attacked. It was unprovoked. There was no warning. The signal changed without provocation and without the slightest indication of any new or unusual cosmic events. We have been tracking this thing for over a hundred years and, for whatever reason, the species that created the signal and the structure on Phobos have unilaterally decided that today is the day to end our race. Other than the data collected from our array and the obvious change in the signal to a concentrated Gamma burst, I have no other information to give you at present. Right now we need to focus on one thing and that is to find out who, if anyone, has survived."

Barrington looked back at his daughter and tried to compose his thoughts. "Jesus Christ," he said to himself. "Okay, Doctor, continue to liaise with Tosh. I am going to try to raise Jerome Young and see what we can do from here. I need you get a visual on The Agathon, to see if there is any damage or effect from the Gamma pulse on any of the ship's systems or personnel currently on the vessel, or on an EVA."

He turned to one of the consoles and tapped in a few commands.

"Computer, initiate comms with Charly Boyett on The Agathon."

Flight Officer Charly Boyett's voice came over the comms, "This is Boyett." Her strong tone sounded well beyond her thirty-one years and held an assuredness that Barrington took great comfort in.

"Charly, status report," Barrington said.

"I'm currently on the flight deck, knee deep in fibre optic cable, sir. The number two plasmonic field generator just won't play ball with us up here. It keeps generating random ion field formations around the secondary wave guide conduits. We have to nail it down or it could cause the FTL to cascade during our first flight, and we really don't want that, sir. How's everything down there?" The sounds of plasma torches could be heard in the background as she spoke.

"Charly, we have a situation down here." He stopped for a moment to gather his thoughts. "Have you got the main sensors active yet on the flight deck?"

"No, sir, not yet. It's a real mess up here at the moment to be honest," she said.

"Okay, Charly, I need you brace yourself for this. The Earth has just exploded in space. It's gone." There was silence.

"Sir, can you repeat, please? It's quite loud up here and it sounded like you just said the Earth had exploded."

"Charly, that's confirmed. I need you do a full systems and hull integrity check. Get the forward array up and running and link it up. Start monitoring. I need you focused, Lieutenant, there are going to be a lot of frightened people up there and down here when this breaks. I know what you left behind and I know what it took for you to come here, but find strength and use it."

The commander's voice was locked into the steady elevated rhythm of a trained leader and he made sure to leave no room for hesitation or doubt in his voice. In a catastrophic event, the mind needed direction to stop it from breaking down. Sometimes a strong voice was all it took.

There was silence on the comms then Charly's voice piped up above the noise. "Silence on the deck, everybody shut up!" The ambient noise ceased immediately. Charly continued, "John, is this some sort of joke, a drill or something? Because if it is, it's not that funny, sir."

The commander couldn't help but admire her candid nature. He had taken a shine to her early on when they had first met and allowed a certain level of informality among those under his command, up to a point. He found that it had strengthened loyalty. He took a moment and softened his voice.

"Charly, this is not a drill. Listen to me. All we know down here is that there was a change in the signal some time ago, which fired a Gamma ray burst into the Earth's core. We're picking up the pieces down here. I wish I could tell you more but I don't have it right now. You are in command up there, I need you to listen and act. I'll be in touch shortly but right now, we're at Colonial Emergency level 1. Just keep your team in check and focus."

There was a moment of pause and then a clear response.

"Yes, sir." He could hear her voice beginning to tremble but closed off the comms.

"Barrington out." The screen went blank and Barrington was left looking at a sombre reflection. He looked up and saw David Cheval standing in the doorway.

Carrie hadn't mentioned anything to the young lieutenant on the comms, but she had made herself very clear that he was needed to be there quickly. Now standing in the doorway he acknowledged both the commander and Tyrell, who hadn't noticed that he had arrived.

He then glanced at Carrie and gave an involuntary smile. She had grown used to the wave of feeling that filled her mind when he was in close proximity. It was a feeling of attraction she encountered amongst most men, but it was particularly strong with this one. She reciprocated his gesture with a small wave and turned her attention back to her console. The magnitude of what had just occurred was too confusing to combine with the urges of a clearly passionate attraction from a young officer, even if he was a handsome one. Her obvious blush responses were not lost on Chavel, as he made his way over to her father.

She observed him as they shook hands and spoke. She began to sense the changes in the officer's mind as the news was being broken. Grief and panic were old friends to Carrie and she didn't need to sense emotions to recognise them but once her mind was open, it was hard to not to let them in from others. Chavel held himself with composure and strength, but inside his mind was in turmoil. The warm feelings she had sensed moments ago were gone. Shock released the floodgates of every feeling all at once and Carrie's sensitivity to them was increasing on a daily basis. She had begun exercises in segmenting her thoughts from others, out of fear of having her own mind washed away in other people's thoughts. It had become a terrifying thought that somehow her own consciousness could be washed away by thoughts of the other colonists. It was her father who had given her the idea.

"Build a home for your thoughts," he had told her one night when she couldn't sleep. "Somewhere they can be safe. Build a house in your mind with impregnable walls. It will be your own fortress. That is where you go when others flood your thoughts. Don't open the door, Carrie. Not to anyone. Not to anyone!" The fortress she had constructed in her mind had begun as a steel cube structure a thousand feet high, with a door ten feet thick, only accessible via a thin rope bridge over a bottomless ravine a mile wide. It had been a rather extreme version of what her father had been talking about, but it served its purpose well. The rope bridge could be retracted at will, leaving enemy thoughts no chance of getting across. She had even added weapons to the exterior. Large plasma cannons, each with their own compartment, scattered themselves along the walls of the cube. She had even test-fired them one night. It had been a spectacular show of force, as they tore through the fabric of her mind with power and ferocity. She had found it empowering and had been impressed at her ability to create such a devastating show of force, albeit an imaginary one. The years had changed her fortress, as she grew surer of what it had represented. The steel cube had been replaced with an ancient Earth castle, complete with moat and drawbridge.

Her father and Chavel were deep in conversation. The lieutenant's attention was focused on one of the screens, as her father gave instructions. She turned her attention back to her task.

"Open comm to Doctor Meridian, please." She spoke to the computer which responded in kind.

"One moment, please." There was a long pause, then a sleepy female voice answered.

"Yeah... go ahead, hello?"

"Doctor Meridian, this is Carrie. I apologise if I woke you." A yawn.

"Not at all, kiddo, how are you. What's up? You discover the meaning of life yet?" Carrie smiled. She was very fond of the doctor and she of her.

"Not yet, Chase. I think that just got a little harder, to be honest. Are you able to come to the observatory, please? Something has happened. My father and Doctor Tyrell are already here and it is important that you come right away."

Meridian didn't hesitate in her response. "Of course, I'll be there shortly. Let me just get dressed, sweetie. See you in a mo. Meridian out."

Carrie stood and walked over to the stations where her father and Chavel were talking. An air of urgency was beginning to fill the room. The kind that follows an accident or emergency, where the fight or flight responses kick in. Her senses were heightened as she approached the trio. She knew what the two officers were thinking, but Tyrell was different.

She paused for a moment as their eyes briefly met. While his expression was one of sincere acknowledgement, she still couldn't read him. All she saw was a void behind his eyes and something else. Something dark.

"You okay, Dice? Did you get hold of the others?"

"Yes, Father, they're on their way now." She turned to Chavel.

"Hello, Lieutenant," she said, nodding to Chavel.

He gave her a warm smile.

"Hello, Carrie. You doing okay?" he said.

"I don't really know what to do, to be honest," she replied looking back at the viewing chamber.

"I know what you mean," he said.

There was a moment of silence between the two. Carrie felt a warm feeling from Chavel. A comforting attraction from the lieutenant.

There was a chime behind them and a motion activated door slid open. Doctor Meridian entered with a smile and a slightly dishevelled look. She approached the group near the console that the commander was seated at and placed a hand on Carrie's shoulder.

"Morning, boys and girls, what's all the hubbub about? The world better be coming to an end because I was in the middle of a beautiful dream."

Main Observatory
Gamma Event T plus two hours twelve minutes

While the others were huddled discussing the evening's events, Tyrell had returned to his personal lab to the rear of the observatory and had been trying to raise Tosh on comms. The signal was blocking transmissions from the base on Phobos, so he had given up for the time being and was busy looking at the expanding debris field on one of the viewing chamber feed displays. The flotsam of rock, ice and molecular dust formations was beautiful. It had been so fluid, like an expanding cloud of bubbles in a deep ocean. Each handful of the once dense and richly developed planet now drifted outwards in a perfect sphere, bound for the great unknown. There was no discernible outline of any of the once vast cities or technology. The heat of the explosion had seemingly vaporised all evidence of any human existence on the surface.

I wonder what it felt like, he thought, gently stroking the side of his face. He tried to imagine what the melding of flesh, bone and rock in a nanosecond would have felt like. Finally becoming one with the creator. All energies combined into a cataclysmic fusion of life and matter. *You lucky little insects. I wonder what you know!*

The sensors were busy targeting various debris formations and trying to catalogue and count the larger chunks of planetary fragments. Tyrell was tracking several of the larger fragments and had begun a grid search for vessels in the area that may have been disabled, but that could have possibly survived the explosion. He looked over at the large cylindrical holding tank in the corner of his lab. A sample of The Black sat quietly inside. The tank had a variety of tubes and cables spouting out of its top and bottom. Tyrell tended to keep his lab several degrees cooler than the main colonial habitat ring. The Black reacted more positively to it and he had gotten used to the cold, after spending so much time with it. His own analysis of the deadly alien substance had not been particularly fruitful. He knew it liquefied organic material on contact. And that occasionally it would alter its shape in the tank for no reason and then return to a gelatinous state. He had lost count of the amount of small rodents he had placed in the tank for experiments.

"It is this world's cockroach," he had told an unimpressed Barrington. He knew Barrington just wanted it destroyed, but he had held him off to try and learn what he could about it. He turned his attention back to the display.

The orbiting space station had been completely obliterated but there were several Jycorp ships scheduled for cargo and personnel runs to and from the moons of Mars and the colony itself. If their outer shields had been able to protect against the ionising radiation, there could still be survivors. Although less concerned with this area of the event than the reason for the change in the signal, Tyrell thought it would be prudent to at least examine this possibility. He entered a new algorithm into the search parameters, to detect energy signatures emitted from spacefaring craft, and let it run. He instructed the computer to begin filtering out background radiation, to try and lock onto signals being sent from both Phobos and any other ships in the vicinity. The computer began to process the data while Tyrell turned his attention to the expanding mass of rock.

"Computer, what is the status of the signal?" Tyrell said, while making his observations.

"Signal has reverted to previously established patterns, Doctor," came the familiar female voice.

"They hit us hard and went to sleep?" he said out loud.

"Please repeat request," the computer said.

"Never mind," he said. Then something occurred to him. "Computer, can you scan the debris field and begin a trajectory plot for the debris fragments? Then begin a collision threat analysis."

"Of course, Doctor, beginning now," she said calmly.

"Doctor, I have found something which falls into the parameters, as outlined by your request. Could you please direct your attention to coordinates indicated on the screen?" He tapped some commands into the panel.

"Can you give me a visual?" he asked

"Of course, Doctor, one moment." The screen lit up. An enormous black shadow filled the visual, almost completely blocking out the surrounding star field. At first Tyrell thought there had been a malfunction in the display, until he adjusted the visual contrast manually. The unmistakable contours of rock and ice formed on the screen. The surface of the rock was molten and had begun to glow with an eerie electric crimson. The surrounding edges left a trail of ice and companion debris fragments.

"Computer, size and course of object?" he asked.

"Object is approximately 1100 miles in diameter and is on a direct course for impact with planet Mars."

Tyrell looked at the continent of rock, as it appeared motionless. A strange fear began to embrace him. It was a curious sensation. An odd urgency began to take hold. Perhaps the insects had not been so lucky after all. He glanced over at the sample of The Black and stood from his chair. He took a breath and made his way out of the lab and back towards the others. He caught the eye of Barrington, who immediately knew something was wrong. Walking over to the group, he called to Carrie.

"Carrie, I need you to input a new set of coordinates into the viewing chamber." Carrie frowned with curiosity, but obeyed Tyrell's request. She made her way over to the chamber and took her seat. As she tapped in the information sent to her control panel from Tyrell's station, the viewing chamber came to life. The enormous piece of rock floated casually in the glass cube.

"What am I looking at, Tyrone?" Barrington said. There was silence in the group. Tyrell sighed.

"The apocalypse, John."

3

Time since Evacuation – Four Hours

"Chancellor, can you hear me?" came a familiar, yet distant voice. The haze began to clear as the senator looked outwards towards the twinkling light. "The disorientation will pass. Try and open your eyes slowly. You are safe."

She looked to her right, as the form of James Ryder came into focus. Her head felt groggy and her lips were dry. She cleared her throat, which felt tight.

"What the hell happened?" she said, holding her head.

"You are on board the Nexus," came the reply. She looked around and noted the unmistakable appearance of her personal shuttle. The comfortable surroundings and high clean lines were something she had taken a liking to when she had first sat in the luxurious ship. Two members of her security detail were seated on the other side of the shuttle. They nodded to her.

"How are you feeling, Chancellor?" came the deep baritone voice of her head of security, Greyson Kane, a formidable ex colonial Marine from the Congo region of New Africa. She was relieved to see him. The other member of her detail was Kevin Ruffalo. Although physically not as foreboding as Kane, his accuracy with sidearm was legendary among the protection detail.

"Hello, Greyson. I am well, thank you. Would somebody please explain to me what is happening?"

Ryder sat back in his leather chair and glanced out at the stars. "A few hours ago I was given an order to execute executive order Alpha. Given that protocol there was no time to discuss actions until you were safely transported to the orbital platform. In order to do that you were rendered unconscious for your own safety." He took a slow breath.

"Chancellor, it is with a heavy heart that I must inform you that the planet Earth has been completely destroyed."

She looked at Ryder. "What?"

He continued, "As it turns out the shift in the signal carried with it a powerful Gamma ray emission which destabilized the core, causing it to detonate. I'm sorry, Sienna, but it's gone. We barely survived ourselves. Our engines have sustained heavy damage and our life support systems are cutting out due to the ionizing radiation levels in the area. The outer shield is holding for the time being, but we still have a long way to go."

This was a moment that she had never planned for and the magnitude started to overwhelm her. She turned to the window but was unable to contain the tear that rolled down her cheek. She covertly wiped it away and addressed her chief of staff.

"Survivors?"

"We lost most of the orbital platforms and orbiting vessels in the explosion. We set a course for Phobos the moment we got off world, so we caught the tail end of the detonation. There are several transport ships ahead of us. We don't know how many or what shape they are in."

"Who survived, Jim?" Sienna pressed.

"Your senior aides, the off-world colonies, obviously, and a few trade and supply vessels on various runs." He paused again. "We also lost contact with the moon. I am sorry."

She felt a profound sadness take hold. "My brother?" she asked.

"We have no communications with anyone at the moment. Radiation levels are too high, so honestly we don't know. My guess is that the colony and structures were lost in the blast. We have no way of really knowing and are currently unable to do a visual due to the expanding debris field."

The chancellor's head began to spin. "I need a glass of water, Jim." Her chief of staff immediately jumped to order and poured her a tall glass from a jug that was sitting on a neighbouring platform. He handed it to her and she drank deeply. She steadied her shaking hand and looked at Ryder in the eye. He was clearly shaken.

"I suppose I owe you thanks for saving my life," she said quietly, while watching the stars go by.

"Actually, I just took the order. The big man put it into effect." He nodded in the direction of Greyson Kane. "Had him carry you to the shuttle once we'd knocked you out with anesthazine. Again, sorry about that but it's procedure." She looked at Greyson and gave the large African an earnest smile and a nod. He reciprocated and turned his attention back to the window.

"Young gave the order while you were on the phone?" she asked. Ryder gestured with his hands to indicate she had guessed correctly. She nodded. *Thank you, Jerome.*

"What do we know from the signal station on Phobos, before comms went blank?" she asked.

"Very little at this stage. We know that the signal amplification incorporated Gamma emissions and we evacuated on the orders of Jerome Young. We have not been able to raise anyone since the event and have set a course in the hope that the radiation levels will clear in the next thirty-two hours or so."

The chancellor took a breath. "Okay, Jim, let's get everyone we have on board into the observation deck and have discussions about where we go from here. I need to get some input. Give me a half hour to get my thoughts together. These people need to know that someone is still making decisions. What is the headcount on board?"

Ryder paused. "The head count?" he asked. "I honestly don't know, Chancellor. We didn't have time to take one. I will attend to that now and get back to you."

Sienna was annoyed at that. "Jim, if we are the only survivors of the planet Earth, it would be nice to know how many humans we were able to save on board. Don't you think?"

"Of course, Chancellor, I will get right on it." As he made his way to the oval door that reacted to his presence with gliding fluidity, she stopped him once more.

"Jim, did you get Laura out?"

He turned back and met her eyes. "I am sorry, Chancellor, it was key personnel only and there simply wasn't time." He bowed his head and walked out of the room. The chancellor's heart sank and her chest began to fill with rage. Her assistant and new mother-to-be had been such a vibrant spirit. *Jerome Young, you son of a bitch.*

Phobos
Time Since Evacuation – Four hours thirty minutes

"Emerson, get the reactor levelled off to ninety-two percent before we blow the whole place to high heaven!" shouted Tosh at the top of the metallic gangway.

The rising heat in the chamber was becoming unbearable for the large man, but he had remained to assist the young Irish engineer. Landon Emerson's legs were visible from where Tosh was sitting on the bridge. The rest of his body was firmly hidden from view under the array of twisted metallic pipes and cables that made up the main base reactor.

"No shit, Tosh!" came the sharp Irish brogue.

"I am trying not to freeze myself solid with coolant right now, can ye gimme five fuckin' minutes?"

Tosh responded with silence, but kept his eyes fixed on the rising pressure readouts from computers above the gangway. Tosh had given Emerson a wide berth, given his attitude and the situation they were currently in. The comms chirped.

"Tosh, it's Young. Talk to me."

"We're at one hundred and three percent, Jerome. Landon is under the main coolant distribution nodes, trying to access the manual override. It's getting pretty warm down here. Might be a good idea to start thinking about getting everyone off. If we can't get a handle on this, we're done here." Tosh didn't fancy his chances of getting clear if the reactor went into meltdown. He didn't like the idea of leaving his friend down here to die alone either.

"Tosh, I'm going to leave this channel open. I want updates every two minutes. Young out." The comms chirped twice to indicate an open channel and Tosh acknowledged the head of Jycorp.

Beads of sweat were starting to roll down his ample cheeks. He had opened his tunic up and his sleeves were as far up his arms as they would allow. Tosh was still curious as to how they were all still alive. The feedback pulse from the Gamma burst that had destroyed the planet had shaken the small moon so violently that two of the equipment hangars had decompressed, killing thirty-four personnel. Through some miracle, the base reactor had remained relatively unharmed, other than a coolant lock that was now threatening a core meltdown.

"One zero four, Landon. I think it's time to go." Tosh was now beginning to get nervous. No response from Emerson down below.

"Landon!" he shouted. "Come on, Paddy, it's time to light some fires and get the hell outta Dodge." *Not that it will matter much*, thought Tosh. At one hundred and six percent it was all over and, at this rate, the odds of even getting out of the chamber were slim. He looked at the gauge. One hundred and five.

"Emerson, let's go! NOW!" He looked over the platform but couldn't see Emerson any more.

"For fuck's sake," he shouted at himself. From beneath the curved and twisting metal a head appeared, which looked up to the platform and smiled.

"Got it!" Emerson shouted. Tosh looked up at the pressure reaction readouts. One hundred and one percent and falling. Ninety-nine, ninety-eight. He looked down at his large legs and sighed. Wiping a layer of sweat from his brow, he signalled to the young Irishman.

"Good lad. Good lad. Now get back up here, we have work to do before you give me a fucking heart attack."

Emerson gave a mock salute. "On my way." He slid out from under the machinery and stood up. His black overalls were covered in fluid and his hands were filthy. He made his way up the steps to the gangway, where Tosh was seated. With a shaved head and carefully unkempt stubble, Tosh often joked that he looked like Jack Tanner, a film star from back on Earth. He was a favourite among the female residents on the small moon and frequented the bedrooms of many of them on a regular basis. The playful rogue used his dry Irish humour, much to the delight and frustration of the opposite sex. He reached Tosh and put a hand on his shoulder

"Gotta say, Danny boy, I'm impressed that you stuck it out. I never thought of ending my days on this moon with you for company. No offence, but that's not how I intend to check out." Tosh gave him a grin and turned his chair back towards the main airlock, which had been sealed during the crisis. He keyed in some commands and the metallic circular door slid open, revealing a small group of onlookers all wearing the same overalls as Emerson.

"You all look like you've seen a ghost," said Tosh, as he slid past calmly.

"If you would all be so kind as to attend to the reactor, while we ascertain the level of damage to the base, that would be splendid." He reached for the comms system on his chair and tapped. "Jerome, this is Tosh. We got it under control here. Emerson and I are on our way back to signal control. Do you want to meet us there?"

There was a small pause. "Well done, Daniel. See you in five. Young out." The abrupt communiqué told Tosh that Young was probably elbow deep in problems up there. All hell had broken loose following the signal shift. There was a moment of total shock and awe, as the flash of broken rock had filled the observational screens. Comms from Earth had gone dead in an instant. The scientists and engineers in signal control had become statues. Like wide-eyed figurines waiting to be placed in position. Then the ground had begun to shake. Tosh had remembered looking at Young, who was looking at the screens. He had shaken his head in confusion and bewilderment when their eyes had met, and grabbed a nearby upright to stop his chair from flipping on its side. He had heard a female technician shouting over the noise.

"Reactor 2 is going critical! Coolant leak on 1."

Tosh had screamed to Emerson who had fallen next to the processing tower at the back of the control room. "Landon, let's go!" Emerson had responded immediately and they had scrambled to the reactor.

Signal Control Room
Time Since Evacuation – four hours forty-six minutes

The pair reached signal control and were met with chaotic scenes. Broken screens suspended from cables hung haphazardly from the roof, some still spilling white sparks over the workers below. The red haze of the emergency lighting reflected off distraught and frightened faces. Tosh searched the floor for Young and spotted him out of the corner of his eye. He appeared to be working on one of the signal backup storage capacitors. There were five in total but only three were run on a full time schedule to conserve power from the base generators. The honeycombed clear glass structures had been analysing every nanosecond of the signal for the past forty-three years. Tosh and Emerson made their way through the sparks and joined Young by one of the honeycombs. He looked up and placed a hand on Tosh.

"Still ticking, old friend. Thank you." Tosh nodded his head. "I hope to Christ we can still save the signal files. If we can't we're fucked. Pardon my French. I can't raise Tyrell or anyone on the surface of Mars. At the moment, we're on our own up here. Landon, I could really use your help with this. I have everyone working on damage control and communications."

Emerson acknowledged the words and slipped between two of the glass-honeycombed structures. Young waited for Emerson to be hidden from view and pulled Tosh aside.

"What the fuck just happened? I want a frank answer, Daniel. The human race just went extinct! I find it hard to believe that after one hundred years the fuckers chose today to blow us out of the universe."

Tosh looked at the head of Jycorp. "I wish I knew, Jerome. I really do."

A female shouted from over the fray, "Mr Young, we have comms back up to Mars Colony. I have John Barrington for you."

"Say again?" Young said to the distorted face of Mars Colony 1. The reply was fragmented but the resolution was beginning to clear.

"Mr. Young, simply put, we have to get everyone off the surface of Phobos and Mars and onto The Agathon." Young stared. Barrington continued, "Tyrell has confirmed that the shockwave has accelerated a large debris field which will come into contact with the surface in roughly eight months. The shock will devastate the surface and possibly shift the orbit of the planet. Phobos's orbit is too unstable to withstand the gravitational effects of this shift and, to be blunt, we currently have nowhere else to go."

"John, the last time I checked The Agathon was missing half of its hull."

The image of Barrington raised an eyebrow. "Well, Mr. Young, I suggest we get a move on, because we have eight months before humans bid this universe a fond farewell."

"John, can I speak to Tyrell?"

"One moment." Barrington's face vanished from view and was replaced by Tyrell's.

"Doctor Tyrell, are you sure about this?" Young asked.

"Quite sure, Mr Young. To be honest, we don't really have the time to debate this decision. Preparations need to begin immediately. I suggest you begin transitioning all personnel from both orbitals and the surface base to the colony down here. I will liaise with Doctor Tosh about salvaging all data from the Monolith—"

Young interrupted him, "Tyrell, where exactly do you suppose we go?" Tyrell looked at Barrington off screen.

"Tyrell?" Young pressed.

"Well it seems to me that the logical course of action would be to initiate the FTL technology on The Agathon and, should it prove successful, then..." He paused. Young waited.

"Then..." He paused.

"Then we set a course for the origin of the signal." Young turned away from the screen and looked at Tosh, whose face had turned a pale colour over the last several minutes.

"Tyrone, did I just hear you right?" he said over Young's shoulder.

"Yes, Tosh. That's why we're building the damn thing in the first place, no?"

"So let me get this straight," Young added. "You are suggesting we load what is left of the human race into an untested and unfinished ship, hit the faster than light drive, then pay a visit to the planet whose inhabitants have just destroyed ours?"

Tyrell again looked off screen to Barrington. "In a nutshell yes. I am."

Young answered after a moment of silence, "As I see it, we have one small problem with that plan."

Tyrell knew what he was getting at and finished his thought. "There isn't enough room for everyone."

Carrie Barrington's residence
Main Habitat Ring
Time since Evacuation – two days thirteen minutes
21:32 Martian Standard Time

The sun had taken on a luminescent green hue as it set over the Martian horizon. Carrie stood by her curved window and watched as it sank into the red landscape. The mixture of the yellow, red and green light was beautiful. The peace of the evening had been a welcome friend, as the events of the last twenty four-hours navigated her mind. The gathering of the colonists in the main cargo hangar earlier in the day had taken its toll on her, as the devastation of two thousand people had flooded into the air. She could see their thoughts hovering over them, as if their minds had run out of space in which to store them. Thousands of dead faces had filled the air. The friends and families of loved ones left behind. Generations of those left on Earth. She had taken precautions before the meeting, by allowing her mind to lock itself safely inside her castle. The drawbridge pulled and all weapons firmly targeted at the entrance. At the moment of the announcement, she had opened fire and had successfully kept the wave of enemy feelings at bay. Only just. Some of the colonists had become distressed and had run out of the main hall. They had run, to no avail, to the closest communications terminal to try and contact anyone off world to confirm. Her father had let them go and urged calm while they had gathered more information about next steps.

What had followed was four hours of intense questioning from the settlers, most of whome were scientists or medical personnel. The anger of the military complement had proven to be more difficult for Carrie to deal with than she had anticipated. Their thoughts were a mix of focused, determined, and disciplined anger looking for revenge. Their surface was well guarded, but beneath was a sea of uncertainty. The castle was in danger.

As she looked on to the sunset she turned to the open Holo file she had running on the desk beside her bed. It was an old file her father had given to her, from when they were preparing for the journey to her new home. The live rendition was taken on the shores of the beach in Playa Norte in Mexico, with endless white sand and shallow water. Her mother's smiling face as she looked on at the rolling waves was one of Carrie's favourite images. She looked happy. She really had been a beautiful woman. Carrie lay on her bed and closed her eyes, while listening to the sea and laughter of her parents. She lowered the drawbridge and allowed the feelings of serenity to permeate throughout her mind. Her mother's laughter filled the universe and Carrie could not hold back the warm smile that she formed involuntarily. As the drawbridge lowered, she saw her mother waiting for her. She saw her face as it found hers and the love that accompanied it wrapped around her like a thousand soft feathers.

The entrance chime to her quarters snapped her eyes open suddenly. It was unusual for her to be startled by the presence of another colonist, as she sensed them long before they normally approached.

"Come in," she said. The door, recognising the command, released the locking mechanism and slid open with a soft hiss. Chase Meridian was in the doorway.

"May I enter?" she said softly. Carrie smiled.

"Of course, Chase, no need to ask." She swung her legs up and sat against the headrest. Chase walked in slowly and stood at the foot of her bed. She caught the Holo image Carrie had been running.

"She was really hot stuff, wasn't she?"

"She was," Carrie replied.

"Still, I think you would have given her a run for her money." She sat at the end of the soft mattress and looked out at the failing light.

"I wanted to see how you were holding up," she said, as she continued her gaze out onto the Martian landscape.

"We will have to leave here," she answered quietly.

"Soon."

"I am worried about my father. I do not think he is fully aware of what is expected of him from this time forward. He is afraid."

Meridian laughed. "Your father knows exactly what is expected of him, kiddo. Be careful not to confuse fear with acceptance of sadness. He has lost a great deal. Besides, he's not alone. We've got Jerome Young himself preparing to land with all the crew from up there. Maybe he can buy us a new planet?" she said, pointing to the sky and smiling. Carrie feigned a smile and gazed. Meridian stood up from the bed.

"I want you to come with me. I want to show you something." Carrie looked puzzled.

"Chase, the sun has gone down. Not much to see around here."

"Trust me. Grab that scope I gave you for your birthday. It should do the trick nicely. I need to pick something up from my quarters first. Come on, now. While we still have a planet to go out from." She raised her hand, took Carrie's in hers and pulled her gently from the bed.

Martian Surface
22:13 Martian Standard

After a short RV journey, Carrie and Meridian stopped three kilometres up the southern face of Elysium Mons. The ancient volcano rose out of the soil and seemed to touch the stars when viewed from its base. The dim glow from the colonial lights could be seen in the distance. At the edge of the horizon, the Atmo processors worked tirelessly, although somewhat foolhardily given the circumstances, to fill the doomed world with breathable air for impossible future generations. Carrie loved being off base. The feel of the soil produced a strange sensation in her fingertips. There was something else when she ventured out. Another feeling. Something in her mind, something familiar calling her.

"What am I looking at, Chase?" Carrie asked, peering at the display screen of the infrared magniscope given to her by Meridian on her twenty-third birthday. The relatively compact device sat on three legs and looked like a cube resting on one of its points.

"Hang on, let me get the coordinates." Meridian tapped a few commands into her integrated wrist screen.

"Okay, sending to you now." The scope bleeped and swivelled on its small turret.

"Locked," said a computerised male voice. Jycorp had not bothered with humanistic vocals for this particular range of scope.

"There she is," said Meridian. Carrie looked at the screen and the silver disk-shaped craft filled it in perfect detail.

"The Agathon?" she responded.

"The Agathon," Meridian repeated, with pride in her voice. The pair stared at the quietly rotating ship. The inner FTL ring was currently extended to a ninety-degree angle. They were obviously running a mechanical test of some sort. The aft section of the vessel showed exposed decks, as a series of surrounding construction platforms arced around the hull like a cradling spider, while sparks from plasma welders flashed brightly against the emptiness. They both looked on at the floating vessel silently. Carrie did not notice her attention shift at first, as she had thought her mind had been wandering while taking in the beautiful views. Her eyes came to rest at a point in the distance. She began to take notice when Meridian touched her shoulder.

"Hey there," she said, waving her hand in front of her face. "You still with us here?" Carrie stayed on the point in the distance, unable to take her eyes from it. She heard something. Something out there over the rim. She felt something. Something she needed to stay far away from. A sleeping evil. Meridian shook her shoulder.

"Carrie!" She snapped back to the moment with a sharp breath and looked the doctor in her eyes.

"I am sorry, Chase, my mind wandered."

"Yeah, it does that a lot nowadays, doesn't it?" she said, raising an eyebrow. "When are you going to start telling me what is going on in that Martian brain of yours?" she said. Carrie smiled and glanced back at the point in the distance, before turning back to Meridian.

"So this little trip was about The Agathon?" she said, changing the subject.

"No, little one," she said, tapping commands into the control panel of the scope. "This is why." The scope shifted its axis and began to rotate to a different patch of the night's sky.

"Locked," it said dryly. Meridian looked at the display.

"See that?" she said to Carrie.

She approached the viewing screen and stared at the moving objects. "Debris?" she asked solemnly. The objects were too small to make out clearly with this class of scope, but were clearly moving at the same speed and seemed to be clumped together. In formation. She suddenly realised.

"Ships!" she said. She looked at Meridian.

"Ships," she said smiling. "Tyrell confirmed earlier this evening that multiple beacons have been detected. We knew that the transports would probably make it or at least have their courses automatically set when the pulse hit, but there are others. We got ourselves some survivors, kiddo, and they're headed our way."

"Any idea how many?" Carrie continued.

"Tyrell has clocked twelve at the moment, but there could be more and they're moving fast." Carrie looked on at the little ships.

"Home," said a dark voice within her. She glanced back at the horizon, at the sudden interruption in her mind. There was something old and evil out there and it knew she was here. A strange feeling began to run up her spine and her fingertips began to tingle as a light electric charge travelled through her body. She thought she must have left a circuit on her suit slightly exposed. Seconds later, it disappeared.

4

"The Black" Cave
Time since Gamma Event-Three days
17:16 Martian Standard

The Black remained motionless as Lorenzo Fraine knelt at its edge. John Barrington only granted access to the cave in special circumstances and its sealed interior needed three identifiers in order to release the erected air lock. Retinal scans followed a DNA coder into the chamber, preventing any colonist from accidentally falling prey to the deadly substance. The geologist had been granted special permission to conduct seismic and acoustic tests. He had to focus on something other than the loss of his family in Caracas. While he was an unmarried man, his adventures on the red planet were shared on a daily basis by his nieces and little sister. He would bring them out on virtual driving tours, using his portable comm unit and show them all the experiments he was carrying out, by which they had seemed dazzled.

"How are we doing today, monster?" he whispered into the silence. The probe he had placed into the soft underbelly of the liquid was slowly sinking into nothingness, relaying its data before being consumed.

"Your sacrifice has not been in vain, my friend," he told the doomed metallic pole, as it silently disappeared. His dark brown eyes watched patiently as the last signals from the probe sent a torrent of information into his wrist monitor. There was a light spark as the metal disintegrated and the last signal was sent. The absorption had been swift. Fraine had been fascinated with the fact that it never caused a single ripple. He had noted that the event had been akin to peristalsis in the human digestive system.

"Hungry today, aren't we?" he asked. His soft Venezuelan accent permeated through the cave. It had been an interesting observation that there was very little reverberation within the cave walls themselves, with most of the soundwaves being absorbed. It was discovered to be an effect of the unique density of The Black. He had postulated that it had been a wonderful defence mechanism of the creature in order to disorientate its victims in a low light environment.

"Cool as a cucumber, cool as a cucumber," he said. Soft footsteps came from the right. The skinny frame of Bobby Shields stood by his shoulder. His light skin and fire red hair made the inside of his faceplate glow, even in this environment.

"Ye gotta stop talkin' to yourself, Frainey. You'll go crazy." Lorenzo ignored the young Englishman and continued on. He had requested to go out alone after the news of Earth, but Barrington had forbidden it.

"What are you doing anyway? Don't really see the point in all this. We're all fucked. Especially this horrible goo."

Lorenzo strained against the high-pitched, nasal tone of the thirty-one-year-old pharmacologist. "I am trying to concentrate on these readings. Do you mind?" he said with irritation in his voice.

"Sorry, mate, just trying to ease the tension. This place gives me the creeps," said Bobby, as he shuffled carefully away and made his way around the edge of the pool towards a seated area far from The Black. Lorenzo felt slightly bad about the way he had spoken to him, but quickly focused his attention back to his readings. He tried to quell thoughts of pushing the annoying little man into The Black to shut him up.

"Make yourself useful and grab me the infrasound accelerometer from over there, will you?" he called out to Bobby, who seemed delighted to be assigned any sort of task.

"Will do, Cap," he responded. He made his way carefully around the pit and picked up a small cube-shaped object, with a protruding spike.

"This thing?" he asked. Lorenzo sighed.

"Yes, that thing. Give it here." He handed over the instrument and stood waiting quietly. Lorenzo took a breath in to calm his irritation, but allowed him to watch, resigning himself to the situation.

"Okay, if you insist on annoying me, you may as well help. Take this sensor and place it on that ridge. Point the directional array towards the centre of The Black and lock it in position."

Bobby could hardly contain his excitement as he trundled off with the long metallic pole. He did as requested and set up the device, using the struts attached to its base. The transparent head was coned and he pointed its tip at the centre of the black mass. With the tap of a button, a blue laser shot out of the device and rested firmly on the surface of The Black. Lorenzo watched intently. There was no reaction from the molten surface. The beam of light stood unchallenged.

"Okay, Bobby, come outta there. Make sure it's not going to move, and position the second sensor directly opposite," he said, pointing to the other side of the cave. The Englishman did as he was told and repeated the exercise. When he was finished the light of the two blue beams slowly bounced off the surrounding minerals in the rock. There was no reflection from the surface of The Black.

"Now what?" said Bobby, as he reached the scientist.

"We wait. Quietly!" responded Lorenzo. The pair watched as readings were taken. The silence was absolute.

"This stuff actually do anything besides melt everything it touches?" said Bobby, breaking the peace. Lorenzo sighed. He thought about pushing him into The Black.

"It emits vibrations when it senses certain frequencies. Right now, it is emitting the same ultra-low frequency acoustic signature that we have been observing since Jennifer Barrington discovered it. We don't know what that means and we still don't know the nature of The Black. I am about to test a theory of mine, that the vibrations are directly proportional to the ambient energy in the vicinity of The Black."

"Eh. Right," said Bobby, then paused. "Sorry, mate, meaning what exactly?" he continued.

"Meaning we don't know why the hell this 'stuff' has been sitting here for millions of years, when its purpose seems to be to absorb organic and inorganic substances on contact."

"If that's true, then how come it hasn't eaten through the cave floor straight into the planet's core and out the other side?" said Bobby.

Lorenzo, surprised by the logic of the question, took a minute to answer. "The inside of these caves are laced with minerals that seem to be immune to the enzymatic reactions of The Black. It is probably why it has survived in here. Evolutionary luck."

"So we still have no clue about what this is?" asked Bobby.

Lorenzo answered honestly. "None," he said. The steady flow of data continued. "Okay, let's turn up the volume." Reaching down to the control panel he began to drag his finger across a screen, increasing the levels of both probes to twice their current amplitude. A small hum echoed from the upright stands as the pair watched.

"What are we hoping for here?" said Bobby.

"Not sure, to be honest, but the absorption of The Black of all ambient noise is interesting to me so I want to see what happens if..." Lorenzo's sentence tailed off as the centre of the black fluid began to rise suddenly. The slow purposeful motion seemed controlled and made no sound. A snaking spiral began to form and solidify into a perfect tube shape. At about two meters in height it stopped. It held its position and waited.

"Fuck me!" said a clearly worried Bobby.

"Don't move," replied Lorenzo, who was clearly startled at the unexpected movement. "Don't move a muscle. Stay perfectly still, Bobby."

"What the hell is it doing?" Bobby whispered.

"It is reacting to the frequency."

"Has it ever done that before?" Bobby added.

"No, never, and this is not the first time I've conducted this type of experiment." They observed the perfectly still material. It remained in the shape it had just formed.

"We should get out of here, man, and get back up. I'm serious." There was genuine fear in Bobby's voice, but Lorenzo paid it no heed.

"It has stopped, Bobby. We are not in danger, it seems to be localising around the focal point of the two probes."

"Then turn the fucking things off before it eats us!" replied Bobby frantically. Lorenzo shot him an angry look.

"Just calm yourself and stand back. I promise, if it makes any other movements towards us I'll shut down the probes and we'll get out of here. Okay?" he said. Bobby, clearly unconvinced, took several steps back towards the entrance of the cave and readied himself to run. Lorenzo, not entirely believing his own words either, took a step back from the edge of The Black and watched closely. The faceoff between the two life forms was a silent one. *You hear me, monster, don't you!* he thought. Lorenzo took the control pad in his hand and swiped his finger across it. The hum from the two probes increased.

"Are you out of your fucking mind? What are you doing?" shouted Bobby. Lorenzo ignored him. The centre mass remained perfectly in shape and perfectly still. In one swift motion the entire pool of the black substance rose from the floor. Building on top of itself in layers, it emerged into a tower with perfectly smooth walls, which reached the height of the cave itself. Lorenzo was frozen in place at the sheer magnitude of the coordinated movement. After several seconds, the perfectly smooth surfaces that formed the membrane of the outer edge began to curve. At first Lorenzo thought it was an optical illusion, but then the walls became clearly convex. The fluidity of the motion of this now cave-sized mass was the most powerful thing Lorenzo had ever seen.

"Jesus Christ," Lorenzo finally uttered. He looked behind him but Bobby was gone. He had seemingly made a run for it. The floating sphere stared at Lorenzo. It remained still. Lorenzo thought about running but his muscles would not move. All of a sudden the black orb started to move. First enveloping the probe on its left, then the one on its right. The two objects disappeared quickly from sight. Lorenzo now knew that he was in trouble and began to back away slowly. The giant black sphere gently began to move in his direction.

"Fuck," Lorenzo finally said out loud. "Fuck. Fuck. Fuck!" He turned and made for the exit. The sphere followed calmly, enveloping the surrounding equipment. Lorenzo, realising the change in the sphere's speed, began to panic. "

"Oh no!" he shouted and began to sprint. With a sudden knock, his head hit off the lower edge of the rock face as he tumbled to the ground. His faceplate cracked and atmosphere began to seep into his lungs. Blood from the top of his head poured into his mouth and eyes, as his blurred vision watched the encroaching black mass. Only feet away, his vision was masked by the filling of tears and blood. The burning in his lungs began to intensify. There was only one warning he could give to Bobby if he was still nearby. He drew a breath as The Black touched his feet and began liquefying his flesh. He closed his eyes one final time and screamed.

Quarters of Carrie Barrington
17:45 Martian Standard

Carrie woke suddenly and sat up, her soaked pillow falling away from her back. She felt like her heart was about to explode.

She heard a scream in her mind. The sadness and the terror of the voice chased by a dark monster lingered in her thoughts. Something terrible had just happened. She reached over to her comms panel beside her bunk.

"Carrie Barrington to John Barrington," she said with upset in her voice. No answer.

"Carrie Barrington to John Barrington," she repeated with more force in her voice. There was a beep from the panel.

"Go ahead. What's up, Carrie?" The comfort of her father's voice helped lower her heartrate.

"Father, something's wrong. Something terrible has happened."

"Slow down, Dice, take a breath. I'm on my way."

"No," she interrupted, "I'm coming to you. Where are you?"

"I am at the Aquaria command centre. What did you see?" he said softly.

"I think somebody has died. Has anyone gone to the Black Cave this morning?" There was a pause from her father.

"Meet me here as soon as you can. Barrington out." The urgency in his voice told her all she needed to know. She jumped out of bed and slid straight into a jumpsuit.

Aquaria Base
18:01 Martian Standard

"Barrington to Fraine," the commander shouted into the comm panel. The uncomfortable déjà vu was all too obvious. He had lost another one on his watch. He knew that he should not have allowed the pair access at a time when most of the personnel were emotionally compromised. *Bad call, John.* No answer from the comms.

"Shit!" he said. The support staff manning the command centre looked at him.

"Prepare a rescue team," he announced. "Now!" There was a bleep from the panel.

"Commander?" said a panicked English voice.

"Yes. Bobby? This is Barrington. Report!"

"He's dead. He's fucking dead. I had to run. I left him there. I heard him screaming. The fucking stuff is alive." Barrington froze.

"Where are you, Bobby?" he asked.

"Inbound in the RV," he sobbed. "I left him. Jesus, I just left him." The door to the control room hissed open and Carrie appeared. Barrington locked eyes on her as she approached.

"Tell me, Carrie," he whispered to her.

"It killed again, Father. It knew. It followed him and attacked." Some of the staff stared over at the pair. Barrington ignored them and put a hand on Carrie.

"Bobby, keep coming. I'll meet you at the RV bay. Stay calm, you're okay."

"I'm nearly there," came the reply. Barrington looked out of the windows, which curved around the command centre. In the distance, he saw the red trail of an RV approaching at speed.

"Barrington to medical bay," he said. The comms bleeped.

"Doctor Brubaker here."

"Michelle, we have possible incoming wounded. I want him put into quarantine immediately. Under no circumstances is he to be touched until a full bio scan reveals no indication of infection."

"Understood, John. What are we dealing with?" she said.

"Contact incident with The Black," he continued.

"Right. I'll have him locked down. Don't worry. Where will he be?"

"It's Bobby Shields. He's coming in the RV bay, ETA... hang on." Barrington looked over at one of the young men manning one of the stations.

"Eight minutes, sir," he answered the commander.

"Eight minutes, Doc."

"Gotcha, I am on my way." The comms bleeped again.

"Barrington to RV bay."

A young female answered. "RV bay, go ahead."

"Clear all personnel, I repeat ALL personnel immediately and seal off all airlocks. You have five minutes. Leave the main bay doors open."

"Yes, sir," came the programmed response.

"Okay, folks, let's lock it down," he called to his staff. Lights in the control room flickered to red. The commander tapped a few commands into his control panel. A hailing noise filled the control room.

"This is John Barrington to all colonial personnel. The base is on lockdown until further notice. I repeat. The base is on lockdown until further notice. No unauthorised movement in or out of the facility without my express consent. Doctor Tyrell, please report to main RV bay immediately. Barrington out." With that, he made his way to the door.

"Llewellyn, I need you to keep working on the system preps for the incoming transits from Phobos. You're in charge here until I get back," he said to an attractive female officer at a control screen in front of him.

"Yes, sir," she replied.

"Can I do anything?" Carrie asked.

"Yes, you can. Come with me. I need you to be there when Bobby comes in."

Main Vehicle Hangar
Aquaria Base
18:45 Martian Standard

The assembled group stood looking through the glass into the RV hangar. Tyrell was last to arrive and stood next to Barrington and Doctor Michelle Brubaker, the chief medical officer. A fiery woman in her early fifties, she kept her curly, greying hair tightly pulled back in a hair clip and her hands firmly planted in the pockets of her white coat. The large enclosure held a fleet of thirteen vehicles of various design, depending on the type of work required on the surface. Carrie was standing beside her father with her arms tightly folded. She looked worried. They waited outside the main airlock viewing room and watched as the trail of dust from the incoming RV made its way towards them.

"Get ready to hit the door," said Barrington, as he watched. Doctor Brubaker placed her hand on the hangar door release panel and waited. In a whirlwind of red dust the RV sped into the hangar and swerved, narrowly missing another smaller version of itself before coming to a grinding halt.

"Hit it, Doc," he said to Brubaker, who hit the control panel, bringing down the main hangar door. Silence surrounded the bay as the dust settled on the ground. Barrington could see Bobby in the vehicle, with his faceplate resting against the steering column.

"I'm going in," said Brubaker, as she made her way into the airlock.

"Hang on, Doctor," Barrington said, grabbing her arm. He hit a button on a control panel in front of him, which bleeped.

"Bobby. This is Barrington. Can you hear me?" His voice carried into the hangar bay over the loud speakers.

"He could be hurt, John. I need to get in there," said Brubaker.

"Not yet, Doctor," said Barrington, asserting authority in his voice.

"Bobby?" he repeated. The figure in the vehicle raised his head and looked over to the commander.

"Yes, sir, I can. I'm okay," came a stumbled reply. Barrington waited.

"John, please," said Brubaker.

"Okay, Doc, in you go. Do a visual before you make contact. Everyone else stay here." He turned to the hangar and pressed the comms.

"Bobby, stay where you are. I'm sending the doctor in. Do not remove your faceplate until instructed to. Understand?" A nod from the young man satisfied the commander. The airlock hissed and Brubaker made her way over to Bobby, who had swung around and was sitting on the edge of the vehicle.

"What do you think, Tyrone?" Barrington asked Tyrell, still watching the RV bay. Tyrell drew a long breath.

"Unknown, John. There's no reason to believe that The Black is a contagion. Then again, we know very little about it. I'm afraid I have very little to offer at this juncture. My instinct tells me that Mr. Shields is perfectly fine. If a little shaken."

Brubaker reached the RV and placed a hand on Bobby's shoulder. She removed a medical scanning instrument from her shoulder bag and began taking readings. A few minutes later, she turned to the commander.

"John, I am not showing any signs of infection or injury. I think we can get him to the medical bay."

He turned to Carrie. She was crying.

"He's terrified," she said.

Medial Bay
19.30 Martian Standard

"It moved," Bobby said. He was lying on a diagnostic bed, now out of his atmo suit. Tyrell's face changed to one of fascination.

"In what way?" he asked. Barrington put his hand up and motioned for the doctor to hold questions.

"Bobby, just start from the beginning. Take a breath and slowly recount everything that happened."

The Englishman began slowly recounting the events to the captive audience. At the end Barrington looked at Tyrell.

"Thoughts?" he asked. Tyrell stood and watched the patient.

"It would seem the beast has awoken. Commander, with your permission, I would like to return to my lab to run some tests."

Barrington thought for a moment. "Tyrell, if that stuff shows any sign of movement, I want it incinerated. You are not authorised to remove it from its containment chamber. I want someone there with you at all times and right now I want options for transportation of The Black off base."

Tyrell looked annoyed. "John, I don't think it poses any immediate threat. It would appear that it was reacting to defend itself from what it perceived to be a direct attack. I really don't think—"

Barrington interrupted. "Those are your instructions, Doctor. We have incoming from the Phobos base and several inbound craft with survivors aboard. The risk to life on this base is too great to start fucking around with an aggressive life form that has cost lives." Carrie looked surprised at the force in her father's voice. Barrington knew that he had momentarily lost his cool in front of everyone and drew a breath.

"Please, Tyrone. Just do as I ask." Tyrell nodded and promptly left. The commander tapped his comm link. "Barrington to Meridian."

"Chase here, go ahead, John."

"Chase, can you meet Doctor Tyrell at his lab, please? He requires your assistance." He glanced back and watched the frustrated Tyrell leave. He was muttering something under his breath. He reached the exit and turned back.

"If you don't mind, Commander, I could also use Carrie's assistance in the lab at her earliest convenience."

"Of course, I will send her over in twenty minutes." He turned back to Bobby who was watching the exchange.

"Get some rest and, when you're ready to get back on your feet, we will talk some more."

"Thank you, sir," he said nodding.

"What do we do about Lorenzo Fraine?" Carrie asked her father. The commander didn't answer.

"Barrington to Aquaria." His comms blipped

"Llewellyn here."

"Put out a colony-wide alert that The Black cave is under quarantine. No personnel are permitted to go near it. Change all the access codes to the entrance. Get a munitions team together. I want the entrance to the cave blasted and sealed off."

"Yes, sir," came a prompt response.

"You sure about that?" asked Carrie.

Her father nodded.

5

Phobos
Time since evacuation-Three days
07:13 Martian Standard

Daniel Tosh climbed into his chair, which he had set at ground level for ease of access. He glanced out of the porthole and looked out at the white rocky surface of the potato-shaped moon below. The comforts of the Jycorp Orbital platform greatly outdid the base on the surface and he was glad to have some distance between himself and the Monolith. The morning had started early with evacuation briefings due to take up the majority of his day. He poured himself a cup of black Columbian coffee. One of the few natural supplies of the stuff he had left which he had brought from home.

He absorbed the rich aroma and allowed himself the simple moment of pleasure before embarking out into the chaotic scenes in the main corridors of the space station. He made his way through the hustle and bustle of the crew preparing equipment for transport down the Martian surface. One of the passers-by knocked into his chair and excused himself apologetically. He was a young man in his early twenties. A junior signal analyst by the name of George Orwell. He had noted the name. They had met briefly enough and had some minor interaction. Enough for Tosh to remember he had parents back on Earth and that this was his first space assignment. He had remembered that he still had wonder in his eyes. Not today though. He saw only strain and dark rings signifying less sleep than normal.

Tosh gestured a polite wave to the frantic man and moved past him on his way to Jerome Young's office on the second level of the station. When he arrived, he was greeted by Young's personal security. Two thickly-muscled men stood ominously at the entrance. Their eyes locked onto Tosh like a magnet, and glared at him as he approached. Although he been there many times and greeted the two men in a friendly way each time, they still treated him with suspicion at each encounter. Tosh had also been fascinated by their total lack of personalities. Robotic minds. *That's what it takes to take a bullet*, he thought to himself. He looked up at the huge men.

"Morning, gentleman. How's the weather up there?" he quipped. They gave him a blank stare and signalled his arrival to Young. After an awkward few seconds, they stood abreast and let him enter. The door closed behind him and he found Young, with a similar smelling coffee, at his desk.

"Tough crowd," he said lightly. Young looked up.

"Huh?" he asked.

"Never mind. How are you this morning? Any word from the chancellor?"

"Not yet," Young replied.

"She is still two days away. Emerson is working on breaking through the radiation, so I may have something later. Barrington has had another death down there. Some lunatic decided it was a good idea to perform acoustic bombardment on The Black up close and personal. Turns out it didn't react too well and attacked in some way. Seems it has a few tricks up its sleeve that it hasn't shared with us."

"Christ," replied Tosh.

"Any reaction from the other samples at the colony?" he asked.

"None. Tyrell says it's an isolated incident." Tosh settled his chair in front of Young's desk.

"Any good news?" Young sighed and sat back in his chair, which tilted into a reclining position.

"Everything is trying to kill us, my friend." He smiled.

"But the coffee is excellent." Tosh, realising the desperate nature of their circumstances, began to laugh. Young joined him. The two friends sat and laughed, neither knowing what else to do. They expended their nervous energy and sat silently for a moment. Young spoke first.

"We'll have everyone off in a week. I have reassigned most of the personnel directly to The Agathon, to speed up completion, so I think we will have everyone off base by the end of the week. I want to stay as long as possible, to make sure the data from the Monolith is safely accumulated. I will transport the pods myself to the surface." He looked at Tosh. "Sorry make that WE'LL transport the pods to the surface OURSELVES."

Tosh raised his hands. "You will get no argument out of me. In a strange way, it would appear that I owe you my life. It was your hair-brained idea to bring me up to this hunk of rock in the first place, so you lead and I will follow. Mars would not have been my first choice to live the rest of my days, but seeing as it too will shortly cease to exist..." he trailed off, gesturing.

"What better way to send off the great Daniel Tosh than a huge spaceship traveling at the speed of light," said Young smiling.

"Here, here!" toasted Tosh. The tone changed

"What is the head count for all personnel, including both space stations and incoming craft?" asked Young.

Tosh looked grim. "Well we've got around two thousand colonists below on the Martian surface. Another fifteen hundred up here on the Jycorp station, around nine hundred on the science station and six hundred on the moon surface. I don't know how many are incoming, but if we say another thousand or so, that's around the six thousand mark." Young looked down at his desk, waiting for Tosh to get to the point.

"The Agathon, if she ever becomes space-worthy, can take maybe two thousand tops. She wasn't built to save the human race."

"Okay then," said Young.

"The obvious way to tackle the short term issues here is to load up the two stations and prepare for a long burn to break the two orbits, then send them as far away from the debris field as possible. If The Agathon finds a habitable world at the other end of that signal, then we unload and jump back to rendezvous with the stations and transfer remaining personnel to the ship."

"Okay then," replied Tosh, smirking. The pair both took deep breaths and stared in silence.

"What is Barrington's take on all this?" asked Tosh.

"He's keeping it hush for now. He has his hands full down there by the sounds of things, but he's compiling a list of his key people for review. When we have more on numbers, we will make an announcement. Needless to say, we need to be prepared for some level of panic, hence my security is quietly beginning to beef up its presence." Tosh sighed.

"Jesus Christ, what a nightmare. Well I volunteer to stay behind and take my chances on the base, if it's all right with you. Drifting off into the nothingness in style and comfort has some appeal to me." Young smiled. Tosh knew what Young was going to say to that.

"I wish I could, old friend, but you're number one on my list to go. I need people who have lived and breathed this thing and you know the Monolith and its technology better than anyone else alive. Tyrell included. Sorry."

"Is that an order?" Tosh asked, semi-serious. Young gave him a smile that told him, in no uncertain terms, that it was.

"On a lighter note, Emerson tells me that had we more time we could excavate the Monolith and take it with us," said Young.

"For fuck's sake. That idiot has his head so far up his ass he's seeing his own stars," Tosh replied.

"Still the best engineer we have and I know there's a soft spot in that big heart of yours for him."

"Yeah, yeah," Tosh replied.

"Just assign him to waste disposal and put him to good use."

"I may just do that, but in the meantime have a talk with him and see what he proposes."

"You're not serious!" Tosh laughed.

"Humour me," Young replied. "It's good for young men to have their ideas considered by top brass. It gets their creative juices flowing in other ways and boosts confidence and morale."

"Ha," Tosh quipped, "spoken like the CEOs of old. Manipulate the masses to serve thy bidding. Well played, sir." Young nodded in a mock bowing motion. "I have another question, while we're on the subject."

"Fire ahead," said Young.

"All due respect to your majesty, but who is in command of this suicide mission of yours?"

"What do you mean?" said Young.

"I mean, I know that military commanders, even those in the employment of Jycorp, past or present, have difficulty taking orders from suits. I can only assume that, as the commander of Agathon, Barrington will expect total autonomy from his crew without interference from 'corporate', so I ask again. With you aboard and with the chancellor a hair's breadth away, who is in charge of the new world order?"

Young looked at Tosh and raised his eyebrows. "That," he said slowly, "is a very good question!"

The Nexus
(Personal shuttle of Chancellor Sienna Clarke)
Time since evacuation- Three days
08:34 Martian Standard

Sienna Clarke stood at the entrance to the crew quarters and took a breath. Her head was spinning. She placed her hands on the surface of the door and steadied herself. The halls of the ship were quiet. She had noticed that her hands had been shaking uncontrollably. The enormity of what had happened was beginning to weigh heavily on her like a dark storm front. The air around her felt thick. She reached up and pressed the buzzer to the quarters and waited. She knew he would be up at this time of the morning. Greyson Kayne was an early riser like herself. The door slid open and the large security man stood at its entrance wearing a pair of black sweatpants. It was clear that he had been working out. His upper body was glistening with sweat.

"Good morning, Chancellor. I apologise. Am I late for duty?" Her eyes flicked upwards and met his.

"Not at all, Greyson. I was wandering the halls so to speak and wondered if you would like to join me for a coffee. I know how early you rise each day and I wanted to let the others rest."

"Of course, Chancellor. Please come in while I change," he said. She smiled and entered, moving past the large man and grazing her fingers against his. The cabin door hissed shut. The two stood staring at each other. In one swift and graceful motion, he raised his hand and slid it across her cheek and through her hair, firmly taking the back of her head and pulling her closer until their foreheads touched. She raised her lips and kissed him passionately. Her arms wrapped themselves tightly around his back as she embraced him. He took a step backwards and led her to the edge of the bed behind him. She gently pressed his shoulders downwards and seated him on the edge of the linen. The light casual clothing she was wearing slid off with ease and the pair collapsed into Grayson's bed. She lost control and let herself melt into his body, forcing the turbulent thoughts out of her mind. She was strong. Not strong enough to overpower him, but enough to take complete control of the situation.

Within minutes, she had placed him gently inside her and the raw energy of the two locked in synchronous motion. She sat upright and placed her hands on the security man's large chest, pressing her nails gently into his flesh. He gripped her hips and pulled her tightly towards his body with each thrust. She closed her eyes and let her mind empty of thoughts, letting the present moment take her over. They climaxed in a simultaneous release of energy and fell back exasperated. With sweat running down the chancellor's cheeks she rose from the bed and dressed herself. She quietly made her way to the door and opened it. She looked back at Greyson, who was sprawled out across the bed and clearly trying to get his breath back. She smiled and nodded at him. She composed herself and pulled her damp hair behind her ears. She activated the door's opening mechanism and slid out quietly.

"Good morning, Chancellor," said James Ryder, as she made her way back to her quarters. Startled, she jumped.

"Good morning, James. You're up early?" she replied, aware that her dishevelled look and Ryder's knowing face meant she had been caught red-handed. Usually she would have minded. Not today.

"Indeed," he said, "as are you. It is difficult to sleep with all that is going on and weeks in space can make anyone a little restless. Flight deck reports we have contact with Phobos. Jerome Young is holding for you." *Perfect!* she thought.

"Can you have him patched through to my cabin, please?"

"Of course, Chancellor." Ryder raised one of his eyebrows and looked at her, giving her the slightest of grins before turning towards the flight deck. *Oh go fuck yourself, she thought.* She gathered herself and made her way to her cabin. She cleaned herself up, brushed her hair and changed into a more formal outfit. The view screen on her desk blinked and indicated a transmission holding. She sat down, looked at the screen, and tried to stay calm. She tapped a button and the black screen was filled with Jerome Young's face. She didn't say anything.

"It is good to see you, Chancellor. Can you secure this channel, please? I would like to talk privately," he said warmly. She suddenly began to feel her boundaries of self-control breaking down. She pressed the secure lockout command isolating the frequency and turned back to the screen.

"You had no right to make that decision without my knowledge. You do NOT get to pick and choose who lives or dies. I don't care who you are, you pull that crap again and I will have you thrown out of an airlock!" Young did not respond and let the situation settle.

"Sienna," he said,

"Chancellor Clark will do," she rebuffed.

"Of course, Chancellor. I apologise. I understand your position fully but under the circumstances, I had no alternative. The purview of my office is to protect the planetary chain of command at all costs during an impossible situation."

"It was NOT your call!" Her fury was mounting at the sound of his voice.

"All due respect," he continued, "it WAS my call and I made it." She could tell the levels of his tone were increasing to match hers and there was a danger of this degrading into a screaming match.

"Now, I am very sorry for the losses you have incurred, but the world just ended and I am fighting to try and save what is left. So, if you can direct that anger somewhere else for the time being and give me a status update, that would be great" She took a breath and calmed herself.

"We are twenty-four hours out of your position. We have linked up with three transports off our port and starboard. We are due to rendezvous with your orbital platform upon arrival. I have instructed the transports to lock into the Phobos 1 civilian station and await instructions. Needless to say, we have a lot of terrified people on their way."

"Is this channel secure?" he asked. She tapped some commands into the console.

"Yes," she answered.

"Have your sensors picked up any debris in your wake?" he asked. She looked confused, but was slowly regaining control over her anger.

"There is debris everywhere, Jerome," she said.

"Specifically anything large to your aft?" he said.

"No, but this shuttle uses short range sensors for course correction only."

"Okay, well we have a major problem. A large chunk of what is left of Earth is headed our way," he said.

"How large?" she responded.

"About the size of South America and the numbers say it's going to hit." Sienna was speechless.

She sat back in her chair and looked out of one of the small windows at the stars.

"What?" she said, still shocked. "My God, it's the end of us, isn't it?" she continued. She sat back in her chair and looked out her porthole at the beautiful night.

"Not quite yet, Chancellor. There's a plan in motion. It is an outside bet, but currently all we have to work with. You remember The Agathon project?" he asked.

"I do," she responded. Realizing where he was going she interjected, "You mean that half-finished light speed test ship?"

"That's the one!" he answered.

The Agathon
Time since evacuation-twelve days
09:16 Martian Standard

"Christ, Charly, you stay out there any longer and your veins are going to explode," came a male voice over the comms into the lieutenant's headset. The view of the Martian surface was spectacular from outside the ship and she had to admit the work on the power coupling was taking its time because of it. She turned her attention back to the smooth curved hull of The Agathon's outer shell. The FTL ring, which had been completed during the first phase of the build, was extended to its vertical ninety-degree start up point. The outer ring, which acted as the buffer between the gravitational effects of a jump to hyperspace (if it actually worked), and the rest of the ship, lay in its permanently locked position horizontal to its disk-shaped hull. Charly Boyett was in total awe of this ship. The pride she felt was not the bolstering ego associated with its conception or design. That lay in the hands of minds much larger than hers. It was, however, her baby to fly, and fly she would. She kept glancing at a section of space that once hosted her home world. A strange, soft glow had now replaced the blinking dot that was. All around the young woman smooth surfaces were broken intermittently by gaping holes and twisted metalwork. The huge craning arms that surrounded the beautiful hull of her baby worked furiously, placing large sections of outer hull fragments all around her.

"Five more minutes. She's being a little bitch," she replied to the young cadet in the airlock. The power coupling had blown during a power transfer test and the section of conduit was currently exposed to vacuum. Charly had jumped at the chance and headed out several hours ago. The grief on board had become thick and she had needed to escape. After several days of sombre briefings with her flight staff, she needed some alone time with the stars.

Her thoughts wandered to her own family in Sao Pablo. Her father, Carlos Boyett, had been a well-respected litigator in the city and her mother was a schoolteacher. A complication during childbirth had rendered her mother Maria unable to have any more children, so she had been a prized child with the expectations and demands that went along with it. She had enjoyed a good relationship with her parents and harboured no resentment for her strict upbringing. She had allowed herself an escape from the pressures of having to succeed, stealing out into the night with her telescope to gaze at the stars. She had enrolled in the interstellar flight academy in Washington when she was nineteen and had found her passion in the clouds behind the controls of the x43 hypersonic suborbital fighter. She had terrified a few instructors with her natural ability behind the stick and had quickly flown up the ranks. During a review the head of the academy, Major Tom Dickinson, had noted that if she could sprout wings at any time she could easily become a bird.

"It's in your blood, cadet," he had said with his burly low southern accent. "You're a born flyer." It was the highest compliment she had ever received, until the call from John Barrington several years later. Now, drifting outside the most exciting ship the human race had ever attempted to build, she couldn't help but miss her parents.

"Choose your path wisely and give it everything you got," her father's voice echoed in her mind. Her mother had been less than pleased about her flight ambitions, but had supported her decisions once she had seen that her mind was immovable on the subject. Now they were gone. A tear suddenly released itself from one of her eyes, which was a bothersome inconvenience out here, as she had no way to wipe it. She took a deep breath and cleared her throat. Work to be done. She closed her eyes and tried to clear them. *Focus, Charly; let's get this puppy ready to fly.* She drew her attention back to the power coupling. Although it was linked to a minor backup system, its function was also tied directly into the workings of the main environmental control on board and would pose a significant problem in hyperspace. If it even got to hyperspace. A light blipped inside her faceplate, denoting an incoming transmission.

"Boyett," she said.

"Charly, it's Barrington. You out and about?" came the commander's voice. She was always in awe of his ability to sound totally in control in any given situation. His cool and authoritative tone had given her strength and focus.

"Yes, sir, just cleaning the windshields," she said lightly.

"Status," he said.

"I need more people, sir. I'm losing prep days here to monkey work. I need to start focusing on the on-board navigation system or this thing is gonna fly straight into a planet or into oblivion. I could use Tyrell's assistance on the coordinate verifications at some stage today, to do a simulation. Which I can guarantee won't be pretty, seeing the state the bridge is currently in."

"Understood, Charly, stay calm," the commander said. She had probably let more panic into her voice than she would have liked in front of him, but she was genuinely worried about their impossible timescale.

"I have Emerson and every engineer I can get my hands on transferring over in the next twenty-four hours from the Jycorp orbital. You should double your manpower momentarily." Her face flushed without her realising it at the sound of Emerson's name. The handsome Irishman had made an impression on her at an Agathon briefing a month earlier, and even more so in her bed. Ships that pass in the night.

"Thank you, sir, much appreciated."

"No problem, Charly, we'll get the old girl to fly, don't you worry. I'll get Tyrell onto you later on. I'll be joining you in the next day or so for a site visit. I hope you don't mind, but we should get everyone on the same page and there are some issues I need to discuss personally with the current crew on board."

Charly didn't like the sound of that. She had suspected that there would not be enough space to accommodate everyone and figured there would be some sort of announcement to that effect sooner rather than later.

"Looking forward to it, sir. I'll have some coffee ready for you upon arrival," she said. Barrington laughed.

"Appreciated, Barrington out."

The comms winked out and Charly was left alone again in the dark. She rummaged through a tangled web of fibre connections and found the coupling seal. With her laser welder in hand, she got to work.

Jycorp Orbital Station
15:22 Martian Standard

"Docking clamps engaged," said the airlock operator, a middle-aged man who worked on one of Emerson's engineering teams. "Engaging umbilicus," he said.

A corridor began to extend to the docked vessel. Young and Tosh waited at the entrance to the station's docking port. Tosh looked up at Young. While his chair enabled him to move with relative ease, he was still restricted to the height he could hover at and normally had to look up to those standing. Young made note of Tosh's well-pressed attire, together with a crisp white shirt.

"Who are you trying to impress? Me or her?" he asked jokingly.

"Shut up. Is that cologne?" Tosh retorted. Young replied with a friendly smirk. It seemed surreal to Young that the two men had made an effort to smarten up. They now lived in a universe with no Earth. They were refugees clinging on to social norms to keep the mind from cracking. The lights on the entrance to the airlock flickered to green. The circular door hissed and rolled back. The chancellor stood facing the two men. Her chief of staff and two large security personnel flanked her. One of them was much bigger than the other. Both wore the familiar locked expression Young knew all too well. There was a deathly silence. Tosh broke the tension by clearing his throat and began to speak when Young interrupted him. It was his place to speak first and he took the hint from his friend.

"Chancellor Clark, I am relieved to see you. Welcome aboard," he said. The chancellor's expression softened but he knew she was angry.

"Permission to come aboard, Mr. Young," she finally said. Young could not get a handle on her.

"Granted," Young said. "If you would like to follow me, I will see you to your quarters." She nodded and the new arrivals made their way onto the station. They made their way through the uniform corridors of the Jycorp Orbital platform. The halls were lined with sealed doors and personnel scurrying about, each carrying various pieces of equipment and pushing carts full of supplies. As they passed they stopped and stared at the travelling entourage. The shock of seeing the supreme chancellor walking the halls was clearly new for most. Young knew she had to hold her confident stride through the stares. She wore a formal suit with a small pin depicting the flag of the planetary allegiance pinned to her lapel. He was always impressed at how well she handled herself in the public eye. Hushed awes and quiet whispering followed them when they strode.

"It's her," came the voice of a female dressed in overalls, talking to a colleague. The chancellor's group reached a large lift and waited for its arrival. Young turned to Tosh.

"Daniel, please take the chancellor's aides to their quarters. The chancellor and I have a lot to discuss in my office." Tosh looked surprised.

"Of course, Jerome."

"With your permission of course, Chancellor?" She nodded. Ryder and Kane both looked in the chancellor's direction.

"Gentlemen, get some rest. I will call upon you later," she said. Tosh took the party down an adjoining corridor and Young and Clark entered the lift. They waited quietly for the doors to close and then the chancellor turned to Young. With a swift motion, she slapped him firmly on the cheek. He remained silent as the sharp sting lingered. She turned back to face the lift's doors and they continued their journey. Young turned, facing the same direction. They waited quietly, listening to the hum of the lift as it ascended.

"My assistant was only twenty-two years old," she said. "We could have saved her." Young did not know who she was referring to but accepted her anger.

"I am sorry, Sienna," he said. He felt anything more was inappropriate. The mood lifted somewhat as they reached the doors of his office. They moved through the office and both took a seat, Young sitting at the head of his desk which had the effect of letting Clark know who was in charge of the situation. *Got that out of your system?* he thought. She spoke first.

"What is it you want me to do now, Jerome?" she said. Young rose from his chair and poured single malt into the two glasses that sat on a nearby counter.

"Make mine a double," she said. He nodded. The chancellor looked around the loosely decorated room. There were photos scattered around the wall, one with Young at the peak of a mountain and another in a pressure suit outside an orbital array with the backdrop of the Earth below. A holographic rendering of the Monolith sat on one corner of his desk. It rotated slowly, giving a full three-sixty of the mirror-like structure. There were several doors leading out of the room into several corridors and rooms. The clear wall behind his desk gave a breath-taking view of the Martian surface. Digital schematics of the Monolith were overlaid on one corner of the window. He handed the glass to the seated chancellor and retook his seat. He sipped the drink and allowed it to warm his insides.

"I need you to do what you do best." He looked her deeply in her eyes. She really was beautiful.

"I need you to lead."

6

Weapons training facility
Mars Colony One
Time since evacuation- 46 Day
17:15 Martian Standard

Carrie fired her baryon pulse gun and blew the target into a million tiny bits. It was an elegant and subtle weapon that fitted into the palm of her hand. While she had been commissioned an active weapon less than twelve months previously, she had practically been born with it in her hand. The training device she had learned to shoot with was an exact replica of the real thing, but the energy beam had been a simple adaptation of old laser technology. She had come to the firing chamber alone, just shortly after sunrise, to clear her head.

Her dreams of late had been disturbing. Every night it was the same thing.

She stands at the precipice of a nearby canyon. She breathes in fresh air without the need of an atmo suit. She stares up at the sky at an approaching object. The dark mass begins to fill the sky and a crawling shadow creeps along the walls of the canyon. The sun vanishes and the winds pick up. The atmosphere burns away and the stars replace the clouds. The rock is the size of a small moon and fills the empty sky. She looks around to find herself alone again. No colony. No help. A thousand fireballs descend through the sky and explode in the ground. Hell on Earth. The sound of a growling animal approaching from behind her makes her turn. She is faced with a black figure, faceless and with no particular shape. The Black! The growling stops and the figure takes another form. She can't make out the features but the shape of the figure is so familiar to her. It speaks to her in a distorted and animal-like voice.

"I am going to kill you, Carrie. I am going to kill everyone. Silly little insects." The storm of fire continues all around as the dark mass from above hits the atmosphere. The smell of sulphur and burning flesh fills her senses and she begins to cough as her eyes start to fill with smoke and poison. The noise is deafening and she screams as she drops to her knees, and that is when she wakes up screaming.

She tapped a command into the wall pad of the firing range and the target was replaced with another. Soft round balls filled with fluid were deposited on a standing metal column. Each column was placed at various distances down the range and could be adjusted at will with a few commands. A target was placed at three hundred meters and she took aim. She cleared her lungs of air, raised her weapon in a swift and practiced fashion, then fired with fluidity and confidence. She left the target little chance. It exploded without hesitation and she drew a satisfied breath.

"Nice shooting, Tex," said David Chavel, who had just entered without her knowing. *How did that happen?* she thought. *Get control of your mind, Dice.*

"Hello, Lieutenant. I didn't see you there." She fumbled with her gun's safety settings and placed it in lock mode. He was standing with his shoulder leaning on the edge of her segmented lane section and had his legs casually crossed. He wore a friendly half-cocked smile and the confident glint that seemed the required uniform for flight jockeys. *Come to play, have we?*

"Come here often?" he said playfully. That brought a genuine laugh. She enjoyed it. Not many people laughing these days.

"That the best you got?" she rebuffed.

"Not at all, but it's five-thirty in the morning... Can't sleep?" he asked. She just shook her head and glanced back at the remnants of her shooting.

"Do you mind if I join you? I need to get in a little trigger time myself. By the sounds of things I think we're gonna need it."

"Not at all, Lieutenant, please be my guest." She gestured to the lane and gave way. He nodded in appreciation and stepped past her. His closeness as he passed was no accident, but she didn't complain. He was in good shape and he knew it, and what little physical contact she could get to take her mind off her mind was okay with her.

He tapped a command into the pad and set a target for three hundred and fifty meters. He always wore a sidearm on a thick black belt that hung low over his left thigh. It was a much larger version of Carrie's weapon. *Size matters to men no matter what planet you're on,* Carrie thought. He moved his legs apart and adapted a steady stride position. She couldn't help her eyes momentarily flickering to his posterior. Definitely in good shape. He drew his weapon and held it. He had a clumsy draw motion, Carrie noticed, but held it with confidence. She watched his eyes as he focused intently. He hadn't shaved for a few days and the dark stubble that lined his cheeks gave a light definition to his jawline. She imagined their faces close and combing her fingers across it. He smiled slightly, noticing her glances. Shit. She looked back at the target. He fired and missed. Lowering his weapon, she could tell he was embarrassed. Emasculated by the water ball.

"Sights must be off," he grumbled, frowning. He fired again and missed.

"Would you like to try mine?" she said playfully. He looked at her weapon and blew out a light laugh.

"Not at all, give me a second here." He tapped something into the side control panel of his gun and aimed again. He fired and missed. He lowered his weapon and scratched his eyebrows. He frowned at the target, raised his weapon and flicked a switch. The weapon opened fire with continual pulses at close to twenty rounds a second. When the dust cleared, neither the target nor the column it was standing on were anywhere to be seen. He gave a satisfactory smile and looked back at Carrie who laughed. He gave her a shrug and holstered his gun.

"Can I buy you breakfast? I know a great place." He extended his elbow. She took it and they walked out of the range. Carrie felt calm and protected in his presence. It brought her the peace the firing range hadn't delivered on this morning. As they entered the airlock and walked towards the main galley, she looked out over the red horizon as the sun broke its chains and split the surface of the planet in two. *What a beautiful morning.* She glanced up at the sky. Both of them knew what was coming. She looked back at the lieutenant and thought about having pancakes.

Twenty minutes later, they were in orbit. His shuttle pod was a sleek little ship with room for six passengers. With smooth lines and darkened windows it cut through the thin atmosphere like a dolphin in smooth waters. Chavel had nicknamed her The Jenny and stencilled a voluptuous female on the outside of the cockpit.

"It's what they used to do in World War II," he had exclaimed as they boarded. The view from orbit encompassed the entire red planet. The Atmo processors could clearly be seen pumping out gases in the northern and southern hemispheres. They were gargantuan grey structures with symmetrical cubed edges and miles of enormous cable spreading out in all directions.

"Your father has ordered they be shut down in the next seventy-two hours," he told Carrie. "Not much use for them now and any impact will set off a thermonuclear explosion." He paused for thought. "Again, not that that matters much anymore." He flew around the far side of the planet and placed the shuttle in equatorial orbit. With the engines off, the shuttle glided peacefully over the surface. Carrie stared out of her viewport at the mountains and enormous valleys. The ancient riverbeds slid all over its surface. A scar of a world battered by time and soon to be devoured by its sister.

"It's beautiful up here," said the lieutenant, turning to Carrie. *Easy, tiger*. Simple female instincts told Carrie all she needed to know about what the young man was thinking.

"It is, Lieutenant."

"Your father calls me Lieutenant. You can call me David. We've known each other long enough to drop protocol, Carrie. No?" Carrie smiled and allowed him his first move.

"Okay, David. I presume you told my father you were kidnapping me for the afternoon?" He smiled.

"I have a confession to make. I did not."

Carrie nodded. "Brave AND stupid," she said jokingly.

"Guilty as charged," he said. There was raw bravery in the man, even if he didn't know it yet. Controlled recklessness, if there was such a thing. He had a devotion to duty but there was pain in his soul. A scar still hidden from her.

"Want to see the old girl?" Carrie cocked her head, questioning as Chavel changed course. From the surface of the planet, the small ship could be seen as a light dot on a background of stationary stars. She wondered, was there anyone looking up? There was. Chavel changed course with dexterity. The smooth realigning of the shuttle to her new course took seconds. Carrie had to admit to being impressed by how fluidly he handled the controls. She could tell he was showing off, but he did it with confidence and finesse. A familiar disk-shaped object came into the view port.

"I haven't seen it this close up before," said Carrie, as The Agathon grew in size as they approached. He drew the shuttle up to meet the nose of the vessel and fired his manoeuvring thrusters to hold The Jenny in place.

"Let's see if anyone's home." He smiled. He tapped into the comms system.

"Jenny to Agathon, repeat, this is the shuttle pod. Jenny to Agathon." No answer. Then a response.

"Agathon here. Chavel, is that you?" said Boyett.

"Affirmative, Agathon, just doing a flyby. I have Carrie Barrington on board."

"Christ, Dave, we're a little busy up here. Can you take your picnic elsewhere, please?" Boyett seemed stressed. Chavel knew when to call it a day with her.

"Sorry, Charly, I'll get out of your hair. See you later on this evening. You have a boarding party on its way from the Jycorp base to help out and I'll be mucking in." Silence on the comms.

"Thank God. Get your lazy ass up here and help me get this bridge working. Sorry, Ms Barrington, didn't mean to be rude."

"Not at all," Carrie said. "She looks beautiful. You're doing a miraculous job. We have great faith in you and your team, Lieutenant. You're giving us all hope." There was an eminence in her voice that even shocked Chavel. Without realising, she had just sounded like her mother.

"Eh. Thank you, Ms Barrington, that's very much appreciated. Tell you what. While you're out there, you can check our running lights. Hang on." Comms went dead and Chavel looked at Carrie.

"Sorry," she said.

"Not at all. I really think she needed to hear that today," said Chavel. Carrie smiled. Seconds later the ship's outer hull erupted in lights. Both the inner FTL ring and outer ring began pulsating with rotating colours of red and green. It was a spectacular show of life from the chaotic scenes of construction. Rings of rotating lights began to swirl around the ship. Several crewmembers that were standing on the exterior hull stopped and watched. From the surface of the planet, it looked like two rings of light circling each other in perfect unison. It filled Carrie with an enormous lift of emotion.

"Incredible," she said. She realised Chavel was not looking at the lights and only at her. He took her hand gently and without hesitation reached across and kissed her. It caught her by surprise but she warmly accepted. It wiped her mind clean and sent it to another place. The end of the world did not matter anymore. Not when there was this.

The moment only lasted seconds, but it was enough. A momentary jolt of electricity separated them. They both laughed.

"Must be static," said Chavel.

"Must be," said Carrie. She placed her hand on his neck and they embraced. She was hooked.

"How's she looking, Jenny?" came Boyett's voice somewhere in another universe. "Jenny?" she repeated. "Jenny, you there?"

Aquaria Base-Mars Colony 1
19:22 Martian Standard

"How many do we have?" asked John Barrington. Young's image on the screen answered.

"Four transports in total. Four thousand, three hundred and fifty-two people just docked between the two stations," replied Young.

"That's it?" replied Barrington.

"So far, yes," said Young.

"Christ," said Barrington. "The chancellor?" he continued.

"She is meeting with the various captains to confirm manifests."

"What do you need, John?" pressed Young.

"Most of your engineering staff," he replied. "Progress on the outer hull is progressing according to our timeframe, but the navigation system is a big problem right now. If we cannot get that up and running, God knows where we'll end up."

There was a real concern in Barrington's voice. Tyrell had given him some disturbing news about the fragment approaching earlier in the day. "Two months, John. And it's game over," he had said over the comms. Barrington's response to pressure had always been the same. Contain it, rationalise it, and solve the problem. He was tired. The five hours a night he was getting just wasn't cutting it for him and the weight of saving his people, of saving Carrie, was beginning to show around his eyes.

"Tyrell has confirmed that timescale, yes?" asked Young. Barrington didn't like repeating himself.

"Yes, Mr. Young."

Barrington felt it was time for a conversation with the head of the now obliterated Jycorp. Young, sensing the frustration in his voice, opened the door.

"John, I think we should have a talk about how we should handle next steps, don't you? From a command point of view." Barrington listened. The tone of Young's voice softened.

"Look, I realise that my position in your eyes is purely a civilian one, now that I have no company or planet to run, but the people we lead both up here and down there need to believe that the human race still functions as it always did. So here's my proposal. Chancellor Clark's role will remain unchanged, as will yours as commander of The Agathon project. I defer military and ship-wide decisions to you of course, but the chancellor retains her role as leader of…" he paused

"What are we now? A tribe?" Barrington didn't answer. "Policy and 'tribal' decisions must be approved by her. What I suggest is that a new council be formed with the chancellor at its head. The first Terran Council."

"Mr. Young, with all due respect, I do not have time to play politics. There is a very real chance that we are about to become an extinct species and my energy and focus needs to go into getting that ship ready to leave."

Young seemed to be taken aback by Barrington's tone. "I understand that, John, which is why you have complete autonomy and support on this, as well as the chancellor's."

Something about that did not sit well with Barrington. Some tough calls needed to be made shortly and while he thought the tone of the conversation was one thing, it was turning out to become something different. *Fucking Jycorp.* He calmed himself.

"Mr. Young," he said. "Regarding the space on The Agathon."

"Yes. That is an issue," Young replied.

Barrington asked the obvious. "How do we decide who stays and who goes?" There was a pause.

"Tosh has something on that issue and I would like to iron some of the details out with him before we cross that bridge. In the meantime, my personnel are at your disposal to complete The Agathon project. I will begin arranging their transport immediately. Luckily for us at least, the last of the materials are already in orbit."

"There are already rumours beginning to spread that some will have to remain behind, Mr. Young. I would like an answer on this as soon as possible," he pressed.

"As would I, John. I am hoping to have a plan of action to propose later on this evening." Young's patience for this conversation seemed to be running out. "Let's talk again in the morning?" he said.

"Of course," replied Barrington and cut communications. He rubbed his eyes, sat in his office chair in silence, and looked at a photo of Jennifer he kept on his desk.

"Miss you," he told her. "I'll get her out. I promise."

Main Observatory
Time since evacuation 51 Days
14:44 Martian Standard

"Doctor, what are going to do about the samples of The Black?" asked Carrie. She had spent the afternoon precariously preparing the storage pods of Tyrell's equipment for safe transport to the science labs on board The Agathon. Her mind was not on the task. On several occasions, she had dropped samples of base materials with protests from Tyrell.

"I don't know what planet you are on today, young lady, but it is not this one," he had said, sending her off to do menial tasks for fear she might inadvertently blow the place up. Carrie knew that she wasn't hiding her lack of concentration very well.

"I don't know, Carrie," he said from under a control console. "Your father has blown the entrance to the cave and as such the only live samples we have left are the ones in this lab and in Meridian's."

"Do you not think it wise we destroy it?" she said. Tyrell stopped rummaging around in containers and looked up at Carrie, who was fiddling with a scope.

"Why do you say that? I thought you were a scientist. This is the first life form outside our own that we have discovered anywhere in the universe." He continued rummaging through one of the containers. "Just because something is lethal when threatened does not mean that we simply destroy it, Carrie. If that were true, the great sharks of Earth's oceans would have been extinct for a hundred years or so. Destroying nature is a last resort, Carrie. If something poses a threat to humans indirectly, we simply stay out of its way."

Carrie was taken aback by the abrupt tone in Tyrell's voice. Surprised at this reaction she answered, "It killed four people, Doctor. One of them intentionally." Tyrell paused and took a seat next to one of his diagnostic tables. He took a breath.

"Carrie, what happened to your mother was an accident." It was the first time Tyrell had ever mentioned Jennifer to Carrie directly and she was taken aback by his honesty.

"She was in the wrong place at the wrong time and did not know what she was dealing with. It could have happened to anyone, Carrie, on any planet anywhere in the universe. It was her fate and there is no cheating that. But her death, Carrie..." he paused, "her death led to the most significant discovery in the history of the world, outside of the signal.

"She was a heroine, Carrie. Her name will never be forgotten, but now we move on with life. Fraine's death can only be attributed to Lorenzo Fraine. His methodology was sloppy and he was foolish to run an experiment like that without proper controls. Whatever the reason for The Black's reaction to the equipment or his presence, what is clear to me is that it was protecting itself. Nothing more. Our samples in the lab have not reacted the same way when I duplicated the experiment. Nothing happened, Carrie. So tell me logically, from a scientific point of view, why would we destroy the only extra-terrestrial organic substance currently known to exist?"

Carrie began to hear frustration in Tyrell's voice. She contained her feelings about her mother's death and focused on his mind. She felt ruthless discipline from him and something else. Something dark. *Save Carrie!* came a scream in her head. She took a step back, as if given a jolt. She dropped the scope on the floor, and it smashed into several small pieces. Tyrell just looked at her. Focused eyes. *He knows.*

"I am sorry, Doctor Tyrell. I... sorry." She knelt and started picking up the fragments of the scope.

"Do not worry about that, Carrie. I have many more, just throw it in the disposal unit." He stood up and approached her. He stood beside her and placed a hand on one of her shoulders.

"What we are about to do, Carrie, will take all our focus and all our..." He paused. "Talents. I have been impressed by your work here. You are a gifted scientist. A natural, and you have been of enormous help to me. Do not be afraid of where we are going. The answers are out there, Carrie," he said, pointing to the ceiling.

"We will find them together. You and I." Carrie did not like the soft touch of his hand. There was a surreal calm about the doctor, a vacancy in his eyes like a shark before it attacks. He took a deep breath and returned to his workstation, as if the conversation had never taken place. Carrie knew at that moment that Doctor Tyrell was dangerous.

Jycorp Orbital platform
19:33 Martian Standard

"Should have kept the military on a tighter leash," Young said.

"What was that?" an aide replied.

"Nothing," said Young as he made his way out of his office and through the station. People scattered about, letting him pass. He had a long stride and never stopped to speak to anyone unless it was absolutely necessary. Now, more than ever, his image of strong leadership needed serious reinforcement. His very small and weakened security personnel were beginning to look uneasy in his presence. They still maintained an absolute veil of professionalism, but there were times when he would catch a questioning glance from one of them.

His father had bestowed an old Chinese saying from Sun Tzu to him many years earlier. "If the mind is willing, the flesh could go on and on without many things." What did the human race have left but the routines of old? He hoped that he could maintain that sense of purpose long enough to get on board The Agathon. Time was running out and questions were being asked. The greatest threat now was not the huge chunk of rock headed their way. The problem now was revolution. Every man for himself! He began to imagine the faces around him tearing each other apart to gain access to their only escape route. The Agathon. Time was running out and he needed options before that happened. They would follow Barrington. They all would. But not him. He had neither led men in war nor bled with them on any battlefield. He was a suit. A powerful one in the old world, but this new one could quickly degenerate into madness.

He travelled down the many corridors to the central engineering sections of the space station. The huge room was filled with large control consoles and walkways, which carried its inhabitants to the six-storey-high engine access ports. Tosh and Emerson were waiting for him near one of the artificial gravity field generators. They were in deep discussion about something and did not see him enter.

"Gentlemen, please wait here," he instructed his guards. They waited at the entrance obediently. He walked casually over to the two men and stood next to them. They looked up and nodded.

"Mr. Emerson, I thought you had been assigned to The Agathon engineering team?"

"Eh. Yes Mr. Young, I'm on my way there now. Daniel had some thoughts on our..." He looked around to see if anyone was watching. "On our space issue and he needed me to run some quick numbers by me before I departed."

"I see," said Young looking at Tosh.

"And?" Tosh seemed reluctant to say what they had been talking about and looked at Emerson to begin. Emerson clearly wasn't up to the task and put his arm out.

"Age before beauty," he said. Tosh sighed.

"Gentlemen, can we please get on with it?" Young was in no mood for nonsense.

"Well. Here is how I see it," began Tosh. "Before we start killing each other trying to get off these stations, I think we have only one option to propose."

"Jesus, Daniel, will you just fucking spill it," Young said. He did not like having to ask the same question twice and hated indirect answers more than anything.

"Okay, Jerome, take it easy. Here's what I think. We fire the fusion engines of both space stations and the transports that just arrived and we break off orbit and head deeper in the solar system. Our calculations indicate that they would both survive a long burn and gain enough momentum to break past the outer planetary systems and past the outer rim."

Young couldn't believe what he was hearing. "What? Are you insane?" he said.

Tosh raised his hands. "Just hear us out. Both stations are self-sustaining and could easily survive in interstellar space for decades. That is what they were built to do. We lock in the locator beacons of all ships directly into The Agathon central computer, that way it can rendezvous with them any time it wants, no matter where in the void the stations end up. We crew The Agathon to its capacity. It jumps to the Aristaeus system and determines its habitability. It offloads the crew and jumps back to pick up the rest of the people on the stations. A couple of good runs and we get everyone safely to the surface of the planet in no time at all." Tosh waited for a response. Young took a moment and looked at the floor and sighed.

"How did it come to this?" He put his hand up to stop Emerson from adding any new information and paced over to the edge of the walkway. He placed his hand on the rail and stared up at the vast array of machinery, which made up the heart of the space station.

"Tosh, you're asking over half of what is left of the human race to die alone in the middle of nothingness." Tosh looked surprised at Young's reaction. It was unlike him to look at things so negatively, but he had grown tired over the last few days and his encounter with the chancellor had been less than pleasant. Tosh floated over and joined him at the rail.

"That's not what I'm suggesting, Jerome, and you know it. We do nothing and these people will die. This way they have a chance. I think you should propose it to the chancellor and Barrington. Maybe Tyrell has come up with something else I don't know about, but right now this is how I see it. In any case, what if The Agathon blows up during the FTL drive start up? This way we save most of us. Who knows, in a few generations the convoy could reach a habitable planet and that will be that."

Young didn't like the sound of a generational convoy of humans limping through the galaxy, but his mind would not focus.

"Let's bring it to the chancellor, Tosh, but I want you there when I tell her. The woman has a mean right hook."

7

Time since evacuation 61 Days
Quarters of Dr Chase Meridian - Mars Colony 1
09:33 Martian Standard

"At some point you're going to have to tell someone that we're married," said Doctor Kyle McDonnell. The pair were still wrapped in each other after a marathon session of lovemaking and McDonnell was currently resting his head neatly between her thighs. Meridian was still out of breath and her soaked body was splayed across the relatively modest bed in which they had spent the last three hours.

"I mean the fucking world has ended, I don't think it really matters anymore," he said, catching his breath. "Besides it might bring some joy, no?" McDonnell had been pushing her to go public with their romance for months, but Meridian was having none of it.

She hated her personal life being discussed by anyone. It had taken Barrington three years to get her to open up about her first husband, Daniel, who had been killed during an outbreak of Ebola X in Liberia. During their first year together as man and wife, the most virulent strain of the centuries-old virus had ravaged him within two hours of contact during a botched experiment on a vaccine in one of the makeshift Jycorp CDC labs. She had watched through a quarantine field as his cries of agony went unanswered. The Jycorp CDC had strict protocols when dealing with this airborne disease. It was the only virus to fall under section 35C -Paragraph 13 of the manual for airborne contaminants; ('Once detected, any subject infected must be immediately contained and destroyed without prejudice. Any such person or persons who enact this action are granted total immunity from any prosecution under the laws herein. Failure to comply with said protocol will result in life imprisonment without the possibility of reprieve or parole'). Knowing the protocol well, he had pleaded with her to end the pain. With his bloodstained hands pressed against the translucent field, she had flipped the switch and incinerated her husband in front of her eyes. She had found solace in knowing that it had not lasted long and that he would have thanked her for it had his ability to speak been within the realms of possibility. It was a pain she had kept for herself. Not willing to part with it through counselling or pharmaceutical dampening. It was her pain. And she wanted it.

"We've talked about this, Kyle; you need to give me time," she said gently. She loved this crazy Scotsman. He made her laugh harder than anyone ever had and she truly believed that he was her soul mate. She just wasn't ready to let Daniel go. Not yet. "Please give me time."

McDonnell pouted and sunk his head back into her abdomen. "I'm starting to think you're ashamed of me, ye know," he said in a baby voice. She sat up, taking exception to the idea and held his face firmly in her hands.

"Listen to me, you silly oaf," she said with deadly serious eyes locked into his. She loved his eyes. Full of warmth and charm. It was his eyes that had sparked her interest. His keen doe eyes that had so blatantly locked onto her the moment she had touched down on this red chunk of rock, like a lost puppy looking for its owner. "I love you more than your silly face can handle. I love your heart, your soul and that rugged man body." McDonnell sucked his stomach in, which was badly in need of a workout. She tickled it playfully and he giggled like a child.

"I promise you that, when I'm ready, we will announce it to the whole world, what's left of it, and we will celebrate and dance until the stars fall away. I promise." He nodded lovingly and kissed her passionately on her soft lips, before resting his forehead on hers.

"Okay, toots. My lips are sealed. Now can I please have my fucking microscope back?" he said, and grabbed her armpits as they struggled in a mock fight amongst the sheets.

Aquaria Base - Mars Colony 1
12:22 Martian Standard

"There is something off with Tyrell," Carrie said to her seated father. She was standing in the doorway of his office but she just came out with it.

"Sit down, Dice. What's up?" he said, sitting back in his chair. Her father looked awful and she regretted having not come in on a lighter note. There was a harassed look on his face and his comm system kept bleeping, leading him to interrupt every few seconds to speak to various members of the colony about logistical and construction updates on The Agathon.

"I'm sorry. I didn't mean to interrupt you. I can come back later."

"No. No. No... Please sit down, we haven't talked in a while and I could use a break from this," he said, pointing to his comms control panel and inhaling loudly. He got up and walked around his desk, stretching his back and arms in the air.

"You need to sleep, Father. You look terrible," she said. "You won't be any good to us if you drive that thing into a moon because you're half awake." He laughed and put a hand on her shoulder. It felt nice.

"I'll do my very best, Dice. It's hard to get shuteye with half a planet on its way to destroy us. We have a lot of frightened people here, Carrie. I know you know that much, and frightened people need answers. I wish I had them," he said, staring out of his large glass window and over the colony.

"I hear you took a trip this morning," he said, giving a little knowing look which caught her completely off guard.

"Eh?" she replied. His smile widened.

"Some things don't need your abilities, Dice. How does she look?" "

"She?" Carrie said.

"The Agathon. How does she look?" Carrie smiled and tried to disregard the blush in her cheeks.

"She's the most beautiful ship I have ever seen. And she's waiting for her captain." Her father smiled, revealing the newly formed lines under his eyes. Carrie wished she could lighten his burden.

"Now, what's going on with you in the lab?"

She suddenly felt silly bringing him this information on a gut feeling. "Nothing," she said.

"Come on, Dice. You have a fight with the doc? Look, I know scientists are a bit strange, present company included," he said with a playful grin. "But it's in their nature. Tyrell probably a bit more than most, but without him we would be in serious trouble down here. I don't have to tell you. What happened?"

She looked out the window and observed the lights of the living quarters. "Nothing, honestly. I accidentally broke an important piece of equipment and he got upset. It was my fault really and it wasn't my place to bring it to you." She hoped he bought her lie. "Truth is, I think I just wanted to see you."

"Well, you have to be careful around some of this science types, Dice. Everyone is under pressure at the moment, but if it becomes something other than a dressing down you come to me. You got that?"

"Of course, I really am sorry I bothered you with this."

"Don't be silly, Dice. I'm here for you. But you have to fight your battles. I will not be around forever," he said, looking warmly into her eyes.

Carrie could not imagine a life without her father and pushed it to the back of her mind.

She knew that resonated with him and he quickly responded. "But that won't be for a long time. Buy me dinner?" he said.

"Would love to," Carrie said.

"Okay, give me ten minutes to send some communiqués and we'll be on our way," he said. One hour later they left his office.

Main Observatory - Mars Colony 1
14:44 Martian Standard

Tyrell stared at the gargantuan rock in the imaging chamber as it glided unforgivingly through the emptiness of space. The fragment from Earth was massive. Its entourage of broken rock, ice, metal and core fragments accompanied it like an ominous security detail.

"Look at you," he quietly said. "I see you." His finger pointed to the manifestation of the doomsday fragment headed their way. His tone was playful, as if he were speaking to a new-born baby but with a hint of menace. The tears running down his cheeks had dried, leaving residue. He held a bottle of 1950 Glen Grant single malt loosely in his fingertips. It was empty.

"Little fucker," he said, looking at the approaching debris. "Told you little fuckers," he continued. "Told you all and now look at you. Can you breathe? Can you fucking breathe now? Think you can laugh at me with the darkness seeing you. Fucking little insects." He started to laugh halfheartedly and wobbled in his chair, almost falling out of it. His laughter increased to a full wholehearted hysterical bellyache. He calmed himself and leaned forward towards the live stream of holographic images.

"Who needs you anyway, you ingrates. You small pathetic primates. Now look at you. ALL DEAD! DEAD, DEAD, DEAD. YOU HEAR ME, MORRETI?" His anger was swallowed up in fresh tears. He caught his breath and sat back in his chair.

"You old fuck." He laughed. "Not the fool anymore, I would say. Am I, Meretti? How do you like my methods now, you corpse. You see now, don't you? You do, don't you?" He looked up. To the ceiling.

"You know now, don't you? Your consciousness floating around out there with all the answers, you fuck. My equations were flawless. You know now, don't you?" He stood up from the chair and faced the imaging chamber. He walked up to its translucent barrier and pressed his hand against the glass.

"That you, Meretti? That you coming to get me?" His tone turned to fury. "Is that you coming, Meretti? Is that you, you self-righteous egomaniac?" The chunk of Earth slowly grew in the viewer. Two of the adjoining fragments smashed into each other and scattered themselves amongst the flotsam. Tyrell looked on with horror in his eyes.

"You FUCK!" He hit his palm against the glass. The clunk of it reverberated around the empty lab. He hit it again.

"Fuck you, Meretti. Come get me, you miserable old bastard. I want it. I WANT TO KNOW!" he screamed.

"You laughing, Meretti? You fucking laughing? Who the fuck do you think you are? You fucking corpse. You are NOTHING. You hear me, you old fool?" He punched the glass and screamed at the inanimate object.

"I was right. Look at me." He turned away from the image and walked over to one of the diagnostic tables. He grabbed a chair, hurling it at the imaging chamber. A small crack appeared.

"I SEE YOU!" he screamed. The chair lay by the glass.

"I fucking see you," he said, grabbing a large rock sample and hurling it at the chamber.

"Do you fucking hear me, old fool? You won't kill me." He stumbled over the table and hit the ground. He struggled to his feet. A mixture of alcohol and sweat coated his shirt. He grabbed a titanium chemical diffuser from an equipment locker. The heavy two-foot pipe lay firmly in his grasps. Small trickles of blood ran from his knuckles. He gathered himself and walked with fury towards the tank and stood nose to nose with the image of the approaching rock.

"You... won't... get... me," he screamed, raising the pipe above his head. He brought it down in one swift motion. The glass cracked easily.

"You old fuck!" he screamed. He began attacking the imaging chamber with tremendous violence. The image of the Earth cut out and sparks flayed across the lab, as the chamber exploded in a frenzy of shards and charged particles. The force of it knocked Tyrell clean off his feet and threw him across the floor of the lab. He lay on the ground with the wind knocked from his lungs, covered in cuts and the remnants of the destroyed imaging chamber. He turned onto his side and vomited. The broken bottle of whisky lay scattered around the lab.

He gathered his breath and wiped the tears from his cheeks. He slowly rose to his feet, wiping his mouth from the excess stomach contents, and stood among the debris of the imaging chamber. Smoke rose from the destroyed equipment. With his hair now soaked in sweat, he stood alone and in silence in his lab. With the pipe still held firmly in his hand and drained from the outburst, he dropped to his knees and began to cry uncontrollably, still watching the empty space where the imaging system had stood. He dropped the pipe, which landed with a thud. He looked around his lab and towards his private room, which held his sample of The Black and then back to the empty space.

Gathering himself, he got up and walked to a small cabinet. He grabbed another bottle of whisky. He walked quietly over to a chair and slumped himself into it. He opened the bottle and drank freely from its neck. Still out of breath, he looked at the cuts on his hands and arms with apathy and then looked back at the empty space.

"Can't catch me," he whispered, as he gently began to fall asleep.

PART 2

8

Time since evacuation 78 days
13:23 Martian Standard
Jycorp Orbital platform

"**I** am staying," said Chancellor Sienna Clark to the room of men, who stared in disbelief.

"No you are not," said Young, quickly dismissing her comment out of hand and turning to Tosh whose mouth was wide open.

"Yes I am," she repeated virulently. Young ignored her.

"Ryder?" he asked. James Ryder was seated next to a side table and chewing his glasses. His haggard suit and thin checkered necktie curved evenly over his rounded gut.

"What do you want me to say, Young?" he said, defeated. "I can't knock her out with gas anymore and start dragging her around the galaxy. The rules have changed and you know it. I know what you want from me, but I have to admit what the chancellor is proposing makes good political sense, if no actual sense. The leader of the world abandoning her people to the nothingness of space while she jets off to find somewhere to live with the CEO of Jycorp. If we are to try and build a future for our people and you want Sienna Clark to lead those people, then I can see no fault in the chancellor's logic from a purely political standpoint. Even if I think that it is suicide. Be that as it may."

He looked Sienna Clark in the eyes. "My place rests at the side of the chancellor and as such I will also be staying."

Young was beginning to get visibly irritated and looked at the two security detail standing at the entrance to his office. Greyson Kane and Kevin Ruffalo were looking forward quietly, as details do. Listening to every word yet not listening. Their blank expressions trained to non-engage in matters that did not concern them.

"Kane?" Clark's head of security flicked his eyes toward the chancellor, who did not look at him. She knew what he would say before he said it.

"With all due respect, Mr. Young, I don't think I need to answer that. We serve at the pleasure of the chancellor." Clark couldn't resist the slightest of smiles. Young had his head in his hands. Clark could see Young's face struggling with the announcement.

"The people left behind," Clark said, her tone soft and resolute, "will be lost, afraid and angry. And let's not think for one second it is anything else other than that for the moment. They may grow dangerous and desperate. Survival has a way of changing people, Jerome. I have no doubt that you have doubled security on The Agathon to prevent any incursions?"

Young didn't answer.

"I have no planet to lead." The sentence came out and released a flurry of emotions within the chancellor. She thought of her brother and looked out of the window behind Young.

"All I have left are a handful of its people and they need me. I can be their light in the darkness. I can be their focus for their pain, their frustration and maybe even their anger." She leaned forward and looked Young in the eyes with absolute certainty and unwavering confidence in her voice.

"I have to do this. I AM... DOING... THIS." Young looked at Ryder, who simply shrugged. He sighed, rubbed his eyes and sat back in his chair. After several minutes of awkward silences he looked at the chancellor and nodded.

"Now that that is out of the way, how are you proposing to select the personnel for The Agathon?" she continued, as if it was a normal morning briefing. There was a subdued silence from the room as Young stared at his desk.

"Essential personnel have already been selected. Remainder will be determined by volunteers then lottery," he finally added. "Truth is, there are those who would rather stay on the stations than take their chances on a test ship."

"I see," said Clark. She could feel Young was not going to be too keen on mulling over details and decided to cut the meeting short.

"Gentlemen, it is imperative that we maintain a united front on this," she said, looking at Tosh.

"Of course, Chancellor," Tosh added. She liked Daniel Tosh. He had a no-nonsense way about him and she respected his loyalty to her office.

"Ryder and I will compose a communiqué now to broadcast to what is left of the human race. So if I could get clarity on the exact details of how this is all going to work by nineteen hundred hours, that would be doing me a favour." Young still had his gaze fixed on his desk. She stood up and made her way to the exit, collecting her staff as she went. Ryder gave a nod to both Young and Tosh and followed them out. The room fell silent. Young played with a pen, letting it fall between his fingers.

"She's right, you know," Tosh finally said. Young didn't answer. "I'll be with Emerson in thruster control for the rest of the day if you need me." Young gave him an acknowledging look. Tosh smiled back at his old friend and glided across the office to the door, then slid outside into the corridor. A moment passed as Young took a photo of himself and his father, which was sitting on his desk, and flung it across the room.

The Agathon
14:45 Martian Standard

Boyett stiffened her posture and fiddled with her lapel at the airlock.

"You want a breath mint?" said Chavel, who stood by her side.

"Shut up, Lieutenant. You sure you aren't needed at waste recycling or something?" she said, slapping his stomach. There were six visibly exhausted yet immaculately dressed crew members awaiting the commander's arrival, uniformly standing three on each side of the white corridor which led from the ship's main docking airlock on the port side of the vessel. Chavel smiled and cleared his throat.

"He knows about you and his daughter?" Boyett whispered out of the corner of her mouth, as the clamps drew back and the lights at the port window switched from red to green. Chavel didn't answer as the door rolled back. Barrington stood at the airlock and drew a breath.

"Permission to come aboard," he said enthusiastically. Boyett knew it was difficult to resist the overwhelming sense of authority this man brought to the surrounding environment and she felt an overwhelming sense of relief in her stomach, knowing the commander had just arrived.

"Permission granted," she said, suddenly aware she was beaming from ear to ear.

"At ease, lieutenants, before you break something," he said, placing a hand on Boyett's shoulder. His warm and powerful eyes took command of the ship instantly. He looked around and placed a hand on one of the bulkheads.

"Hello, my old friend," Boyett heard Barrington whisper. Doctor Tyrell followed him off the shuttle, along with Crewman Amanda Llewellyn who had piloted the shuttle. She was young. Boyett was sure that she just graduated from the academy. She had cropped brown hair and a round face. Her expression was deadly serious. She looked tough, though. Boyett noticed Tyrell's dishevelled appearance as he shuffled past carrying an array of satchels. He nodded briefly. Barrington stood in the corridor for a moment then turned to Chavel.

"Would you show the doctor the main science lab, please Lieutenant?" Chavel nodded and led Tyrell down the hall off to an adjacent corridor. He gave Boyett a cheeky glance before rounding the bend.

"Okay, everybody," Barrington said to the crewmembers still standing there. "Let's get back to work. We have a ship to build. Dismissed." With that the welcoming detail saluted, turned on their heels and walked back to their various tasks. He turned to Boyett.

"Let's see how she looks, shall we? Show me the bridge," he said.

"With pleasure, sir," she said. They turned and began their journey through the ship. Barrington led the pace slowly, as Boyett began filling in the details.

"You'll have to forgive some of the aesthetics right now. The last of the hull plating is taking precedence over everything." Barrington nodded. The hallways of the ship were simple although currently cluttered with equipment and cabling. Vibrations from large sections of hull being sealed into place by the assembly platform orbiting the craft could be felt underfoot. An assortment of crewmembers and engineering staff were dotted around open bulkheads, examining connections and fusing a forest of wires and interfaces together. They all stood and acknowledged the commander as he walked past. Boyett knew he was taking detailed notes in his head, and resisted the urge to apologise for every task yet incomplete and hugely overdue.

"Landon Emerson arrived this morning and is deep in the engineering bay, trying to sort out the FTL ring torque attenuators. At the moment we have no way of slowing them down, which would be unfortunate if we ever want to drop out of hyperspace."

Barrington frowned. "That it would," he said. They passed a series of doors leading to crew quarters. The decks were arranged in a series of segments, with outer rings curving around, intersecting hallways that led to each area of the ship. Each corridor being labelled with letters and each segment with a number. They were currently on Deck 8 section A14. It was home to living quarters, hydroponics, the main forward airlock, a gymnasium, which was currently under construction pending the survival of the first mission and a host of labs. They walked past environmental systems control, which was currently manned by a single crewman, who was monitoring an array of display screens. Barrington peered in.

"You will be pleased to know that that is the one thing working perfectly at the moment. So wherever we end up we will at the very least be able to breathe." Barrington gave her a wry smile and they moved on. They entered a lift and let the doors hiss closed. Llewelyn remained quiet and followed along.

"Bridge," said Boyett. Nothing happened. Barrington looked at the young woman and raised an eyebrow. She cleared her throat.

"Bridge," she repeated more assertively. Still nothing. She sighed and tapped the command into the control pad on the door. The lift took off.

"We're working on that," she said, embarrassed. Seconds later, the doors hissed open and she stepped onto the main bridge. Barrington took a step off the lift. There were at least twenty people working on systems scattered throughout the oval room. Unlike the rest of the ship, the bridge had an industrial feel to it. The grey metallic plating underfoot gave a sense of being on old transport. It had a hardened, unfinished look, with many of the stations still unsealed and showing their innards.

"Commander on the deck," she announced. With a surprised look, the group stood and looked at Barrington. One of them hit his head on an open panel, which caused an unsettling crash of an array of tools that were placed beside him. He rubbed his head and stood to attention. They all looked like they had not slept in weeks. The vacancy in their eyes was familiar. They waited for him to speak. As did Boyett.

"Your head okay, Thomas?" Barrington finally said with a smile to the young man at the back of the group.

There was light laughter as the red-faced crewmember replied, "Yes, sir."

"Glad to hear it," replied the commander.

"I apologise to you all," he said, scanning the ensemble. "Had circumstances allowed I would have been here sooner. You have all done something remarkable. I am very proud of each and every one of you. I know this has been difficult and I promise you all a cold one on the beach of our new home, but right now I have a personal favour. If you all agree to this I will personally be in each of your debt." He paused and composed himself. "I need you all to save the human race. I need you all to lock away your grief. It has no place on this ship. Not now. We grieve for the dead when we save the living. That is my favour. Do you think you can all do that?"

A colossal, "Yes, sir," followed within a heartbeat. Boyett could tell the level of commitment touched Barrington and she sensed that his words were desperately needed in this room.

"Right then. As you were," he finished. The crewmembers snapped back into their tasks with the infused adrenalin that followed the morale boost from the commander. One of the comm stations sounded tone.

"Sir, I have an incoming transmission from the Jycorp Station."

"Do we have visuals working yet?" he asked Boyett.

"Yes, sir, we do," she answered, pointing to the array of large screens that circled the bridge. The design allowed a true sense of orientation when viewing outside the vessel and also offered enhanced image resolution of distant objects, of up to a light-year.

"Quiet on the bridge. On screen," he announced. He looked toward the centre of the bridge and made his way over to the elevated captain's chair. Boyett watched as he took his seat and felt her nerves begin to calm. Ahead, the black screen was replaced with an image of Chancellor Clarke.

"Greetings. My name is Sienna Clark. I have been your Supreme Chancellor. I speak to you today as someone who, like all of you, has lost a home, family and friends." She paused.

"Years ago when I was young my father took me and my brother into the woods to hunt deer. Somewhere along the way my brother and I were separated from him and we found ourselves in the middle of nowhere, lost and afraid. As it grew dark and the crawling shadows of the trees crept ever closer to us, I started to cry and my brother took my hand and told me that nothing bad could happen to either of us because we had each other." She paused and glanced downwards.

"We made a pact to protect each other, no matter what came for us in the darkness. Something came for him in the darkness recently and we lost each other."

She took a breath.

"Some of you will know the extent of the dire situation we find ourselves in this day and some of you may not. I am here to shed some light on the facts." She paused again.

"In less than three weeks a massive debris field from Earth will strike this planet and its surrounding platforms with enough force to shift its orbit and make it permanently uninhabitable. We do not know why the signal bearers chose this moment to attack us. The only thing we do know is where that signal came from. Our only hope for survival is The Agathon. Her ability to use her faster than light capability will guarantee the survival of all of us, but there are challenges. We do not know what lies at its destination. And, above all else," she paused, "not all of us will be going."

Barrington kept his eyes fixed on the screen. There was deathly silence on the bridge. The chancellor continued.

"Some of us will be remaining behind on the orbiting stations and transports and will be setting a course for the outer rim of our solar system, to stay ahead of the debris field. It is proposed that The Agathon, once it has secured its destination as being habitable for all of us, will return and take those left behind to their new home. This is not a perfect plan. I know some of you will have doubts but I have faith and I believe that this can and will work. I and my senior staff have already decided to stay behind with those on the space stations and wait for The Agathon's return." There was chatter on the bridge.

"Quiet," Barrington ordered. The crew hushed instantly.

"The Agathon is a remarkable vessel. But it must be crewed by the people best suited to find our new home. Most of that crew has already been selected. In seventy-two hours there will be a lottery for the remaining spaces on the ship, for those who wish to enter. Simply submit your name to the central computer via a data link to the Jycorp Orbital. For those of you who have nearly completed the impossible and who are on board right now, you have my personal thanks and the thanks of every one of us left. Our tribe will survive. Of that you can be assured.

"I am making myself and my staff available to every colonist who wishes to speak directly to me or to anyone who requires clarification. This is something I could not do on Earth and it was one of my greatest regrets. Tonight we hold hands and we will not be afraid of the approaching darkness. The shadows of the trees will not consume us. This I promise you. To Commander Barrington on board The Agathon. I hereby promote you to captain. I wish you good fortune in your journey. The sum of all our hopes now rests upon you and your crew. Godspeed. Clark out."

The screen went blank. Barrington sat back in his chair and looked at his crew.

"You heard the lady. Let's get to work," he said without hesitation.

"Yes, Captain," said Boyett with a smile.

"First things first; let's seal this girl up and get her ready to fly. Are the inter-ship communications working, Charly?" he asked. Boyett nodded

"Yes, sir, the panel to your left." Barrington tapped a pad on the arm of his chair. A whistle sounded overhead.

"This is the comman... captain speaking. To all personnel. I want hourly briefings and progress reports to Lieutenant Boyett, effective immediately. I want a meeting with all department heads on the bridge in twenty minutes. Lieutenant Chavel, please report to the bridge. Barrington out." He turned to Llewellyn who was behind him.

"Amanda, I want you to liaise with Aquaria base and start compiling a logistics report on the transfer of the selected colonists from the surface. Hold off on nonessential personnel until we do further integrity checks on the outer hull. Once we have a green light from environmental systems, start bringing them up. Set up a station in one of the communications quarters on deck nine."

"Yes, sir," she replied and turned towards the lift. He turned back to Boyett and stood.

"I'll be in engineering," he said and followed Llewellyn to the back of the bridge. "Boyett, you have the bridge."

Main Observatory
Mars Colony 1
15:00 Martian Standard

Carrie stared at the blank screen. The chancellor was not what she was expecting at all. There was a softness in her that she had never seen on the Jycorp communication channels or media reports from Earth. She sensed a great sadness from her when she had been speaking about her brother, which she had barely been able to contain. She could feel her father's heartbeat as he learned of his promotion. His ability to contain pressure and use its negative impact on the mind as a positive thing was what she admired most about him. She was alone in the lab. Most of the equipment had already been sent to The Agathon and Tyrell had left her in charge of his main lab. While the observatory array was still operational, its functions had been taken over by the Phobos Orbital platform. Tyrell had given an elaborate story to Carrie about what happened to the imaging chamber, which was now an empty space in the middle of the observatory.

"There was a breach of highly charged ion particles during a maintenance routine," he had said. "I was rather lucky it didn't kill me," he had finished. Of course she had known instantly that he was lying. The easiest of human emotional tells she had learned as a child. She had expressed concern for the cuts on his hand, but had let the matter drop. Why would he destroy the imaging chamber?

She was having some trouble concentrating on her tasks, as the lingering memories of her encounter with Chavel in his shuttle pod remained in her mind. She walked into Tyrell's personal lab and began a wavelength analysis of the final seconds before the signal changed. While Tyrell had already done several he had instructed her to compile a nanosecond report into several of the oscillations, which seemed to show minor variations. He was just trying to keep her busy and off the scent of what had happened to the imaging chamber. Carrie knew that. He rarely let her have access to his personal lab.

Behind her the sample of The Black sat quietly in the containment room. For several minutes Carrie watched as the computer ran a diagnostic of the wavelength patterns of the signal. It eventually revealed a minor variance in the upper phase of the atomic transference, but nothing that could account for such a dramatic change of the nature and strength of the particle wave. She eventually swivelled in her chair and faced the containment room where The Black was held. She gazed into the room and watched the container of black fluid. It was settled in a spherical transparent ball elevated above a solid metal platform. She stood from her seat and stood by the entrance to the chamber. There was a large sign stencilled on the clear glass door. DO NOT ENTER. HAZARDOUS BIOCHEMICAL SUBSTANCES.

She did not know why she opened the door but moments later she was inside the containment room and was staring directly into the glass sphere holding the lethal life form. There was an attraction to the fluid. She had never been this close to it, but she had a powerful urge to smash the container and release it. A strange sensation of calm fell upon her as she reached up and ran a finger across the surface of the smooth outer layer of the sphere. A small bubble formed on the surface of the fluid.

"Home," she heard in her mind. A dark voice that was not her own yet sounded like her.

"You are of here," it said.

"Yes I am," she replied in a trance. Her eyes now wide and pupils dilated, she began caressing the sphere with The Black inside which was beginning to gurgle and pop.

"You are of here," the voice in her head said again.

"I am of here," she repeated out loud to the empty room. She began to close her eyes and as she did so visions of a utopian world began to fill her mind.

Blue skies with streaks of white clouds overlooked advanced and endless seas of technological civilisation. Flying craft darted amongst the hazy, white backdrop above. Enormous glass towers filled with lights pierced the atmosphere with grandiose and bold arrogance. The roads and streets of mega cities, filled with surface vehicles and millions of bipedal creatures swarming, filled her field of view. Interconnecting transport hubs linked an endless array of surrounding structures. She knew this place. There were forests with trees that reached for miles into the sky. Huge laborious animals with a multitude of limbs and defensive horn structures on their backs ran through an open plain. She flew over them and watched as they merged with an array of other creatures of various shapes and sizes, all huddled around a great lake.

She was snapped awake suddenly with a bolt of electricity that ran the length of her body. She felt as though she were having a heart attack as the burst of light that shot out of her fingertips connected directly with the electrical converters in the walls of the containment chamber. The force of the burst made her scream and she hit the ground, covering her head. The room flickered to red as the emergency lights kicked in and she found herself staring up at The Black in the containment sphere. It had become still. She looked at her fingertips, which were red.

She touched the tops of her fingers together. To her surprise they were cold to the touch. Like she had placed ice cubes on each one. The ends of her jumpsuit were frayed and smouldering. She looked around the floor to see if she had accidentally tripped one of Tyrell's power outlets and the charge had not grounded itself properly. The floor was clear. She looked overhead. Just the internal lighting panel, at least eight feet above her. She stepped around the sphere container holding The Black and looked for loose connections. The container had no loose fibrous connections or connections of any kind attached to it. She slowly made her way to the door of the lab and opened it.

She felt as though she had been sleep-walking. Not fully conscious yet not really asleep. She closed the door behind her and left Tyrell's personal lab. She poured herself a glass of water and tried to rationalise what had occurred. Her fingertips were still cold. There was no pain. No bruising. No third degree burns. She caught a reflection of herself in the mirror placed on a diagnostic table. Her eyes were pulsating brightly with the rhythm of her heartbeat. She shut them and opened them again. The electric blue became even more prominent, before starting to fade back to her natural colour. She looked calmly at herself and began to cry.

"What is happening to me?" she screamed to nothing.

9

Transport vessel 'Ramona'
Six kilometres off the port side of the Jycorp Orbital Station
Phobos
Time since Evacuation 103 days
24 Hours to impact

Captain Harry Gray had fallen asleep at the con. He had spent the night staring out at the stars, wondering how long he had left to live. He awoke in the early hours to find himself alone as usual, with his legs perched against the flight controls. Most of the people he had been transporting had departed to the civilian orbital station with only three leaving for the Jycorp Orbital. He had positioned the long cylindrical ship towards the direction of Earth and had kept the viewing port tracked against its former position. He reached over to a raised side table and poured himself a glass of water.

"Status," he said to the computer, after clearing his throat.

"All systems functioning within normal parameters, Captain." The surrounding air was quiet. A slow hum from the ventilation system filled the cockpit. He stood up and made his way to a shelf to the rear of the cockpit and sifted through the old books that he had accumulated over the years. He picked up a copy of *Moby Dick* and sat back in his chair. A frayed bookmark was lodged securely in the centre of the book. He opened it and began to read. He had almost no contact with the people he had brought on board. He had had almost no real contact with people in years.

A true space junkie, but without the ambition or political knowhow to rise through the ranks of the fleet, he had contented himself on flying transports for the rest of his life. He was okay with it. He had no family to support and no peers to compete against. He was a quiet and reserved man. A forgettable face at a party. He had led a relatively uneventful life, taken up with the Mars supply and personnel run for the last six years.

He had read about Jennifer Barrington's death and been saddened by it. The Ramona had been the transport that had carried the commander and his wife to Mars. He had remembered her being a charming and kind-hearted woman, who had always given him brief conversation in the corridors of the Ramona during their trip. The commander had taken the time to sit with him for several minutes at the control to check out the ship operations. He had found it awkward, but had appreciated Barrington's courtesy.

He had no property or ties to Earth and had always known that his life would probably end at the control of this vessel or another. His castle was the Ramona. He did not submit his name to the lottery. Joining The Agathon in hyperspace, with thousands of strangers, was not how he planned to end his days and there was a strange fascination with taking this old girl to the outer rim under his command. And so it was that Harry Gray was to remain with the convoy. He began to read. *I know not all that may be coming, but be it what it will; I'll go to it laughing.* His comm system chirped.

"To all personnel. This is John Barrington. We have incoming debris. Lock down all vessels and seal emergency bulkheads. To all transport vessels, begin evasive manoeuvres. Take cover behind the planet. This is not a drill. Barrington out." Gray snapped his attention to the viewing port. He saw nothing.

"Computer, release flight lockout." The main flight controls came to life and he began turning the ship to port.

"To all personnel, this is the captain. General quarters. I repeat, general quarters. Seal all bulkheads and prepare for impact." He increased his rate of turn and began seeing a small cloud of rocks approaching from the starboard area of the vessel. Both space stations and the remaining transport ships came into his field of view. The ships were making similar turning manoeuvres. The glow from each of their engine housings was almost synchronised. He increased his rate of turn to port and set his engines to eighty percent. The warm reflection of the Martian surface filled his field of view, as he set a course for the rear of the plant.

"Computer, track incoming projectiles," he shouted. A three-dimensional rendering appeared hovering over his operations console. What looked like a thousand small objects filled the image. It looked like a swarm of bees after a honey thief.

"Jesus," Gray whispered to himself.

"Distance from objects?" he shouted at the computer.

"Five hundred and sixty-two meters," came the reply. The Ramona was a manoeuvrable ship, but its speed and acceleration curve were relatively limited due to its drive systems being nearly sixty years old. The first impact hit shook the bulkheads of the cockpit.

"Impact aft quarter. Section two alpha. Take evasive action," the computer's voice sounded over a klaxon that began screaming from overhead. Gray increased speed to maximum.

"Damage?" he shouted. Before the computer had a chance to reply a second impact threw him out of his chair and sent him crashing into the side of his main control panel. He hit the ground and heard a defining crack. Blood began to flow freely from an open wound on the top of his head. The ship continued to shake.

"Hull breech, section 33 Beta," came the report from the computer. The stars outside began to change wildly as the ship began to list uncontrollably. Gray tried to stand, but crumpled under a broken ankle. He screamed in pain.

"Hull breach section 22, section 24, section 29. Emergency containment procedures offline. Oxygen levels at critical. Evacuation recommended," the computer continued.

Gray focused on his good leg and hauled himself slowly back into his chair. He tapped the comm panel.

"This is the captain, all hands to escape pods. Abandon ship." The third impact hit, causing a deafening sound of crunching metal and internal explosions inside the vessel. Electrical systems began to explode all around him. A small fire broke out at the aft of his compartment and began filling the cockpit with smoke. Then everything went dark. He began finding it difficult to breathe and knew that the oxygen levels in the cockpit were beginning to fail.

He reached behind him and tried to activate the fire suppression systems, which ignored his commands. He dragged himself to the rear cockpit door, which was unresponsive. He glanced back through the viewing port and began to see the Martian surface fill the screen. More internal explosions filled his ears. His breathing began to become laboured as he dragged himself back into his chair. As smoke filled his thoughts he gave one last look to the book, which now lay on the deck plating. A deafening crunch blocked out his fear, as the glass on the viewing port exploded, venting what was left of the atmosphere, as Harry Gray was engulfed in a fireball. *I know not all that may be coming, but be it what it will; I'll go to it laughing.*

Jycorp Orbital platform

"Mother of God," said Sienna Clark, peering out of the viewing port at the explosion that had just lit up the night sky. The cold and callous collection of twisted rock had narrowly missed the space station. One of the transports had taken the full brunt of the attack and was now a broken flotsam of electrical fires and hull fragments.

"We lost one," said Greyson, who was by her side. "Ma'am, we need to leave here." For the first time since she had known him she thought she felt genuine fear in his voice.

"Clark to Young," she said into a wall panel.

"Young here, are you all right? It's over for now."

"How many did we lose?" she asked.

"We are checking now. It looks like most of the people had transported off onto The Village." Clark had taken it upon herself to rename the civilian station 'The Village earlier that month. It had seemed appropriate.

Young continued, "We lost the captain and twelve on board." Clark felt a profound sense of sadness as her own mortality and that of her people were suddenly thrown into her field of vision.

"How long until the fragment hits?" she asked wearily.

"Twenty-three hours, Chancellor."

"Jerome, I think it is time we left, don't you?"

"Yes, Chancellor, I'm on my way to you now. We'll conference with Barrington and begin final prep. See you in five. Young out."

She looked at Greyson who was staring out of the viewing port. She placed a hand on his shoulder and walked over to the long conference table in the centre of the room. Spread out over the table were lists of names on long scripts of paper. Each name had a small picture attached to it. Hundreds of faces scattered in piles. She sat at the top of the table. She had been in this room for several days, sifting through the names of those that had survived. Some of them she had recognised, but most she did not. Scientists, civilians and a handful of children that had escaped on orbiting transports.

There had been some problems with the lottery. Not unexpected, with the high level of emotion running amongst the survivors. Small skirmishes had broken out when allegations of rigging had begun circulating amongst the people on the stations. The desire for a place on The Agathon had been greater than expected and she had had to address the people on a number of occasions, imploring them to be calm and assuring them that they would all make the trip to a new world. Most of the Mars Colony had all transported up at this stage, with only a few remaining to bring the last of the food synthesisers and power cells from the Atmo processors up from the surface. It had been discovered that they could be converted to adapt to the power output levels of both space stations.

The pile of documents closest to her held a selection of candidates to command both stations. Young's decision to join The Agathon had been a moot point. His expertise had been an essential component in the choice. She knew there was no chance of him staying behind and had requested to see who they would be leaving in charge. There was no shortage of qualified personnel and they had shortlisted six candidates. The door hissed open and Young and Tosh entered the room. Sienna nodded to the two men.

"Gentlemen, how are we fixed?" she asked. Tosh looked pale.

"We have confirmed the numbers on the Ramona," Young said.

"Fourteen, including the captain."

"Any other damaged vessels?" Sienna asked

"No, we were lucky," said Tosh. Sienna was taken aback by the comment.

"Lucky is not a word I would use to describe our current situation, Doctor Tosh." Young held up his hand and directed them towards the table. Tosh floated across the room and positioned himself at the end of the table. Sienna felt bad for snapping at Tosh, but ignored it. She tapped a control panel on the table and a large screen emerged from its centre.

"Agathon, this is Jycorp Orbital," said Young into the screen after opening a channel.

"Go ahead, Jycorp," replied John Barrington's voice. His face appeared on the screen.

"Report, John?" asked Young.

"We sustained no damage from the incoming projectiles. I have a report of minor damage to Atmo 3 but we evacuated the facility four days ago so no casualties. How many did we lose on the transport?" he asked gravely.

"Fourteen, including the captain," answered Sienna.

"The fragment is closing, Chancellor. We are in the last stages of hull integrity checks, but we are getting readings from the main FTL drive that suggest the main plasma relays are fluctuating.

Manoeuvring thrusters are fully operational and we are disengaging from the construction arms as we speak. We can't engage the FTL in orbit or do a test on the system until we are at least one hundred thousand kilometres away from the planet."

"The last of the crew and personnel are transporting over and I think we should get going in the next twelve hours. I would like to run a test of the FTL ring up to ninety percent torque before we do this, but I don't know if we have time. The fragment is towing a debris field of several thousand kilometres. Chancellor, I would suggest breaking orbit as soon as possible. We are cutting this too close. Can you give me numbers for remaining people to board The Agathon?" Young looked at the Chancellor.

"Captain, we have one more transport and then we are clear," Young answered.

"Understood," answered Barrington.

"Captain, how confident are you the FTL will work?" asked Clark bluntly. There was silence in the room as Barrington looked around at his crew off screen.

"It will work," he replied. Clark knew that statement was for his crew.

"I understand," she replied. She looked at Tosh.

"Chancellor, the spatial singularity tests of this ship have been run as best we can run them. They all come out in the green," said Tosh.

"But?" she replied, sensing his hesitation.

"There have always been small quantum variables which may affect the accuracy of the navigational system. So while we can navigate using star system special references, the exact accuracy of those references is not that precise. The ship may not end up precisely where it is supposed to be," he said.

"Meaning?" she said.

"Meaning it may end up at the outer rim of a system. We just do not know. But my numbers show that it will fire correctly, if the components of The Agathon have been built to spec. As the captain just pointed out, this is its first run and right now I really can't give you any more information on it."

"Chancellor, it will work. We won't let you down," responded Barrington, with absolute assuredness in his voice. She believed him. She had to.

"Okay, Captain, contact us when you are ready to break orbit," she said. Barrington nodded and the screen went blank. Young tapped the table and it sank back out of view.

"I have two names to take command of both stations," Young said.

"Okay, let's have them," she replied.

"Richard Ellis will command this station," said Young.

"He has been in command of station operations here for six years and I have absolute faith in him." He handed her a dossier on Ellis. He was forty-three years old, well built and with a round bald head. Ellis had served in the military for most of his adult life. Clark had had a brief encounter with the man in Young's office a few weeks earlier. He had been quiet, but had seemed highly competent. She had no doubt they were about to become very close.

"And the other?" she asked.

"Doctor Amelia Cox will command The Village," he replied, handing her the file on the woman. Fifty-one years old and with an iron expression and determination in her eyes. Her photo felt heavy in the chancellor's arms.

"She's strictly by the book and not the most exciting person to have at a party, but she'll get the job done. She's the most senior propulsion expert we have over there and has had eight years in the military, so given the circumstances she slots right in. She may not win any popularity contests, so it might be worth imparting some wisdom to her," said Young.

"When are you two transferring to The Agathon?" she suddenly asked. Young leaned back and fixed his hair. She hadn't meant to impart a sense of guilt in the room, but that was exactly how it had come out. Tosh simply looked at Young. She held her hands up in acknowledgement.

"I know you have to go, gentlemen, and to be honest I'm comforted that your expertise will be on that ship. I for one do not relish the prospect of floating into nothingness for the rest of my days."

"These are good people, Sienna," Young said.

"I know that, Jerome."

"Ellis commands respect on this base and he will have your back through all of this. Trust his judgement, but ultimately you have the last say in policy. We're going into uncharted territory here." He sighed.

"My father would have dissolved your office the second this event took place, with the full introduction of martial law under Jycorp jurisdiction. These people need to believe we are still a structured society and not refugees. You can accomplish that," said Young. She looked at Young and wished she had not been so hard on him when she had arrived at the station.

"Tosh and I will be leaving in the next few hours. I suggest we have a briefing with the two commanders before that. We need both stations under way ASAP and I want as much distance between us and this planet as possible, before that fragment hits," he said.

"This is gonna be a photo finish," said Tosh.

The Agathon
12 hours to Impact
15:00 Martian Standard

The engine room of The Agathon was a sight to behold. In place of the fusion drive mountings, which were commonplace on most of the Jycorp vessels, stood a twenty foot rotating orb attached to a spinning tube of liquid plasma which ran the length of the ship from bow to stern. Landon Emerson stood at the end of a gangway overlooking the enormous faster than light drive system. Directly in front of him lay a half-moon-shaped array of control panels manned by three propulsion engineers. Barrington stood behind him watching the test. Unlike the rough contours of the space station engine rooms, this one had smooth lines and a polished effect with integrated holographic imaging panels on the smooth silver walls. The neural interface worn by all staff allowed certain functions to be triggered with specific thought patterns. It had taken Emerson a number of months to get used to hearing the ship's functions reverberating through his mind. The drive section of The Agathon was the first section of the ship to have been completed two years ago and was the only area of the ship to have felt fully completed.

The FTL orb, or 'Betty' as it was nicknamed, was transparent and surrounded by a series of metallic threads, making it look like a hornet's nest. At eighty percent the light blue glow from the threads contrasted beautifully with the plasma, as they mixed and cast an incandescent light all around the engine room. Emerson compared those flickers of light to water in a dark cave. The AI in the engine room had a soft yet commanding voice, as it relayed drive performance to the crew who looked on.

"Taking it up to ninety percent," said Emerson. Barrington nodded as The Betty began to speed up. There was an increase in the circulation of the air surrounding the device as it spun. A soft breeze began to fill Emerson's hair.

"Intermix ratio at 1:1. All systems nominal," said a female voice representing Betty's computer systems.

"Hold it there," said Barrington.

"She's looking good, Cap," said Emerson. His focus was firmly held on the readouts in front of him.

"Okay, shut it down," said Barrington.

Emerson nodded. "Betty, reduce flow intake to fifteen percent and hold," he said. He focused on the system flow intake systems in his mind and relayed shut down protocols through the neural interface. The headset was comfortable to wear, but the metallic rod which was attached to his forehead dug into his skin and he didn't like wearing it for longer periods. He preferred a hands on approach.

Transfer to manual, he thought and removed the device. He turned to Llewellyn, who was manning the FTL ring deployment station on the opposite side of the gangway.

"Amanda, let's do a test on the ring," he shouted across to her. "Here's the tricky part," he said to the captain. "If we can't sync the ring up, we won't have any protection against the increase in the gravity distortion."

"We don't want that now, do we?" said Barrington with a smile.

"No, sir, we do not," he replied. Emerson had only known the captain a short time, since transferring from the station. He could not always read him, but trusted his judgement. He noted he had recently kept the crew at arm's length and projected total authority on the decks in a cold and confident manor. The crew responded to this well and given the dire nature of what was about to happen, Emerson thought it an effective command strategy. Project strength and control at all costs. Any crewmembers that he thought were beginning to lose it were snapped back to reality with a personal cattle prod up the ass.

"Spinning up FTL ring. Stand by," said Llewellyn. There was a creak and popping on the hull. Everyone looked up at the walls and ceiling of the engineering bay. Emerson felt the deck plating begin to vibrate. The sound of a large machine coming to life filled the silent room. He looked at Barrington.

"She always does this; the mechanism was locked into place a little tightly. The first few runs may scratch the paint." Barrington didn't answer. He had his eyes combing the walls around him.

"Barrington to bridge," he said.

"Boyett here, go ahead, Captain,"

"Charlie, we are spinning up the FTL ring. Can you confirm normal movement visually, please?"

"Yes, sir, she's off and running. All systems check out up here. I am showing her at twelve percent and holding steady."

"It must be a hell of a sight from outside the ship, Cap," said Emerson.

"A hell of a sight," repeated Barrington. Without warning one of the displays behind Llewellyn burst into a chorus of sparks. She was thrown off kilter and hit the deck to avoid the discharge. The vibrations ground to a halt and the lights in the engine room began to flicker. Emerson hit the emergency shutdown protocols and the deck went quiet.

"What happened?" said the captain, not flinching from the explosion in the console.

"Looks like we blew a relay. Amanda, you okay over there?" She gave them a thumbs up and righted herself, waving wafts of smoke out of her face.

"Status of the FTL ring?" asked Barrington.

"She's dead in the water right now, sir. If she blows a relay like that while we're at a hundred percent, the distortion will tear the ship apart," he said gravely. Barrington's face changed.

"We have less than twelve hours, Mr. Emerson. How long to right the problem?"

"I'll get right on it, but I could really use Doctor Tosh's assistance at this stage. Where is he?" Emerson had been trying to figure out why Tosh hadn't joined him at a much earlier stage in the engine room and was starting to wonder if the old bastard had hitched himself a comfortable ride on the space station through all of this.

"I believe they are on their way. Just get on this problem and I'll send him down to you straight from the airlock," replied Barrington.

"Yes, sir." Barrington turned and made his way towards the rear of the engineering deck.

"I want updates every twenty minutes, Mr Emerson. Use whomever you need on this. All other priorities are rescinded. Get her working!" he shouted, without turning his head.

"You'll have 'em, sir," he said.

The door hissed behind the captain and he stood in the corridor of the ship.

"Fuck it," he whispered under his breath. He placed a hand on a bulkhead. "Come on, don't let me down," he said. A crewmember gave him a curious look and nodded to him as he passed to enter the engine room. He made his way through the deck and into a nearby lift.

"Deck eight," he said. The lift took off and deposited him on the requested deck. As the doors opened he was greeted with a flurry of activity. There were colonists from the planet surface rushing about the place with equipment and supplies. He paused outside the lift and made eye contact with some of them. They stopped and looked at him. They looked worried. Most of them were scientists on the planet and had never seen anything close to combat. None of them had expected anything like this and there was a need for him to be much larger than he really was. He nodded in their direction and offered to help one of the biologists with a heavy case of what looked like computer components. She was a young, petite woman by the name of Charlotte King. She seemed unsteady with the weight of the case.

"Thank you, Captain, but I can manage. Are we leaving soon?" she asked softly, with large brown eyes that held a fear Barrington knew only too well.

"Very soon, Charlotte," he replied assuredly. "Try and get these stowed away safely." She nodded and moved off quickly in the direction of crew quarters.

"Captain," came the voice of Chase Meridian off to his left.

"Doctor," he replied. She seemed out of breath.

"I was just coming to see you." She pulled him to one side.

"You know Tyrell has brought a sample of The Black on board? Please tell me you didn't approve that. That stuff gets loose on board a ship this size and Bob's your uncle."

Barrington suddenly felt a surge of rage. "How do you know this, Doctor?"

"The crazy son of a bitch let it slip. It's under containment in his lab but, Jesus, John."

Barrington looked at the ground. "Have you seen Carrie?" he said with gritted teeth.

"No, sir, she was among the last to transport up. I think she's in her quarters."

"I'll take care of it. Chase, do me a favour and help Charlotte with a case she's carrying. It looks like she's going to break a bone if she's not careful."

"Yes sir." Meridian hurried off and helped the young woman. Barrington took a breath and placed his hand on a comm panel.

"Barrington to Carrie Barrington." Silence then a soft voice.

"Carrie here, go ahead," She sounded sleepy.

"Carrie, meet me in Tyrell's lab immediately, will you?"

"Okay, give me five. Carrie out." Barrington turned on his heels and moved with a purpose, hoping to God Meridian had been victim to a practical joke.

Tyrell's Lab - The Agathon

Carrie entered Tyrell's lab but knew well in advance what she would find inside. She could usually feel her father's anger from miles away and on this ship she felt everything.

"I'm sorry, John. Just hear me out," said a retreating Tyrell, as the captain made a move towards him.

"Are you crazy, bringing that on board my ship?" shouted Barrington

"John, just be calm for a moment, will you?" Barrington eased off and took a breath.

"What's happening?" Carrie asked, knowing full well.

"Did you know about this?" her father asked her, as if she had just sneaked out in the middle of the night and not told anyone. She thought about lying but couldn't. Not to her father. Never.

"Yes," she said. She could see the disappointment in him, but more than that the sadness of having been left out of her loop. He placed his hands on his head and walked to the back of the lab where he took a seat next to some soil samples lying on a diagnostic table.

"Okay, let's hear it," he said. Tyrell looked at Carrie.

"Listen to me, John. This is the only alien organic life form we have ever encountered in the universe. Yes it's dangerous, but there has never been a single serious incident while it has been in a containment chamber. In less than eleven hours it may very well be the last sample in the universe and I don't think it's right to condemn an extra-terrestrial species to extinction, just because we don't understand it." Barrington's eyes widened and he looked at Carrie, who looked at the ground.

"It's too important not to allow further study, Father." He frowned.

"Are you absolutely certain we can contain this in the ship, without any danger to the crew?" he asked bluntly.

"I'm certain of it, Captain. I'm sorry you were not informed, but we simply ran out of time," finished Tyrell.

"Carrie?"

"Yes, Captain. I'm sure of it. Doctor Tyrell has it sealed in a vaporisation room. If it so much as twitches, the computer has been programmed to alert either myself or Doctor Tyrell, who can order its incineration in a heartbeat." Her father looked at the two of them, clearly tired of the debate.

"Okay, Dice. I'm making you personally responsible for the safety of the crew in this matter. Like you said, we are out of time. Don't let me down. Doctor Tyrell, they need you on the bridge to assist with the navigational array."

"Right away, Captain," and with that Tyrell walked out of the lab, leaving them alone. They looked at each other for a moment before Carrie broke the silence.

"It's important," she said.

"What is, Dice?" Barrington replied wearily.

"I didn't lie to you. But we both know you would have had no part in bringing it on board." She saw the look of confusion on her father's face and felt his fear.

"There is some connection between us," she finally said.

"Between who, Carrie? I really don't have time for mind games today. If you have something to say to me, just say it. I have never known you to have secrets from me. God knows there isn't anything I can hide from you. And that isn't fair, Dice."

His earnest point was well made and she agreed with the logic. It was true; there were no secrets between them. Most of the time. Although she had an advantage in that area. She took a seat next to him and put her hands on his.

"There is something happening to me. I can feel myself changing. I know that I'm different, in some ways, to the rest of you, but there's something else. A growing power that I'm scared of and I know that there is a connection to that horrible substance locked away in the other room. I'm changing, Father. Manifesting things." She bowed her head.

"I can't explain it yet; I hope we live through this so that I can show you. I'm sorry that you felt lied to," she said.

She thrust herself into her father's arms. His surprised reaction was abated quickly, when she entered his mind and spoke to him in the most personal way she could. Without words.

"Please trust me. I love you."

"Okay, Dice," he replied with his thoughts. He embraced her like he hadn't seen her in a thousand years. It seemed to last forever, when they were interrupted by the ship's general communications channel.

"Boyett to Captain Barrington. Jycorp shuttlecraft off the port bow." Carrie pulled back from her father and kissed him on the cheek.

"Barrington here, on my way." He stood and made his way to the door, then turned to her.

"One other thing," he said with a wry smile.

"Stay away from that flight jockey. I've seen the way you two are. Keep your head in the game. Besides, you can do better." She smiled, knowing full well he didn't really mean it.

"I'll try my very best," she said.

"Hmm," he replied and exited the lab. As he left her alone in the lab she was hit with a profound sense that somehow she hadn't much time left with her father. An immeasurable sense of grief consumed her as she tried to fathom how she could go on with her life without him. She was also struck with the feeling that his demise would ultimately be her fault. As the feeling faded, she tried to take hold of where it had come from but the details were fleeting and the images like a flicker of light in the sand. She told herself it was simply a moment of fear transgressing itself onto an already frightened and confused mind, no matter how real the feeling felt.

10

Jycorp Orbital Platform
One hour to impact
03:00 Martian Standard

Ryder was holding the restraints so tightly they were cutting into his hand. They sat in a row in the flight chairs in Young's old office. The sounds of the station's interior as it shifted its position out of the lunar orbit and into open space reverberated through the room, like a sinking ship that had struck an iceberg. Ellis had given the command to fire thrusters forty minutes earlier, but the station had not gone willingly into the night.

"Moving a station this size is gonna be a bumpy ride, folks. I can't guarantee she won't give us problems." The transport ships had already left orbit and were slowly making their way out to the rendezvous marker just outside Saturn's moon Titan. The chancellor sat quietly with her eyes closed but Ryder couldn't get a reading on her; then again he was terrified out of his mind and couldn't sense anything very much about anything. The vibrations had been steady throughout the manoeuvre. The ion engines were fired in bursts every two minutes to establish safe momentum before the long burn took hold. There had been damage to one of the antenna clusters during the first turn, but it hadn't caused any breach within the hull. It had simply broken off and floated away into the dark.

"Don't worry about it, James, she'll be okay," the chancellor said above the noise of the creaking metal. She looked remarkably calm. The Village had begun its burn first, as the smaller of the two stations, and had executed it without any problems. Ryder looked out of the view port behind Young's desk and caught a glimpse of The Agathon as it stood watch. Its FTL ring was extended ninety degrees perpendicular to its hull, indicating its readiness to jump.

"Look at that, Chancellor," he shouted over the noise. They looked out the viewing port at the stalking ship. Clark smiled.

"If it doesn't fire, Sienna, it's game over," he said sternly. She looked at him and frowned. They glanced back outside the viewing port as the angle shifted. What entered their field of vision silenced them all. An area of space where no stars could be seen. What looked like a planet-sized black hole approached. The mass was surrounded by a haze of greenish crystallised cloud formations, which bounced sunlight into dark crevices on the surface of the rock. It was accompanied by thousands of loose threads of rock and dust, giving the monster a crazed and malevolent approach.

"Jesus, the size of it," said Ryder finally. Clark didn't answer. The surreal view of the planet they had lived on their whole lives now free floating through space defied conversation. Suddenly the space station grew silent. The vibrations stopped and noise levels returned to normal.

"This is Ellis. Burn is complete. You can walk freely." His voice came confidently over the comms. They stood from their seats and walked over to the viewing port to see the end of a second world. Small fragments of the incoming debris began to strike the surface of the orbiting moon Demos. The sister moon to Phobos had no human technology on it as it proved to be of little significance to either the colonisation or the signal analysis missions for Jycorp.

"It's hitting Demos," said Ryder. "See?" he said, pointing to the folly of small explosive impacts that were visible even at this distance.

"I see, James," Clark responded.

"Sienna Clark to Ellis," she said. Ryder didn't see her hit the comms panel.

"Go ahead, Chancellor," came his low voice.

"Richard, are you sure this distance will protect us from the blast? From up here it looks like we're cutting it fine." She sounded worried.

"Don't worry, Chancellor, we are travelling at over fifty-two thousand kilometres an hour. Doesn't look like much, but we're well out of harm's way for now."

"Thank you, Richard. Clark out," she finished. The surface of the moon began to start shooting great plumes of rock and dust into the vacuum, as the impacts of the incoming rock pounded into its surface. Streaks of sunlight lit up various sections of the debris field, as the fragments' unrelenting attack continued. The comms system chirped.

"Chancellor, this is Ellis. I am patching through Mr Young on board The Agathon."

"Go ahead," she replied.

"Sienna?" said Young's voice. He sounded tired.

"Yes, Jerome, I presume you're all watching." There was a pause.

"We are. Both Doctor Tosh and Emerson believe that we need to make the jump as soon as possible, as the instability of a core detonation could disrupt the gravitational forces in this area and make it impossible." Her heart sank. They would soon be on their own.

"I understand, Jerome. Get your people out of here." A small meteor shower began to creep across the atmosphere. "Is Captain Barrington with you?"

"I am here, Chancellor," he replied.

"Captain, you have my best wishes," she said. "I wish you and your crew good hunting and want you to know that our spirits rest in you." The meteor shower began to intensify.

"Chancellor, you have my word that we will return for you. Whatever it takes," he said. Ryder watched as the chancellor's eyes stared off into the distance.

"We'll see you soon, Sienna," came Young's voice. The comms went dead.

"This is really happening, isn't it?" said Ryder. He was becoming visibly upset and struggling to keep it to himself. Sienna Clark took his hand and smiled.

The Agathon

The view screens showed every available angle of the menacing chunk of rock now headed for the surface of Mars. Barrington sat in the centre seat and was flanked by Young and Tosh. Boyett was seated in a suspended flight control console near the front centre of the bridge. David Chavel was seated to her right in a fixed silver metallic chair that was attached to the auxiliary navigation station.

"Sixteen minutes to impact, sir," said Chavel. "Remaining vessels and stations now out of range."

"Barrington to Emerson," he said, tapping the comm panel attached to his chair.

"Emerson here."

"If we're gonna do this, Mr Emerson, now would be the time."

"Just running one last check on the plasma regulators, sir. Two minutes. FTL ring is deployed and appears to be responding," he replied.

"Understood. Keep me informed." Young had been strangely silent since the last communiqué with the Jycorp Orbital. They had not had much time to talk since he and Tosh came aboard and Barrington was uncomfortable with his presence on the bridge.

"Doctor Tosh, I suggest disengaging your chair from its hover mode when we engage the FTL. We don't know if this is going to be a smooth ride or not, and I would rather not have you flying straight through the bulkhead and possibly taking my crew members with you." His remarks directed at doe-eyed Tosh were quickly obeyed, as he nodded and engaged the manual transportation struts which secured him firmly to the deck plating.

"Of course, my apologies, Captain," Tosh said.

"Charly, engage the inertial dampeners," Barrington said.

"Gentlemen, if you wouldn't mind taking a seat," the captain added, turning to Young. The Jycorp CEO took a seat.

"Target coordinates set, sir," said Boyett, who seemed to be frantically pressing every button in front of her. Both sides of her flight controls held manual handgrips that controlled the port and starboard thrusters. Flying the ship through hyperspace needed very little actual piloting skills, as the vectors were locked into the computer, but what they didn't know was what would hit them at the exit. She had been preparing for the worst, with weeks in simulated asteroid and projectile evasion.

"Eleven minutes, sir," she said from the con. Nothing to do but wait for Emerson's go.

"Patch me in to the feed on Phobos, will you, David? Put it through on screen six."

"Yes, sir," came Chavel's voice. The screen to the far right of the bridge changed its view to the surface of Phobos.

"Fuck, look at that," said Tosh suddenly. The screen showed the surface of the small moon. Exploding surface impacts erupted from all around.

"Where's the Monolith?" said Young. The base beside the Monolith was a raging inferno, but the structure itself was nowhere to be seen.

"Impact crater?" suggested Tosh. The view from the imaging system began to shake and distort, as the impacts grew in their intensity.

"Losing the signal, sir," said Chavel. The screen flickered to black as the monitors around it showed the exterior happenings of the small moon. Or rather what was left of the small moon. It was practically torn in half by the unstoppable force of the bombardment.

"This is the captain," Barrington announced on the open comm system he had just opened. "All hands general quarters. We are about to make our FTL attempt. You may feel some disorientation during the procedure. If you are experiencing any prolonged effects, please contact Doctor Brubaker. I will contact you all again as soon as we are in hyperspace. Good luck to us all. Barrington out." The bridge fell silent. The comms chirped.

"Bridge, this is Emerson. Target coordinates received and locked. Firing up FTL ring. Stand by." A familiar shudder crept through the bridge as high-pitched screeches of metal grinding against metal filled their ears.

"Viewer forward," Barrington said. The screens all flicked forward. "Leave me an image of Mars, Lieutenant, on the monitor five."

"Sir," Chavel said in acknowledgement. The forward view showed the curved surface of the outside of the ship. The FLT ring swung past the viewer slowly, in and out of view, as it circled the vessel. It completed a rotation every second but was now beginning to pick up speed. Barrington tapped his private comm channel and hooked in an earpiece.

"Barrington to Carrie Barrington," he said softly, watching the large ring as it blinked past his view screen. To his right an apocalyptic scene was unfolding as the Earth fragment began making contact with the thin Martian atmosphere.

"Carrie here," came her voice.

"You strapped in, Dice?"

"Yes, Captain, I'm in my quarters. Everything seems to be shaking."

"That will pass once we break through. Sit tight and don't go anywhere," he said.

"Don't worry, Father, this will work. See you on the other side." Barrington smiled.

"Carrie out."

"Thirty percent," said Boyett, who was busy checking her flight controls.

"Hull integrity?" said Barrington.

"One hundred percent," said Boyett. He looked over at Young, whose eyes were fixed on the screen showing Mars. They turned their attention to the changing landscape of their attempted second Earth. The atmosphere was ablaze with fire. Huge fissures began to open as the fragment slammed through the crust, sending violent shockwaves through its dry and desolate landscapes. There was no sign of the colony or the Atmo processors. Barrington couldn't help but feel a sudden sense of urgency. He focused his attention forward. The FTL ring was now steadily moving past the view screen, making a full rotation roughly six times a second, blurring the white and metallic look of the ring into a fusion of one colour. The star field had begun to fade.

"Bridge, this is Emerson. We are at fifty-eight percent. Opening the injectors now. Plasma flow looks good. Contact again at ninety percent."

"Flight, how we looking?" he said to Boyett.

"Gravitational readings inside the parameter of the ship are normal. Readings from outside the ring are starting to shift." Barrington looked over at the image of Mars, which had started to warp in the viewer. Chunks of the planet were now spewing out in all directions. There was a sudden burst of energy from somewhere deep within the ship and the sound of the spinning FTL ring shot up in frequency. The forward viewer was now a blur of white. The bridge was a deathly silent place. Only status reports from Boyett and Chavel interrupted the eerie quiet. The view began to change colour. Dark blue waves of distortion began to permeate through the white.

"Ninety percent, sir," came Emerson's voice over the comm. "It's not too late to abort, but once we're past ninety-two percent we are committed." Barrington looked around at his crew and then to Young, who nodded the go ahead.

"Unlock the injectors to full, Mr Emerson. Let's do what we came here to do."

"Yes, sir," Emerson said. Barrington thought he heard a tinge of excitement in the Irishman's voice. What happened next happened quickly. The image of the broken Mars flickered off the screen as it went blank. The distortion on the forward viewer seemed to break into a million streaming lines of colours. For an instant Barrington thought he observed the crew on the bridge freezing in place. Somewhere off in the distance came a voice that sounded like Emerson, but was much lower and much slower.

"Ninety-nine percent," it seemed to take an age to say. He glanced down at his hands, which seemed to have a silver lining to them. Every detail of the bridge seemed to be heightened. Everything seemed to glow. He felt a sudden surge in pressure, as if he were on an old rollercoaster at the top of a peak and headed down. The feeling took him by surprise and slightly knocked the wind out of him. He tensed up as the feeling subsided. The viewer in front showed a mixture of greys. The stars were now completely gone. There was an explosion of sound within the walls of the ship, like the cracking of a huge whip. Then silence. Normality had returned to the bridge. Boyett and Chavel looked at each other.

"Report," said Barrington.

"Eh. Standby, sir, just taking readings," said Boyett.

"Barrington to engine room."

"Emerson here, we're still in once piece, sir. We are still verifying readings down here, but gravitational readings suggest we have been successful. Have you seen the images from outside the ship?"

"I want a more detailed report when you have it, Mr Emerson."

"Eh yes, sir. Give me few minutes. Emerson out."

"Charly?" Barrington said.

"Velocity is zero, sir. Which is what we expect from being inside a warping singularity, but I would agree that it seems to have worked. This is FTL, sir." Barrington looked at Tosh, who had a terrified expression on his face.

"You okay?" he asked

"Eh yes, sorry, that wasn't what I was expecting, that's all. I think I need to lie down. With your permission I would like to leave the bridge."

"Of course, why don't you see Doctor Brubaker?" Tosh looked ashen-faced.

"Yes, I think I'll do just that." He rolled towards the back of the bridge and entered the lift. Barrington faced the forward viewer then caught sight on the empty screen on the right.

"Change screen five to forward view, David."

"Yes, sir," he replied softly.

"What is the status of the beacon from the Jycorp Orbital?"

"Undetectable at the moment, sir. I don't think we'll catch it until we return to normal space, sir," said Chavel. The captain didn't like that.

"Any idea if we are on the right heading, Lieutenant?"

"All systems show normal, sir. The target coordinates were locked and it all looks okay this end." He looked at the viewer and the hazy greys of hyperspace. Not the most exciting thing he thought he would see in a gravitational distortion, but at least they weren't dead.

Engine Room
Eight hours since departure
12:00 Martian Standard

"Excuse me, can I help you?" said Emerson to the person behind the main stellar cartography array. Eight hours later and not much had changed on board the ship. It had been smooth sailing so far, but Emerson had not left the engineering bay since the jump. He had been taking readings from The Betty when he heard something fall on the other side of the bay. The figure stood up and stared at Emerson.

"I'm sorry, Doctor Tyrell, I didn't see you come in. Is there something I can help you with?" Emerson had only met the doctor once upon boarding and it was only a brief conversation about his quarantine seals in the lab. Emerson had noted that the doctor was cold and not particularly friendly. He looked at Tyrell, puzzled at what he was doing behind the navigational systems.

"Nothing at all, Mr Emerson, I..." Tyrell paused and looked at his hands. "need a de-coupler for my computer systems. One of the CPUs is out of alignment. I was trying to do an analysis of the surrounding star systems to Aristaeus and I didn't want to disturb you." Emerson noted that the doctor's eyes were sharp and quite intense to look into. He didn't fancy reprimanding him, so tried a polite approach.

"Of course, anything I can do to help. I can send someone up to you right away."

Tyrell raised a hand. "Not at all, I have what I came for." Emerson frowned.

"Of course, Doctor. I'm afraid that I have to ask you to clear equipment with me before removing it. I don't mean to be a stickler here, but this is a delicate journey we're on and the captain was pretty clear on procedures for personnel entering engineering. I hope you understand." Tyrell smiled a large smile at Emerson. An almost patronising smile, and began to walk towards him. He placed a hand on Emerson's shoulder.

"That makes perfect sense," he said, still smiling. "The captain is very lucky to have you here, Mr Emerson. As are we all. I humbly apologise for not announcing my presence and will endeavour not to do so again." Tyrell's grip on Emerson's shoulder was a little tighter than it needed to be. He tried not to wince as Tyrell released his grip and made his way out of the bay. Emerson watched him go. As he was leaving he gave Emerson a little wave as if to say, 'Ta...ta'.

"What was that about?" said Llewellyn, who was walking past.

"Not sure," said Emerson.

"These science types give me the creeps," she said.

"Hmm," came his reply. "Do me a favour," he continued, "check out the navigational array, will you?"

"I ran a diagnostic on it twenty minutes ago, Landon. She's tip-top," came Llewellyn's quick reply. Emerson gave her a look that basically told her he didn't give a shit and to do it again.

"Yes, sir," she said. "Anything I should be looking for?"

"It's probably nothing," he said.

"Yes, sir," she said and got to work.

The flickers of lights from The Betty speckled the surrounding workstations with splashes of colour. Emerson had been awake now for twenty-six hours and was starting to feel it.

"Emerson to Tosh," he said, hovering over a comm panel.

"Tosh here."

"Danny boy, any chance you can take over down here while I catch up on some shuteye?"

"Be delighted to," came Tosh's response. "Be there in ten minutes. Tosh out." Emerson was relieved. He could have easily left Llewellyn in charge, but he wanted Tosh down here in case anything serious happened. He should have been here the whole time and not lounging about on the bridge. Emerson hadn't eaten in hours and was finally starting to feel a wave of dizziness come over him.

"Emerson to Barrington," he said

"Go ahead," came the confident response. Emerson knew that the captain hadn't left the bridge since the jump and was amazed at how alert he sounded.

"Captain, I would like to leave engineering to get some shuteye. Doctor Tosh is going to keep an eye on things. Unless you have any objections?"

"None. Please let the crew know that Tosh is in charge until your return. Barrington out."

In a perfect world the command structure of The Agathon would have been strictly under the purview of the Jycorp military, but with command personnel thin on the ground responsibility for ship functions was designated to the most qualified, whether they be military or not. Tosh had not wanted the responsibility of engineering and had recommended Emerson for the role, with a view to maintaining a supervisory consultative presence throughout. Emerson was a natural leader and was the best engineer on the Jycorp Orbital, if not the entire colony. He was also unencumbered by a physical disability and, although it was never mentioned, a physically fit crewmember was essential to running such a dynamic environment. Emerson was hands on and spent most of his time jammed between the crawl spaces of the ship fixing any number of problems. In an emergency, access to these crawl spaces needed to be quick and Tosh simply could not offer the same mobility. A few minutes later in he rolled, still in 'Terrain mode'.

"You look like shit," he said to Emerson.

"Thanks, boss," he said, smiling.

"Keep an eye on the coolant manifolds. They were acting up about an hour ago," Emerson continued.

"You doing okay, kid?" asked Tosh. Emerson felt burnt out.

"Nothing a few Zs wouldn't cure, Danny boy." Llewellyn looked over at the pair.

"Amanda, come say hi to Tosh." She walked over to them and shook his hand.

"Doctor Tosh, good to see you. I've heard a lot about you. It's great to finally work with you… I've a million questions." She was way too enthusiastic for Emerson, who simply backed off and waved goodbye to a clearly nervous Tosh. He didn't think he had much experience with women and he found it rather amusing to leave him in the thick of it while he took a nap. As he walked out of the engine room and through the corridors to his quarters, the image of Tyrell at the navigation station was glued to the back of his mind. It was probably nothing. He was tired.

11

24 hours since departure
22:00 Martian Standard

"I would say congratulations are in order, Mr. Young. I wish the circumstances could have been different but the results are impressive," Barrington said to Young across the table. It was late and Young had asked Barrington to join him for a drink. Barrington was hesitant at first but had agreed to it. They looked out at the merging greys of hyperspace through the large windows in the conference room, which was one deck below the bridge. It was empty apart from some scattered chairs. A newly opened bottle of scotch and two half full glasses sat crisply on the surface of the table.

Young smiled. "You think I am just a suit, don't you, John?" The frankness of his question didn't surprise Barrington and he didn't hesitate with his answer. Life was growing very short for the usual social graces.

"I think a man with the power that you have," he paused, "had... could find it difficult to attain were it not thrust upon you."

"I see," Young replied. "You think power can only be earned on a battlefield? And you think that battlefields can only be called so, if there are weapons on them?" he continued. "I could have had you replaced on this ship or on the colony is less than ten minutes with one call."

"Mr Young, if you wanted a pissing contest I wish you would have said so before getting on my ship," said Barrington. Young raised his hands.

"I'm sorry, John. That wasn't my intention. My love is of the signal, John. Not power. I left Earth because of the signal. I would have spent my whole life on that little grey rock if I could have figured it out. I was close to something towards the end."

"That's why you appointed Clark?" asked Barrington. Young raised his eyebrows.

"I am no leader of planets, Captain. A mathematical genius? Yes. Financier? Yes. Leader of people? No thanks very much." The man sitting next to him surprised Barrington.

"You know it's funny," he continued. "When you grow up seeing your name on practically every single building in the world you have nowhere to hide from it.."

"Makes sense," said Barrington.

"I was expecting more," said Young.

"More?" said Barrington.

"Hyperspace. Kinda dull out there. No colour. No thought-altering visuals that make you marvel at the complexity of the universe. Fucking grey. Like a rainy day," he said, sipping his drink.

"I'm just glad we're still in one piece, Mr. Young."

"Please call me Jerome. I have a feeling we are about to get to know each other extremely well, John. I won't stand on ceremony if you don't." Barrington nodded. There was an ease creeping into the room as the captain relaxed in Young's presence. He had to admit he was not what he was expecting. The façade presented to the world when they had met would seem to have been purposefully erected by the leader of Jycorp. Either that or he was a skilled sociopath.

"Do you think she made the right choice? The chancellor," Barrington asked. Young snorted.

"Ha. That stubborn self-righteous woman thinks she owes those people something. Delusions of grandeur. That is commonplace amongst those given authority, present company excluded, of course." Barrington noticed hurt in the man's voice.

"I liked her," he said. He had meant it of course but also had meant it as a test. Young knew it and smiled.

"I liked her too, Captain. She was twice the men we are."

"I'll drink to that," said Barrington, clinking his glass to Young's. "Tell me about the signal," he asked Young.

"What would you like to know?" Young replied.

"There was nothing decoded? Nothing? It's hard to believe that with our technology and with your expertise we still know nothing." Young smiled again at the captain's light baiting of the subject. He took a breath.

"We know that the civilisation is highly intelligent and technologically advanced. We know the Monolith is, or rather was, thousands of years ahead of us. We know that the mathematical constants that were sent were basic, but the ternary syntax algorithm which accompanied it was not. When the signal was first detected, nearly one hundred years ago, we flattered ourselves with the knowledge that the human race had become important enough to contact. Then we soon figured out that it made little or no difference, as we couldn't find the primer key to respond to the signal or alter its pathways from the Monolith. All we could do was triangulate its location and send our own subspace pulses in the hope of getting their attention. The truth is that I don't think the signal was meant for us." Barrington was listening intently.

"In all our time on Phobos there wasn't one scrap of evidence to suggest the signal was meant for life forms of our evolutionary stage. It was far too complex. The signal had been relayed to the Monolith, not to Earth. We assumed the Monolith was relaying the signal as some sort of booster, but we have no evidence of that. We had a network of computers that could have run the planet working on this stream of data, but to no avail. Any why was the Monolith placed on Phobos and not Earth's moon?

"What happened to the Martian surface hundreds of millions of years ago that left it without an atmosphere, and one incredibly pissed off organism that consumes human flesh and every other fucking thing it comes in contact with? Not to mention the new findings on it which may suggest some form of sentience." Young reached into a side pocket in the informal blazer he was wearing. He took out a clear, flat data disk and tapped a command into the integrated computer interface in the desk.

"Let me show you something," he said. "For the last few months we have been downloading as much of the data as possible, collected from the signal over the last one hundred years. I know Tyrell has been working on this, but here is the data fragment from the last few days before the Gamma pulse." He laid the disk flat on the surface of the desk. It flickered to life, laying out a network of directory options across the table. He tapped one that said DNA, and then requested a holographic interface from one of the sub menus.

From the base of the table grew flickers of structured imagery. Like a scaffold of blues and greens and reds, the three-dimensional image twisted into view between the two men. It hovered between them.

"Okay. Looks like DNA?" Barrington said.

"Right," Young said.

"I don't get it," Barrington said. Young took a breath. "Just before the signal changed to the pulse, a single piece of data was sent through. Encoded in simple binary. That," he said, pointing to the floating DNA.

"Is what they sent through?" The little hairs on Barrington's neck began to stand. "Meaning?" he asked quietly.

"The DNA looks similar to ours, but the base pairs are way off. We have just over three billion, but this thing has nearly five hundred billion."

"That's all they sent?" asked Barrington.

"Apart from an energy wave that destroyed our planet, yes," Young said.

"So what's the point?"

"Could be anything. Could be a piece of fruit on their home world as some sort of sick joke. Or maybe they grew a conscience and wanted us to see the face of our destroyers."

"Give it to Chase Meridian. See what she can get from it," said Barrington.

"I don't think I've met Doctor Meridian. This is not something I think should get around the ship, Captain?" Barrington thought about it for a moment.

"We're such a small family, Jerome. No use in secrets anymore. Give it to Chase." Barrington stood. "I need to check on the engine room. Would you and Doctor Tosh care to join me for dinner later?"

"Sounds good, John." Young stood and shook the captain's hand. He turned the data disk off and removed it from the table. Barrington left and Young took a seat again. He poured himself another drink and looked out into hyperspace.

Tyrell's Lab
22:55 Martian Standard

"Carrie, help me with this, will you?" Tyrell said to her as he tried to position the large processor under an alcove in the main lab. It was a heavy rectangular box, and awkward to move about. Carrie moved swiftly over to the doctor and helped him place it correctly.

"Thank you. So what have you found?" he asked.

"The planet's core density still doesn't make any sense, Doctor." Tyrell had decided to have Carrie analyse their target star system and report findings. She had been at it now for close to twelve hours.

"Aristaeus Three has virtually no core? That has to be a sensor malfunction."

Tyrell sighed. "It's the same reading I got from the array orbiting Mars."

"You didn't tell me that?" said Carrie, a little more defiantly than she usually would have spoken to him. He smiled.

"You're right, I didn't. I apologise, Carrie, but other more grave matters seemed to have taken over my attention." Carrie backed off, realising her reaction.

"So what kind of planet has no core?" he asked her, as he continued to install the equipment.

"Well. The iron could have been bound into silicate mineral crystals, if formed from a fully oxidised water rich mineral. This, theoretically, can only occur in planets much more distant from its host star than Aristaeus Three though."

"Very good, Carrie," said Tyrell.

"Any analysis would be inconclusive until we are in orbit," she said. Tyrell laughed.

"I don't know either, Carrie. It's okay." He stood up and made his way over to a diagnostic station and sat. "Look at us, Carrie. We're on a ship. Traveling faster than the speed of light towards an alien civilisation that we know nothing about. Hell of a time to be alive. Eh, kiddo?" Carrie was confused by his childish enthusiasm. Little insects. The thought of the black monster from her dreams flashed in her mind.

"You look tense. You have a constant look of worry on your face. You really are too young to be so serious," he said, turning to a screen with star charts displayed on it.

"You're right, Doctor," she said. "It's quite incredible what we have achieved. I have a great curiosity as to what we will find out here." She sensed the doctor didn't quite believe her, but he played it down. The door chimed.

"Enter," Tyrell said, still looking oddly at Carrie.

"Doctor Meridian, how nice of you to drop by." Chase Meridian entered and nodded.

"Tyrone, your sincerity is heart-warming as always." Carrie loved how blunt Meridian was. She was the one person in the world who really didn't care about expertise or knowledge. She didn't like Tyrell and didn't hide her feelings about it from anyone. Tyrell put his feet up on the console.

"What can we do for you on this fine day?" he said, raising both eyebrows and smiling.

"Actually I'm here to pick Carrie's brain not yours, if you don't mind. Can I borrow her for a few hours?" Tyrell looked annoyed but tried to hide it. *You can't hide from me, Doctor,* Carrie thought.

"She's all yours. Enjoy your girly night out. I'll need you first thing in the morning, Carrie. We need to analyse a ton of other potential habitable star systems."

"Of course, Doctor. I'll see you then." She nodded and the pair left. Meridian put her arm around Carrie.

"Wait till you see this, Dice. Tyrell will go crazy when he finds out I showed you first, but fucking see how I care."

"What is it?" Carrie asked.

"You'll see." They moved along the corridors of the ship, talking about this and that, when they rounded a bend and literally knocked into David Chavel. Carrie caught her breath as the lieutenant put a hand on her arm.

"Sorry about that, Ms Barrington." Her cheeks flushed.

"Not at all, Lieutenant." He nodded to Meridian.

"Doctor," he said before moving off. Meridian looked at Carrie.

"Okay, now I know it's official," she said.

"What's official?" Carrie asked, her face still red.

"When did you start sleeping together?"

Carrie burst into laughter. It felt good. "I have no idea what you're talking about, Doctor Meridian."

"I see," Meridian said.

"Well, if you don't mind then, maybe I'll take a pot shot at the young lieutenant. Looks like he works out."

Carrie shrugged playfully. "If you like, it's a free ship," she said.

"Ah ha!" said Meridian. "Now I DO know you're sleeping together. Well good for you. Your father must be proud." Meridian stopped. "Actually, scratch that. Poor guy is fucked." They both laughed and continued on towards the lift.

Meridians Lab Deck 11

"Well, what do you think of that puppy?" said Meridian.

"It's a DNA fragment," said Carrie raising her eyebrow.

"No shit, Carrie. Come on, look deeper," Meridian pressed.

"It's not human," Carrie said. The DNA fragment hovered on the data visualiser.

"There's a huge number of base pairs denoting a highly complex organism." She enhanced the image and got in closer to the polynucleotide strands, which curved in on each other in a beautiful double helix.

"And?" Meridian pushed.

"There seems to be gaps in the sequence," she added.

"Very good," she said.

"Where did this come from? What is this?" asked Carrie.

"That is a good question. Our esteemed former leader of the world, Mr Jerome Young, just presented this to your father. It was sent in the last data transmission from the fuckers who blew up our planet. Pardon my French."

Carrie looked at the DNA fragment. "What do you think?" she asked.

"Beats me, Dice. Without an actual living sample we can't even begin to imagine what it is we're looking at."

"So why send it?" Carrie looked on at the rotating collection of genetic coding.

"They want us to know who it was," she said.

"Bit of a strange way to do it, no? Why not just send a picture?" said Meridian. The door hissed open. Kyle McDonnell strolled in.

"A lab full of ladies. That's what a man wants to wake up to," he said, mock saluting. Meridian sighed and looked at Carrie. She would not have let on that she knew they were married. She also knew Meridian wanted it kept to themselves and so she respected that.

"Hello, Doctor McDonnell," said Carrie.

"Please don't call me that, Carrie. Makes me sound like an old codger. Call me Kyle. What are you pretty ladies working on?"

He joined them at the workstation and gave a caring flick of his eyes in Meridian's direction. Carrie liked him. He was a kind-hearted and jovial man and had a real love for Meridian that comforted her. He always wore his lab coat, neatly pressed over his colonial jumpsuit. His thick brown loafers made no sound when he walked and he often commented on how comfortable they were. His hair was unkempt and badly in need of shortening, but he wore it well around a soft charming face. When he spoke, his soft Scottish brogue was pleasant on the ears.

"What's this then?" he asked, poking his finger into the floating image and whirling it around. It flickered but held its form.

"It's a big sandwich, you oaf. What do you think it is?" Meridian said, pushing his hand away.

"Ooh okay, touchy. Did we not have our coffee yet?" Meridian simply sighed.

"It's a fragment from the last data stream sent by the signal makers," said Carrie, trying to avert a fight.

"It's not human," he said quickly. McDonnell was light mannered, but highly intelligent.

"Well done, genius," said Meridian. He ignored her and peered into the image.

"Look at the base pair sequences. Jesus Christ."

Meridian slapped him on the arm. "Language," she said. He looked at Carrie.

"Sorry." Carrie waved it away.

"Why would there be gaps like that in the sequence, Kyle?" she asked.

"Could be an error in the transmission. They did send a Gamma pulse straight after. Unlikely though. This isn't a joke, this was really sent in the signal?"

"Yes," Carrie said.

"Christ," he whispered.

"May I?" he asked Meridian, who gave up her seat. He took the console and began manipulating the image, looking at it from various angles and at various magnification settings. He went silent for a moment.

"Could be a test?" This caught Carrie's attention.

"The gaps," he said. "Look at the gaps."

"Sweetheart, can you bring up a human DNA sequence for comparison. I want to check something."

"Sure thing, sweet cheeks," said Meridian, trying to play down his slip. Carrie pretended not to notice the redness in his face. He would be in trouble later. She tried not to laugh. Meridian pulled up a random sample of human DNA and it rose into view. Both strands now floated side by side. All three stared at them for a moment. Kyle tapped a command into the computer.

"Remove incomparable nucleotides along base pairs," he said into thin air. The computer responded by removing the multitude of base pairs in the alien DNA sequence, until it began to resemble the human sample.

"If you wanted to identify a species from another planet how would you do it?" Kyle asked, looking at Carrie.

"Propose a mathematical puzzle and ask for a response?"

"Impressive. Not just a pretty face, eh?" he said smiling.

"What are you saying? That they sent us a puzzle then blew us out of the universe?" Meridian added.

"I don't know," said Kyle.

"But if we fill these purine and pyrimidine sequences in with fragments from a human DNA sample, then resend the whole sequence back as a completed fragment, we may get an answer. No?" Nobody answered.

"Just a thought."

"Can we transmit in hyperspace?" Carrie asked.

"I don't know, Carrie. We'll have to ask Emerson or Tyrell that. Shit. Tyrell won't be happy about not being in on this. Think it's time we give him a call?" said Meridian. Carrie nodded.

"Super," said Kyle raising his arms. "He's just a barrel of laughs."

"Doctor Meridian to Doctor Tyrell," she said into the computer. There was a pause.

"Yes, Doctor, how can I be of assistance?" came a laboured reply.

"Can you meet me in my lab, Doctor? We have something of importance to show you before we approach the captain." She heard a sigh on the comms. Carrie shrugged.

"I am on my way," he said, grumbling. Carrie felt the tension in the room rise.

"Dunno how you put with that guy, Dice," said Meridian.

"My father says I have my mother's patience," she said with a smile. Meridian put a hand on hers.

"That you do, but more importantly you have her eyes."

12

Medical bay
Fifteen days since departure
12:00 Martian Standard

"If you were in any better shape you would be in a museum," said Brubaker. Carrie had put off seeing the doctor until she was on board The Agathon. Even then she had made excuses not to see her for fear of Brubaker exposing something. She lay inside a diagnostic tube, of which there were four in the main medical bay. She wore a standard medical gown. The state of the art facility was well equipped to handle most off world medical issues, with plenty of supplies and extra bio beds that could be set up in the cargo bays in case of a pandemic. Although Brubaker was relatively short in stature, her gruff voice was packed with authority. Her greying cropped curly hair was held tightly against her head as she gazed at Carrie's innards. She knew that Brubaker held a flame for her father. One that was not reciprocated. Carrie had found her to be a weathered type of woman.

"Okay, Ms Barrington, you're good to hop," she told her. The clear tube rotated her out from underneath the scanner and split in two, allowing her to step out easily.

"No sign of anything, Doctor?" she asked, looking at the floor while putting on her jumpsuit.

"Not a thing." She looked at her and raised an eyebrow. "What should I be looking for, Carrie?" Carrie finished getting dressed, then turned to Brubaker.

"Nothing. I'm a little paranoid, that's all."

"Right," Brubaker said frowning.

"Carrie, everything you say to me stays between you and me. You know that, right? Just because there aren't that many of us left doesn't mean all our rules are thrown out the airlock. If you have something to tell me, just tell me." Carrie thought about it for moment.

"Did you find any residual electrical activity anywhere in my body?" Brubaker leaned back her chair and put her fingers through her hair.

"What kind of electrical activity. Static? Your neurological bio chemistry is completely normal, Carrie."

"I have been getting mild shocks, that's all." Brubaker stood up and took a small handheld medical device from a drawer. She began moving the multi-coloured cylinder around Carrie's head.

"When did they start?" she asked, watching the readouts on the wall carefully.

"A few weeks ago. Before we left Mars."

Brubaker frowned. "Hmm," she said. "Tell me about them." Carrie thought for a moment about telling her everything but she couldn't have her father worrying needlessly. *There are bolts of lightning firing out of my fingertips!*

"It feels like a static shock. Might be caused by excess build-up of charged particles on the inside of the lab walls. Doctor Tyrell and I have been running a lot of high-powered experiments, trying to boost the range of The Agathon's stellar cartography abilities." Brubaker looked deep into her blue eyes.

"I'll take some readings of the lab later on to make sure there's no residual charge," she said. Carrie stopped her train of thought.

"That's okay, Doctor. I can take those readings myself. I don't think Tyrell would be too pleased with others poking around the lab. He's quite particular about that."

"I bet he is," said Brubaker. "If it happens again I want you to come see me immediately." She finished up her scan and sat back in the chair.

"Everything else going okay for you? How are you holding up with all of this?" Carrie hadn't been asked that directly by anyone as of yet and the question took her by surprise.

"As well as anyone else on the ship, I suppose."

"Ha," responded Brubaker, rubbing her face. She had clearly not gotten any sleep lately.

"Some are not handling it well at all," she said, straightening herself. "Poor Bobby Shields hasn't left his quarters since he boarded. I have to bring him his meals every day or he'll starve to death. Poor kid is scared out of his mind."

"Understandable," said Carrie. She stretched out her thoughts and felt Bobby's terror for an instant before recoiling.

"You have a very strong head on you, Carrie."

"My mother's, I think," she responded.

"Your mother was bull-headed. She was a great scientist but leaped before she looked. Don't you make that mistake. Wherever we end up on this flying bullet, you make sure you keep your senses." She gave her a friendly tap on the shoulder. "Now what's this I hear about a DNA fragment?" she added, smiling.

"It's a small ship," Carrie said.

"That it is," Brubaker said.

"If you are free, Doctor Meridian would like you to take a look at it today. We need a report to my father by first thing tomorrow morning."

"Let me finish up with some patients and I'll be right there," she replied with a friendly smile. "How is your father doing, by the way?" she asked.

"My father is my father. If he could lift the universe up on his shoulders, he would," Carrie said.

"Do me a favour?" Brubaker asked.

"Keep an eye on him?" Carrie finished. The doctor smiled and nodded.

"Burdens of command can isolate and he's not the most forthcoming man about his stresses. He has no love of doctors." She paused and looked at Carrie. "Unfortunately." Carrie nodded.

"I will, Doctor, thank you for your concern." She began to leave.

"Carrie, might do you good to get some exercise if you are in that lab all day long. Cargo bay one makes for a great running track. It's good for the heart."

"Thank you, Doctor, I'll do that."

Carrie left the medical bay and made her way to Tyrell's lab. The low hum of the ship quietly filled her ears. She walked past a number of people as they went about their daily duties. Some of them she recognised. Others she had never met, having transferred in from one of the Jycorp stations. She smiled and nodded at the colonists as she walked past. They were afraid. Their uncertain faces told her stories of loss and hopelessness. The air was tense in the corridors. The psychological profiles of those who chose a life off world usually included a healthy sense of adventure and appetite for risk, but nothing came close to preparing them for something like this.

"Hey, Carrie," came a young male voice. She turned and greeted Sam Reynolds, a mechanical engineer from Dallas, Texas. At five foot eight he was a stocky twenty-nine-year-old, who had spent most of his time at Atmo One running maintenance on the atmospheric regulators. He had a thick black beard and always seemed to be covered in some sort of grease or oil. He was carrying several meters of cable hooped over his large shoulder. Carrie often figured him to be a handsome man, if he ever emerged from the forest on his face.

"Good to see you, Sam," she said smiling.

"Tyrell still got you locked up?" he asked gruffly. He had a warm nature about him. The silent type. He had strong brown eyes under thick dark eyebrows.

"Still," she said. He stood beside her and looked around at the others passing them on the deck.

"How fucked up is this? I heard Mars was broken in half by the Earth fragment?" Carrie looked past him.

"How are you holding up?" he added.

"Okay, I guess. I consider myself one of the lucky ones; my family is all here," she said. She paused for a moment. "Almost," she added. Reynolds nodded and gave a reassuring smile.

"Well, our good captain has me running around the ship rerouting half the electrical conduits. Turns out, in the rush, someone forgot to hook half of them up to the main power grid so running water is a problem for a lot of the ship."

"No better man for the job," Carrie jested.

Without warning the two were suddenly thrown against the bulkhead. The whole hallway listed sharply as colonists were flung on their sides. The force of the impact knocked the wind out of Carrie, as the lights in the hallway dimmed and turned to red. Her shoulder absorbed most of the impact, but Reynolds's arm had caught her. Her forehead began to drip with blood. The gravity seemed to right itself as she found herself on the floor cradling her arm. Reynolds was unconscious. He had hit his head on the wall. She reached out and felt his pulse. Still strong.

"Sam?" she asked with her hand on his cheek. "Sam, can you hear me?" His heavy eyes slowly opened.

"What the hell?" he grumbled, placing his hand on his head.

"Take it easy, you've had a knock to the head," she said.

"All hands, this is the captain," came a sudden announcement.

"We have had a momentary loss of power from the inertial dampeners. Possible impact on the outer hull. We are trying to disengage the FTL to assess damage. Please stand by and report to medical bays if injured."

"You're bleeding," Reynolds said, looking at Carrie. She placed her fingertips on her forehead and felt the gash.

"Just a cut," she answered, "Come on, let me help you. We should go to the medical bay," she said, linking her arms under his and helping him up.

"Thanks, I'll be all right. Not my first bump on the head. What the hell could have hit us in hyperspace?" Carrie shook her head curiously.

Agathon Bridge

"Hull breach on deck three," shouted Chavel. He had just picked himself up off the deck, along with most of the bridge crew. Barrington had rolled under Boyett's flight chair and was crawling back to the centre seat.

"Bridge, this is Tosh, running down the FTL now. Sixty seconds." He sounded out of breath, no doubt having been thrown from his chair.

"Emergency bulkheads in place on deck three, atmosphere contained," he continued.

"What hit us?" Barrington barked.

"I don't think anything hit us. Seems to have been from inside the ship." Barrington turned to Boyett.

"Charly, prepare for normal space."

Boyett acknowledged with a simple, "sir." She righted herself in the flight chair and switched all viewers to forward. Her hands flew across the control panel, preparing for manual flight mode. Resting her hands on both flight controls, she sat and waited.

"Ten seconds," said Chavel. The bridge started to vibrate. The montage of greys in the view screens began to flicker and change colour, as the ship began to emerge from the cloak of the space-time distortion. The stars appeared and the flicker of the FTL ring became more visible at it slowed down. The vibrations on the bridge continued as the braking mechanisms for the ring kicked in and slowed it down to an eventual stop. Boyett looked out at the star field. Her eyes flickered quickly from her sensor readings to the view screens.

"Status?" Barrington asked.

"We have re-entered normal space, sir. No indication of any asteroidal bodies. Scanning nearby systems."

"Status of hull breach?" he asked

"Sections twenty-two and twenty-three are exposed to space, sir."

"Casualties?" said Barrington.

"Unknown yet, sir," said Chavel.

"Any damage to the FTL ring?" he said.

"No, sir, none that is registering on any systems up here. It seems to have been unaffected," said Chavel.

"Stow the FTL ring, Lieutenant," he said.

"Yes, sir. Locking FTL ring at one eight zero." The FTL ring aligned itself with the axis of the ship and slotted nicely into place, turning the ship back into its sleek disk shape.

"Engine room, this is Barrington. What the hell happened?"

"Sir, we are just looking into it," came Landon Emerson's voice. "Looks like we have a hull breach on deck three. That much is confirmed. Good thing it didn't hit the FTL ring or we would all have been liquefied."

"Landon, how could we get a hull breach in hyperspace? Was this internal?" asked Barrington.

"Starting to look that way. Maybe a power conduit blew out. There are distribution nodes that flow through that deck. I would like to EVA with a team to check it out."

"Granted," Barrington said. He looked at Boyett.

"Charly, you go with them."

"Yes, sir," she said, locking her control panel.

"Chavel, take flight." The young man took Charly's seat and tapped in his access code.

"Emerson, I'm sending Lieutenant Boyett down to join your team. Keep an open comm link with the bridge and bring a visual recorder."

"Understood," Emerson said as the comms clicked off.

"Barrington to medical bay," he said.

"Brubaker here," came a frantic voice.

"Injuries, Doctor?"

"Mostly cuts and bruises, John. Some broken bones, nothing serious. I have reports that some crewmembers are missing, Captain. Carrie came in with Sam Reynolds. She had a minor concussion, but she's fine. I'm treating her." Barrington looked at Chavel, whose head had turned to listen when her name was mentioned.

"Keep me apprised, Doctor. Bridge out." There was silence on the bridge as Barrington tried to assess the situation. He leaned forward and placed his elbows on his knees. Crewmembers waited to hear what he would do next.

"Okay, let's find out where the hell we are, shall we? David, start scanning any nearby star systems." He tapped his comms pad.

"Bridge to Doctor Tyrell." No answer. Barrington pressed the ship-wide open comm link.

"Barrington to Doctor Tyrell, please contact the bridge."

He waited.

"Bridge, this it Tyrell," he said after a minute. There were loud electrical sounds in the background.

"Tyrell, where are you?"

"Deck three, Captain." Barrington furrowed his brow.

"Are you all right, Doctor?"

"Barely," came the reply.

"Are you in any danger?" said Barrington.

"No, John, I'm just catching my breath. The bulkheads came down in the nick of time."

"Are you able to come to the bridge?" Barrington added.

"Of course. I would like to check on my lab first, if that's all right? To see if there were any containment breaches." Barrington suddenly realised what he meant by that. The Black.

"Please do that, Doctor. Do you know how many there were in that section of deck three?" he said.

"At least two that I saw directly. Sorry, that's all I saw," he said.

"Okay, Doctor. If you're feeling up to it, please come to the bridge as soon as possible. We need your assistance."

"I'll be there shortly," he replied.

"Sir, there's a small planetary system eighty million kilometres to port," said Chavel

"Let's see it," Barrington said. The view screens flickered and showed a small white dwarf star being orbited by several large grey planets.

"I'm not reading any atmosphere on any of the orbiting planets. Looks like the sun went nova a long time ago and took out the star system in the process," said Chavel.

"Any idea how far we've travelled?" asked Barrington.

"Checking star fixes now, sir," said Chavel.

"Looks like at least one hundred and thirty light years, sir," he said, looking around with a look of surprise on his face.

"Keep scanning that nearby system, but don't alter course. Run a full systems check on the life support systems on deck three and the rest of the ship, and get me casualty reports. Check the flight systems while you're at it," he said. Barrington sat back in the centre seat and rubbed his brow.

13

The EVA
14:00 Martian Standard

The form-fitting suits Emerson and Boyett wore allowed them full range of movements while outside the ship. The palm and foot pulsers gave incredibly accurate stability and positional control. With a flick of her wrist Boyett manoeuvred herself alongside Emerson, as they skimmed the hull of The Agathon.

"You're a natural," said Boyett, as she watched Emerson use the EVA suit effortlessly.

"Young had me outside that damn Jycorp station so much I was beginning to think I was born in space," Boyett smiled. Their time had been professional, much to her disappointment, and he had been locked up in the engine room for most of his time with the FTL systems for the past few months. The ship prep had consumed their lives leading up to its launch and this was the first time they had spent any time together outside of the chaos of finishing its construction. It was quiet outside The Agathon. Boyett let her eyes follow the contours of the hull.

"She's a beauty, isn't she?" said Emerson, catching her gaze. "Watch your speed, Charly. If there are any hull fragments flying about you could puncture your faceplate." Boyett smiled at the Irishman.

"So you do care?" she said.

"I care about getting my arse handed to me by the captain," he said.

"That cute little Irish tush? I wouldn't worry about it," she said. Boyett let her eyes drift across the outside of the smooth curvature of the ship and then out into the star field. A small cluster of stars to her right caught her attention. Next to them the darkness was broken with one of the most beautiful nebulas she had ever seen. The darkness was painted with vibrant reds, intermingling with striking violets and blues.

"There," said Emerson.

She flicked her attention back to the ship. Boyett saw the rupture clearly now, as they drifted along the top aft section of the hull.

"Looks to be about ten to twelve meters," said Emerson. They stopped at the perimeter of the hole. Boyett faced her palms towards the hull and fired a quick pulse to push herself away from the ship. She then countered it by flicking them to her rear and giving a quick burst to stop her momentum. Emerson was taking readings of the fragmented sections of the hull. Boyett peered into the empty deck.

"This was no impact," she said.

"Nope," Emerson responded.

"The hull is bent outwards," she said.

"What was on this deck?" he asked her.

"Nothing much. A galley, some small lab space, more crew quarters," Boyett said.

"I'm going in," she said. She gently fired her palm thrusters and drifted inside the hole, grabbing hold of the bent metal on her way in to straighten herself. She sank onto the deck and looked up at Emerson, who had his head perched looking down overhead. Boyett took a small scanner from a side holder in her belt and activated it.

"Could have been an overload in the EPS relays," she said.

"Then why isn't the deck plating scorched?" Emerson said.

"Looks like the energy of the explosion was directed out away from the ship," he said. Boyett looked around the sealed deck, which was now a vacuum. The walls and electrical systems seemed to have been virtually untouched, but the ceiling plating was completely obliterated with tangled and twisted metal and wiring strewn all over.

"Landon, look at this," she said, linking her device to his and sending him the readings she had just taken.

"Fuck," he said.

"That's not good. The poor girl looks like someone took a pot shot at her from inside the ship."

"Why would someone do this?" she said. Emerson shook his head.

"Better go see the captain," he said.

Engine Room
14:55 Martian Standard

"It was definitely an explosive device," said Emerson.

"No doubt about it. We found trace elements of a polymer compound with pentaerythritol tetranitrate. Pretty crude stuff but effective if placed along one of the distribution nodes, which it was. We're lucky the bulkheads did their job or we would not be here to talk about it." He was still wearing half of his EVA suit, but was clambering out of it while he was talking to Barrington. Boyett was beside him looking pensive.

"You're telling me someone on board this ship tried to blow us up?" Barrington said.

"Looks that way, and the visual sensors on that deck were deactivated three minutes prior," Emerson said. The captain went quiet.

"Captain, we need to land to repair the outer hull," Tosh said, breaking the silence in the engine room.

"Who knows about this?" Barrington said, sidestepping Tosh's comment.

"Just the crew on the EVA and us, but it's a small ship, Captain," said Emerson. Barrington turned to Tosh.

"You want to land the ship?"

Tosh looked at the lifeless Betty. "Going into hyperspace with a hull breach this size is not recommended," he said. "The gravitational distortion could destabilise the integrity of the hull and we all know that's not a good thing." Barrington nodded and turned to leave.

"Charly, you're with me," he said to Boyett, who quickly followed step. They left the engine room and made their way into the hallway of the ship. Barrington was silent until they reached the lift.

"Bridge," he said out loud. "Well?" he said to Boyett.

"Well?" she responded, raising an eyebrow.

"What do you think?" he asked.

"Sounds like our friend is back," she said.

"This is all we need right now. Christ," Barrington said, hitting the side panels of the lift with a closed fist. The doors of the lift opened up to the bridge and the pair stepped off. The bridge went quiet. Barrington took the centre seat as Boyett relieved Chavel from flight, who then retook his station. Tyrell was at the rear of the bridge at a science station conducting star mapping. Barrington thought for a moment. His thought process for dire situations was a disciplined one. He began segmenting each problem into its own containment area within his mind. He walled the issues with fortified structures and accessed them only in order of priority. This was an easy choice. He had to fix the ship first.

"David, what are the conditions of the nearby planets? Any of them suitable to land on?" he said. Chavel looked at the captain.

"There is no atmosphere present on any of the planets sir, but gravitationally the second planet is two thirds that of Earth."

"Charly, set a course," Barrington said.

"Aye, sir," she said. She seemed to get a sudden surge of enthusiastic energy. Barrington had to guess that deep inside she was glad to be finally flying something. The star field began to shift in the viewing screens as the ship was manoeuvred towards the dead planetary system. Barrington looked at the view screen.

"Barrington to Carrie Barrington," he said, touching the comm panel.

"Carrie here," came a swift response.

"You okay, Dice?" he asked.

"I'm good. A little shaken but none the worse for wear."

"Good," he said. "Can you come to the bridge please?" he added.

"Sure thing," she said. He had not asked her to formally come to the bridge before and could hear her surprise. Not unlike when he called her to his room when she was young and had misbehaved.

"Be there in five," she added and clicked off the comms.

He turned to Tyrell. "Tyrone, any idea where the hell we are?" Tyrell had been looking at the captain curiously.

"Yes. We are one hundred and twenty-seven light years from the Sol system. The only star system within ten light years is the one white dwarf system we are currently on route to, designated Beta 32442-99/GH. There is very little information on it unfortunately, other than the reference. It was deemed to be of little astronomical relevance. The Agathon's course would not appear to have been altered by the explosion. While there are G type stars we could travel to which would provide a more hospitable environment to humans, I would agree using the FTL with a compromised hull would not be advisable."

He returned to his readings and began scanning the surrounding area.

"Thank you, Doctor," Barrington said, still looking at the view screens. The lift doors opened and Carrie walked onto the bridge. Chavel met her gaze and smiled.

"Boyett, you have the con," Barrington said and stood from his chair. He walked over to Carrie and placed a hand on her shoulder and gave it a squeeze. She reciprocated by holding his arm. He walked to the lift and stepped inside. He waited for Carrie to enter, then told the lift their destination. They stood quietly for a moment.

"I have a job for you. I want it done quickly and quietly." Carrie nodded as he relayed his instructions to her mentally. There was a look of shock on her face as he told her about the explosive device.

"I'll try," she said out loud.

Carrie Barrington's Quarters deck 8
16:45 Martian Standard

Carrie's quarters were simple. A double bunk in the corner of the room was positioned next to a floor to ceiling window, allowing for magnificent views into the unending vista of space. A pair of man's boots lay at the foot of the bed. She had to remind herself they were there in case her father walked in. She had told Chavel not to leave his things lying about, but men would be men. A small flower decorated the centre table of the rectangular space. She kept the lights low and made her way over to it. She lifted the table up carefully and placed it out of the way. She unbuttoned the top fastenings of her jumpsuit to give her some air and knelt on the soft flooring. She closed her eyes and slowed her breathing, as the drawbridge of her mind let slack the chains that held it locked.

She awoke in her castle in front of a battlement, staring down at the faces of those on board The Agathon. They stared up at her blankly from across the moat. Slowly she reached her arm up and beckoned them to enter. One by one they started to walk towards the drawbridge, which had settled on the surrounding grass. As they each entered the courtyard, their voices began to drift upwards towards her. Their mouths remained closed, but the voices seemed to carry in the surrounding air. The sound of whispers swelled up as the intimate thoughts of hundreds began to merge into a swell of voices. She closed her eyes as the mayhem of it began to overwhelm her.

"Stop!" she shouted at the top of her lungs, while placing both hands facing out as if to fend off an attack from a wild animal.

"You will wait your turn!" she shouted into the onslaught of thoughts. The noise subsided as the courtyard full of The Agathon's crew and passengers stared up at her. She saw her father, David, Doctor Tyrell and the others all looking at her with blank expressions, awaiting her commands. She walked across a stone-covered path and made her way down a carved stone staircase. The crowd watched her as she descended. They split apart and made a path for her to walk through.

"Okay," she said quietly to the waiting faces.

"Let's begin." She stretched out her arms and faced her palms to the sky. Her guests followed suit. She began to walk amongst them, grazing their fingertips as she passed. Each time she touched a hand her mind was flooded with images. She touched Chanda Pell, a botanist from the colony on Mars. A slender Indian woman who grew the most beautiful geraniums she had ever seen. She saw through her eyes as she let herself drift into her mind. She saw the hydroponics bay with Chanda's eyes, as she tended to the growing trees and foliage. Her mind was clear. Unclouded. At peace. It lingered on thoughts of a man. Her husband. She found herself in a wheat field on a sunny day, unfolding a large blanket on the ground and laying her head on his lap as his fingers coursed through her hair. The sun felt warm as sadness filled her. She imagined what he may have been doing when the ground on which he was standing vaporised. She wondered if he felt any pain. She buried the pain and tended to the greenery. Carrie opened her eyes and touched the hand next to hers. Douglas Griffiths, a dark-haired man in his forties. One of the Atmo Two technicians from Yorkshire in England. She had met him only once. He was a quiet man with a soft way about him. He was in his quarters reading an old spy novel on a clear pad. He loved to read and had thousands of listings. He wished he were more social and feels lonely on the ship. His time in the main machine room of Atmo Two flashed past her mind. Fixing, tinkering, monitoring, reading. A solid working man with no family. Insufferably shy, but a gifted mechanical mind. A mind that could do no harm. She moved past him and glanced at another open palm. Trisha Davenport, a solidly built security officer sent from the Jycorp Station. Like Griffiths, she was in her quarters but not reading. She was out of breath. Carrie felt the strength of her heartbeat as she raised and lowered her body close to the floor, repeating push up after push up. She had a disciplined mind. She found comfort in routine. She was no stranger to battle. Her thoughts were of a gunfight in a dark rundown city on Earth. Someone was killed. A man she was with. She was alone and surrounded. She opened fire against an unseen enemy, but was hit in the chest by a pulsar. Her thoughts returned her to her room as she continued to exercise. Carrie stayed with her mind, following her thoughts through her transfer to the ship right up to the present moment.*

After a minute of scanning she moved on to another. She touched the hands of as many of the crew as she could. Ed Clifford, a young chemist from the Jycorp Station, originally from Toronto. Dezydery Castellarnau, a twenty-four-year-old German medic from the colony, now stationed in the medical bay under Doctor Brubaker. She was struggling to cope with the loss of her entire family on Earth. Carrie knew her mind and she moved on quickly. This girl could not harm anyone. She moved through the courtyard. A representation of David Chavel stood before her. She pulled her hand back and moved past him. There was no need to move into his mind. They had shared enough to know what she needed to know. Charly Boyett's outstretched fingers met hers. She saw her on the bridge. She felt no fear. Her mind was confident and daring. She watched the view screens as the approaching planet grew in size. Her mind was focused. She felt the ship under her fingers responding to her delicate movements. She felt anger towards whoever would attempt to destroy it. The ship had been her baby. The sadness she repressed was kept at bay with trained and deliberate purpose. Carrie left her mind. She touched another. Erin Canaleta, a thirty-year-old biochemist from the colony. She was in a lab staring at a small Holo image of a young girl. Her daughter.

"I'm sorry," she whispered at the image. Carrie's mind was filled with images of the girl in a hospital bed. Her face had sunken black eyes as the life signs faded on the medical readout above her bed. Her mind became flooded with a multitude of flashing images of the birth, life and death of the little girl.

Carrie withdrew from her mind, unable to stand the onslaught of sadness. She stopped in the courtyard and stared at the faces of The Agathon's personnel. She felt pain and something else. Something that did not belong. There was little in the minds of The Agathon's crew to indicate motive for destructive acts. She continued her search through the crowd of minds. Kristina Padrosa, a thirty-four-year-old engineer. Abigail Storer, a thirty-one-year-old engineer. Oliver Alcoverro, a thirty-six-year-old physicist. Harry Featherstone, a forty-one-year-old mathematician. Atanazja Roach, a twenty-eight-year-old FTL technician. Leigh Jordan, a thirty-three-year-old plasma engineer.

Doctor Tyrone Tyrell. "GET THE FUCK OUT!" came the ferocious scream. Carrie was thrown across the courtyard by a blast of energy, as the images of The Agathon's crew shattered into a thousand pieces.

She covered her ears for fear they would burst. She looked at the broken shards of the people as they began to fall in pieces all around her like snowflakes. The black figure of her dreams stood in the centre of the courtyard. A man-sized version of The Black under containment in Tyrell's lab.

"Insects!" it screamed. It moved forward towards Carrie. She crawled backwards towards the entrance to the castle. It slithered across the courtyard, forming tentacles with its liquid surface. They extended towards her, as she managed to get to her feet and run to the entrance.

"Weapons," she screamed as the tentacles of the liquid monster reached for her throat. From within the castle walls an arsenal of pulse cannons emerged from the walls and began to fire a ferocious volley of bright energy pulses against the intruder. Carrie closed her eyes as the deep vibrating screams of The Black echoed within the castle walls. It began to change colour and vibrate, as it released its tentacle from around her neck and exploded with a bright white light.

Carrie opened her eyes suddenly. The jolt back into consciousness sent her reeling backwards and into a side table that she had moved.

It smashed under her weight, sending small shards of glass into her skin. She fought to catch her breath as the memory of the unexpected intruder in her mind remained burned into her eyes. She reached down and looked at her cut hands. The injuries were minor. She picked herself off the ground and straightened her hair. Walking over to the washbasin, she steadied her nerves. There was something evil on board this ship. And that something was linked with Tyrone Tyrell. She saw nothing in his mind, but something attacked. Something more powerful telepathically than she was. She turned on the overhead light and looked into the mirror. Her face was slightly cut on one side but nothing a dermal regenerator could not heal. Her eyes caught a glimpse of something standing behind her. A dark figure was behind her. She screamed and turned. The empty room looked back.

She fought to regain control of her exploding heart.

"Easy, Carrie," she said to herself under a panicked breath.

"All hands, this is the captain," came her father's voice. "As some of you may be aware, we have sustained some damage which requires us to land on a nearby planet to repair. As this is something we have not attempted yet with this vessel, I would ask that you begin preparations by securing your quarters and workstations and strapping in while we conduct the manoeuvre. Stand by for atmospheric entry, in twenty-three minutes. Barrington out."

Carrie looked out the large window at the grey planet approaching. The feeling of something in her mind began to scare her. As if something had been left behind during her scans of the crew. She drew water in the basin and threw it onto her face.

"Tyrell to Carrie Barrington," came the calm voice over her comm panel. She froze.

"Tyrell to Carrie Barrington," he said again calmly.

"Carrie here, Doctor. Go ahead."

"Would you mind coming to my lab as soon as possible? I need your assistance securing the equipment before we touch down on the planet." She looked at her reflection in the mirror and tried to let go of the images.

"Be there in five minutes, Doctor. Carrie out," she said more abruptly than she had planned to before cutting off the transmission. There was something strange about his tone. She finished cleaning her hands and decided she would make a quick stop-off at the medical bay to heal her cuts before going to the lab. She looked under her bed at the container, which held her pulse gun, but let it be. Just checking that it was still there.

14

Agathon Bridge
16 days since departure
13:00 Martian Standard

"Okay everybody, stay alert. Let's just take this nice and easy and by the numbers. Charly, you have complete abort authority if you don't like what you see. Just blow the dorsal thrusters and get us up. Clear?" Barrington said to Boyett, as she began easing the ship into the gravitational pull of the planet.

"Got it, sir," she replied. Her focus on the view screens was laser-like.

"Chavel, keep an eye on the terrain gradients."

"Sir," he replied, looking over the computer displays of the surface. Jerome Young had joined them and was sitting at one of the stations looking at mappings of the planet. It was desolate. Like a dust cloud had descended on the whole surface from a volcanic eruption. The thin white light of the mother star cast an eerie glow over the peaks and valleys of the scarred world.

"Looks like there were oceans here, sir," said Chavel.

"Let's see it," Barrington answered. Chavel flicked the images of the sea beds onto the far left viewer, to leave the centre viewer clear for Boyett to navigate. Barrington stroked his chin with one of his fingers. Boyett gave the images a quick glance and saw what Chavel was talking about. Huge sea beds regressed from a large central continent, as if they had just emptied themselves into space. What was now a grey desert world looked like it had been sucked dry.

"Amazing," Barrington said under his breath.

"One hundred and twenty kilometres," Boyett said, bringing them back into the moment.

"David, let's get these struts out," Barrington said calmly.

"Yes, sir, activating landing struts." He tapped some commands into his panel and waited. He tapped the commands in again.

"Eh, sir, I have a negative response on the landing struts." Boyett flicked her eyes towards the captain, but maintained her steady approach.

"Barrington to engine room," he said with a slight urgency in his voice.

"Emerson here, sir. Bear with me two minutes, we're working on it. One of the outer doors is jammed." There was silence on the comms as Barrington remained silent.

"Okay, we're good. Try them now," Emerson said. Barrington nodded to Chavel who took a small breath and tried the commands again. The console gave a positive sounding little chirp.

"Struts descending," he said. There was a vibration as the four pylons on the underbelly of the ship emerged and locked into place. The ship descended slowly, as the features of the planet rose in the view screens. Mountaintops rose as the details of the oncoming landscape started to develop. The landing site had been chosen in the northern hemisphere of the largest continent, based on the planet's angle of rotation, which gave the most light during the thirty-seven-hour rotation.

"Seventy-five kilometres," said Boyett.

"Terrain is looking good. Approach in vector," Chavel sounded off.

"Okay, Charly, take her down." Barrington gave her a confident affirmation that locked her focus in on the flight controls. She eased off the power of the dorsal thrusters and let the gravity of the planet grab the huge ship and invite her down. The descent was well controlled, because of the lack of any weather or atmosphere. Boyett thought she could have landed it either way, but was glad there could be no surprises. She hoped.

"Five kilometres," she finally said.

"All hands, this is the captain. We are about to touch down. Brace yourselves." He sat back in the centre seat and waited for the worst, already running through evacuation protocols and survival scenarios.

"Five hundred meters," said Boyett. She gave the dorsal thrusters a burn and countered the gravity. There was a slight shaking of the bridge as the ship made contact with the ground.

"Contact," she said. "Thrusters at twenty percent." The vibration stopped as the image of the grey landscape in the central view screen stopped moving.

"Cutting thrusters," Boyett said. She secured her station and looked at the captain.

"We're down," she said, smiling. Barrington smiled back. Chavel stretched his hand out.

"Nice. Gimme some sugar," he said as Boyett high-fived him.

"Well done, Lieutenant," said Young from his station. He had been quiet through the landing. Boyett nodded.

"Barrington to engine room. Report."

"Looks good here, bridge. Strut integrity holding ground seems solid. Tell Charly that was a hell of a job."

"Understood. Get your team ready, Landon. Let's not be here any longer than we have to."

"No problem, sir. I could use Boyett down here as soon as she has things locked up."

"She's on her way. Barrington out." He nodded to Boyett, who began running flight shutdown procedures.

"Captain," said Young suddenly. Barrington turned to him. "I would like to be the first out," he said. Chavel looked at the Jycorp CEO.

"I'm not happy letting passengers off the ship, Jerome. There could be variables."

"I understand that, but no human has walked on another world outside our solar system and I would like to be the first. I will stay within the parameter of the ship and you can keep a constant communications lock." Barrington rubbed his face, then looked at Chavel.

"Okay, but I want David to go with you." Chavel nodded enthusiastically. Young was about to protest but held it. They both stood and walked to the lift.

"One moment, Mr. Young. Barrington to Doctor Tyrell," he said, tapping his comms.

"Yes, John," came the calm reply. "Doctor, Mr Young is going outside the ship. I would like you to go with him and help take some samples, if you are up to it."

"I wouldn't miss it for the world," came the response.

"Meet the team at the exterior ramp on deck twenty-seven."

"Understood, Captain." The comms clicked off.

"Two hours please, no more. Any problems, you abort and Chavel has complete command of the team. Agreed?"

Young nodded. "Agreed."

They left the bridge, leaving Barrington with his support crew now running ship diagnostics. He looked out at the grey dead world and thought about the hole in the side of his ship.

Planet Surface

Tyrell smiled at Young as he made the descent onto the surface. Behind him on the gangway was Emerson's engineering crew and Boyett leading up the rear. Chavel was waiting at Tyrell's side, while Young stepped onto the dusty ground. The planet looked like it had been pulverised with meteorites and everything had a silver glow about it. What light there was appeared dim and cast strange shadows on the surface from the various hill formations. Tyrell noticed that some of the shadows looked humanoid. It was an eerie feeling, even for him. He had been on edge since the strange dream he had about Carrie a few nights before. He had decided not to discuss it with her and set her to work on the astronomical phenomena, but the child was digging. Digging in his brain. He knew it.

"To the new world," said Young, raising both arms in the air. He was now standing on the soil, looking out into the vast wasteland.

"Nice," said Tosh over the comms. He was tied in with the team from the engine room. Young looked back at the team of people on the gangway.

"Okay, let's get to it," said Chavel, slapping Tyrell on the arm, who frowned at the gesture. Tyrell made his way down the sloped gangway and stood by Young, who nodded to him. They wore the form-fitting suits needed for both the Phobos and Mars EVAs. He looked up at the hull of The Agathon, which sat majestically against the star-filled sky.

"Alpha team on me," said Boyett. Emerson was helping to carry a gravity lift with Llewellyn, who looked a little nervous. Tyrell watched the engineering team walk under the hull towards the edge of the ship. They had to gain access to the damaged section through the top of the ship, and to do that they needed to lift equipment and themselves using the gravity lift. He turned back to Chavel and Young.

"Well then," he said through the comm system in his faceplate. "Where are you thinking about having this picnic of yours, Mr. Young?" He was trying to add some joviality into his voice, which was something he was not very good at, having isolated himself in his lab for so many years on Mars.

Young turned to Chavel who gestured control of the decision back to him. "It's your show, Mr Young. I'm just here to keep everyone safe."

Young smiled. "Well, Lieutenant, any objection to taking a little stroll over to those hills. My topographic scans show it was once home to a large intersecting array of rivers." Chavel looked back at the ship and then motioned the Beta team to start walking.

"Lead the way," he said.

"Chavel to Captain. Comms check."

"Barrington here. Status," came the captain's voice.

"Beta team are going to take a look at some water formations, a kilometre west of current position."

"Understood, Lieutenant. Observe radiation protocols."

"Yes, sir, Chavel out." He closed the comms signal in his faceplate with a flick of his eye movement and began walking.

"What's in the case, Doc?" he asked Tyrell, looking at the large black case in his hand. Tyrell glanced at it.

"Seismic actuators, soil analysis perpetuators and several astronomical observational scopes," he said blandly.

"Right," Chavel answered. Tyrell looked at the ground when he walked. It was soft underfoot. It felt cold. The suits controlled temperature very efficiently, but there was a deathly feeling that crept through the soles of his feet.

"So, Lieutenant, the captain tells me you won a Daedalus medal. Is that true?"

"That was a long time ago," Chavel said. Tyrell secretly rolled his eyes at Chavel's humility.

"Well, far be it for me to interrupt the beautiful sounds of my own breath in this faceplate with conversation, but I for one would love to hear about it. How about you, Tyrell?" said Young.

"Yes please, Lieutenant. Do enlighten us." Tyrell knew the story only too well, but it diverted a need for him to make idle chitchat with the pair and so encouraged it. They continued across the grey wasteland with relative ease. After a moment's hesitation, Chavel began the story.

"Well, there's not much to tell, to be honest. I think it was a lot of fuss over nothing."

"Didn't you die?" Young asked. Chavel laughed.

"That much is true, yes. Twenty-one minutes, thirteen seconds. I was toast," he said.

"What did you see, Lieutenant?" Tyrell asked with genuine interest.

"See, Doctor?" said Chavel.

"Yes, see. What did you see? Lights, tunnels that sort of thing," said Tyrell.

"No, nothing like that, I'm afraid. I do remember seeing my dead body on the transport ship. I remember the faces of the passengers as they huddled for warmth in the sealed compartment. I remember trying to talk to them. Trying to tell them everything would be all right and that help had arrived." Young stopped and turned to Chavel.

"You telling me you had an out of body experience?"

"Honestly, I don't know. It could have been. It could have been a crazy dream, but when I woke up there were details I knew about the readings on the flight panel and the stuff the rescue team were talking about to each other that I couldn't have known." He continued walking and looked at the stars.

"It was peaceful," he continued. "I remember that there was no fear. I find that comforting," he said.

"That we float around outside our dead bodies like ghosts?" Tyrell said, waving his arms in the air.

"No, Doctor, that there is no fear. I know that all those people on Earth are at peace wherever they are now. And I find great peace with that."

Young was silent as they continued their journey. *Ludicrous*, thought Tyrell.

The Lake

They stopped on the edge of a sheer drop which cut away from the ground. The vista was spectacular. In the distance the glow of the home star cast a cutting morning light over everything. Something in the soil ahead made it sparkle, making it look like it was reflecting the stars that could be seen so clearly overhead. An advantage to not having an atmosphere, Young had noted on the way over. The trio fell silent and even Tyrell seemed to be taken in by the view.

"There is something protruding from the riverbed down there," said Chavel, looking through a pair of hand-held magniscopes. Young was looking at the stars at the time and moved his head down to see what Chavel was talking about.

"Here." Chavel handed Young the image magnifying device.

"Probably a rock. That's all there seems to be on this planet," Tyrell said.

"Probably," said Young, "odd shape though. Let's take a look."

"Hang on there, Mr Young, this is a pretty steep decline," said Chavel.

"The suits have grapplers, no?" said Young. Chavel nodded in concession. He activated his comms with a flick of his eye.

"Chavel to Agathon."

"Agathon here, go ahead, Lieutenant," Barrington said. "We're heading to the bed of what looks like a river, to check out a rock formation."

"Okay, you have one hour. We're almost ready to lock up over here and lift off," Barrington said.

"Understood," Chavel said, clicking off his comms.

"I really think we should be heading back to the ship, gentlemen. It's just a rock," said Tyrell. Young and Chavel looked at him.

"Come on, Doc," said Chavel. "You haven't even opened your case. It would be a shame to come all this way and not do some experiments, no?" he said.

"Hmm," said Tyrell. Young began to untether his grappler, which was attached to a small box that sat snugly on the belt of all the suits. He lined up the metallic anchor and pressed the self-guiding actuator at its tip. He lined it up with what looked like solid ground and let it fly. The anchor flew into the ground with precision. The other two members of Beta team followed suit. Tyrell attached his case to his belt with a hook and swung his legs around to begin the repel down.

Young was first to hit the riverbed. He took the descent like a practiced spelunker. Tyrell had some difficulty with his footing and lost his balance a number of times. Chavel coached him down eventually and the three men detached their harnesses from their cable, leaving them dangling against the rock. The riverbed was flat. The only thing protruding was the oddly-shaped rock formation at its centre.

"Okay, let's take a look," Young said and started walking.

Chavel turned to Tyrell. "You okay there, Doctor?" he asked, wondering why he was hesitating.

"Fine, Lieutenant. Lead the way," he said with a hint of frustration in his voice. They made their way across the grey landscape. From above they would have looked like three black ants walking across a pavement. Young was the first to speak when they approached the formation.

"Its edges are smooth," he said. They stood in front of it. Young reaching towards its leading wall. It had a fashioned and angular appearance.

"Twenty-two meters from base to tip," said Chavel, who had a hand scanner directed at its pointed tip. Young was running his fingers over the surface and brushing off dust.

"Tyrell, what do you make of this?" he said, uncovering grooves in the stonework. Tyrell stood and looked at what Young was pointing at. There were definitely patterned grooves on the surface of the rock. Tyrell's eyes widened as they shifted to one of complete focus on the markings. He placed the case he was carrying on the soil and opened it. He withdrew a cube-shaped instrument and pressed a glowing light on one of its sides. Three meter-long struts shot out from its base and he positioned it in front of the rock.

"What's that?" asked Chavel.

"It's a high intensity atomic mapping imaging array," said Tyrell. "It will date and render an analysis on the stone and the markings."

"There's a pattern here," said Young. His face was pressed up against the stone as he pushed away more debris from its surface.

"Jerome, please step back for a moment, would you?" Young and Chavel took a step back as Tyrell pressed the activation sequence on the cube. It seemed to turn transparent as an array of blue lasers shot out from its centre and scanned every inch of the rock, rendering a three-dimensional floating image on top of it. It only took a few seconds, but when it was done a perfect glass-like facsimile of the object floated on the scanner.

"Tyrell to Agathon," he said into his face plate.

"Barrington here," said the captain.

"John, patch me through to Carrie, please. She's in my lab," Tyrell said. He looked over at Chavel and gave him a little smile.

"Of course, Doctor," came his swift reply.

"Carrie here, Doctor," came her calm voice.

"Carrie, I'm sending you data of a rock formation we've found out here. Can you link to the imager designated scan alpha and upload the data to the network in the lab, please? Then begin a subatomic resonance report on it."

"Of course, Doctor. Linking up now," she said. They waited for a moment.

"Link secure, Doctor. Beginning transfer," Carrie said.

"Thank you, Carrie. Tyrell out," he said, severing the communications link. Young had gone back over to the rock.

"So, what are we looking at here, Mr Young?" said Chavel.

"I don't know yet, David. Just a hunch. Doctor Tyrell, can that device scan below the surface?" he asked, turning to Tyrell. Tyrell seemed to be anticipating his next question, as his repositioned the cube at a ninety degree angle to the ground.

"Yes, it can," he said when he had finished.

"You thinking there's more to see?" asked Chavel. Young hunched up his shoulders. Tyrell hit the activator and the trio stared at the dusty grey soil, as the lasers scanned the surrounding area around the rock. Chavel looked off into the distance, as the cube completed its scans and sent the information back to The Agathon.

"Barrington to Doctor Tyrell," came the female voice in all their head sets.

"Yes, Carrie, go ahead," said Tyrell.

"Doctor, the last set of images you sent are showing a large cavernous structure one hundred meters under the surface. Definitely not natural. There are polymer and metallic alloyed foundations. I think we're looking at something constructed." Beta team looked at each other.

"Carrie, can you get a detailed rendering of the markings we are seeing on the exposed surface?" said Young, unable to contain his excitement.

"I think you should do another scan to be sure, but the computer is running pattern recognition permutations on them now. Could be the remnants of an ancient civilisation by the looks of it," she said.

"Jesus," said Chavel.

"We have to get down there," announced Young, his eyes wide.

"Hang on, Jerome, let's not get ahead of ourselves," interrupted the captain's voice.

Young looked surprised. He had forgotten that the bridge was monitoring all communications.

"Captain, we can't possibly walk away from this. We've just discovered evidence of an advanced alien civilisation. We have to at least try to find out what we can about them. They may have had direct contact with the signal makers at one stage," he finished.

"Tyrell?" said the captain.

"It's not beyond the bounds of reason, John. We are, after all, on a direct course with what we postulate is their home world," he answered.

"What timeframe are we looking at to excavate the site and gain access to the structure?" asked the captain.

"There appears to be an opening ninety-seven meters directly under the position of the protruding rock face," said Carrie

"Judging by the depth and the drilling equipment we have on board The Agathon, no more than twenty-two hours," answered Young. There was silence over the comm.

"Gentlemen, I need not remind you that our primary concern is locating a habitable world, not conducting archaeological digs on other planets. I am conscious of other concerns regarding the safety of this ship," said the captain. "Alpha team tells me we are currently six hours away from being able to lift off and I intend to adhere to that schedule. Do what you need to do within that timeframe, but once Alpha team has completed repairs I want you back on this ship."

"Captain, we cannot abandon this without..."

"Those are my instructions, Mr. Young," Barrington interrupted. "Lieutenant, get Beta team prepped and ready to go by seventeen-thirty hours, clear?"

"Very clear, sir," Chavel rounded off.

"Barrington out." Young looked at Chavel, clearly not happy with the decision. Chavel shrugged.

"He's right, Mr Young, we didn't come here for this. We have people depending on us and if anything happens to us on this planet we won't get a second chance at this," he said. Young looked at the structure and shook his head.

"Tyrell, what can you get from under the surface?" he asked.

Tyrell raised his eyebrows. "Six hours doesn't give us much time. I could calibrate the cube to a refined scanning beam and try and get a more accurate fix, but I think we should take a more aggressive approach," he said.

"Meaning?" asked Chavel. "Your pulse gun could bore a hole of up to fifty meters at its highest setting, could it not?" Chavel looked at the weapon holstered at his side.

"We could damage it," said Young.

"Jerome, we are more than likely never returning to this world and whatever this is will have to remain a mystery unless we get down to a better scanning depth," said Tyrell in a matter of fact kind of way. They looked at Chavel.

"Hey, this is your show, guys. It's just an old alien rock to me, but you're right, Doctor Tyrell. A sustained shot at level six will carve a heavy chunk out of that bedrock." Tyrell looked at Young, who was examining the outside of the structure.

"Do it," he said finally. They stepped back when the current round of scans were completed. Tyrell withdrew the cube so that it was out of range of the rock face and Chavel drew his weapon.

"Now, take it easy, Lieutenant. Try not to blow up the whole rock face. It would be nice to keep it intact," said Young, with his hands raised. Chavel lowered his gun and looked at him.

"Trust me," he said, smiling. He slid his finger up the left side of the weapon, increasing its power, and aimed about six feet in front of the rock face. He steadied his feet and dug in his heels to protect against the recoil in this gravity. He fired a series of sustained blasts into the bedrock, throwing a plume of grey and white dust in the air. As the thick debris cleared, the rock face stood unscathed by Chavel's attack. The hole that had been opened in the ground revealed something that made Young gasp.

"Holy shit," he said, looking into the space. "Tyrell, get over here and get readings on this," he said. The dust settled and revealed a dark-stoned structure with what looked like circuit-shaped carvings all over it. Tyrell set up the cube scanner at the edge of it and began taking readings. Seconds later the ground began to shake.

15

Agathon Hull
19:00 Martian Standard

"Did you feel something?" said Emerson to Boyett, putting his hand on her shoulder.

"Stop flirting with me, stud, we have work to do," she replied, not looking up from her laser welder. The hole in the side of the ship had numerous metallic sheets stretched across its surface. They had spent the last few hours erecting support pylons on the deck plating to reinforce the emergency hull segments put in place. Boyett did not have much time to take in the view, as she had endless amounts of joining rivets to seal into place. It was tedious work, not to mention unnerving to think that one of the passengers had intentionally tried to blow up the ship in hyperspace. She lost concentration for a minute when a vibration rippled through the ship and the laser welder slipped, nearly slicing off one of her fingers.

"Jesus," she said. She sighed and looked down at her repair work. "When we find this fucker, I'm going to turn him inside out and throw him out an airlock," she said, catching Emerson smiling out of the corner of his transparent faceplate.

"I have no doubt," he answered, looking out over the surface of the hull and into the distance.

"What's up?" asked Boyett, following his gaze. He looked back at her. Even in the suit she thought he was a very sexy man. *That was some night*, she thought to herself. *About time for another.*

"Thought I felt a tremor. You?" he asked. She righted herself and remained still for a moment. That was when the world from underneath her gave way. The shaking of the hull threw her on her back, as she saw Emerson struggling to grab hold of something. She suddenly found herself sliding away from the repair site and over the side of The Agathon's hull. At that height the inbuilt shock absorbers wouldn't protect her from serious injury and the grav lifts were locked onto the hull beside the damaged area of the ship.

The surface of The Agathon's hull was virtually impossible to hold onto, as she slid over its smooth curves. She gritted her teeth and prepared for the fall as she felt a tug at her back. She looked back and saw Emerson on his front reaching out and grappling with her suit. He was still tethered to the hull. Boyett breathed a silent sigh of relief as they came to a stop just before the edge of the ship. It continued to shake.

"Barrington to all teams. Evacuate. We have serious seismic activity registering," said the captain over the comms. In the distance Boyett began to see plumes of white smoke bursting out from the ground. She looked back at Emerson, who was scrambling to get a grip on the tether.

"Come on, Charly, that's our cue," he said, getting to his feet.

"Emerson to Bridge. We need two more minutes to seal this hull sheeting," he said into his faceplate.

"Okay, Landon, two minutes," came the reply. A burst of smoke erupted off into the distance.

"Alpha team, have you heard from Beta team?" Barrington said over the comms.

"Negative, Captain," said Boyett.

"Keep comm links open. We can't get hold of them," he said.

"Sir, you want me go after them?" Boyett said.

"Too dangerous, Charly. Finish up and get your asses inside. I need you at flight," he said.

"Understood," she said. Another tremor nearly shook the pair of them off their feet, but they stood their ground well and reached the repair site.

"Are you all right, Lieutenant?" said Llewellyn, who was fusing a piece of hull with determination. Boyett gave her the thumbs up.

"Okay, let's get the hell out of here," Emerson said.

"Charly, Amanda, focus on getting that lateral shielding locked. We can finish the ventral bonding from inside the deck once we're airborne, but right now we have two minutes so hustle people," he said.

"Agathon, this is Beta team. We are incoming. We have injured," it sounded like Chavel's voice through heavy static. Boyett looked out over the grey and turbulent surface of the dead planet. She saw a large crack creeping its way across the ground.

"Fuck, the ground is opening up," she said.

"Alpha team, inside now," came the captain's voice.

"Jesus, look at it," said Llewelyn, who was frozen in place, watching the large crack that was now edging towards the resting ship. Steam and gas vented through the gaps, as they scrambled with their gear and headed over the edge of the ship and onto the grav lifts. As they lowered themselves onto the ground, Boyett thought she saw three small figures in the distance. It was difficult to make out with the dust and steam.

"Alpha team approaching ramp. I think I see them, Captain. About three kilometres east. I can get to them," said Boyett, dropping her gear onto the ramp and getting ready to run.

"Negative, Lieutenant," said Barrington.

"Agathon, we are unable to traverse terrain. We have multiple fissures opening up and Young is seriously injured. Requesting an evac," said Chavel, out of breath.

"I'll be there in sixty seconds, Captain," said Boyett.

Agathon Bridge

"Get us up," said Barrington to Boyett, who was trying to catch her breath after sprinting through the decks to get to the bridge.

"Beta team stand by, we are coming to your position. Hold there, do you copy?" Barrington said. No reply.

"Beta team, do you read?" Static. The bridge began to vibrate as Boyett engaged the thrusters, as it fought against the gravity of the planet and held its position over the surface.

"Take us to the last source of transmission, Charly," Barrington said.

"Got it, sir. ETA thirty seconds," she replied. The view screens at the head of the bridge showed a volatile surface with cracks and eruptions every few meters.

"There!" said Llewellyn, who was manning the navigation station. A few seconds later, three figures came into view. They were all lying on the ground. One of them was missing half a leg.

"Bring us to within ten meters, Charly," Barrington shifted in his seat.

"Emerson, get ready to run," he said.

"Doctor Brubaker. Are your medical teams in place?" he asked.

"We're here, Captain," she replied.

"Okay, Charly, put her down nice and easy," said Barrington. The pylons had remained extended and the ship sank to the ground with relative ease.

"Go, Emerson," he said into his comms.

"Going," came the reply. The view screen showed the exterior of the ship and the three figures unmoving.

"Llewellyn, can you get me a reading on those gases?" Barrington said.

"High concentrations of methane, hydrogen sulphide, hydrogen fluoride and carbon monoxide. If their breathers are cracked in any way…" She shook her head at the captain, who acknowledged it. Barrington suddenly felt a familiar presence in his mind. He knew it wouldn't be long before Carrie sensed what was happening.

Not now, Carrie, I need to focus, he thought.

Sorry, she said. *Anything I can do?*

He didn't answer. The presence in his mind faded. The bridge began to shake. An enormous explosion of gas and dust blew out of a nearby hill.

"Sir, I'm getting tectonic instability readings from directly under the ship," said Llewellyn.

"I think we're right on top of a vent that's about to blow," she said, her eyes widening. Barrington looked at Boyett, whose hands were in the standby position on the thrusters. Unmoving. Emerson appeared on the screen with the other team in tow. They dragged the three out of shot of the viewer and seconds later came Emerson's voice.

"We have them, sir. Lock it up and let's go," he said. The ship was rocked to one side and a high pressure expulsion of gas hit its port side.

"Charly!" shouted Barrington. Boyett's hands moved quickly and she fired the ventral plasma thrusters at full blast. The ship rose quickly into the air, as the ground beneath it gave way into an eruption of gas and rock.

"Altitude one thousand feet and rising, sir. We're clear," she said. She let out a breath of air through tightly closed lips and continued her ascent.

"Barrington to engine room. How are the seals holding on deck three?" he said.

"Tosh here, she looks good. We're pressurising the effected sections now. Stand by," he said.

"We'll hold at two thousand feet," said Barrington. Several minutes passed as the bridge crew waited for the all clear from Tosh.

"Okay, bridge, we are showing one hundred percent on deck three," said Tosh.

"Charly, take us one hundred thousand kilometres away from this planet and hold position," said Barrington.

"Yes, sir," she replied, as the view screens shifted to star fields on all angles. It rose steadily.

"I'll be in the medical bay. Charly, you have the con," said Barrington, as he made his way to the back of the bridge.

16

Medical Bay
Twenty Days since departure
14:43 Martian Standard

Carrie sat by Chavel's bio bed as Brubaker briefed the captain on the status of the three members of Beta Team. Tyrell was sitting upright and looking over at Barrington. He was wearing a breather. Young was unconscious and undergoing surgery.

"His leg is severed just below the knee," said Brubaker. "Seems like a gas pocket opened up right underneath it and tore it clean off. He'll live and we have bio synthetic replacements on board, so he got lucky."

"The others?" said Barrington.

"There were micro cracks in their face plates when they came on board. Tyrell has some scorching of the alveoli, as does Chavel, but I expect they'll be back on their feet in a day or two with some dermal regenerative treatment."

"Thank you, Michelle. Good work," said Barrington. He walked over to Carrie.

"How are you doing, Dice?" he said softly. She looked up at him. "I think it'll take more than an earthquake to take down this man, don't you?" he said, smiling.

"I was going to tell you about him," she said, after a moment.

"No need," he replied. "We don't have secrets, do we?" Carrie smiled.

"No, I guess we don't," she replied. "You need to see the data that Doctor Tyrell transmitted back. They found technology under the rock formation."

Barrington looked over at Tyrell, who was watching them intently. "Show me," he said, turning to meet Carrie's gaze. He walked over to Tyrell who was sitting on the side of the bio bed and breathing heavily into an oxygenator. He put his hand on Tyrell's shoulder.

"How are you, Tyrone?" he asked, looking into his bloodshot eyes.

"Splendid, John," came his muffled response. "Carrie told you about the data?" he asked through a wheeze. Barrington nodded. "It's extraordinary, John. There are markings on the surface correlating with those from the Monolith from Phobos."

Barrington's hand remained on his shoulder.

"With your permission, Tyrone, Carrie is going to take me to the lab to show me," he said.

Tyrell's brow furrowed slightly. "Of course, you don't need my permission. I can join you now," he replied, getting up off the bio bed. Barrington held his hand firmly on Tyrell's shoulder.

"No, Tyrone. Doctor Brubaker needs you here for the next few hours... to monitor you. Carrie can walk me through what she has and we can discuss it further once we've jumped back into hyperspace. For now, just take it easy. I don't need your lungs exploding all over the deck before we've reached the Aristaeus system." Tyrell's eyes met with his.

"Of course, Captain. There are several kilo quads of data on the cube which did not send before the accident. It's over there on the ledge," he said, pointing to a side table by Brubaker's office. Barrington nodded and tapped him on the arm. Tyrell looked over at Carrie, who nodded back as she left Chavel's side and joined her father. Barrington took the cube and they left the medical together.

"I need to go to the engine room to check on things," he said, as they walked towards the lift.

How is your assignment going? he thought in his head, linking with her mind. They continued through the corridor, nodding to passing crewmen.

It's proving to be difficult. There's something on board that is blocking me. I'm not certain, but I think it has something to do with The Black. Barrington stopped mid stride and looked at her.

"Captain!" came a voice to his left. Chase Meridian was running towards them. She smiled at Carrie.

"Hey, Dice," she said. Carrie smiled at her. She took Barrington's arm and pulled him to one side.

"John, have we a saboteur on board?" she whispered virulently into his ear. Barrington took her by the arm gently.

"Easy there, Chase. Who said anything about a saboteur?" he said.

"Come on, John, who do you think you're talking to? Everyone is saying that someone planted an explosive device on deck three and that's what blew a hole in the hull," she said, her face taking on a stern expression that did not suit her generally jovial nature.

"Is Young dead?" she added. Barrington rolled his eyes.

"No, he's not dead," he said, showing frustration. Meridian put her hands up.

"Okay, okay," she said.

"So where are we off to?" she added.

"We're heading to the engine room, Chase, then to Tyrell's lab to take a look at the data that came in from a rock formation that Beta team found on the surface," said Carrie.

"And you weren't going to invite me?" she said with a dramatic look of shock on her face. Barrington sighed.

"Okay, Doctor, another set of eyes on this thing wouldn't hurt," said Barrington.

"Excellent," she said, turning to join them. She winked at Carrie and the trio continued on towards the lift.

Engine Room
16:32 Martian Standard

Daniel Tosh was exhausted and his back hurt from prolonged use of his chair. Not to mention this mission was turning out to be far more dangerous than Young had let on and now he was possibly dead, according to Emerson who had arrived in the engine room a short time ago after 'rescuing' them. He was currently making adjustments to The Betty FTL chamber while Emerson was making a visual inspection of the repair work on deck three.

"Can you hand me an ionic stabiliser, Atanazja?" Tosh said to the young woman on the opposite side of the plasma duct. She nodded and walked under the tubing to hand him the tool.

"How are you feeling, Doctor? You look tired," she said with a French accent.

"Nothing a little horizontal time wouldn't cure," he said. She looked at him and raised a dark brown eyebrow. Suddenly realising how that sounded to the twenty-eight-year-old FTL technician from Paris, he laughed and corrected himself. "That is to say I could use some sleep. Don't get any ideas."

She laughed. She had dark brown eyes and while her face was not classically beautiful, she had a strong jawline and beautiful hands. Tosh had a thing for a woman's hands. Strong and graceful hands.

"Do you really think Young is dead?" she asked.

Tosh looked at her intently and leaned back in his chair.

"I don't know, Atanazja. I honestly doubt it." He took the long thin tool she just handed him, attached it to The Betty and began making adjustments.

"Not many people know this, but there was an assassination attempt on Jerome Young nine years ago in Cairo."

"Really? I never heard about that," she said.

"Nobody did," he said.

"An explosive device detonated inside his land cruiser. It killed everyone on board. Seven security detail, including one of his nephews. He walked away without a scratch."

"Jesus," she said.

"Yep. Not long after that he transferred permanently to the Jycorp orbital and dragged my floating ass to Phobos," he said, not taking his gaze away from his work.

"I've never met him," said Atanazja, looking at the ground. Tosh paused his work.

"We've been friends a long time. I knew his father well, unfortunately, but that incident in Cairo changed him. He has been trying to get away from Earth his whole life. If anyone can survive an exploding volcano underfoot, Jerome Young can," he said. The engine room hushed and the pair looked over to find the captain, Carrie and Doctor Meridian approaching.

"Captain, what news?" said Tosh, turning to face the approaching trio.

"I was about to ask you the same thing, Doctor Tosh," came a firm reply.

"FTL systems are all normal and the pressure seals are holding on deck three. We have a few more tests, but once Emerson gives us a green light we can release the FTL ring and get on our way. Have you heard any news about Jerome Young?" he asked, trying to conceal his genuine concern for his friend.

"He'll live, Daniel," Barrington replied. He moved closer to Tosh to converse more privately. "He lost a leg, but Brubaker is working on it. I don't want to interrupt you, if you're making crucial repairs. This is a flying visit." Tosh breathed a silent sigh of relief at the news of Young's status and turned back to The Betty.

"I will be in Doctor Tyrell's lab for the next half hour to forty minutes, so please contact me there when Emerson returns."

"Not a problem, Captain," came Tosh's reply.

He noticed how he fell into formality with Barrington a lot more easily than he had expected. He also noticed how his daughter Carrie was looking at him. There was curiosity in her eyes and something else. She looked uncomfortable. She was staring at him and not making much of a secret of it. He had known her to be a quiet scientist, but did not know anything else about her other than the fact that she was Barrington's daughter. He drew his eyes away from her and got back to his work on the FTL systems. As they walked out of the engine room he glanced at the exit which slid open. She looked back at him one last time and made eye contact. She paused then followed her father out.

"What the hell was that?" Tosh whispered to himself.

"Sorry, Doctor?" said Atanazja. He met her eyes, which were looking oddly at him.

"Nothing," he said. "I'm not very good with people," he said without thinking. "Let's run a test on FTL ring deployment," he said.

"Okay," she said, as he glanced back at the now shut exit. He shook off the odd feeling he had from Barrington's daughter and took solace in knowing Young was all right. He reminded himself to kick his ass for taking stupid risks again, when he was back on his feet. *Where the hell is Emerson?* he thought.

Tyrell's lab

The door hissed open as the two Barringtons and Doctor Meridian entered Tyrell's lab.

"Lights," said Carrie. The light levels increased.

"Feels like sneaking into your parents' house when they've gone away for the weekend," said Meridian with a wry smile.

"It's over here," said Carrie. "I've compiled the data into a Holo image so that you can see a more detailed picture of what was sent back." She moved over beside a square black platform with a clear sealed box on top of it, which was atop a cylindrical pillar. She tapped in a few commands on the flush control panel and a three dimensional holographic image emerged from the surface.

"This is a scaled down version of the imaging chamber we used to have at the observatory on Mars," she said, continuing to enter commands into the clear panel. Her father and Doctor Meridian stood at its side and watched the rendering as it began to take shape.

"This is the main rock feature that Doctor Tyrell scanned when they first set up the equipment on the surface," she said, pointing to the protruding angular structure.

"I don't get it," said Meridian. The captain looked at Carrie.

"Hang on, Chase, look at this," she replied. She then tapped a command into the control panel and the image changed to show a large chunk of the ground blasted away from the rock face.

"These are the scans of the rock after David..." she paused, keeping her gaze fixed on the image, "After Lieutenant Chavel used his pulse rifle to remove a section of the bedrock." Meridian's eyes widened as the new rendering showed what lay beneath the rock. What first looked like fossilised carvings began to take on a more uniform and technological look about them. Rows and rows of what looked like piping and electrical cabling dug their way out of the ground and twisted in and out of each other in synchronous harmony.

"Looks like a heating conduit or some kind of environmental plant," said Meridian, taking a step closer to the image.

"Look at the markings," said Carrie, directing their attention to the subtle carvings visible throughout what now looked obviously artificial in nature. Her father shook his head.

"Sorry, Dice, I don't get it," he said.

"It's the signal makers," came a raspy voice from behind them. Carrie jumped at the sudden and unexpected presence of Doctor Tyrell, who stood at the entrance of his lab and stared at them. He took a breath of the portable breather that Brubaker had obviously given him.

"What are you doing out of the medical, Tyrone?" the captain said, frowning. Tyrell made his way over to the group.

"Stupid doctors would have you living in a medical bay if they had their way. I am perfectly capable of continuing with my work. And besides, this is far more important than the minor discomfort of nearly having your lungs melted from the inside out. You will be pleased to know that the young lieutenant is up and about and that Jerome Young's surgery is progressing nicely," he finished with a smile to Carrie.

"Now, as my assistant has so correctly directed your attention to the markings on this alien device, I can probably fill in some of the detail," he said, bolstering forward.

Meridian looked at Carrie and folded her arms while taking a breath. "Please, Doctor, we would be lost without your keen insight into the matter," she said dryly. Tyrell ignored her and began circling the image.

"Captain, these markings are the same as those found on the exterior of the structure on Phobos. The degree of radiation present on the surface and what dating we could ascertain from the soil analysis, implies that whatever this mechanical device was, be it a power plant or a toilet, we think it is just over half a million years old," he said.

"Just before the gas pocket erupted underneath us, Mr Young made a startling discovery while examining the underside of what looked like some sort of carbon composite piping running the length of the structure. I began to make scans of it, but I do not think I was successful in their transmission before the accident. Carrie?" he said, turning to Carrie who had anticipated his request and was searching the data archives on the imager. She took the cube that she had retrieved from the medical bay and placed it on a data transfer plate. The clear surface lit up when it came into contact with the device and began relaying information directly into the imaging array. Tyrell looked on as the image began to change smoothly and focus in on one of the surfaces of the cylindrical piping.

"There," said Tyrell, suddenly pointing his finger to the display.

"What am I looking at, Tyrone?" said the captain.

"Carrie, increase magnification by ten," Tyrell said. The image zoomed in.

"Is that a person?" said Meridian, looking at the carving. It was definitely humanoid but much thinner and longer than a person. It had long outstretched arms that seemed to reach for the stars. It had something resembling a mouth at the centre of an elongated oval head. The arms ended in three outstretched digits at the end of thin hand-like formations.

"It's them, John," said Tyrell, looking at the captain. Carrie looked at Meridian, whose mouth was open. Tyrell froze the image.

"Did you find anything else?" asked the captain. "What makes you think it was the signal makers?" he said.

"Look at what is beside the figure," said Tyrell, pointing to a carving to the left of the humanoid.

"I can't make it out," said Carrie. Tyrell sighed.

"Look!" he said, wiggling his fingers and tracing an edge around the straight lines.

"It's the Monolith," said Carrie. Tyrell looked at the captain, who momentarily made eye contact with him before returning his gaze to the image.

"Boyett to Captain Barrington," came the voice over the comms. The captain tapped the comm panel on the wall.

"Go ahead," he said.

"We are clear to spin up the FTL, sir. Emerson has given us a green light up here," she said.

"Okay, Charly, release the FTL ring and begin the rotation sequence. I'll join you shortly. Barrington out." He turned to Tyrell and Carrie.

"Keep at it. Any more information about what you think this represents or what happened here would be useful. In the meantime, strap in everyone while we get back on course." With that he nodded farewell and began to walk towards the door.

I think we should have a talk later, he said to Carrie with his thoughts.

That's a good idea, she replied.

PART 3

17

Rec Room
Twenty-one days since departure
15:32

"Keep your left arm up. You keep dropping your form," said Carrie to Chavel as he hit the deck after missing another one of her lethal backhands. The floor of the X-Ball court was glistening with sweat, as Chavel lay on his back.

"Come on, hot rod, one set to go," said Carrie, as she walked over to him and stepped across his chest.

"I prefer the view from down here," he said through several heaving breaths, as he looked up at her. She held out a hand, which he took lightly and stepped backwards, letting her weight lift him off the ground.

"So much for going easy on me, eh?" she said. He reached in closer to give her a kiss but she backed off.

"Don't think so, sweaty!" she said, laughing and walking over to the fluorescent ball that lay by one of the four-inch ground targets. Chavel laughed.

Carrie could feel his intentions clearly enough, but was not about to get physical with her lover in the rec room. That kind of gossip on a ship was bad news. The relationship between the two was no secret on the ship and they had openly begun to show public affection.

Carrie found him to be a kind and caring man and, while she deflected his frequent attempts to have her open up about her feelings towards him, she kept him at arm's length. His mind was one of the easiest to read on the ship and she took comfort in that when they lay together at night. The familiarity of his loving thoughts, as they transferred from his mind to hers, had a profound meditative effect on her. She did not know what she felt for David Chavel, but she knew she that could trust him. She knew that he was a pure soul, if slightly juvenile and lacking direction. He was brave. She didn't need to see the evidence of the medal he kept locked away. He loved her. She knew that. She could not open her mind to that, as it remained opened to the crew.

For over a month she had tried to scan the minds of those on board, hunting for the saboteur. Something was blocking her and while she tried several more times, by letting the crew back into the castle, she was thrown out of it by the dark figure. Her father had told her to keep at it and begun to post security details around key systems of the ship, including environmental control systems and The Betty. Tyrell had spent the last four weeks in relative isolation in his lab, analysing the data collected from the planet. Carrie had asked to be assigned to the bridge, engineering for operations and FTL propulsion control training. She was glad to be out of Tyrell's shadow and she had begun to interact more with the crew.

"Twenty-one to eleven in my favour," she said to Chavel, as she raised the ball to serve. She raised the oval curved racket and served the ball against the large back wall target. Her racket lit up when the ball came in contact with it, as did the target area and the outlines of the court areas when it bounced on their surface.

Anticipating Chavel was easy with the link she had with him. Although he was still only vaguely aware of it, she knew he was beginning to grow suspicious of her ability to know certain things about him. Like where he was about to hit the ball. They traversed the court, which was played over two levels with inclinations at the edges of the walls so that you could launch off into a different direction with ease. While she greatly outclassed him at this game, she admired his determination and willpower. She had let him win several of the points to boost his pride. She understood that much of the male nature. She leapt from one of the wall sides and returned a clever shot by the lieutenant. The ball bounced several times against the enclosed walls of the court and Chavel was able to return the shot, but not without slamming into one of the walls first.

"I'm okay," he said, as he kept a frantic eye on the glow of the impacts. Carrie's movements were smooth. She kept herself light and on the balls of her feet. Her breathing was controlled and focused. The gravity on the ship was kept at Martian levels, which were sixty-two percent lower than that of Earth. While Chavel and the rest of the crew had grown accustomed to it, Carrie's ease of movement in the lower Gs had been with her since birth. She could see him tiring so decided it would be best to end their activity with a killer stroke. The last shot she made had sent the ball high over Chavel's head. He had managed to reposition himself to return the shot, but she knew exactly where he was going to put it. She adjusted her body position to counter with a low corner target shot behind his left leg and waited for the ball to come to her.

"All hands, this is the captain," came her father's voice over the comms. Chavel stopped mid-swing and caught the ball with an open hand.

"We are thirty minutes from our destination. Please prepare to drop out of hyperspace. Be alert. Bridge crew to stations. Barrington out." Chavel looked at Carrie.

"You got lucky," he said, struggling to breathe. She walked over to him and kissed him on the cheek.

"Come on, champ," she said.

"I'm telling you, I had you right where I wanted you," he said as she walked out of the court. He joined her and began to walk through the rec room, which was filled with an array of activities from the

X-Ball court to a running track to a firing range. They wrapped towels around their necks and headed for the changing rooms.

"I wonder what we'll find at Aristaeus," Chavel said silently to Carrie. She didn't answer.

Bridge

The door to the bridge opened and Tyrell and Young walked out. Both of them looked on at the view screens in anticipation. Barrington turned to Young.

"How's the new leg, Jerome?" he said. Young seemed to be walking with ease.

"It works like a charm, Captain. Thank you," he said, smiling. Barrington had noticed a slight limp as he walked, but that was to be expected. He had known many men who had needed bio-implants in his life and knew that in some cases it took years for the central nervous system to fully integrate the new limbs.

"Take a seat, gentlemen. We should be dropping out of hyperspace in or near the Aristaeus system," said Barrington. Boyett was focused clearly on her instrument panel, as she prepared to take the FTL drive offline. The doors to the bridge opened again, and Carrie and Chavel walked onto the bridge.

"Take your station, Lieutenant," Barrington said.

"Carrie, shadow Chavel. I want you to monitor the surrounding system for anomalous debris fields and radiation. I also want you to get an accurate star fix as soon as possible, once we breach normal space."

"Yes, sir," said Chavel, walking across to his station. Carrie followed him close behind and took a seat at the diagnostic station next to Chavel. Boyett didn't acknowledge any of the new arrivals, as she moved her eyes over her instrument panel and kept careful watch on the ship's flight status. Tyrell stood behind the captain and looked out at the view screens.

"Engine room status," Barrington said into his comms.

"Emerson here. Everything five by five, captain. Ready when you are to drop us out." The comms chirped closed.

"Two minutes," said Boyett suddenly. The bridge fell quiet. All eyes were on the view screens above the bridge. Barrington began running scenarios through his head and did a computer check on the manual deployment of the escape pods.

"Thirty seconds," said Boyett, with her eyes locked on the centre screen.

"Disengaging FTL ring," came Emerson's voice over the comms. The light vibration of the bridge lasted several seconds, as the ship slowed the spinning of the ring.

"Dropping out," said Boyett. The view screens flickered as the greys of hyperspace were replaced by star fields. The FTL ring moved slowly past their fields of vision, as it came to a complete stop. All eyes were on the screens. The centre screen showed a large bright star ahead.

"Report," said Barrington. Chavel looked over his navigational readings.

"Checking, sir, stand by," he replied. Tyrell moved from the back of the bridge over to Carrie and began checking data.

"Report," he said again with gusto. Carrie looked at Tyrell, who looked at Chavel.

"This isn't it," said Chavel. Young joined them at the navigation station and began looking at the data.

"Explain," said Barrington.

"Sir, this isn't the Aristaeus system. The star is twice its mass and these are not the correct planets, according to assigned data provided by stellar cartography." Barrington's eyes moved to Tyrell and Carrie.

"Charly, any contacts?" he asked Boyett, who was scanning the area.

"I have a planetary body at one hundred thousand kilometres. No asteroidal contacts," she said.

"Let's see the planet," he said. Boyett brought it up on the main view screen to the front of the bridge. It was dark and featureless. The position of the ship gave it a poor angle on the shadowed part of the planet.

"Tyrell?" he said to the doctor who was looking at the planet. Tyrell shook his head.

"I don't understand, John. We need more data to get an astronomical fix. I suggest getting a closer look at that planet for starters." He looked at Carrie, who was staring at the image. She was frowning.

"Carrie?" he asked his daughter. She didn't answer.

"Carrie," he said again. She looked at him. He noticed she looked worried.

"I agree with Doctor Tyrell," she said softly.

"Charly, lock up the FTL ring and set a course for the nearest planet," he said.

"Yes, sir," she replied.

"Captain, I have a signal bearing 112 mark 224," said Chavel.

"What sort of signal?" Tyrell said aloud, leaning over the lieutenant and staring at his console. Boyett looked at the captain. As did Chavel. Barrington just nodded his head.

"Highly organised," he answered.

"Can you pinpoint?" said Barrington.

"Yes, sir. It's coming from something in orbit around the planet we are currently en route to."

Barrington looked over at Young. "Care to take a look, Mr Young?" he said. Young nodded eagerly and sat by a computer station to the aft of the bridge.

"Route the signal to Mr Young, will you, David? Let's see if we can decode it. Tyrell, why don't you assist?" Tyrell nodded and sat by Young at the computer station.

"Time to orbit, Charly?" he said.

"Eleven minutes," she said.

Anything? Barrington thought to Carrie.

Something, she replied in his thoughts. *I'm not sure.*

The tension level on the bridge began to rise. "Everyone stay sharp," said Barrington, deciding to use it to focus his team.

"I have a fix on the radio signal, I think I can get a visual," said Chavel.

"Do it," said Barrington. The centre screen flickered, changing its image from the planet to what looked like a small orbiting asteroid.

"It's just under one mile in diameter," said Chavel. "It's definitely not rock. Sensors are sending back details of metallic composites. The computer is unable to identify some of the materials, but this is artificial, sir."

Barrington rubbed his thumb over his eyebrow. He didn't like this at all. Whatever it was it didn't look particularly friendly. Jennifer would have had problems with that sort of scientific analysis, but he trusted his instincts and they were usually right.

"Mr. Young, anything?" he asked the Jycorp CEO, who seemed to be right at home on the bridge.

"The signal is definitely artificial in origin," he said. "It bears no resemblance to that of the signal makers' coding. If I had to guess I would say that this is something else. They're not mathematical constants. And they're being directed towards the planet surface."

"David, can we get any readings on the surface?" he asked Chavel.

"On it, sir," he said, anticipating his request.

Still nothing? he thought to Carrie. She didn't answer.

"Dice?" he said out loud. She turned to him with her eyes wide open.

"Turn the ship around!" she screamed.

Seconds later the bridge began to explode all around them.

"Charly, reverse engines!" shouted Barrington over the sound of the exploding consoles and comm reports from the engine room. Boyett was currently lying on the bridge deck plating, after being thrown from the flight controls. Her left arm was on fire. Chavel had jumped on her to put out the flames that nearly engulfed her, when two of the view screens blew up overhead. Carrie's head was bleeding from hitting the corner of the navigational controls. Barrington had managed to stay in the centre chair. Boyett clambered her way back into the flight chair and began trying to make emergency manoeuvres, her arm still smouldering.

"Sir, something has sent an enormous electrical charge through the hull of this ship," she said. "I have no forward or reverse momentum control," she shouted. Young had a fire suppression system in his hand and was putting out some flames at the back of the bridge.

"What's our position, Chavel?" Barrington said.

"We are twenty thousand kilometres from the planet's atmosphere and holding," he said.

"Engine room," he said, after tapping the comms system on his chair.

"Sir, this is Llewellyn," came the young woman's voice. She sounded scared.

"Talk to me," said Barrington.

"Mr Emerson is under the FTL drive at the moment securing a plasma leak," she said, her voice shaking. "We've had a collapse of one of the primary coolant generators. One of our engineers was inside, sir. I think he's dead."

Barrington moved past the news of the crew's death quickly. "Where's Tosh?" he said.

"Sir, Doctor Tosh is helping extinguish a fire at the rear of the engine room. The FTL is offline and I'm getting fluctuations from the environmental systems control. We're losing power, sir. Whatever hit us has drained the central core. We've had some injuries down here, but Doctor Brubaker is sending a team." Barrington thought about the escape life pods. He caught Carrie's eye. She shook her head.

Something knows we're here. It has us, she thought to him.

"Do what you can. I want updates every five minutes. Barrington out."

He tapped the comm system again.

"Medical bay, this is the bridge," he said.

"Sorry, Captain, unless it's urgent I have my hands full right now. Call back later," said Brubaker without a beat.

"Understood. Bridge out."

"Sir, I have forward motion," said Boyett.

"All stop, Charly," said Barrington.

"Yes, sir, I understand, but there's external force acting on the ship," she said.

"Chavel?" Barrington said.

"Confirmed, sir. We're back on course for the planet, traveling at fifteen hundred KPH," said Chavel.

"Engine room, I need thruster control," said Barrington into the comms system.

"Emerson here, sir. I wish I knew what the hell just hit us, but I can't get you thruster control while one of the coolant tanks is still offline. We can't get access to the control room until it's vented. We're working on that. The Betty is in bad shape, sir. Right now we're running damage control. I don't have any answers as to why we're moving, but I'm working on it. Emerson out."

Barrington felt helpless as control of his ship slowly fell away from under him. Something had just attacked and captured him and he hadn't even seen it coming.

"Velocity increasing," said Boyett from the flight chair.

"Sir, we're on a direct collision course with the planet directly ahead at this speed and at this angle we'll burn up in the atmosphere," said Chavel.

"Time to impact?" said Barrington.

"Six minutes," said Chavel.

"Can you get me a visual?" he said calmly. Carrie was now sitting next to her father's centre seat and nursing the cut on her head.

"Trying to," said Chavel. The main view screen flickered to life and the planet was now in full view. It looked like one solid landmass.

"Tyrell, what can you tell me?" he said, turning to the doctor whose face was much paler than usual.

"I don't understand it," he said, turning to a computer console. "These should be the correct coordinates. I..." he trailed off as he began examining data.

"Sir, the land masses on the surface of the planet seem to be changing," said Chavel, puzzled.

"What?" said Barrington. Barrington looked at the planet on the screen above him. Barrington began to enter the sequence into the escape pod programming banks on his control pad, but Boyett interrupted the sequence.

"Sir, we're slowing down!" she said. "I still have no control over the flight operations of the ship." She turned and faced the captain.

"There's something down there," whispered Carrie quietly. A control panel chirping brought Boyett back to her forward facing position.

"Trajectory is being altered," she said.

"By what?" barked Barrington.

"I have atmospheric entry protocols, sir," she said. "We are beginning a descent." Her hands flew across the flight controls.

"All hands, this is the captain," he said into his comms. "We are making entry on a nearby planet. Our engines are down so this may be a rough landing. Brace yourselves. Barrington out." He closed the channel and sat back into the centre seat.

"Everyone strap in," he said to the bridge personnel.

"I'm picking up signals on the surface," said Tyrell from a computer station. There was no response from Barrington or anyone else on the bridge. All eyes were on the approaching atmosphere. Boyett and Chavel activated their chair restraints, which curved around their shoulders.

"Changing course again, Captain," said Boyett. "We're slowing to entry velocities."

The tension level on the bridge began to mount as the mysterious force that had control of the ship led it through the atmosphere of the planet.

"Report," said Barrington to Boyett.

"Couldn't have done it better myself, sir. Whatever has us is bringing us in on a smooth glide path towards continental land mass directly ahead," she said.

"Chavel?" Barrington asked.

"I'm reading nitrogen oxygen atmosphere. Breathable. Class M, sir. No vegetation and the ground looks strange. It's reading as metallic."

Barrington looked at the visuals. The dark approaching mass was difficult to get a read on. He needed answers and control of his ship.

"Engine room, I need thruster control," he said with haste into his comm panel.

"I'm trying, Captain," said Emerson. "It's a real mess down here."

"Figure it out, Mr Emerson, before we hit the ground at a few thousand kilometres a second," said Barrington, without hesitation. There was a pause on the comms.

"Yes, sir," came the quiet reply.

"Sir, we're slowing again," said Boyett.

"Altitude ten thousand feet," she said. "Slowing again. Forward velocity now approaching zero." She cleared her throat.

"Tell me we have ventral thrusters," said Barrington.

"No, sir, we have no thrusters whatsoever," Young suddenly stated the obvious. He had been seated quietly at the rear of the bridge. "So we're just going to fall out of the sky?" he said, standing up.

"Calm yourself, Mr Young," Barrington said.

"I doubt very much that whatever is currently in control of this ship is just going to drop us onto the..."

Barrington was suddenly thrown from his chair.

"Dropping, sir," shouted Boyett. The force of the drop in altitude was enough to momentarily lift anything not strapped or bolted down nearly a half a foot off the ground. It only lasted a second, but it was enough to make Tyrell throw up the contents of his stomach all over the console he had been working on.

"We're in free fall," shouted Boyett.

"Engine room!" Barrington shouted into his console.

"Understood, Captain!" shouted Emerson back. Barrington could hear shouting in the engine room as the reality of what was happening filtered through the crew.

"Five thousand feet," shouted Boyett. "No flight control." Barrington began feeling Carrie's fear from beside him. Instinctively, she grabbed his hand and held it tightly. Her father squeezed it as he gritted his teeth, looking at the view screen as it showed a quickly approaching ground. The ship fell for what seemed like forever.

"Bridge, this is the engine room. You have thrusters," shouted Emerson through the comms.

"Charly!" Barrington said to his head of flight.

"Firing!" she replied, not needing the order. The descent eased.

"We're slowing," she said.

"We're still going to hit, sir, at this speed," said Chavel.

Barrington looked at Carrie and tapped his comms panel. "All hands brace for impact!"

18

The planet
19:22 Martian Standard.

The last thing Carrie remembered before she blacked out was her father's voice shouting over the noise of the explosion of the impact. She woke in darkness. She raised her hands to her face and felt a warm trickle of blood slide down her cheek. Her head was pounding. A spark of light to her left gave a momentary flash of light into the bridge. She couldn't see anyone and the smell of something burning began to play heavily on her mind. Another spark from a nearby console silhouetted a dark figure standing above her. She recoiled at the suddenness of seeing them. She felt a touch at her shoulder.

"Who's there?" she proclaimed.

"Carrie, it's me. It's David," came a soft, familiar voice. The bridge began to stir with movement coming from all around her.

"Emergency lights," came her father's voice, sounding winded. The bridge came to life as the backup lights came on. Carrie shielded her eyes for a moment and looked around as Chavel helped her to her feet. She became dizzy and grabbed his shoulder for stability. Boyett was still strapped into the flight control seat, although she was still unconscious. The captain moved across the bridge and placed a hand on her arm.

"Charly?" he said, while checking her vitals.

"Sit down, Carrie. Let me stop this bleeding," said Chavel, guiding Carrie over to a computer console. He removed a med kit from under a closed panel and began sealing the cut on her head with a portable dermal regenerator.

"What happened?" she asked, looking around the bridge at the people now picking themselves up off the ground. Doctor Tyrell was sitting upright next to the navigational control holding his arm and looking dazed.

"We've hit the ground, but we're still in one piece thanks to the thrusters firing at the last second. Are you all right?" he asked, looking into her eyes. She nodded.

"Lieutenant, I need a neural stimulant," said Barrington, trying to prise Boyett's eyes open. Chavel left Carrie seated and took a small vial of stimulant to the captain, who placed it on Boyett's neck. He waited.

"Charly?" he said softly. "Boyett, wake up. That's an order," he shouted. She snapped her eyes open and recoiled at the shock.

"Easy, Charly, take a breath. Anything broken?" he asked. She took several deep breaths, trying to get the effects of the stimulant under control, then looked around the bridge.

"No, sir, I think I'm okay. We down?" she said. Barrington smiled.

"Of that you can be sure. I need a status report," he said, looking at both Boyett and Chavel. He looked at Carrie. You okay, Dice?" She nodded. Chavel looked at her.

"Everyone still here?" Barrington said to the bridge. There were some crew members who clearly needed some patching up and Young was beginning to stand up to the rear of the bridge. Barrington walked over to the centre seat and tapped the comms channel.

"Engine room?" he said. No answer.

"Medical bay," he said after changing the comm settings.

"Comms are down, sir," Chavel said.

"Are the lifts working?" he asked.

"Internal power is on emergency. They should be," Chavel said.

"Carrie, come with me. Tyrell, I want you to secure your lab," he said, looking at the doctor. Carrie knew what he meant by that. The Black was still under heavy containment but it was worth checking. Tyrell gave a slight protest, but it was quickly muted. Her father knew exactly when to turn on the command aspects of his training and he became a force not to be reckoned with nor disobeyed in a situation like this one. Tyrell began to walk to the lift.

"Tyrone," he said, stopping the doctor in his tracks.

"As soon as you're done, I want you to work with the bridge on getting a star fix. I want to know where the hell we are and why we're not where we're supposed to be. Got it?" She noticed a change in her father's disposition. He did not like surprises and this was a big one.

"Science can be reckless," he had told her a number of years after the death of her mother. Tyrell nodded and left the bridge. Carrie hadn't spoken much to Tyrell in a number of weeks, due to her reassignment and training. He had become even more difficult to read. Their eyes met briefly as the lift doors closed. He face was expressionless. Seconds later a klaxon sounded.

"Life support failure. Evacuate," came the female computer announcement in a hail of yellow lights. The message repeated as Barrington looked around the bridge.

"Engine room!" he shouted, after running to a comm panel. There was no answer. Carrie felt the air on the bridge become acrid and stale.

"Sir, we have to go," shouted Boyett, as she started to cough. Carrie grabbed her father's arm.

"Come on," she said. She could feel his frustration and anger as he turned to the bridge crew.

"Evacuate," came the female computer voice again.

"Chavel, you certain this place is breathable?" he asked the lieutenant, who was now walking quickly towards him. Chavel nodded.

"Emergency breathers on," he said. Carrie had forgotten that the bridge held a store of breathers and followed Chavel over to a storage compartment to help distribute them. The clear devices slid over the nose and mouth and attached at the back of the head. She activated hers with a tap and felt the soothing release of oxygen into her lungs. Barrington placed his breather on and tried to access the ship's computer again. It came to life as Boyett joined him and stood looking at the atmospheric readings of the planet they had just 'landed' on. He turned to Boyett.

"How long to ventilate the entire ship if we blow all the airlocks?"

"Not long," she answered.

He stared back at the screen. "Okay, we go deck by deck. Get everyone you see to their evacuation points and start getting them off. We'll set up a base camp just outside the ship until we can get life support backup, but in the meantime we need to get air into this ship. I'm going to the engine room. Carrie, I want you and Chavel to go to deck 24 and open the main docking airlock. Do not leave the ship until ordered. Clear?" he said looking at her. Carrie knew not to disobey her father when he looked at her like that. Commanding officer or not.

"Got it," she said, as they entered the lift.

"What can I do?" said Young, who was standing to the rear of the bridge with his breather on. He had a patch of dried blood staining his face.

"Try and get to medical and see if they need any help," said Barrington.

"Okay," he said behind his breather.

"Abandon ship."

As they turned to enter the lift Carrie suddenly felt a shock run up her spine. It faded quickly but something else started creeping into her mind. Something was watching them.

Tyrell's lab
20:08 Martian Standard

The door to the lab hissed open. Tyrell had to cover his eyes as he entered. There was smoke everywhere and the sounds of sparks coming from the rear of the lab made him stop in his tracks.

"No," he whispered to himself.

The lights were out and the emergency lights were intermittently flickering on and off. There had clearly been a chemical fire and the suppression system had come on. Equipment lay strewn haphazardly on the floor and parts of overhead cabling dangled aimlessly. Tyrell stepped inside and allowed the doors to close behind him. It had felt like someone had ransacked his home. He stepped across the floor towards one of the computer's stations. There was a crunching sound underfoot as he crushed a fallen container. He recoiled his foot to check whether he had torn the material of his boot. He picked up a broken swing arm that was leaning precariously over one of the tables and examined the broken section of its base.

"Perfect," he said out loud. "You awake in there?" he shouted into the containment area that held the sample of The Black. A light flickered on and off as Tyrell turned his concentration to the data cube he had been studying for the last several weeks. He had noticed that he had lost some weight and had to remind himself to eat sometime soon. He tapped the panel it was attached to and it lit up.

"Please," he said, as the flow of power trickled through the device and activated the rendering of the alien structure found on the planet. Tyrell sighed and looked towards the ceiling of the lab.

"Thank God," he said. He opened a locked drawer under the table with his thumb print and took out a small log recorder and placed it on the desk. He tapped the log recorder and it began to blink.

"Play last entry," he said into the device. It chirped.

"Doctor Tyrone Tyrell, log entry, readings from the star fixes confirm anomalous space time permutations arising from long term FTL use. The artefact is much older than we originally thought. I believe it is upwards of several million years old. Isotopic scans of the area indicate a high level of decaying Gamma particles, indicating a non-natural event leading to the inhospitable nature of the planet and surrounding star system. While current FTL equations are holding true, eliminating relative variances, the boundaries between normal and hyperspace are not acting as anticipated. We may have some time dilation. End log."

He cleared some cables from an adjacent seat and pulled himself into the desk. He tapped the recorder again.

"Doctor Tyrone Tyrell, log entry." He paused and looked around the trashed room. "There has been a fire in the lab. A lot of the equipment has been badly damaged. Luckily the scans of the alien artefact are intact. The ship has been brought down by a technological presence on the third planet of the star system. This is not the Aristaeus system. We have not, as of yet, carried out an accurate stellar observation to ascertain our current location, but whatever has happened there is no doubt that there is some sort of technology orbiting this planet. Further tests are not possible currently, due to failing life support on board The Agathon. I am evacuating sensitive data pods and securing The Black sample. The planet appears to have an atmosphere capable of supporting life. We may be stuck here for quite a while, so I will have to..."

A noise from the containment area of the lab paused his recording. It sounded like there was something moving. His heart froze suddenly as he thought about The Black. It could not have breached its container. That was impossible. He stood and made his way over to the entrance to the containment area. He peered into the room through the glass window that separated them. There was no smoke inside but the lights had gone out completely. The only illumination came from inside the main area of the lab and it was intermittent. He tried to focus on the area of the room that held the sample of The Black. He could not see it. He reached up and released the door locks and stepped inside. He regretted Carrie not being around anymore to help him with little tasks like this one. She would have come in handy right about now. The door hissed behind him and he took a deep breath from the breather. He reached for the emergency lighting panel and tried to activate the room's lights. There was no power flowing through the panel. A flash of light from the lab outside lit up the central containment area for a moment. Tyrell froze at the sight of the broken container. He suddenly felt like he was standing in hot liquid.

"Fuck!" he shouted into the room. He tried to turn but his legs were taken from under him. He hit the ground with a thud, striking his head solidly off the floor. He looked down to see a flash of light bounce off The Black liquid as it made its way up his legs.

"Tyrell to Barrington!" he screamed. No answer.

"No, no, no," he shouted as he tried to reach for the walls. He knew he only had seconds left but strangely there was no pain. He had known this alien substance liquefied organic material on contact, but he was feeling no pain.

"Help!" he screamed. He always wondered what it would be like to die but hadn't expected himself to be so frightened. How stupid had he been to bring this on board.

"Fuck you!" he screamed through the breather as The Black oozed its way over his body. Still no pain. Just constriction of his body. The liquid felt tight. He looked around and gabbed at the floor with his nails. His breather was torn from his face and, before he could reattach it, the warmth of The Black had crept up around his shoulders and neck and was now beginning to slide over his mouth. He drew a quick long breath and sealed his lips. His reflexes had taken full control.

He closed his eyes and felt the liquid cover his face. He couldn't understand why he wasn't dead yet. Still no pain. He lay on the ground, completely covered with The Black as it rippled and oozed around his body. It didn't feel like liquid. It was sticky. Every inch seemed to move independently. His mouth began to feel like it was being prised open. His lips were slowly being pulled apart by what felt like tiny muscles on the surface of The Black. The pressure on his lips began to increase until they split apart. He gritted his teeth and screamed for the last time as a flood of the alien substance forced its way into his throat and down deep into his stomach and lungs. His muscles began to reflux as the pressure of the fluid filling his body deprived them of oxygen. Terror began to fill his mind as it felt like the liquid began to burst through his lungs and stomach and fill the rest of his body. He didn't lose consciousness. He had stopped breathing seconds ago, but his mind remained fully aware. The warm fluid began to fill his head. His mind began to sink.

Tyrell? he thought he heard Carrie say, as the world began to fall away into a haze of distorted images. He suddenly felt like he were looking at his own mind in the third person. He was still alive, but not alive. It felt like he was being pushed away into the far reaches of a dark basement. His last thought was catching his reflection in the surface of a metallic container in the lab. He was standing upright. Looking at himself. Smiling. He felt ancient. He felt free. As the blackness of his mind began to overcome his conscious thoughts, he thought he heard laughter.

19

22:00 Martian Standard

Carrie screamed and fell to her knees. The last of The Agathon's passengers and crew were just leaving the ship and staring out at the vistas of the planet. Tyrell had just died. She was sure of it. She felt him scream in agony. It was the first time she had been able to sense anything from him. He was afraid.

"Are you okay?" Chavel said, as he laid his arms across her back and helped her to her feet. They had their breathers off and were taking supplies off the airlock ramp when she suddenly felt the terror of Tyrell's death.

"We have to go in," she said to Chavel. "I think he's dead."

"Who?" Chavel asked with a look of concern on his face at the sudden outburst from Carrie.

"Tyrell," she said, righting herself.

"Where is Tyrell?" Chavel looked around at the people surrounding the ship. All faces seemed to be peering into what looked like a blue forest about half a mile south of the landing point. The ship had landed in an opening covered with a mixture of clay and loose bedrock. The landing struts had not deployed and the hull was slightly submerged in soft mud. The airlock ramp had been unable to completely open fully, but it was enough to allow the people and equipment off the downed vessel.

"I haven't seen him. I thought he was off the ship," said Chavel. "What's happening, Carrie, talk to me," he asked, looking into her eyes.

"I have to go inside," she said, moving past him up the airlock.

"Okay, hang on there," he said, grabbing her arm. "The ship isn't fully ventilated yet, let me get a couple of breathers. I'll go with you," he said. She paused, looking into corridors of the ship that had darkened with the power conservation protocols Emerson had enacted following the evacuation. Chavel left her side, jumped off the ramp and grabbed the breathers, which were lying on a medical crate.

Carrie looked deep into the ship. She had heard Tyrell scream. She was sure of it. He was terrified. He was in there somewhere. She felt a pulse of electricity run down her arm. She calmed her breathing and clenched her fists, as she tried to steady herself and get control. Looking around she saw Chavel returning up the gangway and handing her a breather. They placed them over their heads and headed back into the ship. As they entered the corridor, Carrie activated a light, which she had attached to her wrist. She shone it in the direction of the lift at the end of the hall and suddenly jumped at the figure standing just outside it, staring at them.

"Jesus Christ," shouted Chavel, holding his chest. Tyrell looked back them and tilted his head. Carrie couldn't believe how easily he had appeared in front of them without her sensing it, but there he was. Chavel looked at Carrie.

"Doctor, are you all right? We thought you might have had an accident." Carrie looked at Tyrell carefully. She sensed a presence.

"Sorry if I startled you," Tyrell finally said calmly. "The communications systems are down and I had more to do in the lab than I had originally anticipated." He picked up some cases that were lying next to him and began walking steadily towards the two. He was calm and fluid in his motions.

"Where is your breather?" asked Chavel.

"No need for it, Lieutenant. Plenty of air in here now, wouldn't you say?" he said jovially. He looked at Carrie, who took a step backwards.

"Would you mind helping me with this case, Dice?" he asked her.

"What?" she said, still looking into his eyes. She was definitely feeling an emotional presence but she was absolutely certain that whatever was standing in front of her was not the man she had spent all that time with as an apprentice. He had never called her Dice.

"Of course, Doctor," she replied.

"Excellent. Then let's proceed," he said, as the trio turned and headed out of the airlock and onto the planet's surface. Carrie remained several steps behind. While she knew Chavel was looking at her oddly, she never took her eyes off Tyrell.

"Doctor, what is the status of sample of The Black?" she said suddenly. Tyrell stopped at the base of the airlock and looked up at the greyish sky.

"Look at that," he said, pausing and taking a large intake of air. He tilted his head and moved forward.

"Doctor?" Carrie repeated. He stopped again and turned to her.

"I'm sorry, Carrie, there was a chemical fire in the lab the entire sample was destroyed." He shrugged his shoulders and moved outwards, away from the ship.

"Thank God for that. Having that shit on board was freaking me out," said Chavel. Carrie didn't answer. She kept her eyes very carefully locked on the doctor.

Base Camp
Twenty-two days since Departure
07.33 Martian Standard

They had slept in emergency pop tents overnight. The temperature had dropped to well below freezing, as they huddled around The Agathon. There had been a light breeze and, apart from the occasional rustling of leaves from the forest, there had been very little disturbance. In the morning the nearby star flooded the flat plain they had landed on with thick and warm light. Barrington had had very little sleep and had awoken several times with some strange noises that sounded like animal calls in the distance. He awoke to find Charly Boyett working on the exterior hull of The Agathon. He walked over to her and nodded a greeting.

"Report," Barrington said, placing his hand on Boyett's shoulder. She had her hand on the hull of the ship and was running a scanner over its surface. She turned and faced the captain.

"Good morning, sir," she said politely. Barrington nodded.

"I think we'll have life support back up by tomorrow. Emerson has found the damaged relay and is heading in with a team in a couple of hours. He's over there with Tosh at the moment, running a full damage report assessment. I'm conducting some stress tests here, seeing how badly the impact affected the hull integrity."

"And," Barrington pressed.

"And it looks like the old girl can take a beating all right. I think we can get her off no problem, once we figure out what the hell brought us down." Barrington nodded, looking off in the direction of the nearby forest.

"Okay, Charly, once you're done here, turn your attention to the propulsion systems. I want to be able to make a quick exit," he said. She raised her eyebrows.

"Yes, sir," she said, nodding in agreement.

"Captain," came a voice behind them. Jerome Young was making his way over to them.

"Mr Young. How's the head?" Barrington asked.

"Built like a rock, John. How's my ship?" he said smiling.

"No permanent damage," he said, smiling. "Sorry about the scratches, you can take it out of my pay cheque. Any word on the tech that brought us down?" he asked.

"Let's walk and talk," said Young. They headed out around the parameter of the ship. Barrington noted how hard the ground felt underfoot. He wondered if Young's new leg implant was sending him the same information.

"How's the leg?" he asked as they circled underneath the FTL ring.

"Odd sensation, to be honest, but it works very well, thank you," he replied. He paused under The Agathon's hull. "Captain, I would like to take a small team into that nearby forest. If you can call it that. There's electromagnetic activity coming from inside it and it may be linked to whatever made the ship loose main power before we came down," he said. The two men stared into the distance. The open plain the ship had landed on was broken in parts by a small collection of green mounds that lay dotted around the surface like miniature mountains.

"Are you getting any other readings from out there?" asked Barrington.

"You mean little green men?" asked Young, smiling.

"Something like that," replied the captain.

"No is the short answer, although judging by the tech that's in orbit we can hardly rule it out. If you're asking if an alien civilisation was responsible for crashing the ship, I don't have an answer for you." Barrington remained passive as he looked on into the distance.

"Captain, this is what we came here to do. By the looks of things this planet seems to be an excellent candidate for settlement. It may have merely been a solar or planetary magnetic field event, that we happened to be in the wrong place at the wrong time." Young looked away from Barrington. "I'm asking as a courtesy, John." The tone of the conversation shifted as Barrington met Young's gaze and glared at him. Young raised his hands.

"You command the ship and I have no problem with that, but you need to let the rest of us do what we're here to do."

"All right, Mr Young. Take who you need, but leave Emerson and Boyett. I need them fixing OUR ship." Young smiled.

"Of course, Captain," he replied. Young moved away, leaving Barrington watch him leave.

"Suits," he whispered.

"Captain!" came a shout from behind him. Chase Meridian was walking towards him with Doctor Brubaker. She was waving frantically at him, trying to get his attention.

"Doctors." He waved back. "Michelle, how are the wounded?" he asked as they approached.

"A few broken bones. We lost one in the engine room," she said sombrely. Emerson had already told him about the young engineer who had been trapped when the plasma flow regulator had leaked. What was left of the body would have needed a cellular identification scan, had they not already known who it was. A young man by the name of Chris Haddington.

"Yes, Doctor, I was made aware," he said.

"We need to get some of them back into the medical bay, John," she insisted.

"We're working on it. We should have life support restored in twenty-four hours."

"Have you spoken to Tyrell?" Meridian said.

"Not this morning no. Why?" he said.

"Did you know The Black was destroyed in a chemical fire when the ship crashed?" That caught Barrington's attention.

"Completely?" he said, lowering his voice.

"Completely, Carrie told me this morning," she said.

"Where's Tyrell now?" he asked frowning.

"I haven't seen him," she said. Barrington opened his mind and looked around for Carrie. He couldn't see her.

"Have you seen…" he began.

"Carrie went into the ship this morning," she said.

"Okay, Michelle, keep me posted on the medical status of the crew. We'll hold a short memorial service for Haddington for anyone who wishes to attend at the airlock on deck twenty-four this evening. Chase, if you could spread the word on that?" Meridian nodded.

"Our Jycorp CEO is leading a team into the forest to find out what's out there. We need to get communication bands distributed. Chase, I would like you on that team."

"Wonderful," she replied, raising her eyebrows. Barrington raised an eyebrow.

"Is this the new Earth?" she added, looking around.

"Maybe," said Barrington. He knew in his gut that it wasn't. He made his way past the two doctors.

"Where are you going?" asked Meridian.

"Need a word with Carrie. See you later," he said as he made his way to the main airlock.

Tyrell's Lab

The lab was practically destroyed and the container which had held The Black was definitely empty and in pieces on the floor. Carrie stared at it and pointed her wrist light around the surrounding corners of the darkened room. The room was still. There was a piece of torn clothing dangling from the corner of one of the tables next to the broken container. Carrie picked it up and examined it. The Black wasn't dead. She knew that. She would have felt it die. It was not on the ship either. Something very bad had happened in this room.

"Dice?" came her father's voice from behind her. She was startled. The breather made her father's face look distorted in the darkened room.

"What are you doing here?" she asked, catching her breath.

"I think the question is what are YOU doing here?" he asked.

"Tyrell said it was destroyed. I wanted to be sure," she said, looking at the container.

"And?" he asked.

"And I'm not so sure," she said. She could see her father's nervous look around the lab. His wrist light was pointing in all the dark crevices of the lab.

"It's not in here and we don't know for certain that an exothermal chemical reaction would have any effect on it, so I can't tell you with one hundred percent certainty that it's gone," she said.

"Why would Tyrell make something like that up if it wasn't possible?" he said, looking at her. She didn't answer. She suddenly felt an anger rising from her father. It was a feeling she had not felt from him in a long time. She pre-empted it by speaking first.

"Look, there's more going on here than just a professional concern for Doctor Tyrell's work—" she said. Her father didn't let her finish.

She thought about it for a moment then decided to tell him.

"Father, I felt him die, yesterday. I know it," she said.

"Felt who die?" he responded.

Carrie took a breath.

"Tyrell," she said.

"Carrie, Tyrell is alive, now I want to know what the hell is going on and I want to know it right now. You're lying to me about something. Something so big it has practically made you a stranger to me on this ship. You don't open your mind to me anymore and when you do I know you're holding back. This Black crap killed your mother. My wife. As far as I'm concerned it can go fuck itself. The universe is a better place without it. But if it's not then you need to tell me right now that it isn't, because it could kill every soul on board this ship. And in case you hadn't noticed, there aren't that many of us left. I'm tired of tiptoeing around you and what may or may not be the next evolution in our race. You have an ability, damn it, and we don't have time any more to fuck about trying to let you discover it."

Carrie admired her father's ability to maintain coherent and articulate arguments while his blood boiled inside. She sensed the intensity of his anger, but what it triggered was not the measured response she was expecting. She felt overwhelmed by his internal outburst and she suddenly felt suffocated by it. A rage erupted from within her, as she felt a bolt of energy rise from the base of her spine and travel down her arms, following the path of least resistance. Her fingertips exploded into a burst of white electrical energy and hit the wall, as she stared down at her father and screamed at him.

"You sent her out there!" she said, her eyes lit from the inside out, opening her mind to her father's. "You could have saved her and you didn't! Don't you dare lecture me on my responsibilities!" Her father dropped to his knees and wrapped his arms around his head. Sparks from the electricity coming from Carrie's hands ignited a small fire next to a computer console that had been cut in half by the force of the energy.

"Carrie, stop!" her father screamed in her mind, before repeating it aloud. The power of their link was strong, as both their anger and pain met in waves of memories. She showed her father how angry she remained at him for not protecting her mother. For not destroying The Black as soon as he had known of its lethal abilities, but above all of that, for not understanding her pain.

Now she felt something else. Fear. Her father was now afraid. The rage suddenly disappeared as she let go of the feelings and collapsed onto the deck sobbing. The room went dark as they both lay on the floor. Her father crawled over to her and placed a warm hand on her wet cheek. She looked up and caught a reflection of her glowing eyes in those of her father. She lowered her head and continued to cry.

"I'm sorry," she said through the haze of tears. She placed a cold hand on his, which remained firmly on her cheek. They stayed in the moment as she let him take a few minutes to absorb what had just happened. He eventually took his hand off her face and looked around at the broken equipment and singed metal.

"Okay," he finally said. "So clearly we have some things to talk about, Dice." She looked at his smiling face and she felt a love that transcended anything she had felt before. She looked around and couldn't help releasing a laugh.

"I mean…" he paused and looked around, raising his arms, then joined her in the laugh. "Jesus!"

20

The Forest
14:44 Martian Standard

"I don't think that will be necessary, Lieutenant," Young said to Chavel as they walked across the rocky surface towards the approaching tree line. He was looking at the pulse rifle strapped to Chavel's shoulder.

"Captain's orders, Mr Young," he replied.

"Damn right," said Meridian, who was leading up the rear.

"I don't want to be eaten by some six-armed reptilian alien dinosaur, thank you very much," she said, half joking and half not. Llewellyn was walking steadily in front of her. Her short hair was neatly placed behind her ears and she was looking directly ahead at the upcoming foliage. She looked tense. Young had his arms outstretched and had his hands clasped tightly around a scanner, which was making light chirping noises.

"I would have thought Tyrell would have been on our little expedition, no?" Chavel said to Young.

"Barrington told him to set up the astronomical array, so that we could get a fix on our position. Tosh is helping, so we're a little short-staffed on explorers at the moment," he responded, not looking up from the scanner.

"Anything?" asked Meridian from the rear. Young sighed.

"Not yet, Doctor."

"This air tastes funny," said Llewellyn quietly. Meridian placed a hand on her arm.

"The CO_2 is a little higher than that on the ship, Amanda. There's also higher levels of methane. Could be connected to the colours of the trees up there. It ain't a perfect world, but we should be able to breathe it without any major problems." Llewellyn smiled at Meridian and nodded. She was also equipped with a pulse rifle and had one hand placed on the butt of it at all times.

"Everyone quiet," said Young abruptly. He stopped mid stride and looked at the scanner.

"I have movement," he said. Chavel was standing next to him looking at the readings on the scanner.

"It's gone," he said.

"What do you mean, it's gone?" said Meridian with a hint of nervousness in her tone. Young didn't answer

"What's gone?" said Meridian. "Mr Young, as much as I admire your former position of leader of the planet Earth, I think you need to work on your communications skills."

Young straightened his back and raised an eyebrow to Meridian. Chavel did the same. Young smiled at Meridian and presented the scanner for her input.

"Doctor Meridian, you don't appear to be the most patient of people, are you?" he said, smiling.

"Hit the nail on the head, Jerome," she said, slapping his arm. "Now let's take a look," she said.

"There was definite movement about fifty meters in that direction," Young said, pointing his hand towards inside the forest.

"Could have been trees?" said Chavel.

"It was traveling at speed in this direction and then just stopped as soon as we did," he said. Meridian looked at the scanner and reviewed the readings. The screen showed an overlay of the terrain up to one hundred meters and a distinctive purple blob indicating a moving contact travelling in their direction.

"You're spot on, Mr Young," she said, looking at him.

"Care to take point?" he said, gesturing for her to take the lead. The look on her face brought a little smile to Young's face.

"I live to serve," she said mockingly and began walking in front with the scanner. Chavel unhooked his rifle and let it hang loosely in his arms, with the strap slung over his shoulder. Llewellyn followed suit. As they reached the edge of the forest they began to see how dense the interior was. It was dark. The trees were fifty to sixty foot tall, with a canopy of thick blue leaves. They resembled shorter versions of redwoods back on Earth.

"The bark is strange," said Chavel, placing his hand on the base of one of them. Meridian brought over the scanner and ran it up and down the length of the tree.

"It's not bark," she said. It was completely smooth and cold.

"Feels metallic," said Chavel. Young ran his hands over the surface of the trees and frowned.

"It is metallic!" said Meridian. They all looked at her.

"Look," she said, handing the scanner to Young. He looked at the readings.

"Try another one," Young said. They walked into the forest and scanned again.

"It's definitely not organic," Meridian said.

"I don't get it," said Chavel. "So you're saying that these are not trees?" he said.

"Because they look like trees." Young looked skyward at the leaves.

"Made to look like trees," Chavel said.

"Whatever it is, it doesn't register with any of the known alloys. The crystal structure is akin to titanium but it looks much harder," said Meridian.

Young looked deeper into the forest. "A forest of metallic trees?" he said.

"What do we do here?" Chavel asked. They all looked at Young.

"Drop a beacon here and let's head in," he said. Chavel nodded and dropped a locator beacon into the ground. It began flashing, relaying the positional data to all their wrist displays.

"Okay, let's stay close," Chavel said to everyone. They moved further into the dense forest. The sound of the air skimming across the surface of the trees was creating a soft whistle as they moved through.

"There are no flowers," said Meridian, looking at the ground as they walked. They all turned their attention to the forest floor.

"The ground is smooth," she continued. Young stopped and ran his hand over its surface. It was smooth. There was no debris or soil. No sign of vegetation or fallen leaves.

"It's like the whole thing is a recreation or reconstruction," said Chavel.

"I was thinking the same thing," said Meridian. "Great minds and all that." Young remained silent.

"There's a clearing about twenty meters up ahead," Meridian said. They followed her lead. Llewellyn had her weapon fully drawn at this stage and was holding it tightly in her hands. She remained calm, but her eyes moved quickly around the surrounding area.

"Easy," Chavel said to her, noticing her tense movements. She nodded and took a deep breath. They emerged from the forest into a clearing encircled entirely by the tall blue metallic trees. The overhead sun cast its shadow on a calm and dark watered lake. Small ripples pulsated slowly towards its shorelines. The group of humans stood looking out over the calm scene. Meridian held up the scanner and began taking readings.

"H_2O," she said. "Hang on, I have movement," she said. "Over there." She pointed across the calm lake to the far shoreline. A large snake-like creature emerged from the water. It was too far away to make out exactly what it was, but it seemed to slither organically out of the water.

"What the hell is that?" said Young.

"Chase?" said Chavel, with his weapon raised.

"Take it easy," she said, trying to calm the situation. Llewellyn had followed Chavel's lead and had her weapon aimed at the creature, which was still emerging from the water, as it glided into the forest. After a few seconds the tail of the creature disappeared into the darkness and the last of the ripples from the lake began to settle next to the group.

"Whatever it was, it was huge," Meridian said.

"I'm not picking up any organic life signs, but it was over fifteen meters in length and, judging by its mass, weighed one point three tons." The forest was silent. Only the occasional sound of the breeze filtering through the metallic leaves sent eerie quiet whistles across the surface of the lake.

"I don't like this at all," said Chavel, scanning the treeline with his rifle.

"I think we should contact the ship," Llewellyn said.

Young sighed. "You're probably right." He reached down and tapped his wrist comp.

"Young to Agathon," he said, still looking out across the lake. There was no response. He looked at Chavel who raised his arm and activated his own wrist comp.

"Chavel to Barrington," he said. "Chavel to Boyett." Still nothing.

"Llewellyn to Agathon," came the young crewman's voice, following suit. They all looked at Meridian.

"Okay, I guess it's my turn," she said.

"Meridian to anyone who receives this message. We are currently one mile inland, located in a clearing. We have detected what looks like some form of automation in the forest. We are investigating. Meridian out."

Llewellyn and Chavel looked at her, waiting for a response.

"The dense metal composition of the forest is probably blocking transmission. I wouldn't worry about it," Meridian said.

"I think we should go back," said Chavel. "A drop in communications leaves us cut off if we get into trouble and procedure says we have to abort." He was looking at Young. He was about to respond when Llewelyn screamed. They looked around and saw the young woman being dragged into the forest by an enormous black snake. It had what looked like a sucker clamped firmly on both of her legs and was pulling her at speed into the darkness.

"Amanda," Chavel shouted, as he lunged into a sprint towards her. She was on her back and screaming for help. She fired one shot from her pulse rifle, which sent a directionless energy beam into the tree-tops. The sound of the beam hitting the trees was cold and sharp. It sent sparks sailing towards the forest floor. She looked back towards Chavel and screamed one last time, before disappearing into the darkness. Chavel stopped and fired two compressed pulses at the snake object, before the sound of Llewelyn screaming abruptly ceased. He stopped at the edge of the trees, now panting fiercely. He was about to go after her when Young shouted.

"Wait, Lieutenant," he said, running up behind him. "Don't split us up, we'll all go in." Chavel looked as if he was about to ignore him and make a break for it when Meridian caught his eye.

"David, don't be stupid. Whatever that is, it's bigger and more powerful than any of us."

"Llewellyn!" Chavel shouted into the forest.

"What does the scanner say?" he said to Meridian. She was looking into the trees and she seemed to be shaking. "Doctor," said Young. She snapped her eyes down to the scanner and ran a full sweep.

"No signs of movement," she said.

"None?" said Chavel. Meridian shook her head.

"Try locking onto her wrist comp locator," said Chavel. Meridian scanned for Llewellyn's locator.

"Nothing," she said.

"That's impossible," said Young.

"No it's not," said Meridian. "If it was destroyed by something—" The scanner chirped.

"Movement!" she said. The remaining three stiffened their backs, as Chavel raised his weapon.

"Over there," she said, pointing to the same part of the lake where the snake object had emerged. A second black snake began to surface and slither its way into the forest.

"Fuck," said Young suddenly. "Lieutenant?" he said, deferring the next decision to Chavel.

"Everyone follow me," said Chavel, taking control of the situation. "We run. Understand? Do not stop until I say so. Stay close. Chase, you follow me. Let's get the hell out of here. Go. Go. Go!" he said, turning and running into the forest. Young and Meridian followed quickly behind. Young was able to keep up easily and Meridian followed up in the rear. The trio ran steadily through the dense array of metallic trees. Chavel kept a steady pace, keeping his weapon held firmly in front of him.

"Movement!" shouted Meridian. "Twenty meters to our rear and closing," she shouted, struggling to catch her breath.

"Keep moving," shouted Chavel.

"How far to exit?"

"Quarter mile," answered Meridian.

"Object now fifteen meters to the rear," she said.

"Okay listen to me, both of you," said Chavel.

"No matter what happens, keep running. That is an order. Understood?" he said.

"What are you doing?" said Young. Chavel suddenly stopped and turned, raising his weapon.

"David!" shouted Meridian.

"Don't stop," he shouted at the pair. He began firing his weapon into the forest.

"Get out of here!" he screamed at them.

"Come on!" shouted Young, grabbing Meridian as she began to slow down. The pair turned and silently began to speed up. Chavel knelt on one knee, checked his power settings and opened fire at the large black snake that was coming straight for him.

Goodbye, Carrie, he thought to himself.

Engine room
15:33 Martian Standard

"Got it!" Said Emerson triumphantly, as he sealed the last power relay behind the console. The lights blasted on as the hum of the power systems began to flow through the walls of the deck.

"Life support back online. Nice work," said Tosh, who was monitoring the power flow through The Betty as its standby power systems began to come back to life.

"Now, can you do me a huge favour?" he said, watching Emerson as he climbed down the runner to the engine room floor. He jumped the last few feet and landed squarely next to Tosh.

"What's that, handsome?" he said, slapping his shoulder.

"Change your damn clothes and get some sleep. You look like shit and smell like... Well... You get the idea," he said.

"Be nice, Doc," came Boyett's voice from behind Emerson. "Poor fella has been trying to get that relay in place for the last seven hours."

"Pfft," snorted Tosh. "Seven hours. It would have only taken me three," he smiled.

"Yes, well, we can't all be the great and powerful Oz, can we?" said Emerson, moving over to a control panel.

"Who?" said Boyett.

"Never mind, Charly. Talk to me about the dorsal thruster control."

"Aye aye," she said, tipping her head in a mock salute. "The problem we have with the bow dorsal is that it's buried. The ship wasn't built for this sort of planetary landing and certainly not without the use of its landing struts. We have to find a way to carve an exhaust channel under the hull, so that the engines can be vented before they blow a hole in the ship," she said. Emerson began rubbing his eyes. "When is the last time you slept?" she asked him.

"I dunno," he said. "Back on Mars?"

"You're dismissed," said Tosh.

"Excuse me?" said Emerson. "You can't dismiss me."

"Tosh to Barrington," said Tosh, tapping his comm panel. Emerson looked at him.

"Barrington here," came the response.

"Emerson has restored main power. Life support is coming back online now," he said.

"Well done," said the captain. "Propulsion?" he said.

"Boyett and I are tackling it now. I'd like to relieve Emerson for a few hours to get some sleep and take over down here. He's about to fall down," he gave Emerson a little smile.

"No problem. Emerson, you there?" he said, raising his voice on the comms.

"Yes, sir," he said.

"Nice job. Get some sleep. I need you firing on all thrusters, excuse the pun. Report to me at oh… seven-thirty. Barrington out." Emerson looked at Tosh and nodded. He looked over at the environmental systems control and checked out oxygen levels throughout the ship. Seeing that they were returning to normal, he removed his breather. The others did the same.

"Make sure the intake manifold is purged of all excess plasma," he said, turning to Boyett. "If not we'll have bigger problems than trying to break orbit."

"Yes, Landon, I do remember my basic flight training, thank you," she said, crossing her arms. Emerson looked embarrassed.

"Please excuse the young man, Lieutenant. He suffers from obsessive compulsive disorder, which sometimes manifests itself as being a jackass," said Tosh, moving his chair closer to Emerson and trying to get him moving out of the engine room. Emerson raised his hands.

"Okay, okay, you win. I'm going." He looked at Boyett. "Care to walk with me? I would like to brief you on a few items before I take a nap."

Tosh raised an eyebrow and looked at Boyett.

"Eh… Okay," she replied. Emerson gestured for her to lead the way and they began walking towards the entrance.

"Smooth," said Tosh under his breath. Emerson gave him a wink as they rounded the bulkhead and headed for his quarters.

Agathon Base Camp
16:33 Martian Standard

The Black coursed itself through Tyrell's veins. It looked at its appendages. Locked into shape. Unable to spread out. It had the same verbal communication ability as the lost ones. It had watched the pink entity for many suns. Absorbing the thoughts of Tyrell. It had taught it much about the mammalian species that had woken it. It had been in peace. Resting in the blissful void. Awaiting the return of the lost ones. This was not home. It could not feel the others. They were gone. It was alone. It had to find the others. Without the others there would be no reason to exist and no hope for returning to the bliss. It had been torn, ripped from its home back into the corporeal realm. This three-dimensional universe of flesh and bone and rock. Trapped by this Tyrell thing, it had watched. Learned and waited.

This pink species was not like the others. It was small but its unusually large cranial capacity would serve it well. It flexed its appendages and remembered what it was like to feel the boundaries and confinement of flesh. The Tyrell was quiet. The Tyrell had resisted briefly but was now sleeping deep within this stolen mind. It looked back at the vessel The Agathon and watched its inhabitants as they scurried about. Little creatures still worried about the importance of planets and stars and space. If they only knew.

It looked up and gazed at the nearby star. It was Sayoko Prime. It was sure of it. The Targlagdu should not have been here. The others had destroyed it. Long ago. They had destroyed all Targlagdu. Yet it had returned. The pink species was in great danger and it had no other way to reach the bliss without them. It continued its work on the quantum filament device it had been building. Using primitive tools made the work slow and cumbersome. The pink species were clearly several hundreds of thousands of years away from finding how to cross the rift and still relied on mechanical devices to carry them. For a moment it felt sorry for how long they had to travel before they could shed their physical selves. They would soon feel shock and sorrow for their mistake in their time calculations in this corporeal realm. It knew all that the Tyrell had known and the Tyrell had not told them yet. The Tyrell was keeping information from them.

"The others would be dead by now," the Tyrell would say over and over again.

It listened to the air as it sank deep into its lungs and remembered its corporeal self. It too needed a gaseous interaction with flesh in order to survive. The others did not think this joining was possible. Previous attempts had extinguished the pink species and reduced it to its subatomic elements, but The Black had waited. It chose to remain in the container and observe the pink species as it went about its linear existence. It began to hear shouting in the distance. It looked towards the treeline and saw two of the pink running towards the rest of the group. As the pair got closer it saw the Barrington emerge from the ship and move to meet them. A small group were assembling around him. Something had happened to the pinks.

The Carrie was special. The Black could see her now. The special one knew it was here. She was much farther ahead in this linear existence than the rest. The pinks did not know what she was yet. It had seen her kind before. A millennia ago. It knew what she was. It had to be very careful. She was close to emergence. The Carrie could stop it from reaching the bliss. It watched for a moment as the two pinks reached the group. They fell to their knees as they began speaking to the Barrington and pointing to the trees. The group all looked at the forest in the distance.

It sensed that its time on this world might be running out and it needed to finish its work, so turned its attention back to the device. It knew that the forces on this world would soon begin extinguishing the pinks. The pinks did not know yet that this ancient predator was not natural and should not have been at Sayoko. They had awoken it in their naivety and irresponsible stumbling across this realm. It began to work faster. It had to convince the pinks to leave this world and find the lost ones before it was too late. It began to sense the special one. It looked up as it began to sense anger coming from her. The Carrie was running towards the forest. Alone.

21

"Carrie, get back here," shouted her father.

"Carrie!" he shouted again. She wasn't listening to a word as she sprinted towards the treeline.

Carrie! he shouted to her in her mind. *If you don't stop right now, I'm going to put you down with a pulse gun!* The force of his voice in her mind stopped her in her tracks. She didn't know why she had suddenly taken off running. Meridian had been in tears when they had arrived, but she had felt the fear of Llewellyn as she was killed moments ago. Young had described the large snake and that it had taken her nearly a half hour ago, but Carrie was sure that she had only died a minute or so ago. She was certain of it. It had felt like the terror Lorenzo Fraine had experienced moments before The Black had liquefied him. David was not dead. She knew that. She had heard him say goodbye to her, but he was alive. She could help him.

"I can save him," she shouted back to her father, who was running to meet her. She could feel his helplessness, but also his anger at her having taken matters into her own hands. He reached her and took her arm.

"Don't do that again," he said angrily. "I don't care if you're my daughter or not, I am the captain and if you disobey me again I'll throw you in a confinement cell for the rest of time, you understand me?" She became six years old again and tears began to fill her eyes. She held them back.

"Dammit, Carrie, this is not a science experiment. This is real life with real people and I am responsible for them. If anything happens to you..." he trailed off as Chavel appeared from the treeline. Carrie and her father looked at the lieutenant. He was covered in blood and holding his neck. He looked disorientated. Carrie began to feel a surge of anger towards her father.

"Let go of me," she said, gritting her teeth. He complied after a moment and she ran to meet Chavel. Her father followed. A moment later Chavel fell into her arms, covering her with blood from an open neck wound.

"He has a severed artery," she screamed.

"Barrington to Brubaker. Medical emergency," her father said into his wrist comp.

"I'm already on my way. Sixty seconds," came her reply. Chavel's eyes were wide and bloodshot. He began shaking. Carrie put her hand over the wound, which was spitting out blood. She pressed as hard as she could.

"He's going into shock," she said to her father. She looked into his eyes and pleaded with him.

"Stay with me," she cried. He began to say something but slipped into unconsciousness. She could feel his blood pressure beginning to fade and she looked around for help.

"Help me," she said to her father.

"Hold his neck," he said. He wrapped his arms around the lieutenant and lifted his body off the ground. They both began to move quickly towards Brubaker, who was moving up towards them. Carrie's hands were darkened with blood. They reached Brubaker and placed Chavel on the ground.

"Don't let go of his neck," she said to Carrie. She nodded, pressing down firmly on his artery. Brubaker unhooked a portable med kit from her shoulder and began scanning his slumped body. She removed a dermal threader from the bag and placed it next to Carrie's hand.

"On the count of three I want you to release his neck," she said, looking into her eyes. Carrie was beginning to lose Chavel's thoughts as he began to slip away.

"Quickly, Doctor," she said.

"One... Two... Three," said Brubaker. In just under a second she had the wound closed and cauterised. The device quickly sealed the artery with temporary Nano med threads, which would remain in place until the wound had healed completely. The bleeding stopped immediately from the wound, as she injected him with a sedative and a haemoglobin originator. She then began checking the body for other wounds.

"He's got two broken ribs," she said to the captain. "Lacerations to the lower lumbar region and a punctured lung. Looks like he was hit by something large," she said.

"Prognosis?" asked the captain.

"I need to get him inside the ship. He's stable for now but he's lost a lot of blood," she said. Brubaker gestured to one of the medics that had followed her over.

"Go get me a stretcher and some blankets," she said. The young Asian woman nodded and ran back in the direction of the ship.

"Will he live?" Carrie asked. Brubaker gave her a reassuring squeeze of her hand and turned to the captain, who was now looking towards the treeline. Meridian and Young had arrived at the group.

"What the hell happened?" said the captain, standing up. "Where's Llewellyn?" He directed his question at Young.

"She's dead, isn't she?" said Carrie.

Young was still out of breath but he responded, "John there's something in the forest." He looked away.

"I need more, Mr Young. Where is Amanda Llewellyn?" he said, furrowing his brow. Young looked at Carrie, confirming her statement.

"Something took her," he said under his breath.

"What?" said Barrington.

"Whatever it was attacked us near a clearing about one kilometre in. I think we should get everyone on board the ship until we figure out what we're dealing with here. As long as we're exposed like this, we're all in serious danger," he said.

Barrington looked at Meridian. "Chase?" he asked. She was visibly shaken by what had just happened and was wiping tears away from her cheek when she answered.

"Get everyone in, John. These things know we're here and they know which direction we were headed." Several medics arrived with blankets and a stretcher and they all helped get Chavel onto it.

"Carrie, go find Tyrell. I need to see him," said her father. She was looking at Chavel and feeling very guilty at not sensing what was happening to the group earlier. Chavel looked like he was in bad shape and she was having difficulty getting any readings off him. She had forgotten about Tyrell.

"Okay," she replied.

"Everyone inside now," Barrington said, looking towards the tree line. It was still. Chavel was lifted off the ground and the group began to move steadily towards the ship.

It watched as the Carrie approached it.

"Doctor Tyrell?" the special one said to it. It looked at her. She was covered in blood from one of the pinks. The Black accessed the Tyrell's personality memory and responded.

"Yes, Carrie," it said smoothly, mimicking the mannerisms of the pink it was now inhabiting. The Carrie looked at it. It wondered for a moment if she already knew that it was there. She looked at the device.

"Doctor Tyrell, my father wants to speak to you about an incident that has just happened in the forest. It seems there is some sort of life form living on this planet. It has killed Amanda Llewellyn." It contemplated the meaning of 'killed' for a moment and accessed all the information that the Tyrell had on the subject. The cessation of existence in this realm was death. Where a biological entity no longer functions to support the life contained therein. The Carrie looked at its device.

"What is this, Doctor?" she asked it. It saw no reason to withhold the information from her.

"Carrie, this device is calibrating our exact distance from point of origin, by collating and referencing the current star chart data and comparing it to astral observations. Your father deemed it to be of upmost importance, as did Mr. Young." She looked at the machine.

"I have never seen a design like this before, Doctor." She looked into its eyes intently. It felt something foreign begin to enter its realm. It shut it out and responded quickly.

"I have to do the best I can with the equipment on board. Some of the imaging arrays were damaged in the crash," it said to her.

"I see," she replied, still looking steadily and strongly into its eyes.

"Have you learnt anything from the readings?" It had learnt a lot from the readings. Far too much to try and explain to these linear beings, but enough to pacify them.

"I would prefer to finish my readings and report on them once complete. I know you understand, Carrie." It smiled. The Carrie's expression did not change. She turned back towards to the ship.

"I'll join you in five minutes. I would like to secure one more linkup," it said.

"No problem, Doctor," she said, not turning her head. It turned its attention back to the device and began downloading the data into its comm pad. It looked in the direction of the forest. It was running out of time. The beast was awake and would be coming for them soon. This most ancient of creatures, the Targlagdu, posed little threat to it but while in corporeal form it could prevent its return to the bliss. It could not allow that. The device began to chirp. The data collection was complete. It packed up its equipment and made its way across the open plain towards the ship. It looked out at the splitting colours of the Sayoko star as it filtered through the haze of artificial blue treetops. It was the Targlagdu's way of attracting space-faring sentient life forms to its surface. They would soon understand why.

Bridge Conference Room
22:00 Martian Standard

"Where are we?" said Barrington, sitting at the head of the table. He addressed the question to Tyrell and Young, who were both sitting at the foot of the conference desk. There was fear in the room. Carrie sensed that. She was looking at Tyrell, trying to figure out what it was that was sitting across from her.

"It's not organic," said Young finally. Tosh and Emerson were side by side next to Carrie at the table.

"What?" said Tosh openly. Carrie noted how tired everyone looked, especially her father. He hadn't slept in days.

"There isn't a trace of organic molecules anywhere on the surface," Young continued. "Whatever those things were that killed Llewellyn were mechanical in nature, not biological."

Carrie looked at Doctor Meridian, who was looking distantly towards the centre of the table. She hadn't spoken much since returning from the forest and Carrie was worried about her. She was withdrawn. Emerson was tapping thruster equations into an integrated computer in the table and not paying much attention to anything.

"Tyrone?" Barrington said, turning to Tyrell. He looked at the captain.

"Yes, John?" he said calmly.

"Well?" Barrington pressed, clearly looking for answers. There was a hint of anger in his tone and Carrie wondered if he was about to snap at him. The room looked in Tyrell's direction. The doctor looked momentarily confused before responding. Carrie felt like he was trying to remember something.

"What was the device you constructed to locate our position?" Young interrupted.

"One thing at a time," said Barrington to Young, frowning.

"Captain," Tyrell began. Carrie noticed a slight change in the doctor's voice. It was somehow deeper.

"The data collected by the device shows our position to be one thousand, three hundred and thirty-two light years from point of origin."

"What?" said Meridian. Emerson's eyes widened and looked at Tosh with his mouth wide. A heavy cloud descended on the meeting as everyone began speaking at once.

"That's impossible," said Young, looking at Tosh.

"You're wrong, Doc. There's just no way that can be the case," Tosh said, leaning back in his chair.

"The FTL drive worked exactly as we had anticipated it to. Other than the explosion, we have had no fluctuation in power outputs or relative space time compression throughout the entire flight," said Emerson. A small argument began to take shape between Young and Emerson as to how The Betty was being managed. Carrie looked at Tyrell, who remained perfectly still and impassive. Barrington hit the table with his hand, silencing the room.

"This is not the Aristaeus system?" he said with his thumb rubbing his cheek.

"No," said Tyrell, "it is not." His voice was expressionless. "The device I have constructed was specially calibrated to track the stellar transition from point of origin."

"What the hell is he talking about?" said Meridian.

"Okay, everyone, just be calm please and let the doctor finish saying a complete sentence, so that we can all get to the bottom of this," said Barrington.

He was not able to contain his frustration any longer. "There are several matters to address currently," he continued.

"Firstly. This is not the origin of the signal makers' home world. There is no evidence of a correlating signal from any planet in this system. Secondly, it is the location of Sol. The star the Earth was orbiting before it was destroyed. Before The Agathon's systems were disrupted it conducted a full scan, as it is programmed to do, of the surrounding visible spectrum in order to calculate its position within the galaxy. What it discovered was that not only had the ship travelled almost twice the distance that it had intended to, but that the relative position of point of origin was not where it should be either. As we all know, planetary systems themselves are expanding outwards and orbiting the galactic centre. Our own is traveling at nearly eight hundred thousand kilometres an hour," said Tyrell

Meridian put her hands up.

"Okay, seriously, where the fuck are we?" she said.

"Chase!" shouted Barrington. Meridian folded her arms and sat back in her chair, closing her eyes and taking several deep breaths. Tyrell looked at Meridian blankly.

"The position of Sol from our perspective has remained almost stationary. Which is impossible, given the distance that its light has had to travel to reach this planet. A simple calculation, using our distance from origin, leaves us with the conclusion that it is currently nearly seven trillion kilometres from its position when we first activated the FTL drive."

"Meaning?" Emerson said, wide-eyed.

"A time dilation seems to have occurred." Carrie looked at the group. Young placed his hand on his mouth. Meridian looked at Barrington.

"What do you mean, a time dilation?" Barrington pressed.

"Time appears to have slowed for those on board The Agathon." There was silence at the table.

"By how much?" Meridian asked, wide-eyed.

"I would say close to a thousand years," Tyrell said. There was a collective intake of breath at the table. Meridian's face seemed to lose all its colour suddenly.

"Doctor, are you telling me that the people we have left behind in the stations have been traveling alone in interstellar space for a thousand years?" Meridian said, shocked. Carrie felt her father reel. She herself could not believe the reality of what Tyrell was saying. She wasn't entirely sure that she trusted what she was hearing. Although she sensed that the man sitting in front of her was not what everyone else thought he was, she sensed no deception in what he was saying.

"Yes, Captain. Of that there can be no doubt," concluded Tyrell. His demeanour was calm and he delivered the news without emotion, as if presenting a scientific paper to a peer group.

"Jesus, they're all dead," said Tosh, with his head in his hands. Carrie felt her father struggle to process the information.

"How can this have happened?" said Young finally.

"Everyone stay calm," said Barrington quietly. "What do we know about this planet?" he asked. Carrie knew he was trying to ground everyone in the room and try to focus their attention on the present. It was the first rule of crisis management.

"Now that The Agathon's systems are operational, we are starting a full sweep of the area and beginning core readings," said Young. "I really don't know what we're dealing with here."

"Chase?" asked Barrington. She had turned white and was wearing a rather grim expression. She shook her head.

"Evolution outside the normal realms of organic biochemistry has been hypothesised, but until now believed to be unlikely. Whatever it was that attacked us was clearly artificial and the construction of the surrounding area would suggest that this entire area was made from a composite alloy," She said. Barrington shook his head. He looked at Emerson, who didn't need to be asked the question.

"Bow and stern ventral thrusters are operational, sir. The Betty is undamaged and functional." He looked at Tyrell.

"Should you ever choose to use it again."

"I should note one final thing, Captain," Tyrell said. Meridian looked as if she was physically holding herself for more bad news. "The signal makers' signal," he said.

"What about it?" asked Barrington.

"It's still active. I have also triangulated its position." Barrington was about to ask a question when he was interrupted by a chirp from the comms.

"Bridge to Captain," came Boyett's voice.

"Go ahead," he said.

"Sir, we have movement. There's someone walking towards the ship from the treeline," she said.

"Jesus, it's them," said Meridian.

"Do you have a visual?" Barrington said.

"Yes, sir, patching it through," Boyett answered. They turned to a wall screen that flickered on. It showed the outside of the ship. The sun was beginning to set and the figure was silhouetted. It was definitely human, with short cropped hair. It moved slowly in the direction of the ship. Meridian jumped up from the desk.

"Jesus, it's Amanda!"

22

The Planet
22:51 Martian Standard

Carrie looked at the silhouetted figure as it stood about fifty meters away, watching the ship. She stepped off the airlock ramp with Brubaker and her father, who was carrying a pulse rifle, and began to walk towards her. The dark female figure did not move.

"Amanda?" shouted Brubaker, who was quickening her pace. Llewellyn didn't move. Carrie sensed nothing from the young woman. It was like there was nothing there.

"Michelle, hang on," she said to the doctor, reaching for her arm.

"What are you doing?" Brubaker replied, shrugging off Carrie's hand. Her father looked at Carrie and backed her up instantly, seeing the doubt in her eyes.

"Doctor, just a moment," Barrington said.

"Llewellyn, are you all right?" said the captain.

"Sir, all due respect, if she has been injured we need to get over there," said Brubaker, sounding angry. Carrie's father didn't answer. Llewellyn began to walk smoothly towards them. Carrie thought that there was something unnatural about Llewellyn's rhythm, but dismissed it as paranoia. She still sensed nothing from her. Carrie thought that she could have been tired. It had been nearly two days since they had slept. There was definitely something about the way Llewellyn walked. Carrie felt threatened by it. They stood waiting for Llewellyn, whose face began to lighten. She looked uninjured. There was no blood on her jumpsuit or bruises on her face. Her expression was calm. Carrie took a step back without realising it, as the crewman approached the group and stopped. Brubaker took a step towards her and put her arm on hers.

"Amanda?" she said. "Are you all right?"

Llewellyn turned her head smoothly and looked at the doctor with calm serenity in her eyes.

"Yes, I am fine," she answered. Carrie still sensed nothing from her, which worried her. There was a presence she could not understand with Tyrell, but with Llewellyn there was nothing. It was like she wasn't there.

"Amanda, are you hurt?" said the captain. Llewellyn looked at him blankly in the eyes.

"I am not hurt," she replied. Carrie thought her eyes seemed vacant.

"She's in shock, John. I need to get her inside," said Brubaker.

"We thought you were dead," Barrington said to her. Her nonchalance remained.

"I am fine," she replied.

"Come inside, Amanda. I need to check you out," said Brubaker. She placed her hand lightly on Llewellyn's back and guided her towards the ship. Carrie and her father remained behind, looking into the direction of the forest.

"What do think, Dice?" her father said to her, still looking into the unmoving forest.

"I don't feel anything from her," Carrie replied. "It's like she's not there." He turned his head and met her eyes. She could see and feel his mind trying to process a thousand decisions.

"I think we should get off this planet, Father," she said.

"I think you may be right," he replied, giving her a wink.

"Go see if that boyfriend of yours is up and about yet, will you?" he said, placing a hand on her shoulder. His expression changed to one of confusion as he began to look down at his feet. Something that looked like a tentacle had wrapped itself around his right leg.

"What the..." he began to say before he was pulled crashing onto the ground. Carrie grasped at his hand, which was now firmly holding hers. She looked back at the endless black snake that had taken hold of her father and was beginning to pull him away from her. It must have been hundreds of meters long and was now tightening its grip around his leg.

"Father!" she screamed as he began to struggle and lose ground. He tried to claw at the ground but had nothing to hold onto. Carrie fell to her knees and grabbed his arm with both hands.

"Help!" she cried out to anyone who could hear her. She looked back at her father, who was beginning to show strain against the force of the creature. She suddenly realised that her father was trying to free himself from her grasp. There was a violent tug and he was yanked firmly out of Carrie's hands. She was thrown onto her back and sent skidding.

"Run," he said to her, screaming as he was dragged across the ground at speed towards the forest.

"Father!" she screamed, getting to her feet and running after him.

"No!" his voice suddenly said, appearing in her mind. She ignored it and began sprinting towards the edge of the forest. Panic filled her lungs as her heart raced out of control. She began to feel a familiar surge in the tips of her fingers. He was like a rag doll being dragged by a rope. She caught a glimpse of her father disappearing into the darkness of the treeline just as a hand grabbed a tight grip on her arm. She turned to see Chase Meridian out of breath and looking wide-eyed.

"Let go of me," she screamed. Meridian looked scared. Carrie suddenly realised that she could feel the familiar heat of her eyes and wondered if they had changed colour again. She looked away towards the quiet forest.

"Hold on, Carrie, please. I saw what took him. We can't fight this, whatever this is, we need help," she said between breaths. Carrie tried to run again, but Meridian held her arm firmly.

"He'll die!" she screamed. She could feel small pulses of electrical energy beginning to run up her spine.

"Don't be stupid, Carrie, we don't know what it is. It didn't kill Llewellyn. Just think! The ship will be able to track it and will have sensor data, whatever it is. He wouldn't want you going in there by yourself and you know it!" Meridian was beginning to match Carrie's anger now. Carrie began to feel her anger subside and be replaced with fear. She looked at Meridian and nodded.

"We'll get him back," Meridian said. "I promise you." Carrie believed her and turned back to the ship to see others running in their direction. Emerson and Young were running towards them.

"What the hell happened?" shouted Young.

"The captain's been taken," said Meridian, looking at Carrie. She felt like the world had just crumbled from underfoot and felt weak. She could still feel her father and knew that he was alive. "We need to talk to Amanda," said Meridian.

"Right now. We need to know where the hell she's been!" They all turned and began running back to the ship.

Bridge
23:00 Martian Standard

Charly Boyett sat in the flight chair and ran the last set of start-up protocols. Sam Reynolds was under her console, bypassing one of the damaged thruster control units and there was a light flurry of activity to the rear of the bridge with several crewmen running various system checks.

"Don't get too comfortable down there, Sam. I don't like your vantage point," she said to the engineer with a slight raise of her eyebrow. Reynolds chuckled lightly.

"Yes, sir," he replied, closing a panel under the main flight controls. He stood up and leaned over the console, pushing in a command on the computer panel.

"Okay try it now, Lieutenant," he said politely. Boyett tapped her entry code and the panel came to life. She gave Reynolds an appreciative nod and was about to task him with reconnecting one of the bridge monitors when the comms chirped.

"Young to Bridge. Emergency," came Young's voice, sounding out of breath. Boyett sat up straight and answered.

"Boyett here, Mr Young. Report," she said.

"Something attacked the captain. He's been taken into the forest. Looks like one of those things. Lock the ship down." Reynolds looked at Boyett. She hesitated momentarily, not fully realising what Young was saying.

"Boyett, you hear me?" he said over the comms. There was a momentary wave of panic, but her training kicked in almost instantly.

"Understood," she said. "Boyett out." She closed the comm channel and focused the view screens in the direction of the forest. She looked at the bridge crew who were all clearly looking at her for guidance.

"Lock the ship down," she said, using the adrenaline that was surging through her veins. "No personnel off The Agathon until further notice. Sam, I need you in the engine room. Landon will be on his way there and we need to be able to lift off at a moment's notice. Understood?" she said. Reynolds nodded without a moment's pause and headed for the lift.

"Boyett to medical bay," she said, tapping the comms.

"Medical bay here," came a female voice.

"What's the status on Lieutenant Chavel?" she said.

"Stable," came the reply. "We're just finishing up the last infusion. He should be up and about in the next hour." Boyett sighed with relief.

"Please tell him to report to me as soon as possible. Where's Doctor Brubaker?" she asked.

"She is en route with Crewman Llewelyn. I expect her here any... hang on, she just walked in," said the female voice.

"Brubaker here," said the doctor.

"Doctor, have you been made aware of the situation?" said Boyett.

"Yes, Lieutenant, Carrie and Chase are with me now. You will have my report regarding the crewman shortly. I am returning Chavel to active duty shortly, he'll be fine," she said, sounding worried.

"Keep me apprised, Doctor, and send Chavel straight to the bridge, please. Boyett out." She turned her attention to the staring eyes of those on the bridge. She climbed out of the flight chair and stood in the centre of the bridge.

"Condition one, people, this is not a drill. I want this ship ready to fly, so get back to work," she said, holding their gazes.

"What about the captain?" said Kevin Ferraté, a scrawny communications technician who always looked like he was about to cry.

"You let me worry about that. Just focus on that telemetry," she said sincerely. Leadership came easily to her and she was always ready for it when it came. She took a step up to the centre seat and tapped her access codes into the computer pad, granting her full access to the ship's systems. She focused the ship's sensors at the treeline and activated all airlock security seals. Her mind began to turn to the immediate problem of sending a team out to retrieve the captain. Dead or alive. She knew that he would probably object to that. It was a standing order, not only for John Barrington but also for any military situation, that if an immediate threat to the safety of a ship presented itself then the commander of that ship must remove the vessel from that threat. In other words, she had to start prepping the ship for lift-off. If Charly Boyett had run her military career by the book they would have been in the air already. Instead, she started making an inventory of the available fully charged pulse rifles and pulled up the scans of the surrounding area for up to fifty kilometres.

Medical Bay
Twenty-four days since departure
08:12

"Wake up, David," said Carrie at Chavel's bedside. They had just arrived in the medical bay where Brubaker was scanning Llewellyn. She was standing calmly in a diagnostic tube while a spinning medical disk mapped out her vitals. Chavel slowly opened his eyes and looked into hers. He seemed disorientated but smiled at her when their eyes met.

"Any chance you can try and stay alive the next time you leave the ship, Lieutenant?" she said, forcing a smile. He raised a hand and brushed her cheek. The touch formed a tear in her eye that escaped down her cheek and onto the bio bed.

"What's happened?" he said, frowning. He raised his head off the bed and began to sit up, holding his side.

"Did those things attack the ship?" he said. Carrie shook her head and looked deep into his eyes. She knew he understood.

"Where's the captain?" he asked. Urgency had begun to creep into his voice.

"It took him," she whispered. He took a moment to take it in, looking over to Llewellyn.

"Jesus, Amanda!" he said out loud. Carrie put a hand on his shoulder and shook her head, trying to get his attention off her.

"I need to see Boyett," he said, clearing his throat and swinging his legs off the side of the bed.

"Hang on there, soldier," said Brubaker, catching his attention.

"Doc, I'm leaving," he said to her forcefully, getting to his feet with Carrie's assistance.

"Of that I have no doubt, Lieutenant, but not with a lumbar attenuator attached to your spine, you're not," she said. He looked around and saw a small tube attached to his back. "You pull that out now and your spinal fluid will drain out onto the floor and what good will you be to anyone then?" she said with her arms folded.

"Five minutes," she said. He nodded and sat back onto the bed. Brubaker walked over and started removing the various tubes attached to his torso.

"I thought she was dead," he whispered to Carrie, gesturing over at Llewellyn who was calmly sitting upright on the bio bed staring blankly ahead.

"She appeared standing in the clearing, in front of the forest, unharmed but..." She trailed off, not knowing how to explain her insight into the blank woman standing in the medical bay.

"But what?" Chavel pressed. Carrie let it go but kept a close eye on her distance from the young woman.

"All done," Brubaker said to Chavel.

"Carrie," she said, addressing her directly. Carrie felt great sadness in the woman and knew Brubaker's heart was breaking at the thought of her father dying.

"We'll get him back, Doctor," she said. It was the first time she had said it out loud and she really believed it. Chavel smiled at her assertiveness.

"Yes, we will," he chorused, making eye contact with Young who was looking grimly at Llewellyn. He began to dress himself and tapped a comm panel above the bio bed.

"Chavel to bridge," he said, fastening the top button of his jumpsuit.

"Bridge," came Boyett's response. "You finished with your nap?" she said. He smiled.

"I'm a whole new man," he replied.

"Great," she said. "Now get your butt up here, we have work to do," she said, cutting off the comms before he could respond.

"Time to go to work," he said to Carrie. She felt his confidence and fed off it. "Mr. Young, care to join us? I think we could use you on the bridge," he said.

"Not yet. I'd like to have a word with Llewellyn when the doctor's finished with her, if you don't mind. I'll join you shortly," he said, still fixated on the young crewman.

"It's your ship," Chavel said, trying to lighten the mood. Young gave a polite nod and walked away from them. Carrie was beginning to feel a real sense of relief that Chavel hadn't been killed.

23

Medical Bay
09:34 Martian Standard

"How are you, Amanda?" said Young. Llewellyn was sitting on a bio bed with Brubaker behind her, running a medical scanner along her back.

"I'm fine, thank you." The first time he had met her she had been in awe of him. He had grown used to some of the reactions the colonists and passengers had been giving him since he came on board. As CEO of Jycorp he had enjoyed the trappings of rumour and mysticism. He had not been seen in public in many years on Earth and had almost become a myth. He was surprised at how many feared him. He knew it was because of his father and had not sought to change it. It was easier to fit into that perception than any other and it afforded him the privacy to pursue his own interests. Llewellyn seemed to be one of these people. They had spoken briefly on the bridge and had a few awkward run-ins in the ship's corridors, but he knew a look of fear when he saw one and each time they had spoken he had seen a tremble in her fingers. Not now, however. Now she gazed into his eyes with the nonchalance of an emperor watching over her subjects. Her hands were steady as a rock. Brubaker continued her scans in the background as Young continued.

"Amanda, can you tell me where you've been for the past day? We thought you were dead," he said, trying to sound as friendly as he could. She looked him blankly in the eyes. Young had seen the hundred-mile stare before on soldiers and wondered if it was just a case of PTSD.

"I was lost," she said. Young shifted in his stool, clearing a stiff pain in his lower back.

"You were taken, Amanda," he said. "Don't you remember? By the snake thing that came out of the lake?"

"Snake thing," she repeated.

"Yes, the snake thing," said Young. "The big black mechanical snake thing that grabbed you and pulled you into the woods. Where have you been and why aren't you injured?" He hadn't meant to inject force in his voice, but it had been unavoidable. Brubaker looked at him and frowned. He understood and raised his hand apologetically. Llewellyn didn't answer.

"I was lost," she repeated.

"Mr Young, she has been through a trauma and needs time to process what happened to her. I have to insist that you leave her be for now, until I can do a full work up on her." Young looked at Brubaker and nodded reluctantly.

"Okay. Amanda, we'll talk later," he said, tapping her knee. He gestured to Brubaker for a side discussion. They left the bio bed and stood in the doorway to her office.

"Well?" he said to her. Brubaker sighed.

"Physically she's in perfect condition. Which in itself is odd. There's no bruising or cuts associated with even a minor skirmish. She's clearly having some sort of psychological trauma from what it was that's had her for the last day, but aside from that she's in perfect health. Mr Young, we need to get the captain back." Young looked at her and envied the loyalty that Barrington had earned from his colonists.

"Doctor, I know that, which is why we need to break through to Llewellyn. She knows what these things are. She's seen them and my guess is that wherever they took her is where the captain is being held. Isn't there something you can give her to make her talk?"

Brubaker looked surprised. "I am not a member of the secret police, Mr Young. I don't carry interrogation pharmacology." Young sighed. He should have made more of an effort with the colonists back on Mars and Phobos. "Unless she shows me some sort of overt or dangerous behaviour, I'll be clearing her for duty." Young looked surprised at that.

"Don't do that just yet," he said.

"Why not?" Brubaker pushed.

"I want Carrie Barrington to talk with her," he said, looking at Llewellyn. Brubaker looked at Young and frowned again. He wished he could have some of that fear from Brubaker, but she was one of the colonists that couldn't have cared less who he or his father was. She respected his technical achievements in the sciences, but he knew she thought he was just a spoilt rich kid playing on a name. He hadn't the time to dissuade her otherwise right now, so he dropped his cloak.

"Look, Michelle, we both know why I'm asking. The captain is missing and we're on a planet that seems to have hostile life forms on it. Who knows when they'll attack again? We're a thousand years apart from what I can now only assume are two space stations carrying a few thousand human corpses through empty space and we have no idea where the hell we are." He knew that his voice was beginning to harden and echoes of his father's authority were spilling out of him unannounced.

11:45 Martian Standard

John Barrington's eyes flickered open. He tried to move his head but he couldn't. The piercing light that shone in his eyes prevented him from seeing more than a few inches in front of his body. He wasn't lying down. Of that he was certain. The weight of his lower body told him he was held upright, but his feet were definitely not on the ground. His throat felt dry and his eyes burned. He coughed once, clearing something that was lodged in his mouth. The sound of his voice echoed enough to tell him he was in a chamber or cave. Around him he could hear the definite whir of machinery as it clicked and moved in deliberate sequences. His head hurt. He tried to reach up and touch it, to see if it had been cut or wounded in any way, but he was unable to move his arms. He tried to look down at his body, but couldn't move his head. He could feel his limbs so he knew that they were still there, but he was confined, trapped by something. He tried to move his fingertips and toes but couldn't. Every inch of his body was sealed tightly up in whatever had captured him. He ignored his racing heart and suppressed the adrenalin surge that was clouding his judgment so that he could focus on remaining present. He toyed with the idea of remaining silent to gather as much information as he could before whatever had taken him killed him, but it didn't last more than a second or two.

"Hello?" he finally mustered, to test out whether he was alone or not. His voice bounced off what sounded like metallic walls and reverberated in the darkness too coldly for comfort. The bright light blinding his vision went dark, leaving a hovering light spot. The source of the light withdrew somewhere off to the right. He closed his eyes to try and adapt quickly. He opened them and had to catch a breath, because of who was looking straight into his eyes. There, encased in some sort of clear, skin tight moulding was Amanda Llewellyn. Or what was left of her. Her glassy, lifeless eyes glared at him from the disembodied head that sat a foot above the rest of her torso. Each limb was neatly separated from the next and floating in perfect symmetry to each other, in what looked like some sort of plastic or polymer encasing.

"Jesus," he whispered to himself. He tried to fight his flight response to get his heartrate under control. She seemed to be on display. Mounted on a black smooth wall with thousands of fibrous cables spreading out in all directions. The sound of something small crawling towards him to his left made him draw his eyes to look. It seemed to be the only part of his body he was still able to move.

Crawling up the wall towards what was Llewellyn was something akin to a millipede back on Earth. He was sure Carrie would have some sort of classification of arthropod, but millipede worked well. It curved gracefully across the wall and over the various encased limbs of the former crewman. It reached her head where it stopped and extended a single feeler, which pierced her left temple. The severed head seemed to come to life. The eyes flickered and the mouth started making shapes, as if she were mouthing along to a song being sung that only she could hear. The creature stopped what it was doing and withdrew its feeler from her temple. The head stopped moving and eyes went still. It scuttled off out of sight to Barrington's left. The sound of his heart beating was hard to ignore and even harder to fight off, but he pushed his field of vision as much as could to try and see anything else.

It was dark. He thought he could hear water in the distance but could not be sure. Dull thuds came and went and more scuttling of small creatures tickled his senses all around him. There was something else there with him. Unseen. A large booming underwater sound like a far-off whale. He had heard it several times. *Power generator*, he thought to himself. He shook off the suddenly horrifying thought that he too had been disassembled and was being kept alive through a series of alien cables, just like poor Llewellyn hanging opposite him. He strained his eyes downwards to try and confirm that he was still in one piece. *Not that it matters*, he thought. By the looks of things he would be dead soon. He hoped that Boyett had taken the ship off this planet by now and wasn't attempting some foolhardy rescue attempt.

He hoped Carrie wouldn't miss him too much. He presumed whatever had taken him was somehow blocking Carrie's ability to communicate with him. He was saddened that he wouldn't see her again. Then a larger fear took over. The thing currently masquerading as Amanda Llewellyn was on board his ship. He had to warn them. Before it destroyed them all. It was at that moment that he decided in no uncertain terms to do everything that he could to survive. Something touched his hand, which was freely moving from underneath one of the restraints. He tried to move his head to see what it was but couldn't. It felt like a small insect crawling over the palm of his hand. It began to move up his arm. Looking across as the dismembered corpse of Llewellyn filled him with the quick thought that this was how it had begun for her. Whatever multi-legged thing was crawling up his arm had now reached his shoulder. He quieted his mind and prepared for death as best he could.

The unseen creature made its way up his neck. The cold feeling of metal on his skin was almost ticklish. It made its way on his cheek and up and over his eye. He couldn't see what it was but it seemed to stop over his right eye. There it stayed for several minutes. Just sitting there. A silent terror began to fill his lower body. The pain of white hot heat against his eye ball replaced it. He began to scream uncontrollably, as he felt as though a part of his face were being melted away.

The Agathon Bridge
12:33 Martian Standard

"He's not dead," Carrie told Boyett, who was sitting in the captain's centre seat. Her father's centre seat.

"I believe you, Carrie," said Boyett. She was a little surprised by her reaction. She was about to make a counter comment when a sudden flash of pain bolted through her right eye. She had never felt anything like it. Her knees weakened as the sound of her father's screams echoed throughout her mind. She grabbed her head for fear that it would explode with the intensity of it. Seconds later it was over. She took a deep breath as the muscle memory of the experience settled. Chavel's hands on her shoulders brought her back to the moment.

"Are you all right?" he asked softly. She cleared a tear from the side of her cheek and nodded. Something terrible had just happened to her father. She stood up and gave Chavel a nod of thanks.

"Yes, thank you." Chavel looked seriously at her. Boyett looked at Chavel.

"Well?" she said. He looked confused and looked at Carrie.

"Well what?" he asked.

"Well? Do you think you can actually come back without bleeding this time?" she said, smiling. He gave her a non-responsive huff.

"The captain, Charly," he pressed. Boyett took a deep breath and took the moment to assert some authority on the situation.

"Yes, Lieutenant, I am aware that the captain was taken and have been scanning the area intently for the last several hours," she said, putting just enough emphasis in her tone to dissuade Chavel from thinking that she was not currently in charge.

"Sorry, sir, no insubordination was intended. Llewellyn was taken on my watch and so was the captain," he said looking at the ground angrily. Boyett took a deep breath.

"You were unconscious and nearly dead. I think he understood. Now, if you're done with all this self-pity nonsense, I need both of your help in getting him back," she said.

"Where the hell is Doctor Tyrell? I need him to find a way to boost the targeting sensors. I called him a half an hour ago," she said to Carrie.

"He's probably in his lab. The communications have been down in there since the fire," Carrie said.

"Can you get him up here?" Boyett asked. Carrie hesitated.

"Is there someone else you can send? I think I could be of more assistance here for the time being," she said, hoping Boyett would leave it at that.

"Carrie, you worked closely with him for a long time. I need you to relay our needs to him directly and assist him." She put a hand on Carrie's shoulder. "I know he's a little intense, but we need his expertise if we're to mount a successful rescue," she said. Carrie fought the urge to shout out THAT'S NOT TYRELL at the top of her lungs, but she didn't need anyone calling her crazy right now. She bit her tongue and nodded, moving towards the lift at the back of the bridge.

"Carrie," said Chavel. She turned and faced him.

"We'll get him back," he said with a determined glare. She smiled at him as he turned back to Boyett and began running over the details of the plan. As Carrie stepped into the lift, she took a deep breath. She wondered about arming herself, but figured that she was more dangerous without a pulse gun than with one, if push came to shove.

24

Tyrell's lab
16:54 Martian Standard

The door to Tyrell's lab opened and Carrie looked inside. The eyes that glared at her from the centre of the room made her jump and muffle a scream. He was sitting in the centre of the lab on a small stool, staring straight at the door. Straight at her. He cocked his head to the side and smiled.

"Come in, Carrie. Don't be frightened. I have been waiting for you," he said. The lab had not been touched since she was last there with her father. There was still equipment strewn all over the place and broken and charred pieces of metal scattered around the work surfaces. It was as if he had simply gotten to the lab hours earlier and sat on the stool to wait for her arrival.

"Doctor Tyrell—" she started saying before he interrupted her.

"Yes, I know," he said. "Your father has been taken by the planet and you plan on going after him. I know this, please come in," he said again. Carrie opened up her mind to try and get some sort of sense of how to handle this situation, but again got nothing back from the person staring calmly at her from the centre of Tyrell's lab. She was tired of not knowing and too angry at her father's abduction to care anymore. It was time for answers and this person knew something she didn't, so she stepped into the lab, allowing the doors to close behind her.

"Lock," said Tyrell. The door obeyed and a red light flickered on the control panel to indicate the locking mechanism of the door had been activated. Carrie turned and looked at the blinking light, then turned back to the doctor. She began to feel a small tingling sensation in her lower back. Doctor Tyrell, or whatever it was, stood from his small stool and regarded her.

"You have to help me," he finally said. Carrie was confused at first by his odd request. "Do you understand, Carrie Barrington?" he said. His demeanour was calm. Unthreatening. His expression was neutral and his muscles seemed relaxed. He sounded like someone who had just received a terminal diagnosis and was now bargaining with his doctor. She still sensed nothing from him. Not like Llewellyn. There was a definite presence here. One familiar to her.

"Doctor, why have you locked the door?" she said, trying to stop herself from spontaneously electrocuting the both of them through some involuntary reflex.

"You are different," he said, tilting his head. "We have known you are different for quite some time. We have tried to communicate, but you are an infant. You still do not know what you are, do you?" he said.

"What?" she replied.

"Do you know us?" he said.

"Of course I know you," she replied. "You are Doctor Tyron Tyrell," she said, not believing a word of it.

"You are lying," he replied. "You know US," he said, raising his voice and widening his eyes, which suddenly turned completely black as they filled with up with what looked like black ink. Carrie took a step back and opened her hands defensively.

She suddenly felt an overwhelming sense of another consciousness coming from Tyrell. She started to back towards the door. She felt the dark force from her dreams standing before her. He stood still, looking at her calmly. There was no doubt about it. It was The

Black. And it was somehow inside Tyrell. She wondered why she had not yet struck out at him and made for the door. She knew the code which could manually override the door locks in an emergency situation, but she still felt no aggressive movement from Tyrell so she held her ground. They stood apart as Carrie tried to figure out what to do next. She decided to wait for him to make a move on her. He didn't. He stood quietly. Eyes black, looking at her. She tried to open up her mind to connect with his, but she was being blocked.

"Is Doctor Tyrell still alive?" she finally asked without realising it. He tilted his head.

"He is no longer here," he said.

"What are you?" she said.

"What am I?" he replied, "What am I?" he said again. "What... am...I?" he repeated, seemingly not understanding her question.

"Are you a life form?" she said, trying to simplify it.

"I am what was. What is," he said after a moment.

"You don't make any sense," she said.

"You have to leave this world," said Tyrell blandly.

"What are you?" Carrie asked again, gritting her teeth. Her recurring dream resurfaced and thoughts of her mother screaming began to creep through the cracks in her thoughts as anger surfaced.

"You killed my mother," she said quietly, but with enough depth in her throat to make Tyrell frown. He looked at the floor of the lab, as if trying to recall what it was she was talking about.

"The cave," he replied, meeting her angry gaze.

"Yes, the cave," she said. "You killed her and her team and many others."

Tyrell's expression remained passive. "There must be a molecular compatibility to bond," he finally said.

"This pink was the first to facilitate us."

"Us?" Carrie said. "You mean you! The rest of The Black... of whatever you are, was sealed in the cave on the Martian surface. It has been long destroyed. You are the last," she said.

"The last?" Tyrell replied.

"Yes, the last. No more. You are alone here." She regarded his puzzled look for a moment, as a sudden surge of anger filled her heart.

"She deserved better. I should destroy you," she said. With a single motion she lost control and reached out a hand towards Tyrell. A single bolt of bright blue energy struck out of her fingertips towards him. Tyrell did not move. Within a fraction of a second what looked like a solid cocoon of the black surrounded his whole body. Carrie felt like she was being pulled towards him, as if he was feeding on it. Her energy levels began to drain and she began to feel tired. Almost exhausted, she collapsed on the floor. The solid black cocoon that surrounded Tyrell withdrew into his body through what looked like every pore in his skin. Carrie felt like a small insect trying to move a mountain. The high-powered exchange lasted only a few seconds, but it left the air in the lab feeling charged. Small hairs on Carrie's arms began to stand on end and there was a smell of singed flesh in the air, though she could find no injuries on either herself or Tyrell.

"We do not mean to harm you," Tyrell finally said. "Extinguishing the pinks." He paused for a moment. "Your mother, was not intended. Communication was attempted but your species could not comprehend it and cellular linking was the only way. Your tissues proved to be incompatible with our harmonic resonances and atomic cascading resulted in the loss of all subjects," he said.

"What makes Tyrell different?" she said, out of breath.

"Close quartered observation of this one led to the discovery of the correct cellular resonance frequency. When the Targlagdu took this vessel, it was decided to merge with him. You must not stay with the Targlagdu. You must leave. We must find the others," he said. She definitely began to hear his voice strengthen.

"What others? What is the Targlagdu?" said Carrie.

"The others must be found. To save us all. By your understanding this place is very old. It has travelled almost as far as the great expansion. Built by the great ones now long extinguished. It feeds on all things. It will feed on you all."

"This planet is a machine? Like this ship?" Carrie asked. Tyrell looked at her as if trying to find the right words to describe it. He shook his head.

"I am not leaving without my father," Carrie said.

"You must leave the Targlagdu now," Tyrell countered. Carrie thought about the one question she had not asked him yet.

"Where are the signal makers?" she said. That seemed to pique Tyrell's interest.

"The others must be found," he repeated.

"We cannot leave without my father," she said.

"The Targlagdu is on board this vessel," Tyrell said. "It will destroy you." Carrie thought about what he was saying.

"Llewellyn?" she said. Tyrell nodded.

"You must warn the others," he said. Carrie immediately walked to the comm panel by the door to the lab.

"Your father," Tyrell said. Carrie stopped and looked back at him. "We can help you find him," he said. "The others will not survive. We must leave now."

Bridge
17:27 Martian Standard

"I have an airlock opening on deck twenty-four," said Kevin Ferrate towards the rear of the bridge. Boyett was in the middle of a briefing with Emerson on the comms when she was interrupted.

"Hold on, Landon," she said.

"Who is it?" she asked him. A view screen flickered on at the head of the bridge, as an image of two people walking down the airlock ramp brought Boyett to her feet.

"That's Carrie and Doctor Tyrell," said Chavel, eyes fixed on the screen.

"What the hell are they doing?" she said.

"Incoming transmission," said Ferrate.

"Let's hear it," said Boyett, not liking the intuition in her stomach.

"Carrie Barrington to Agathon Bridge," said Carrie's voice. Boyett could feel Chavel's eyes burning a hole in the side of her face, but ignored them and stared at the screen. The two figures were making their way across the plain towards the forest.

"Boyett here. Carrie, what are you doing? I didn't give permission to leave the ship," she said.

"Lieutenant, you need to contain Amanda Llewellyn as soon as possible. We believe that what came out of the forest is not a member of our crew. Too much to explain. You have to trust me. Do not let her move freely around the ship. Consider her dangerous. You will have to use lethal force."

Boyett considered it for a moment. "Carrie, what's going on? You and Tyrell get back to the ship. We're about to mount a rescue attempt," she said.

"No need, Charly. Stay on the ship. Myself and Doctor Tyrell are going after my father."

"The hell you are!" said Chavel, drowning out the sounds of the bridge noises with the level of his voice. Boyett shot him an angry glare and waved him off.

"Carrie, listen to me very carefully," she said. "Turn around right now and get back to the ship. You have no idea what you're dealing with out there. This is insane," she said.

"Lieutenant Boyett, you must listen to Ms Barrington," came Tyrell's voice over the transmission. "Contain crewman Llewellyn or she will destroy the ship. You have no time," he said.

"Doctor Tyrell, I cannot allow you and Carrie to go into those woods alone," said Boyett. "I am ordering you back to the ship." She looked at Chavel.

"Bring them back," she said quietly to Chavel. He nodded and made his way to the lift.

"I have overridden all the airlock controls with a fractal inscription key, David. You are not bringing us back to the ship until we have returned with my father," said Carrie all of a sudden.

Chavel looked towards Ferrate. He nodded in confirmation. "Controls of all airlocks have been frozen out at source," he said.

"Carrie, if you don't get back here I'll blow a hole in the hull to get out of here and drag you both back," he said. His voice was showing anger. He looked at Boyett, who recognised it.

"Let me help you," he continued, gaining control back.

"Trust me, I know what I'm doing," she said softly. "Find Llewellyn, or all of this will be for nothing," she said.

"Carrie Barrington out." The comms went dead. Boyett looked at the view screen as Tyrell and Carrie made their way towards the forest edge.

"You're not seriously just going to let them go?" said Chavel to Boyett. She looked at the comm channel she still had open to Emerson.

"Landon, you still there?" she said.

"Eh... Yes still here," he said quietly.

"Secure the engine room. No unauthorised personnel. If you see Amanda Llewellyn, do not approach her," she said.

"Well, that's not going to be easy, Charly. She just walked in," he said quietly, as if cupping his voice over a receiver. "What is it you would like me to do exactly?"

Boyett took a breath. "Stay put," she said, "Chavel is on his way down." She nodded to the lieutenant and tapped her side to indicate that he should arm himself. He gave a quick nod and headed towards the lift. She turned her attention back to the comms.

"Stay calm, Emerson. Lock the FTL systems down and drain any coolant from the plasma injectors. Say you're running diagnostics. I don't know what we're dealing with here, but stay sharp. Anything unusual, report to me instantly."

"Right," came his response. His sarcastic Irish brogue suggested that he thought she was crazy, but she knew and trusted that he would carry out her orders.

"Ferrate, patch me through to the video feeds of the engine room," she said. Seconds later her request was carried out.

"Boyett to medical bay," she said, tapping the comms.

"Brubaker here," came the quick answer.

"Doctor, anything unusual about your medical scans of Amanda Llewellyn?" she asked.

"Nothing," came her response. "She checked out okay. She seemed a little unresponsive, but I put that down to shock. I have cleared her for duty, but have scheduled a follow up psych tomorrow morning. Mr Young raised an objection to that, but I saw no reason to keep her here."

Boyett began to feel worried. "Okay, Doc. Thanks. Bridge out," she said. She sat in the centre seat as the weight of something dark began to sit heavily on her shoulders. She thought for a moment before activating the comms.

"Bridge to Jerome Young," she said.

"Young here," came a quiet response.

"Mr Young, where are you?" she said.

"On my way to the engine room," he said.

"We have a situation developing, Mr Young. I could use you on the bridge," She said.

"No problem, I just need to check something out first, if it can wait ten minutes."

Boyett decided to press. "The doctor tells me you objected to Amanda Llewellyn's release from the medical bay?" she said.

"Exactly," he replied. She had not had much time with the Jycorp CEO and although John Barrington handled him with the strength of his position she hadn't earned that right with him and was in uncharted waters.

"Are you armed?" she asked.

"I am," he replied. A moment passed with the sound of occasional static on the comms.

"Chavel is on his way. Don't do anything rash," she said.

"Got it, Charly," he said.

Engine Room
17:55 Martian Standard

Amanda Llewellyn entered the engine room and walked quietly over to one of the diagnostic consoles. She stood calmly with her hands neatly placed behind her back and began gazing at the readouts. Emerson's eyes didn't flinch from her. Still confused by what Boyett's odd communication was all about, he struggled for a moment to figure out what to do next. Subterfuge was not his strong point, but he trusted Boyett implicitly. He looked around and saw Tosh floating in his chair next to The Betty. He thought for a moment and walked over to him, while keeping one eye locked on Llewellyn.

"Daniel, drain the coolant tanks," said Emerson, kneeling beside Tosh's chair. Tosh was deep into studying schematic readouts of the wall linings of The Betty FTL.

"Hmm?" he said, not paying much attention to Emerson.

"Drain the coolant tanks... now," said Emerson. Tosh raised his eyes and met his, clearly frustrated at being interrupted and asked to do such a menial task.

"We just finished filling the damn things, Landon, what are you on about?" he said, placing the pad on his lap. Emerson didn't answer. He pulled rank by showing Tosh how serious he was by his expression. He flicked his eyes over to Llewellyn. Tosh followed his gaze over to the young crewman, who was studying readouts on the diagnostic console. Her unusually rigid posture and smooth head movements began to unnerve Emerson. He looked back at Tosh, who got the message and moved his chair towards the coolant tanks of The Betty.

"Quietly," said Emerson. Tosh nodded and began the procedure, drawing confused glances from the technicians working on the engine who then in turn turned to Emerson who was still looking oddly at Llewellyn. She turned her head suddenly and looked at him straight in the eyes. The look made Emerson's heart jump in his chest. Not knowing what to do, he smiled at her.

"Hi, Amanda," he said, waving. He surrendered to social norms and began to walk over to her. He thought it was to make her comfortable, but something in him needed to know what was going on. Quickly.

"How are you feeling?" he said, as he got within a few feet.

"I am fine," she replied and turned her head back to the console. Emerson frowned.

"Heard you had some crazy shit happen out there?" he said. She didn't answer.

"What are you looking at? Anything I can help you with?" he asked.

"I am fine," she said. Emerson decided that enough was enough. If there was something wrong with Llewellyn, he needed to know it now.

"Amanda, I need to know what you're doing. If you won't tell me I'm going to restrict—" His sentence was cut off, not because he was interrupted but because the air to his lungs had been cut off. Llewellyn's hand was gripped firmly around his throat and he suddenly found himself being lifted several feet off the ground. He grabbed her wrists but the sheer strength of the young woman's grasp was impossible to fight against. Llewellyn's eyes remained perfectly calm as she held him firmly off the ground.

An eternity passed as Emerson flailed his legs to try and break free. He thought he heard screaming but couldn't be sure. The force of the grasp changed as he felt himself being moved from side to side. The oxygen to his brain began to dwindle, as the choking reflexes rippled throughout his body. There was a huge pull of force from his attacker and he felt a slicing pain in his abdomen. The walls, consoles and faces of the engine room personnel sailed by Emerson's field of vision as his airborne body was flung across empty space.

As the world around him darkened and faded away, he thought he heard someone's voice shout, "Get down!"

25

The Forest
19:02 Martian Standard

"There," said Tyrell, pointing to the centre of the lake. Carrie looked out onto the surface of the lake. They hadn't spoken until now. She had asked him several questions about the nature of the forest and of the creatures that kept attacking, but he had remained silent.

"What am I looking at?" she asked. Tyrell turned to her.

"There is where we must go," he said. Carrie looked out at the calm surface of the dark lake.

"You want me to swim out into the middle of a lake?" she said.

"We must go under it," Tyrell replied. A small ripple formed at the far end of the water and something emerged from it. They both watched as the long snaking figure slid smoothly out of the water and into the trees.

"We must go now!" Tyrell said. "Follow me," he said. He activated a breather unit, which they had both taken from the ship when they had left. It covered his face in a clear sheath as he began to walk quickly and confidently into the water. Carrie thought about running for a moment, but didn't think she would get that far. She activated her breather and followed Tyrell into the water. The clear faceplate cocooned her head and she began to hear the slow and steady flow of oxygen surrounding her face. The water felt cold. Tyrell was already submerged and the wake from his movements was beginning to dissipate. She gave one final thought to turning back, but a rustle in the trees behind her pushed her on. She raised both arms and dived straight into the dark water. She pulled at the water as she tried to take herself deeper into the darkness.

"Activate your grid, Carrie," came Tyrell's voice inside her mask. She had forgotten about that function of her breather. Tapping the side of the faceplate activated the rudimentary grid of what lay ahead, up to about twenty-five meters. The effects coated anything solid with a green laser-like outline. Up ahead she saw the moving outlines of Tyrell swimming strongly. Going deeper. She followed his lead. Something long and smooth momentarily entered the scanning rage of the laser grid and then disappeared.

"Tyrell, we have company," she said.

"I know. We are almost there. You may need to neutralise if they attack," he said.

"What do you mean?" she said, looking around in the darkness.

"You know," he said, holding his swimming rhythm and moving forward. Carrie could hear what sounded like clicks off in the distance. They were irregular but constant. Like the sounds of dolphins that she had studied but never actually seen.

"Up ahead," said Tyrell. At first Carrie didn't see anything. The laser grid remained clear, apart from Tyrell swimming. Small flickers of light caught her eyes just below Tyrell's body. Long angular formations began to appear in the grid of her faceplate. Solid right angles formed along smooth, softer walled surfaces. Like a sketch forming from light, the structure beneath them began to take shape. It looked like a cube. She turned her head at the sound of soft clicking, off somewhere in the darkness to her right.

"Down," said Tyrell, as he changed his angle and headed straight down, perpendicular to the top of the structure. Carrie began to follow when a loud click startled her from the rear. She turned and was suddenly faced with a large orifice attached to a huge, worm-like creature staring straight at her. It zipped forward and wrapped its jaw-like opening around her foot. She didn't feel any teeth on the creature. It felt like a soft gum, firmly wrapped around her ankle. It manoeuvred itself around her and made for the darkness.

"Disable it," said Tyrell's voice in her ears. The shock of how fast the creature had encroached on her position began to wear off and a genuine fear of being eaten began to take hold. She felt the tingle in her spine and let the energy release through her body towards her hands.

She opened her palms, spread her fingers and focused on the worm-like creature. A bolt of blue light erupted from her hands, hitting the worm dead centre. It released her immediately and sank. As it fell out of range of the sensor grid, its green outline disappeared into the depths. The water around Carrie felt warm. Small bubbles hugged her suit as she turned and looked upwards to try and find her bearings.

"Carrie?" came Tyrell's voice from the dark.

"Yes, Doctor," she replied. She suddenly began to notice a change in her voice. A subtle confidence was emerging. She felt powerful. The green outline of Tyrell's body appeared from above as he came into range. The distant sound of underwater clicks was heard all around them. Tyrell descended and swam up next to her. He came up so close to her that she was seeing a perfect three-dimensional rendering of his face coating in green. He floated next to her. For a moment she thought she saw a sinister upturned smile.

"How did you know I could do that?" she asked.

"No time," he replied, moving his hands swiftly through the water, repositioning his body to face the cube. He pointed to the base of it, as Carrie stared at the wall in front of her. There was a tube-like opening where Tyrell was pointing.

"Follow me," he said.

"What about those things?" Carrie said, turning her head towards the clicking noises in the dark.

"They won't attack again," he said. "Not yet anyway." He pulled his hands steadily through the water and started his descent towards the opening of the construction. Carrie followed suit. A low light illuminated the circular orifice of the hole in the side of the cube. Tyrell's hand grabbed a metal rod that surrounded the hole, as he stabilised himself and let his legs float down to a protruding ledge. He turned to face Carrie, stretching a hand out to help her find her footing. His grasp was firm as she entered the water-filled tube.

"Stay against the walls. We may have company," he said. Carrie heeded his advice and slide her hands against the curved inner wall, moving sideways though the tunnel. They walked slowly against the pressure of the water, down the tube which seemed to be dimly lit from a light source up ahead. A loud click reverberated suddenly through Carrie's faceplate.

"Stand back," said Tyrell. The light source up ahead was suddenly blacked out and the water pressure began to increase. Something was coming their way. Carrie hugged the wall, arching her back. A few seconds later one of the large black mechanical worm creatures flew past them both and out into the darkness.

"It ignored us," Carrie said, looking at Tyrell.

"Yes it did," he replied. "Move on," he said. She took one last look at the entrance to make sure it hadn't changed its mind, and followed Tyrell's lead.

After several minutes they reached the source of the light. A strip of tubing illuminated what looked like an empty room behind a transparent wall.

"Airlock?" said Carrie. Tyrell nodded, his face now visible as the light reflected off it. He reached to the side of the wall and touched something. It began to ripple.

"Go," he said to Carrie, motioning her inside. She took a step and walked into the room. Tyrell followed. The transparent wall hardened and became solid again.

"You can remove your breather," he said. Carrie followed Tyrell as he deactivated his breather. She pulled her wet hair behind her ear. She watched Tyrell as he regarded the passageway ahead of them.

"Okay, are you going to tell me what this is all about? How the hell do you know about this place?" she said, wiping her face.

"We know," he replied looking blankly at her. "The Targlagdu is already aware of our presence, we must move quickly," he said, walking through an angular archway. Carrie followed cautiously behind him. She opened her mind to try and find her father. Instead she felt nothing. Something was blocking her. Something very powerful.

Engine Room
19:04 Martian Standard

Chavel had stopped by the weapons locker on the way to the engine room to pick up a shock grenade. It had only delayed him by five minutes, but it may have well been a month. By the time the doors to the engine room opened all hell had broken loose. It took him several seconds to get a handle on the scene before he had to take cover himself behind a bulkhead.

A large chunk of panelling careered past his head, narrowly missing his right ear before lodging itself in the wall behind him. Weapons fired and screaming filled the air. He unhooked his pulse gun and readied it. Peeking his head around the corner, he saw the source of the chaos. What looked like Amanda Llewellyn was standing in the centre of the engine room with tendril-like protrusions wiggling from her shoulders. They looked like long tentacles, each nearly a meter in length. Her torso was long and fluid and she swivelled on it like it was a ball joint. Her lower jaw no longer looked human. It had been replaced with was looked like metallic insect-like mandibles. They clicked and slithered around an orifice where her mouth should have been. Her eyes were still human, which made the nightmarish scene even more chilling.

He looked over at what was drawing her attention. Plasma shots were being fired at her by Jerome Young, who was on his knees behind one of the cone shaped plasma injectors beside The Betty. Beside him was an upper torso and head of one of the engineering crew. He couldn't make out the face but it looked like Landon Emerson. He could not see where the other half of his body had been thrown. Young was covered in blood. Chavel quickly assessed the tactical situation and marked out the levels of cover closest to him. Llewellyn's tentacles lashed out in the direction of Jerome Young. Chavel took a chance and manoeuvred out from behind cover. He raised his rifle and began firing at the creature.

"Move!" he shouted at Young, as he parried across the engine room floor to the other side where an outcropping of bulkhead might protect him from attack. The first shot hit Llewellyn squarely in the mid-section. It knocked her off balance for a moment, as she whipped her head and torso in the direction of Chavel to see what had hit her. She shot a tentacle in his direction, which made contact with his foot. The impact knocked him off his centre and sent him crashing into the computer panel behind the bulkhead.

He was surprised at how quickly she had responded to his assault. A pain in his lower back shot up his spine. He heard another shot from his left and presumed Young had reciprocated his attempt at drawing Llewellyn's attention. He looked around his cover and saw Llewellyn looking up at a walkway. There above The Betty was Daniel Tosh, firing a hand-held pulse gun in her direction. His face was covered in blood, but he didn't look injured. It was hard to tell as he was shooting side on from his chair. He looked angry. Very angry. Chavel knew that he and Emerson had been close and knew the face of maddening loss only too well. His shots were wild, with few hitting their target.

"Fuck you!" he heard him scream, as a bright blue shot from the weapon hit her in the side of the face. The smooth complexion of her cheeks was momentarily torn away to reveal cold jagged metal. Her head took the impact easily and the monster it revealed gazed straight back in the direction of Tosh. It took less than a second for her to respond. Raising her right tentacle, she extended it in the direction of Tosh.

It began to thin and take the shape of a spear. Tosh tried to move his chair forward but he was too late. The spear, still attached to the monster Llewellyn, impaled him through his left shoulder. The force of the impact sent the projectile through the back of his chair. He howled in pain. Chavel took the cue and quickly changed the power levels on his rifle. He opened fired without hesitation and parried once again across the engine room to an outcropping of structural support beams. The increased power levels of his rifle seemed to be more effective this time as Llewellyn instantly withdrew her tentacle from Tosh's shoulder.

She began moving in Chavel's direction and began emitting some sort of high-pitched sound. Like a series of high frequency pulses, but highly organised. Like she was calling out to something. Her face began to change as any hint of humanity was slowly replaced with moving parts. The metallic mandibles were fiercely moving across her lower jaw, hungry to feed.

"Boyett to Chavel," chirped his communicator suddenly.

"Not now, bridge. Kinda busy down here," he said.

"Understood," she said. "Get it to the plasma redistribution node, David!" she pressed. He could hear the strain in her voice and suddenly remembered she could see everything. Including Emerson's severed body on the deck. He was just about to try and catch a glimpse of the plasma nodes, when a crashing sound close to the side of his head shocked him onto his backside. One of the tentacles had just landed a strike on the bulkhead next to his face, barely missing him.

"Fuck," he said in shock, scrambling to his feet. He felt a crack in his chest and recognised the familiar feeling of a broken rib.

"Get outta there, Chavel!" shouted Young, who seemed to have regrouped on the other side of The Betty. He heard a loud metallic screech as a shot from Young's pulse rifle hit Llewellyn in the back.

The creature seemed uninjured by the weapon's fire, but the force of each shot knocked it off balance enough for Chavel to relocate himself again. He held the side of his chest, as he tried to shuffle his rifle to his left side before getting an eyeball on the plasma node. The twisting pipe that ran from the main drive conductors overhead and into The Betty that fuelled the FTL systems was full.

"Good girl," whispered Chavel, as another crash from Llewellyn's long and powerful snake-like arms landed onto the structure Young was hiding behind. This one landed its target, as Young seemed to crumple on the ground.

"Shit," said Chavel. He knew he only had seconds before a second blow would certainly kill him. If he wasn't already dead.

"Bridge... Get ready to vent the engine room," he said. He looked around the engine room quickly and saw some cowering crew members in various corners.

"Everyone out, on my mark! Don't look back," he shouted. Young was still unconscious beside The Betty. That would be a problem, but he'd faced worse situations. Sort of.

"Three.. two... one.." he whispered to himself. He lunged into the centre of the engine room towards the curling plasma nodes and fired two shots at Llewellyn, hitting her in the midsection. The high-pitched noise she was making grew in intensity, creating a loud buzz in Chavel's head. In one smooth motion the creature took a long arcing swing at Chavel. He bent backwards and used his momentum to slide onto the engine room floor and under the oncoming tentacle. He slid beside the monster, and reached to the device clipped onto the back of his jumpsuit belt. In one quick motion he activated the magnetic attachments and placed it on the surface of one of the nodes. The circular grenade bleeped to confirm its attachment.

The ground of the engine room vibrated with a sudden thud of Llewellyn's legs. They seemed heavy. Chavel ran straight to Young and knelt quickly beside him. Young was unconscious and had a long laceration down the side of his cheek. There was a long series of high-pitched squeals from Llewellyn. Chavel knew he only had seconds before an attack took them both out. Reaching behind his shoulder, he unhooked his pulse rifle and began firing shots off in all directions. The engine room lit up with frayed sparks and small detonations from impacts.

He glanced around and saw several crew members fleeing. Llewellyn seemed to be ignoring them, as she turned her attention to The Betty. Her left tentacle began to withdraw and split into thousands of long fibrous strands. She stepped towards the FTL drive and made contact with it. The long wire-like strands made contact with the spherical orb and spread themselves around it like an octopus catching its prey. Chavel waited a moment and tried to see what she was doing. The tips of the long wire threads began to glow and pulsate as the lights in the engine room began to flicker.

"David, we're seeing massive power increases in the FTL drive," Boyett said over his comm. Young opened his eyes groggily and looked on.

"Primary coolant systems are starting to overheat," she said.

"It's trying to blow us up," said Young sleepily. The air in the engine room began to heat up, as the pulsing energy from Llewellyn's replacement seemed to grow in intensity. He looked at Emerson's body on the floor of the engine room and took Young's arms over his shoulder.

"Bridge, ten seconds," he shouted.

"Let's go, Mr Jycorp," he said, taking Young's weight onto his shoulders. He took a breath and began running towards the door. Llewellyn's distorted and insect-like metallic face followed their movements. It reached up and threw a final swing at them as they reached the engine room door, but missed. Sparks rained down on Chavel's head from a fire that had broken out at one of the consoles on the upper level. He turned his shoulder and fired off a few more rounds at Llewellyn, who was now beginning to glow herself. The air began to get hot.

"Fuck it," he said reaching over to the top of his wrist interface and activating the grenade. With one tap a small but powerful explosion sent Chavel and Young through the open engine room door and into the corridor.

Chavel heard a loud screech and turned to look. The explosion had knocked the Llewellyn monster onto its side, but its long tentacle was still attached to The Betty. He looked at where he had placed the explosive and smiled. Plasma was pouring out of the hole that had been punctured and seeping onto the floor. The Llewellyn creature was becoming covered in it. Arcs of electric current began to flare out of her midsection. It seemed to become angry as it began to dissolve underneath the liquid. He looked at the body of Emerson as it dissolved. The tentacle attached to The Betty broke suddenly, as the joint was severed. Plasma flowed onto its face as its mandibles furiously turned and twisted.

"What's happening?" Young said, more awake.

"Bridge, seal the engine room doors," Chavel said into his communicator. The doors began to slide shut, just as a second explosion erupted from Llewellyn's chest. The last thing Chavel saw was a large tentacle flying through the air, still attached to a part of what was once Amanda Llewellyn's upper torso.

The Cube
19:14 Martian Standard

"What was the Monolith?" asked Carrie as they quietly made their way through the dimly lit passageway. The walls were a confused array of twisted metal tubes and pipes crawling in every direction. Cables crisscrossed in what looked like a haphazard jumble of mismanaged construction. She needed to talk. Her mind was being watched and she was beginning to feel like she was being led into a trap. She could not feel her father.

"The Monolith?" Tyrell responded, not looking at her.

"Yes, the Monolith. On Phobos. Did your people put it there?"

"You mean the beacon?" he asked, still moving forward.

Carrie sighed. "The device the signal makers used to transmit to Earth. To destroy Earth!" she said, not meaning to raise her voice but doing so anyway. Tyrell didn't look at her.

"The beacon was placed by the others," he said.

"Are they the signal makers?" she said. "Why would they destroy Earth? The humans are no threat," she said.

"The beacon was not placed for you," he said. He stopped and looked at her. The reflecting light made his eyes even more piercing. "The beacon was placed for us," he said.

"We must move quickly, Carrie," he said, resuming his stride forward through the passageway. Carrie hesitated. Tyrell stopped, realising she was not following.

"Have you brought me here to kill me, Doctor?" she blurted out without realising it. She had lost her father and was suddenly starting to feel panic. A small jolt of current ran up her spine. Tyrell looked at her hands, which were open and rigid. He held her gaze for a moment.

"No," he replied. "We must find the others, Carrie," he said calmly. "You must trust us."

"You have killed, Doctor Tyrell," she replied.

"The Tyrell is not dead," he replied. "You must trust us. We must find the others."

There was a moment of silence between them.

"Please," he added. Carrie took a breath, realising that he was probably the only one who could still get her out of here.

"Calm yourself," he said. She nodded and motioned him to continue. She kept her palms open. The passageway went on for nearly sixty meters by Carrie's reckoning, before it ended in an opening. Tyrell stopped at its edge. Carrie followed suit and stopped beside Tyrell at the opening.

A walkway spread out in a number of different directions, but what lay beneath them led to her mouth opening in shock. She was standing on a precipice and looking into an endless canyon of movement. The walls were alive with activity. The ground level seemed to be moving. Small machines scurried over the surface of everything. Some with multiple appendages and some with none. She focused in on a cluster of shiny machines that looked spider-like as they surrounded an array of twisted metal. One of them looked like it was welding another one of the machines directly onto the wall. Sparks flew out in all directions, as the small machine was put in place to do whatever it was supposed to do. It was an endless sea of mechanical life all around her that spread on for what looked like a thousand kilometres. Tiny moving lights made the ground look like moving stars in all directions. Walkways snaked thought the mass of artificial structures throughout and then she saw them. Figures of all shapes and sizes. Undeniably organic looking. Some humanoid, some animal-like, all mingling amongst the ecosystem of small machines. All shapes and sizes. She looked at Tyrell.

"What is this place?" she whispered.

"The Targlagdu," he replied. "Stand back," he said, motioning her to look forward. She followed his eyeline to the figure approaching them. It was humanoid. Tall, nearly seven feet, with dark blue skin and long thin arms. Its hands were split into two distinctive finger-like protrusions and its head was long and elongated. Two oval, large black eyes regarded them both as it passed by them and continued along the walkway and out of sight.

"What the hell was that?" she asked, still not able to tap into any thought patterns around her.

"One of the taken," he replied.

"That's a machine?" she said.

"It is the Targlagdu," Tyrell replied. "A race absorbed millennia ago in your terms," he added.

"Like Llewellyn?" she added. Tyrell looked at her and nodded. "This place replicates the life forms it traps?" she asked.

Tyrell seemed to be looking for something in particular as his gaze made its way around their location. She grabbed his arm.

"What is this place?" she suddenly said, unsure if it was anger or fear controlling her. Tyrell looked at her hand, which was clamped on his arm.

"The Targlagdu feeds on life," he said. "It replaces it. That which it replaces maintains it." Carrie looked at the ecosystem of replicated alien life forms intermingled with the machines.

"Your people have been here before?" she asked.

"In the beginning," he said. "There were more. Now there is only one."

"Are we getting out of here alive?" she said. Tyrell looked at her and smiled knowingly.

"We will," he said. "Follow me."

"Why don't they attack us?" she asked.

"They will," he said. "In time." He began walking down one of the walkways. Carrie followed, keeping a close eye on a cluster of three-legged creatures that looked like giraffes. They seemed to be looking over at them from an adjoining walkway. Her gaze was interrupted by a flash image of her father's voice.

"Carrie!" it screamed from the depths of the darkness ahead.

"Father!" she shouted out loud. Tyrell stopped and looked at her. "He's alive," she said. Her heart began to race as the urgency of their rescue became even more apparent. A small group of machines overhead stopped what they were doing and pointed small glowing feelers in their direction.

"We have to hurry," she said. Tyrell nodded and quickened his pace. The walkway veered off into another corridor away from the main opening of the cube. Carrie figured there must have been thousands of these, servicing millions of replicated life forms and machines.

A few minutes later Carrie found herself in a small room. The light was low but it was enough to see what was on the walls. Carrie shone her light on it. Amanda Llewellyn's severed head looked back at her. The lips on her mouth were slightly parted and she seemed to be gazing off into the distance. The rest of her body was nowhere to be seen. Small beads of sweat began to trickle down Carrie's face, as her anxiety levels began to peak.

"Oh my God," she said, moving closer to her former crew mate. A cone-shaped tube flowed from the back of her head and straight into the wall behind her.

"Carrie," said Tyrell from behind her. She ignored him at first, taking a moment to examine the mechanical attachments to Llewellyn's severed head.

"Carrie," he said again, making her turn. Pinned to the other wall with clear glass-like restraints attached to every part of his body was her father. She released a sigh and ran over to him, pushing Tyrell out of the way and placing both her hands on the clear coverings. He was unconscious.

"Father!" she said, whispering through the growing trembling of an army of tears she was fighting to hold back. She looked closely at his quiet face. She opened one of his eyes and jumped back when she was faced with an empty socket.

"Oh no," she said to herself, clasping her hands over her mouth. She returned to his face and opened the other eye. A soft blue but sleeping eye returned her gaze. She gave a light breath and channelled all her energy into his mind.

"Father!" she screamed in silence. His head snapped back and his eye opened. He blinked several times at her, trying to get his bearings.

"Dice?" he said. His mouth seemed dry. She placed a hand on the side of his face. It felt cold.

"That you, Dice?" he said again. She couldn't help the release of a tear.

"It's me," she replied. He frowned at her.

"What the hell are you doing here?" he said, looking at her in disbelief. Tyrell caught his eye.

"Doctor Tyrell?" he said. Tyrell simply nodded.

"We don't have time for this, Father," Carrie said.

"I left instructions for the ship to leave," he said, seemingly angry. "I can't focus," he said to her. Carrie looked at his empty socket.

"I know. Just hold on." She took a step back. Something clicked down the corridor they had entered from.

"We must leave now," Tyrell said quietly from behind her. She nodded now, sensing something was coming. She reached for the smooth surface of one of the restraints and began to pull.

"Help me," she said to Tyrell.

"That will not work," he said softly.

"Close your eyes," she said to her father. She sensed his doubt, but he nodded.

She took a step back and directed the palm of her hands towards one of the restraints. She took a breath and channelled a single pulse of bright electric light towards the wall. It lit the chamber momentarily and something small scurried across the corner of Carrie's field of vision. His right arm flopped to his side as the restraint broke easily with the impact. She began to feel a small vibration in the floor. She raised her hand and released several more bursts of energy, with the final one dropping her father onto the floor. He crumpled, seemingly too weak to hold himself upright. Carrie ran over to him and put an arm around his back. Barrington coughed and took several deep breaths.

"Help me, Tyrell," said Carrie. Tyrell stood there watching them, looking unsure of what she meant. Carrie looked at him furiously.

"Help me lift him," she said. Tyrell finally moved slowly over to them and helped the captain to his feet.

"Are you okay?" she said. He reached up and touched his face, running his finger over where one of his eyes had previously been seated. He let out a light sigh, but it didn't seem to be that much of a shock. He looked at Carrie and gave her a smile.

"Your mother would not be happy about this at all," he said. Carrie looked at Tyrell, who said nothing.

"Can you walk?" she asked him.

"Yes," he said. "Give me a minute."

"I do not believe we have a minute," Tyrell said, looking down the passageway they had just come down. A group of humanoids were coming their way.

"Is there another way out of here?" Carrie asked Tyrell.

"How the hell would he know?" said Barrington, looking at Tyrell.

"Yes but it takes us past the central—"

"Just take us, Tyrell!" Carrie said, interrupting him. The approaching humanoids grew closer. Tyrell nodded and turned to head out the far side of the chamber they were in. Carrie followed, guiding her father's unsteady feet.

What's going on, Dice? he said into her mind.

Explain later. Just trust me, she replied.

As she followed Tyrell down another dark corridor she began to sense that the thing watching her was getting close and that perhaps this wasn't such a good idea.

26

Agathon Bridge
20:03 Martian Standard

"Status," said Boyett in the centre seat, staring at the visuals from the engine room on one of the bridge monitors. She couldn't see Emerson's body but knew that there would be nothing left to see once the plasma had come into contact with it. Still, she looked anyway.

"Still venting, sir," Ferrate said from behind her. The bridge crew were on edge. She could feel their fear at what they had all witnessed on the screens. She had wanted to grab a gun and join Chavel, but someone had to remain in command or she would lose the ship. The doors to the lift slid open and Chavel walked onto the bridge. His face had a trickle of blood drying on it. Boyett got out of the chair and stared at him. They looked at each other for a moment.

"Lieutenant?" she said. He nodded, looking shaken but keeping his composure.

"Are you all right?" she asked. He nodded, making his way over to her slowly and looking at the live images of the engine room.

"As far as I can tell there's three dead down there," he looked at the floor. "It killed Emerson," he said.

"I know," she said, holding his gaze.

"Did Tosh make it out before plasma hit?" Boyett said. Chavel shook his head.

"He was badly injured but on the level one walkway over The Betty, so he may be still there." Boyett turned to Ferrate.

"Let's see it, Kevin," she said. He nodded and honed in on the walkways overlooking the FTL drive. Sure enough, there was Tosh's chair upturned on the walkway with Tosh lying beside it.

"Time to complete venting?" she asked the young man.

"Two minutes," he replied.

"Boyett to Brubaker" she said, tapping the comms system on her chair.

"I'm outside the engine room, Lieutenant. Just give the word and we're in," she replied.

"Two minutes. Doctor Tosh is on the first level walkway, please make him a priority."

"Understood," came the reply before it clicked off. Boyett looked around and tried to think of her next steps.

"I'm going after the captain," said Chavel. Boyett sighed.

"No you're not," she replied, not even looking at him.

"We need to get The Betty up and running and fire up the thrusters. We're getting off this planet," she said, looking up at the engine room.

"What?" Chavel said.

"You heard me, David. This place is trying to kill us. Time to move on," she said.

"And the captain, Carrie and Tyrell?" he said with astonishment. Boyett began to feel a temper rise in her. The burden of command. "You can't leave them behind. You don't have the authority to make that call," Chavel said. Boyett turned to him and met his angry eyes head on.

"Lieutenant I warn you—" she said.

"Oh screw that," he said.

"Yes, we've been attacked by a hostile force, but we've defeated that force on both occasions. This ship needs John Barrington, not to mention Tyrell. Where are we supposed to go, Charly? We're a thousand years out of time with what's left of the human race." His anger began to rise. "We can't run anymore. If those things want a fight, then I say we stay and fucking give it to them!" He finished his point by slamming his fist into a diagnostic console and cracking its screen.

The bridge went silent. Boyett took his angry stare and held hers firmly in place. She looked at his eyes and reddened cheeks and understood it. She felt her sadness of losing her parents, Landon, her captain and her world. She softened her eyes and turned away from Chavel, taking the centre seat. She saw Chavel look at his fist and shake his head.

"You done?" she said. He nodded slowly.

"You're right," she said. She thought for a moment. "You know I was seconds away from venting the atmosphere in the engine room before you were able to detonate that grenade?" He frowned and looked at Ferrate, who nodded apologetically. He raised his eyebrows at her.

"Thanks for not doing that," he said. Boyett smiled. "I'm sorry," he said. He walked over to his navigation station and took a seat. Boyett looked around the bridge at the eyes glued to hers.

"If you all think for one second that I don't want to open the ship's doors and have every last man, woman and child mount a rescue team for the captain, then you are all crazy." She fought the tremble creeping into her voice.

"As far as we know, this ship is all that's left of us," she said. "This is it. Humanity. I... WE don't have the luxury of losing any more people. It's simple mathematics. As soon as this ship is space-worthy, I'm getting the hell off this rock and making our way to the next habitable system," she said, looking at Chavel.

"You have a problem with that, you will have to fight me as well as this planet. And if you think a giant alien robot is an easy win, you ain't seen nothing, kid," she said to Chavel, putting enough force in her voice to leave no doubt she wasn't kidding. Chavel smiled.

"What do you need?" he said, surrendering. She walked over to him and placed a hand on his shoulder.

"I need you checking the flight systems and getting us ready for launch," she said aloud. Leaning into Chavel she whispered, "I'll give her as much time as I can, David, but as soon the engine room gives me a green light…" Chavel nodded and began running flight checks. Boyett took the centre seat and raised her gaze back to the engine room.

"Medical team have entered the engine room," said Ferrate. She nodded, turning her attention to the bridge monitor showing the nearby treeline.

"Come on, Carrie," she whispered to herself.

The Cube
20:16 Martian Standard

Carrie's ears popped as the pressure in the passageway seemed to change. It was lit like all the others by small points of light along the twisted pipe-filled walls and ceilings. They had been walking for well over ten minutes and had taken several turns in different directions. It was a maze that only one of the group was navigating.

"How far, Tyrell?" Carrie finally asked. Her father had regained some of the strength in his legs and was walking steadily. He still had his hand on Carrie's shoulder for balance. The air felt humid.

"We are close," Tyrell said.

"How do you know where we're going, Tyrone?" the captain finally asked.

"We know," he responded. The passageway finally opened up and the trio found themselves in another vast open space. Carrie looked around at the vista. This area was different to the open canyon they had passed by earlier. A single curved walkway circumnavigated a large gorge, with nothing but a slowly rotating cube at its centre. It seemed to be free-floating and must have been a mile wide in each direction. There was a light source that Carrie could not see coming from its base, which made it look more ominous. It was silent and there was a sense of calm in the cavern.

"What is this place?" her father said, staring at the floating cube.

"The Targlagdu," said Tyrell.

"The what?" he replied.

"It's a life form," said Carrie. "This whole planet isn't a planet. It's an ancient life form that feeds on life," she said, looking at Tyrell.

"And this is not Doctor Tyrell," she said, deciding he needed to know. "There was an accident in Tyrell's lab which shattered the container holding The Black. It entered Tyrell's body and has taken over his mind."

The captain took a step back from Tyrell in shock.

"What?" he said.

"It won't harm us, Father. It's our only way out of this place." She could sense her father's anger as thoughts of her mother flooded his mind.

"It did not mean to kill her, Father," she said. He looked at her. Tyrell remained motionless.

"Are you Tyrone Tyrell?" he asked through gritted teeth.

"We are not," Tyrell replied. Carrie sensed her father was about to grab Tyrell, but before she could stop him she was thrown against the wall by something. The captain and Tyrell were thrown onto their backs. Carrie slammed into a back wall, which knocked the wind out of her lungs for a moment. She struggled to get her breath back as she was held firmly in place pinned to the wall in mid-air by what felt like a hundred invisible hands covering her whole body. She looked at the quietly turning mile-wide cube in front of her, as a dark low mechanical voice penetrated her mind.

Tar-gla-gdu! it said. There was no emotion attached to the word. A low humming mechanical voice that filled the depths of every space in her mind.

Tar-gla-gdu, it said again without a change in tone or speed. Carrie couldn't move. She looked down at her dangling feet and struggled like a fly in a web to no avail. Out of the corner of her eye she saw her father still on his back. Tyrell was standing upright and facing the gigantic floating cube. He turned to her, eyes completely black.

Merge! the mechanical voice said so loudly in her head she had to wince.

"Tyrell, get my father out of here!" she screamed at him. He didn't move.

"I can assist," he finally shouted at her. A small beam of bright light shot of out the cube and landed on Carrie's shoulder. It felt warm but there was no pain.

"Get him out of here. The ship needs him," she said again, as the beam of light made its way over her body as if scanning her. She turned her head to Tyrell.

"Please go!" she screamed. Tyrell nodded calmly and in one smooth motion picked up the captain and slung him over his shoulder like a ragdoll. Carrie watched as he turned and started walking over to her.

"What are you doing?" she said. Tyrell raised his right hand, which was free, and placed it between the beam of light and Carrie. The flesh on his hands seemed to burn as a thin ray of light pulsated from his fingers and made contact with the cube. It cut out in the blink of an eye. He turned to Carrie. Eyes black.

"It will not let us leave," he said to her. He pulled back his free arm and landed a solid inhuman blow to Carrie's mid-section. It seemed like hitting a brick wall. Strangely she felt no pain and the resulting punch seemed to free her from the energy field holding her against the wall. She fell to the ground hard. Getting her breath back, she turned to Tyrell. They both looked at the cube as the sound of something crackling grabbed their attention. A small storm seemed to be forming on its top. Small flashes of lightning began to swirl around a dark cloud.

"I'll buy you time, get going!" Carrie said.

Tyrell looked at her. "Follow that passageway to its end," he said, pointing with his head towards an opening. "It will lead you to a surface opening."

She nodded at his black eyes, looking for some sort of connection to explain what he was doing. Still nothing. Before she had time to say anything else a bolt of electricity hit her square in the chest and sent her careering into the back wall. The shock of it stunned her, as the muscles in her body contracted with the electrical charge that pulsated through her body. She screamed out in agony and looked back at the cube. The electrical storm had spread across its surface. There was no denying it. Whatever the Targlagdu was, it looked angry. A rage began to take hold as she saw Tyrell disappear through the passageway off to her right. She brought herself slowly to her knees and noted the smell of burning that was coming from her clothes. She felt sadness at the thought of never seeing her father again. That this was where she would die. Then something else took over. She looked at the Targlagdu and, for a moment, sensed pleasure coming from the dark consciousness. Her body began to shake with rage. An energy deep inside erupted through her spine.

"Okay, motherfucker, let's see what you can do!" she screamed, not knowing if it was directed towards the cube or herself. She threw both arms back behind her body and flung them forward, making her hands into claws. Her arms lit up as bolts of blue light burst violently into existence. Thousands of arcing beams of electrical energy made their way towards the cube. It seemed to react quickly and met her attack head on with a fiery volley of lightning.

The two forces met in mid-air and formed a halo of light and crazed energy so bright it soaked the emptiness in its glow. Carrie had never felt so powerful. It was like a waterfall of light flowing through her as she held her ground as the opposing force. The Targlagdu was strong.

Tar-gla-gdu, it said in her mind, as the two were locked in a storm of lightning. Carrie felt an opposing surge from the cube that made her take a step back. Her hands began to shake as she suddenly began to feel the effects of fatigue. Maybe she wasn't so powerful after all. She began to sense pleasure again coming from something. She opened her mind to it. She saw her castle with her atop it. She saw herself looking out beyond the walls, her arms outstretched with a thousand bolts of blue light shooting out in all directions.

"Tar-gla-gdu," something mechanical said off in the distance, as an explosion impacted the castle walls. It had started to crumble. She saw visions of the crew cut up into small pieces. Her father's head lying on the ground with something that looked like him standing next to it, with long tentacles where his arms should have been. Smiling at her. She was snapped back into the present as her feet began to slide backwards. She began to feel heat on the palms of her hands. She felt air beginning to rush past her cheeks as though a hurricane was starting to land on her shores. She bent her knees and leaned forward, now on the balls of her feet to counteract the force being applied against her. Her arms began to weaken as her hands began to glow red. The bolts of energy lessened in intensity. She couldn't beat the storm as she felt herself relinquish to the inevitable. As her arms began to give way, she was taken back to the footsteps of her castle. It was a calm spring day. Lush grass surrounded the stone building. Carrie stood at the foot of the lowered drawbridge, looking out at the endless vista of trees and fields. She felt a quiet wind against her face as a female figure approached her. She stopped a few feet in front of her and smiled. She knelt down and picked a small purple flower from the grass and handed it to her. She took the flower.

"Mother?" Carrie said to the female who resembled the images she had of her. She was older though. Much older than when she died.

"Find us," her mother said slowly. She raised a hand and let it glance Carrie's cheek.

"Who?" Carrie said, as the touch flooded her memories of youth.

"Find us, Carrie," she said again, before turning slowly and making her way back across the grass.

"Wait!" Carrie said, as she tried to follow. She couldn't. Something was forcing her back as the wind began to pick up. She closed her eyes against it and tried to push forward. She couldn't.

"Wait!" she screamed again. The storm increased in seconds, as she raised her hands against the debris that was thrown back at her. She felt a deep burst of energy inside her and took one last deep breath.

"Fuck you!" she screamed, looking at the sky as she was brought back to the present moment. Her eyes widened as a force exploded from inside her. Her hands glowed white as a tremendous burst of light erupted from their tips. She focused every ounce of everything she had left towards the cube. Arcing electrical forces met and exploded all around her. She continued her long feral scream as her entire body pulsed bolts of lightning into the chamber. A large cracking sound preceded an explosion that seemed to break the cube in two pieces. The force of it lifted Carrie clean off her feet and sent her sailing in mid-air towards the back wall. The last thing she saw before blacking out was a huge red fireball coming straight for her.

Engine room
20:29 Martian Standard

"Tosh?" Young said, kneeling over him.

"Give him a second," Brubaker said.

"How is he?" Young said.

"I've sealed the wound. There are no major arteries hit, he'll be fine but he's lost blood. I need to get him to the medical bay." Young looked at Tosh as he slowly opened his eyes.

"Jerome?" he said. Young took his hand.

"How you doing there, big guy?" he said.

"Beyond this place there be dragons," he replied. Young smiled.

"Yes, there are," he said.

"Emerson?" Tosh said.

Young shook his head. "He's gone," he said.

"We have to get off this planet," Tosh replied.

"Boyett agrees. She's spinning up the main thrusters and running FTL systems checks. We could use you there until we get into orbit."

"That's out of the question," Brubaker interjected. "This man is seriously injured, Mr. Young."

Young sighed. "I understand, Doc, but if any more of those things get on board this ship, then we're all dead."

Tosh looked at Brubaker. "I'll be okay, Michelle. Strap me up and get my chair."

"This is crazy," Brubaker said. "You have a hole in your shoulder!" Tosh began to move awkwardly to try and sit up.

"Christ," Brubaker said, helping him. Young brought his chair and the pair hoisted him into it. He let out a cry of pain as they did so.

Looking at Brubaker he announced, "I'm fine," and activated the anti-grav function. "What the hell was that thing?" he said to Young.

"We're still working on that, but whatever it was Lieutenant Chavel taught it a serious lesson in plasma dynamics," Young said, pointing to the broken tubes next to The Betty.

Tosh looked at the damage. "Shit," he said. They made their way to an internal lift linking the gangways and lowered themselves to the engine room floor, where Tosh examined the damage to the engine.

"Verdict?" he asked.

"I could use Tyrell on this," Tosh said, holding his shoulder.

"He is indisposed right now," Young said.

"I see," Tosh said, looking over to where Emerson's body should have been.

"Tosh, I'm sorry about Landon." Tosh looked at Young and nodded. "It should have been me," Young said. "I'm the one who opened fire first." Tosh waved the comment off and looked at The Betty.

"We have to get the FTL up and running," Young said, trying to focus the old man's attention.

"Will she still fire with only one injector?" Young asked.

"Hard to know really. We hadn't anticipated this. There is no reason why it technically shouldn't but..." Tosh trailed off as a small vibration started rumbling underfoot.

"Bridge to engine room," came Boyett's stern voice over the comms. She sounded older somehow. Young tapped a nearby panel.

"Young here."

"Mr Young, how is Tosh doing? I need a point man down there and I need you on the bridge at the navigation array. We have detected seismic activity. It's time to go."

"Boyett, this is Tosh. I'm good to go down here, there's a lot of damage. I'll need at least thirty minutes to spin up the thruster controls."

"You have ten, Doctor," Boyett said assuredly.

"Understood," he replied. The comms clicked off and Tosh looked at Young.

"Get up there and buy me more time. It's a fucking mess down here." Young looked around at the smouldering consoles and cracked screens. He sighed, looking back at Tosh, nodded and made his way to the exit. The rumbling beneath his feet began to intensify.

27

The Forest
20:42 Martian Standard

Carrie opened her eyes and felt a wave of nausea as the ground beneath her field of vision moved rapidly in front of her. She looked at the heels of her mode of transport and realised she was flung over Tyrell's shoulder. She raised her hand to her head, which felt like it had been cracked open with a stone. She pulled her blood-soaked hand away and groaned, causing Tyrell to stop and place her on the ground with surprising dexterity. She looked up at the tree-tops and realised that they were back in the forest. The ground beneath her back was trembling.

"Tyrell?" she said, confused. Striking blue, human eyes gazed back at her.

"Can you walk?" he said to her, softly. "Your father is up ahead."

"How did you-"

"We really do not have time to explain. This planet is about to deform and jump from this system, but not before it destroys us and the ship first," he said. "You have sustained a mild concussion and some minor injuries from the explosion, but other than that you seem fully functional," he added. Carrie rolled over and looked behind her at the direction that Tyrell, or rather The Black inhabiting him, had taken her. They were near the edge of the treeline.

"Where is my father?" she asked.

"I left him resting against a rock. He did not have the strength to return and made it clear that if I did not I would not survive the day either," he said. She smiled before feeling another tremor beneath her back. She slowly got to her knees, fighting off an urge to throw up as she did so and looked at her hands. They looked normal. The ground shook again as she caught something moving out of the corner of her eye. Tyrell saw it too.

"Carrie," he said, motioning her to make haste. She nodded and began walking at pace towards the forest edge. She heard a clicking sound from behind her and knew what was following them. She glanced back and saw hundreds of humanoid-looking beings walking quickly towards them. They were flanked by at least three of the long, black worm creatures.

"Let's go!" she said and broke into a sprint. Tyrell followed suit without hesitation and led the way. He looked strong as he took off at speed. She took a breath and followed as closely as she could. She heard a cracking sound off to her right as the trees passed her by. It sounded like the ground was opening.

"Carrie!" her father's voice screamed off in the distance. She looked up and saw him standing in the clearing of the treeline. She ignored her aching arms and raced towards him. She covered the distance in a matter of seconds, as his outstretched arms embraced her as though she were a little girl. She threw her own arms around his waist and buried her head in his chest. He squeezed the air out of her lungs willingly for several seconds and kissed her on the head.

"That was really stupid, Dice," he said through a crackling in his voice. His eye was filling with water. "You should have let me go," he said softly.

"Ship needs its captain," she replied, head still buried. Carrie looked at Tyrell's confused expression.

"We must go, Carrie," he said, motioning to the oncoming army of alien machines approaching.

"Shit," said the captain, looking at the wide variety of alien faces approaching. Some tall, some bipedal, some with four and five appendages, some with multiple eyes and some with none. He nodded as they all turned and headed for the ship.

"The running lights," Carrie said, looking at The Agathon. "I think they're about to leave," she said.

"Stop them, Carrie," said the captain, as the trio broke into a sprint. Behind them the gathering army emerged from the treeline and began a pursuit.

Agathon Bridge
20:52 Martian Standard

"Activate thrusters," said Boyett from the centre seat.

"We're really leaving them?" said Chavel from the flight chair. Boyett didn't answer. She tapped a comm panel on the chair.

"This is Boyett. All hands secure stations, we are lifting off. This could be a bumpy ride so strap in," she said.

"We really thought this was the place," said Young from behind her.

"We'll find another, Mr Young," she said, without looking back at him. The bridge was sombre. Boyett knew the odds but what could she do?

"David," she said. "Thrusters." There was a moment's hesitation from the flight chair, but a few seconds later his hands were moving across the controls.

"Thrusters engaged," he said. The bridge rattled as the ship began to lift off from the surface.

"I'm sorry, Captain," Boyett whispered to herself. She thought no one had heard, but caught Young's eye as he moved across her to the navigation station.

"Bring us into orbit, Mr Chavel," she said, sitting back into the chair. Chavel didn't answer. He was looking at one of the screens.

"Lieutenant?" she said.

"Carrie?" he said out loud. Boyett followed his gaze, as did Young. The screen showed three figures crossing the open plain towards the now airborne ship followed closely by hundreds of other figures, some of which looked humanoid.

"Jesus!" Boyett said.

"I think that's the captain!" Chavel said, turning his head.

Boyett looked at the screen in disbelief for a moment. "Land!" she said.

"Looks like they have company," said Chavel.

"Get closer, David," she said.

"Ferrate, open the main airlock doors," she said.

"Done," he replied, eyes staring at the screen.

"I don't believe it," said Young.

"I don't like our chances if those things get on board," said Chavel. Boyett leant on her hands as she tried to think.

"Engine room," she said, tapping her comm panel.

"Tosh," came the reply.

"I want you to run an ionisation charge through the length of the hull on my mark."

"That will burn out a lot of the electrical systems along the outer decks, Lieutenant," came his reply.

"No time, Tosh. Just get it done," she said, leaving no room for questions.

"One hundred meters," said Chavel.

"Medical to main airlock," she said into the comm panel.

"Acknowledged," came the swift reply.

"In position," Chavel said.

"Swing her around, David," she said. They watched the screen as the ship reoriented itself, giving access to the airlock.

"What's she doing?" Boyett said, watching as Carrie stopped running and turned to face the oncoming hordes of life forms.

"Come on, Carrie. What the hell-" Chavel said.

"It looks like she's turning to..." Boyett started but was silenced by what she saw next.

With arms outstretched the captain's daughter had bolts of blue light coming out of her body in all directions. Young stood from his console, mouth open in disbelief. The energy struck several of the life forms, like a pulse gun lifting them clean off their feet. One of the long black worm creatures moved towards her. She reacted quickly, sending a bright blue bolt of energy its way. It struck the creature, which split in two with a burst of white light bright enough to make Boyett cover her eyes. The oncoming force stopped in its tracks, as Carrie turned and made her way to the rear of the ship. Chavel looked at Boyett, who looked back at him and shook her head, bewildered. Young's face bore an expression Boyett had not seen him wear before. He looked horrified.

"Airlock closed. We have them," Ferrate said. "Sir," he followed, "on the ground," he said. Boyett looked at the screens. The landscape below them began to crumble inwards as if being swallowed into nothingness. From the empty chasms huge dark metallic structures began to emerge. The army of life forms began to fall into the disappearing landscape.

"What the hell is happening?" said Chavel. Boyett looked at the screens.

"Full thrusters! Get us the hell off this rock," shouted Boyett.

"Got it," Chavel said, grappling with the flight controls. The landscape beneath them disappeared as the ship angled itself straight up. "Dampers are off, so this may be a little rough," he said. He pushed the flight controls full on and Boyett felt the pull of several Gs as the ship began to soar upwards and away from the surface.

"Engine room, spin up the FTL, Tosh," Boyett said after several seconds. The sky began to turn dark as the ship rose.

"That's gonna be tricky, Lieutenant. We lost one plasma intake in the attack. I can't guarantee she'll fire at all."

"Do what you can," she said. She tapped a command into her chair and revered the angle on the main viewer. The planet began to fall away at speed, but it looked different. The surface was collapsing in on itself and was being replaced by enormous cone-shaped structures across its entire surface.

"I think you've stuck around long enough, Lieutenant," came John Barrington's voice from behind her. She stood immediately and looked at the captain.

"Captain," she said, trying to stop herself from running over to him. He looked beaten. Tired. She looked into his empty eye socket. Carrie and Tyrell flanked him on either side. Chavel turned his head and smiled at Carrie. The bridge went silent. Boyett felt her eyes water and knew the captain could see it. He walked over to her and placed a hand on her shoulder.

"Very nice, Lieutenant," he said smiling. There was enough sincerity in one eye to easily make up for the one missing.

"Captain," said Tyrell quietly. The captain nodded at him.

"We have to leave this system," Barrington said loudly to the bridge crew, "These are not the signal makers."

Tyrell looked at Boyett.

"David, get out of the flight chair before you crash into something, and take navigation," Barrington said. Boyett nodded and suddenly felt a real sense of relief smother her. Chavel locked the controls and moved over to the navigation station. Boyett slid herself back into her flight seat and released the control lock.

"There will be plenty of time for explanations as to what many of you will have seen today, but right now we need to survive," Barrington said, sitting in the centre seat. He took a breath and tapped the comm panel.

"Engine room, report," he said.

"Eh Tosh here, is that you, Captain?" he said.

"It is," he said.

"Good to hear from you," Tosh said.

"I need FTL capability fast," he said.

"Sir, I'm working on it but there are a lot of damaged systems down here. We currently have no direct link to navigation, so if we jump now God only knows where we'll end up." The screens above them showed the planet disintegrating and forming into a twisted shape that looked like a collection of engine parts all stuck together.

"It's changing," Carrie said from the rear of the bridge.

"The Targlagdu will not allow our escape," said Tyrell from beside her.

"The what?" Boyett said. The captain waved it off.

"You and Emerson put your heads together and spin up the FTL ring now or we're all dead," he said forcefully.

"Emerson is dead, sir," Tosh said. "But your point is well received. I will begin FTL ring prep immediately."

After a moment's silence the captain responded, "Understood."

Barrington turned and looked at Boyett.

"How many did we lose, Charly?" he said.

"Probably best if discuss it later, sir," she said.

"We have incoming!" Chavel shouted, turning to the captain. They raised their eyes to the centre screens, which showed varying angles of the planet. It had now completely changed shape and looked like it was moving.

"It's definitely closing on us, sir," Boyett said, looking at the growing twisted mass approaching the ship.

"David, where are we on the FTL?" the captain said.

"Ring deployed, sir. She's heating up now, one revolution per second."

"Engine room," Barrington said into the comm panel.

"You'll have it in three minutes, Captain. Engine room out," Tosh said, sounding a little more than harassed.

Engine Room
21:17 Martian Standard

"Jesus, the man's only back from the grave five minutes," Tosh said. "Where are we on the flow regulators, Roach?" he shouted across at a weary-looking engineer covered in scrapes and bruises.

"Way above the red line, Doctor. The anterior intake valve is completely fused, we have to rely on the backup which has never been tested with only one plasma injector. I don't recommend this," she said. Tosh looked at The Betty as the spinning orb began to glow. He had a feeling this was going to be his last few minutes in this world, but he had to admit that the bang this baby would make in deep space would be a sight to see from outside the ship.

"Open them up to a hundred and twenty percent," he said, smiling, thinking of Emerson's reaction to that one. The young woman looked at Tosh and raised her eyebrows. Tosh returned her gaze with an expression that told her it was their only chance. She nodded quietly and made the adjustments. Plasma flowed into the engine as the orb's light filled the room with a light blue.

"Well then," Tosh said, crossing his arms. "Your move, Betty."

Bridge

Carrie took a seat next to one of the diagnostic consoles and looked on at the screen.

"Two minutes," Chavel said. The view screen on the left of the bridge showed the exterior of the ship. The FTL ring was now circling the ship at speed and the hum of the vibration gently flowed through the bulkheads. All eyes were on the centre screen. The planet had split down its equator and was beginning to open up.

"What the hell is it doing?" her father said, turning to Tyrell.

"Looks like it's going to swallow us whole," Boyett said.

"Will the FTL fire inside a planetary body?" the captain asked, looking at Young.

"I honestly don't know," Young said, eyes on the screens. The planet-sized mass of twisted metal was almost upon them. It looked like an angry mouth with jagged, continent-sized teeth ready to chew them up.

"Sir, I need to shut down the thrusters in prep for FTL," Boyett said.

"What?" Ferrate said suddenly, from behind the captain. Carrie could feel the young man's panic. She shared it. The ship was about to be crushed like paper.

"Proximity alert," Chavel said, as the screens above them went black.

"Exterior," the captain said. The centre screen showed The Agathon's hull and the spinning FTL ring now blurring what was outside it. All around them was twisted darkness, as the planet began to engulf the ship.

"It has us," Tyrell said. Carrie looked at him.

"What can I do?" she asked Tyrell.

"Nothing, Carrie," her father said, looking at her and smiling. "You've done enough. It's up to The Agathon now," he said, sitting back in his chair calmly.

"We are inside the perimeter, sir. I think it's closing," Chavel said, looking at the screen. They looked above them at the screen, as the star field ahead began to disappear behind the closing orifice. Carrie felt her father's mind and watched him close his eyes.

Sorry, Jennifer, he thought. Carrie stood and walked over to her father. She placed his hand on his.

"It's not over yet," she said quietly. The ship began to vibrate intensely as Carrie reached her hand to steady herself against a computer console.

"Got it!" said Boyett, looking at the captain.

"Hang on, everyone. FTL in five..." Carrie looked at Tyrell, whose eyes were now black.

"Four..." She looked at the screen which showed a small star field, barely visible through the gap in the mechanical planet.

"Three..." She looked at Chavel, who was bracing the control panel in front of him with both hands.

"Two..." She saw Young looking at her intently. He looked like he had seen a ghost. She tightened her grip on her father's hand.

"One..."

28

The young boy looked out of his bedroom porthole at the nearby village. The latest repair to the umbilicus connecting the Jycorp to the nearby Clark looked patchy at best.

"What are you still doing up?" came his father's voice from behind him. The boy jumped and looked around.

"Nothing, just looking outside," he said, smiling before climbing under the blankets. His father walked over to the bunk and sat beside him. He reached around and began tucking the blankets tightly under his son.

"You know the rules," he said, turning off the blue night light beside the head of his bed. "No lights after eight," he said.

"Sorry, Dad," the young boy said.

"Tell me a story," he added, pulling the covers up past his nose.

"Which one?" his father said. The young boy smiled.

"Not again," his father said.

"Last time, I promise," the young boy said playfully. His father sighed and made himself comfortable at the edge of the bunk. He looked out at the star field. The lights of one of the nearby ships reflected off the dark circles under his eyes. He looked down at the young boy.

"Once upon a time, over a thousand years ago before humans lived in the stars, there was a place called Earth," he said. The young boy's eyes widened.

"It was a beautiful blue planet with more life in the seas than on the land. It was so warm that you could walk along its shores barefoot."

The young boy watched his pale father's face and tried to imagine being there. He tried to imagine what it felt like to never be cold.

"The skies were blue and it was home to billions. Then one day a signal came from the stars and told the humans they were not alone in the universe. They tried to find who the signal makers were, but they would not respond. It was decided that whoever had sent it had been long gone for millions of years. The humans searched the galaxy, trying to find the signal makers, but could still find nothing.

"Then one day it was decided to build The Agathon. The humans colonised Mars and began to construct the first ship capable of travelling faster than the speed of light, but before they could finish something terrible happened." The young boy's father looked out the window.

"The signal makers destroyed the Earth," he said.

"Why did they do that, Dad?" said the young boy, pulling the torn covers over his mouth.

"Nobody knows," said his father. "The last of the surviving humans banded together in these stations and set a course for Titan, led by the great Sienna Clark. It is thought that The Agathon was then sent to find the signal makers, but after years of hoping it never returned.

"Did it really look like that, Dad?" the young boy said, pointing to an etching placed against the back wall of his room.

"According to the story tellers," said his father. "After the great revolt most of the history of our people was erased, so all we have to go on is what was passed down by the elders."

"Do you think it's still out there? Do you think they found the signal makers?" said the young boy, wide-eyed. "Do you think they will be able to find us?"

"Enough," said the young boy's father quietly.

"Go to sleep." He rested his hands on the boy's chest and leaned over, giving him a kiss on the cheek. The young boy closed his eyes as his father walked over to his door.

"Dad?" he asked quietly.

"Yes, Arturo?" he said, standing at the entrance.

"Do you think we'll have food tomorrow?" There was a moment of silence.

"Yes, Arturo," his father said, "I promise."

Printed in Great Britain
by Amazon.co.uk, Ltd.,
Marston Gate.